Praise for the Rosato & DiNunzio Series

"Scottoline's merging of the themes of her family-driven stand-alone thrillers with her ongoing legal series continues to work splendidly." —*Booklist* on *Damaged*

"Scottoline is an A-lister all the way, and her Rosato series is always an A-plus." —*Booklist* (starred review) on *Corrupted*

"Scottoline's third entry in her Rosato & DiNunzio series does not disappoint. Fans will be on the edge of their seats eager to discover what happens next." —*Library Journal* (starred review) on *Corrupted*

"There is nothing as riveting as a skilled writer creating tense courtroom scenes and Scottoline does that in *Corrupted*." —*The Huffington Post*

"Scottoline excels at turning societal issues of the day into suspenseful plot points, a proclivity she takes to a whole new level in *Corrupted*, out-Grishaming Grisham. After twenty-plus books, she has written her best ever, as tightly fashioned as it is nail-bitingly suspenseful. A masterpiece of pitch-perfect storytelling balanced against emotional angst." —*The Providence Journal*

"Pop culture's current crop of female lawyers owes a great deal to the attorneys at Rosato & Associates . . . The deliciously dramatic and slightly over-the-top *Betrayed* reaffirms that after more than twenty novels, the Edgar Award–winning Scottoline is still able to create surprising, suspenseful plots with likable, daring heroines at the center." —*The Washington Post*

"*Betrayed* is populated with the kind of smart, funny women you love to watch working crime scenes." —*All You* magazine

DAMAGED

Also by Lisa Scottoline

Rosato & DiNunzio Novels
Corrupted
Betrayed
Accused

Rosato & Associates Novels
Think Twice
Lady Killer
Killer Smile
Dead Ringer
Courting Trouble
The Vendetta Defense
Moment of Truth
Mistaken Identity
Rough Justice
Legal Tender
Everywhere That Mary Went

Other Novels
One Perfect Lie
Most Wanted
Every Fifteen Minutes
Keep Quiet
Don't Go
Come Home
Save Me
Look Again
Daddy's Girl
Dirty Blonde
Devil's Corner
Running from the Law
Final Appeal

Nonfiction (with Francesca Serritella)
I Need a Lifeguard Everywhere but the Pool
I've Got Sand in All the Wrong Places
Does This Beach Make Me Look Fat?
Have a Nice Guilt Trip
Meet Me at Emotional Baggage Claim
Best Friends, Occasional Enemies
My Nest Isn't Empty, It Just Has More Closet Space
Why My Third Husband Will Be a Dog

DAMAGED

A Rosato & DiNunzio Novel

Lisa Scottoline

ST. MARTIN'S GRIFFIN ❧ NEW YORK

DAMAGED. Copyright © 2016 by Smart Blonde, LLC. All rights reserved. Printed in the United States of America. For information, address St. Martin's Press, 175 Fifth Avenue, New York, N.Y. 10010.

www.stmartins.com

THE LIBRARY OF CONGRESS HAS CATALOGED THE HARDCOVER EDITION AS FOLLOWS:

Names: Scottoline, Lisa, author.
Title: Damaged / Lisa Scottoline.
Description: First Edition. | New York : St. Martin's Press, 2016.
Identifiers: LCCN 2016016827 | ISBN 9781250099624 (hardcover) |
    ISBN 9781250119308 (signed edition) | ISBN 9781250099631 (ebook)
Subjects: LCSH: Rosato & Associates (Imaginary organization)—Fiction. |
    BISAC: FICTION / Mystery & Detective / Women Sleuths. | GSAFD:
    Legal stories. | Mystery fiction.
Classification: LCC PS3569.C725 D36 2016 | DDC 813/.54—dc23
LC record available at https://lccn.loc.gov/2016016827

ISBN 978-1-250-09964-8 (trade paperback)

Our books may be purchased in bulk for promotional, educational, or business use. Please contact your local bookseller or the Macmillan Corporate and Premium Sales Department at 1-800-221-7945, extension 5442, or by email at MacmillanSpecialMarkets@macmillan.com.

First St. Martin's Griffin Edition: August 2017

10 9 8 7 6 5 4 3 2 1

This book is dedicated to Franca,
a great friend, a great lawyer, and a great heroine, in her own right.

If you want to go faster, go alone.
If you want to go farther, go together.

—African proverb

DAMAGED

CHAPTER ONE

Mary DiNunzio hurried down the pavement, late to work because she'd had to stop by their new caterer and try crabmeat dumplings with Asian pears. Her stomach grumbled, unaccustomed to shellfish for breakfast, much less pears of any ethnicity. Her wedding was only two weeks away, and their first caterer had gone bankrupt, keeping their deposit and requiring her to pick a new menu. She had approved the mediocre crabmeat dumplings, proof that her standards for her wedding had started at Everything Must Be Perfect, declined to Good Enough, and ended at Whatever, I Do.

It was early October in Philly, unjustifiably humid, and everyone sweated as they hustled to work. Businesspeople flowed around her, plugged into earbuds and reading their phone screens, but Mary didn't need an electronic device to be distracted, she had her regrets. She'd made some stupid decisions in her life, but by far the stupidest was not using a wedding planner. She earned enough money to hire one, but she'd thought she could do it herself. She'd figured it wasn't rocket science and she had a law degree, which should count for more than the ability to sue the first caterer for free.

Mary didn't know what she'd been thinking. She was a partner at Rosato & DiNunzio, so she was already working too hard to take a honeymoon, plus it was a second job to manage her wacky family in full-blown premarital frenzy. Her fiancé, Anthony, was away, leaving her to deal with her soon-to-be mother-in-law Elvira, or El Virus. Meanwhile, tonight was the final fitting for her dress and tomorrow night was her hair-and-makeup trial. She was beginning to think of her entire wedding as a trial, a notion she hated despite the fact that she was a trial lawyer. Maybe she needed a new job, too.

Mary kicked herself as she walked along, a skill not easily performed by anyone but a Guilt Professional. She had no idea why she always thought she should do everything herself. She only ended up stressed-out, every time. She was forever trying to prove something, but she didn't know what or to whom. She felt like she'd been in a constant state of performance since the day she was born, and she didn't know when the show would be over. Maybe when she was married. Or dead.

She reached her office building, went through the revolving door, and crossed the air-conditioned lobby, smiling for the security guard. The elevator was standing open and empty, so she climbed inside, pushed the UP button, and put on her game face. She was running fifteen minutes late for her first client, which only added to her burden of guilt, since she hated to be late for anything or anyone. Mary's friends knew that if she was fifteen minutes late, she must have been abducted.

She checked her appearance in the stainless-steel doors, like a corporate mirror. Her reflection was blurry, but she could see the worry lines in her forehead, and her dark blonde hair was swept back into a low ponytail because she didn't have time to blow it dry. Her contacts were glued to her eyes since she'd spent the night emailing wedding guests who hadn't RSVP'd. She had on a fitted navy dress and she was even wearing pantyhose, which qualified as dressed up at Rosato & DiNunzio.

Mary watched impatiently as the floor numbers changed. Her legal practice was general, which meant she handled a variety of cases, mostly state-court matters for low damages, and her client base came from the middle-class families and small businesses of South Philly, where she'd grown up. She wasn't one of those lawyers who got their self-esteem from handling big, federal-court cases for Fortune 500 clients. Not that she got her self-esteem from within.

Mary was the Neighborhood Girl Who Made Good, so she got her self-esteem from being universally beloved, which was why she was never, ever late. Until now.

"Hi, Marshall!" Mary called out to the receptionist, as soon as the elevator doors opened. She glanced around the waiting room, which was empty, and hurried to the reception desk. Marshall Trow was more the firm's Earth Goddess than its receptionist, dressing the part in her flowing boho dress, long brown braid, and pretty, wholesome features, devoid of makeup. Marshall's demeanor was straight-up Namaste, which was probably a job requirement for working for lawyers.

"Good morning." Marshall smiled as Mary approached.

"Where's O'Brien? Is he here already? Did you get my text?"

"Yes, and don't worry. I put him in conference room C with fresh coffee and muffins."

"Thank you so much." Mary breathed a relieved sigh.

"I chatted with him briefly. He found you from our website, you know. He's an older man, maybe in his seventies. He seems very nice. Quiet."

"Good. I don't even know what the case is about. He didn't want to talk about it over the phone."

Marshall lifted an eyebrow. "Then you don't know who your opposing counsel is?"

"No, who?" Mary was just about to leave the desk, but stopped.

"Nick Machiavelli."

"Machiavelli! The Dark Prince of South Philly." Mary felt her competitive juices flowing. "I always wanted a case against him."

"Machiavelli can't be his real name, can it? That has to be fake."

"Yes, it's his real name, I know him from high school. His family claims to be direct descendants of the real Machiavelli. That's the part that's fake. His father owns a body shop." Mary thought back. "I went to Goretti, a girl's school, and he went to Neumann, our brother school. We didn't have classes with the boys, but I remember him from the dances. He was so slick, a BS artist, even then."

"Is he a good lawyer?" Marshall handed Mary a few phone messages and a stack of morning mail.

"Honestly, yes." Mary had watched Machiavelli build a booming practice the same way she had, drawing from South Philly. The stories about his legal prowess were legendary, though they were exaggerated by his public relations firm. In high school, he had been voted Class President, Prom King, and Most Likely to Succeed because he was cunning, handsome, and basically, Machiavellian.

"Good luck."

"Thanks." Mary took off down the hallway, with one stop to make before her office. Her gut churned, but it could have been the dumplings. The real Niccolo Machiavelli had thought it was better to be feared than loved, and his alleged descendant followed suit. Nick Machiavelli was feared, not loved, and on the other hand, Mary was loved, but not feared. She always knew that one day they would meet in a battle, and that when they did, it would be a fight between good and evil, with billable hours.

Mary reached her best friend Judy's office, where she ducked inside and set down a foam container of leftover dumplings amid the happy clutter on the desk. Judy Carrier was one of those people who could eat constantly and never gain weight, like a mythical beast or maybe a girl unicorn.

"Good morning!" Judy looked up from her laptop with a broad grin. She had a space between her two front teeth that she made look adorable. Her cheery face was as round as the sun, framed by punky blonde hair, with large blue eyes and a turned-up nose. Judy was the firm's legal genius, though she dressed artsy, like today she had on a boxy hot pink T-shirt with yellow shorts and orange Crocs covered by stuck-on multicolored daisies.

"Please tell me that you're not going to court dressed like that."

"I'm not, but I think I look cute." Judy reached for the container. "What did you bring me? Spring rolls? Spanakopita?"

"Guess what, I have a new case—against Nick Machiavelli."

"Ha! That name cracks me up every time I hear it. What a fraud."

Judy's blue eyes lit up as she opened the lid of the container. "Yummy."

"I'm finally going up against him."

"You'll kick his ass." Judy opened the drawer that contained her secret stash of plastic forks.

"Don't underestimate him."

"I'm not, but you're better." Judy got a fork and shut the drawer. "What kind of case is it?"

"I don't know yet. The client's in the conference room."

"Meanwhile, I thought you were going vegetarian." Judy frowned at the dumplings. "This smells like crabmeat. Crabmeat isn't vegetarian."

"It's vegetarian enough," Mary said on her way out. "I gotta go."

"There's no such thing as vegetarian enough!"

Mary hurried to her office, dumped her purse, mail, and messenger bag inside, grabbed her laptop, and hustled to conference room C.

CHAPTER TWO

"Good morning, I'm Mary DiNunzio." Mary closed the door as O'Brien tucked his napkin in the pocket of his worn khakis, which he had on with a boxy navy sports jacket that hung on his long, bony frame. His blue-striped tie lay against his chest, and Mary noticed as she approached him that his oxford shirt had a fraying collar. Edward's hooded eyes were an aged hazel green behind wire-rimmed glasses, with visible bifocal windows. His face was long and lined, and his crow's-feet deep. Folds bracketed his mouth, and age-spots dotted his temples and forehead. His complexion was ruddy, though Mary could smell the minty tang of a fresh shave.

"Edward O'Brien," O'Brien said, walking over, his bald head tilting partway down. He was probably six-foot-two, but he hunched over in a way that made him seem like a much older man than he was, which was probably in his seventies.

"Please accept my apologies for being late." Mary shook his slim hand.

"Not at all. And call me Edward."

"Great. Please, sit down." Mary sat down with her laptop and gestured him into the seat, catty-corner to her left.

"Thanks." Edward sank into the fabric swivel seat, bending his long legs slowly at the knee.

"So how can I help you, Edward?"

"This is a free consultation, correct? That's what it said on the website." Edward frowned, his forehead lined deeply.

"Yes, completely free." Mary opened her laptop and hit the RECORD button discreetly, so he wouldn't be self-conscious. "I hope you don't mind if I record the session."

"It's fine. I'm here because of my grandson, Patrick. I'll begin at the beginning."

"Please do." Mary liked his reserved, gentlemanly manner. His teeth were even but tea-stained, which she found oddly charming.

"Patrick is ten, and he's in the fifth grade at Grayson Elementary School in the city. We live in Juniata." Edward pursed his lips, which turned down at the corners. "He's got special needs. He's dyslexic, and I think I need a lawyer to help with his school. I should have dealt with it before."

"Okay, understood." Mary got her bearings, now that she knew this was a special education case. Under the Individuals with Disabilities Education Act, a federal law, students with learning disabilities were entitled to an education that met their needs at no cost. She'd been developing an expertise in special ed cases and had represented many children with dyslexia, a language-based learning disability. There were differences in symptoms and degrees of dyslexia along the spectrum, but most dyslexic children couldn't decode, or put a sound to the symbol on the page, and therefore couldn't phonetically figure out the word because the symbols on the page had no meaning.

"He can't read at all. He thinks I don't know, but I do."

"Not at all, even at ten?" Mary didn't hide the dismay in her tone. Sadly, it wasn't unheard of in Philly's public schools.

"No, and his spelling and letters are terrible."

Mary nodded, knowing that most dyslexic children had spelling problems as well as handwriting problems, or dysgraphia, since handwriting skills came from the same area of the brain as language acquisition.

"I read to him sometimes, and he likes that, and I guess I kind of gave up trying to teach him to read. I thought he'd pick it up at school."

"Have they identified his learning disability at school?"

"Yes. In second grade."

"Does he have an IEP?" Mary asked, because under the law, schools were required to evaluate a child and formulate an individualized education program, or an IEP, to set forth the services and support he was supposed to receive and to help him achieve in his areas of need.

"Yes, but it isn't helping. I have it with me." Edward patted a battered mailing envelope in front of him, but Mary needed some background.

"Before we get too far, where are Patrick's parents?"

"They passed. Patrick is my daughter Suzanne's only child, and she passed away four years ago in December. On the twelfth, right before Christmas." Edward's face darkened. "I have no other children and my wife, Patty, passed away a decade ago."

"I'm sorry."

"Thank you. My daughter Suzanne was killed by a drunk driver." Edward puckered his lower lip, wrinkling deeply around his mouth. "I retired when that happened. I'm raising Patrick. I was an accountant, self-employed."

"Again, I'm so sorry, and Patrick is lucky to have you." Mary admired him. "How old was Patrick when his mother passed?"

"Six, a few months into first grade at Grayson Elementary. He took it very hard."

"I'm sure." Mary felt for him and Patrick. Special education cases could be emotional because they involved an entire family, and nothing was more important to a family than its children. Mary felt that special ed practice was the intersection of love and law, so it was tailor-made for her. This work had made her both the happiest, and the saddest, she'd ever been as a lawyer.

"Finally, he's doing great at home. It's school that's the problem. The kids know he can't read and they tease him. It's been that way for a long time but this year, it's getting worse."

Mary had seen it before, though dyslexia could be treated with intensive interventions, the earlier the better. "How's his self-esteem?"

"Not good, he thinks he's stupid." Edward frowned. "I tell him he's not but he doesn't believe me."

"That's not uncommon with dyslexic children. The first thing anyone learns at school is reading, so when a child can't do something that seems so easy for the other kids, they feel dumb, inferior, broken. It goes right to the core. I've had an expert tell me that reading isn't just about reading, it's the single most important thing that creates or destroys a child's psyche." Mary made a mental note to go back to the subject. "Are you Patrick's legal guardian?"

"It's not like I went to court to get a judge to say so, but we're blood. That makes him mine, in my book."

"That's not the case legally, but we can deal with that another time. What about Patrick's father? How did he die?"

"He broke up with Suzanne when she got pregnant. She met him up at Penn State. She was in the honors program but when she got pregnant, she dropped out. Suzanne could have been an accountant, too. " Edward shook his head. "Anyway, we heard he died in a motorcycle accident, two years later."

"And when Suzanne dropped out, did she come home?"

"Yes, and I was happy to have her. Patrick was born, and Suzanne devoted herself to him. Since she passed, I'm all Patrick has now. I'm his only family."

"I see." Mary's heart went out to them both, but she had to get back on track. "When did you notice his reading problems?"

"Suzanne did, in kindergarten." Edward ran his fingers over his bald head. "Then after she passed, I would try to get him to read with me, and we'd get books from the library. He didn't know the words, not even the little ones like 'the.' He couldn't remember them either. But he's smart."

"I'm sure he is." Mary knew dyslexic children had high IQs, but their reading disability thwarted their progress in school. They often had retrieval issues, too, so they forgot names and the like.

"He does better when there's pictures, that's why he likes comic books. He draws a lot, too. He's very good at art."

"So back to the IEP. May I see it?"

"Sure." Edward opened the manila envelope and extracted a wrinkled packet, then slid it across the table.

"Bear with me." Mary skimmed the first section of the IEP, and the first thing she looked at was Present Levels, which told her where a student was in reading, writing, math, and behaviors. Patrick was only on a first-grade level in both reading and math, even though he was in fifth grade. The IEP showed that Patrick had been evaluated in first grade but not since then. Mary looked up. "Is this all you have? There should have been another evaluation. They're required to reevaluate him every three years."

"I didn't know that. I guess they didn't."

Mary turned the page, noting that Patrick had scored higher than average on his IQ tests, but because he couldn't read, he had scored poorly on his achievement testing, which a district psychologist had administered, and the IRA, the curriculum-based assessment test that the teachers administered. She looked up again. "Is he in a special ed classroom or a regular classroom?"

"Regular."

"Are they pulling him out for help with his reading?"

"No, not that I know of."

"How about any small-group instruction? Does he get that?"

"No, I don't think so."

"So what *are* they doing for him?"

"Nothing that I know of."

"So they identified him as eligible for services, but they're not programming for him or giving him any services." Mary wished she could say she was surprised, but she wasn't. "They're supposed to be giving him interventions, and he can learn to read if they do, I've seen it. I've seen wonderful progress with dyslexic children."

Edward brightened. "What kind of interventions?"

"A dyslexic child needs to be drilled every day for his brain to connect sound and symbol, then language. There are many great research-based programs, and they work."

"He hates school, more and more."

Mary had seen this before, with dyslexic children. Early on, they might use pictures to make it look like they were reading, but by fourth grade, when pictures were gone and the words took over, the fact that they couldn't read became more evident. They couldn't read aloud and avoided group projects. The axiom was that children learn to read, then read to learn, but that was a heartbreak for dyslexics.

"Patrick gets nervous, and when he gets really nervous, lately, he throws up. He did it in school a couple times, already this year. They sent a note home, then they called me. The teachers don't want to deal with it anymore. But it's not his fault, it's his nerves." Edward pressed his glasses up higher on his long nose. "The kids make fun of him, call him names. Up-Chucky. Vomit Boy. Duke of Puke. They make throw-up noises when he comes into the classroom."

Mary felt for the boy. "First, have you taken him to a pediatrician?"

"Yes, but she said there's nothing medically wrong."

"It could be from anxiety. Have they evaluated him to determine if anything else is going on?"

"Not that I know of." Edward blinked, uncertainly.

"They should have done a social-emotional assessment, like the BASC test, which will pick up how he's feeling. It's a questionnaire that asks the child a series of question and it tells the psychologist if he's anxious, depressed, or shutting down. The evaluation determines what his programming should be. If they don't do the evaluation, they don't know what services or counseling he needs."

"The teasing only makes him more nervous, and his teacher sends him to the guidance counselor. They say they send him there to calm down, but I think it's because they don't want him to throw up in the classroom. They said it's normal, they call it something."

"It's called a 'cooling-off room,'" Mary said, supplying him with the term of art.

"But he sits there for hours, like a punishment."

"The school can't punish him for behaviors associated with his disability. For example, a child with ADHD will have a problem completing assignments on time. The teacher can't say to the child, 'you have to stay in for recess or you can't go on a class trip.' They can't punish him for the manifestation of a disorder that he can't help. It's illegal and it's just plain"—Mary searched for the words, then found them—"cruel."

"But wait, Mary." Edward leaned over with a new urgency. "The worst of it is Patrick got hit in the face by a teacher's aide, Mr. Robertson."

"My God, what happened?" Mary asked, appalled. She had heard horror stories, but this was the worst. Teacher's aide was a misnomer; aides weren't teachers, they could be a bus matron or a cafeteria worker. They couldn't teach, nor were they trained to work with children with behaviors.

"Patrick threw up and Robertson made him clean it up. Patrick got some on the desk, so Robertson punched him in the face and told him to 'cut the crap.' "

"That's an assault!" Mary said, angry. "Robertson should have been arrested on the spot."

"Patrick didn't tell anybody what happened, and Robertson told Patrick that if he told, he'd beat him up." Edward frowned, deeper. "Patrick was so scared, he didn't say anything. When he came home that day, I asked him about the bruise on his cheek, it was swollen. He told me that he fell against the desk. I gave him Advil, I put ice on it. I believed him because he does fall, he can be clumsy."

"Were there any witnesses to the assault?"

"No."

"Any surveillance cameras that you know of?"

"No, only in the halls." Edward shook his head. "The next day Patrick was really afraid to go to school. He begged me not to make him, so I didn't. By Friday, I started to think something was really wrong, and over the weekend, he finally admitted it to me."

"Poor kid." Mary felt a pang. "Did you call the police?"

"No, I called the school and I told them what Patrick said, and they said they would look into it. So then the school called back and said that Robertson had quit. They denied knowing anything about Patrick getting punched. They said they were going to investigate the matter." Edward dug into the manila envelope again and pulled out a packet of papers. He grew more upset, his lined skin mottled with pink. "Then the next thing I know, yesterday, I'm being served with a lawsuit."

"Who would be suing you?" Mary asked, incredulous.

"Robertson hired a lawyer named Machiavelli, if you can believe that, and they're suing me and the school district, claiming that Patrick attacked Robertson with a scissors."

"What?" Mary felt her blood begin to boil.

"It's a complete fabrication." Edward handed Mary the suit papers. "Here, take a look. But I know my grandson, and he did not attack anybody with a scissors. He's not aggressive. He doesn't have it in him. It's not possible."

"Bear with me while I read this." Mary skimmed the cover letter on Machiavelli's letterhead, then she turned to the facts and read aloud: **". . . the Defendant Patrick seized a scissors from the teacher's desk and lunged at Plaintiff with the weapon, attempting to do him grievous bodily harm."**

Edward scoffed in disgust. "That's false."

"Has Patrick ever been disciplined in school, for fighting or violence?"

"No, not once."

"What about when the other kids tease him?"

"No, never. He just cries or gets sick. He won't hit back, he's little."

"Does he tell the teacher?"

"No, he hides it, like with Robertson. He doesn't want trouble."

"Poor kid." Mary flipped the pages to the causes of action, where it set forth claims against the O'Briens for battery, assault, and intentional infliction of emotional distress. Again, she read aloud, **". . . Plaintiff was so frightened by the assault and battery by Defendant Patrick that Plaintiff has been unable to return to his position and was compelled to terminate his employment and seek psychiatric counseling . . ."**

Edward groaned. "Can he win on that?"

"Doubtful. He has proof problems with the assault and battery claims, and to qualify as intentional infliction, an action has to be extreme and outrageous. I doubt a court would find it met by a little boy lunging at an adult male, even with a school scissors."

"God, I hope not." Edward frowned. "Why are they doing this, then? Is it a money grab?"

"Yes, but you're not the deep pocket here, the school district is. Wait 'til they find out it's not so easy to sue the district, they have immunity." Mary returned her attention to the Complaint and flipped to the causes of action against the school district, which were for Negligence and Breach of Contract. She read aloud: **"Defendant School District has a duty to keep the Plaintiff safe from harm while performing his jobs on school grounds and also has a duty to train Plaintiff on how to deal safely with violent and emotionally disturbed 'special education' students at the school. Defendant School District breached each such duty to Plaintiff and Defendant School District was grossly negligent in compelling the Plaintiff to deal with a violent, emotionally disturbed 'special education' student on his own, untrained and unsupervised."**

Edward shook his head. "Robertson punches my grandson, then turns around and sues us and the school?"

"It's hard to believe." Mary wondered if Machiavelli knew that Robertson was lying, but she wouldn't put it past him. To Machiavelli, the end justified the meanness.

"Robertson's asking for half a million dollars in damages, claiming he can't return to work, and he'll have psychiatric and medical expenses."

Mary fumed. "But wait, if Patrick really attacked Robertson, why didn't Robertson report it to the police? Or the school?"

"I don't know."

"I bet I do. Robertson didn't think of it right away. It's some story he thought up later, to drum up a lawsuit. Robertson will have to think of some reason to explain it, but it argues in our favor."

"Good point." Edward nodded. "The school called me this morning after they got the Complaint and they said Patrick broke a school rule, using a weapon like a scissors, and he had to stay home on an at-home suspension pending their investigation. They said if he did it, he's getting sent to disciplinary school."

"Oh no." Mary knew that if a child was found with a weapon in a Philadelphia public school, he could get transferred to a disciplinary school, after a hearing. The problem was that disciplinary schools contained kids with more serious anger issues.

"Mary, so what do I do now?"

Mary collected her thoughts. "There are two different legal matters here, and we have to run them on parallel tracks. One is the civil tort case, which is the Complaint just filed against you, and the other is the special education case. Both have to be dealt with. First, we have to respond to the Complaint. I would like to call Machiavelli right now and tell him we won't be offering him anything in settlement."

"I agree." Edward nodded. "I'll be damned if I'll pay a penny, it's extortion."

"Second is Patrick's special education case. He needs to be in a school where they can program for his dyslexia and his anxiety, where he feels safe and nurtured, and can get remediation. The district is threatening to expel him, but I'm not sure I'd want him back at Grayson anyway. I know an excellent private school, Fairmount Prep in the Art Museum area."

"*Private* school?" Edward grimaced. "I have some savings and a trust set up for Patrick's expenses, but I had expected it to last his lifetime. We live frugally."

"Don't worry. You don't have to pay for private school, the school district does."

"Really?" Edward's sparse gray eyebrows flew upward, the first bright note in their meeting.

"Yes." Mary felt happy to give him some good news. "Legally, if the school did not program appropriately for a child, they owe that child compensatory education, that is, funding for tutoring, educational services, and materials. But if the school district *cannot* educate him where he is, then they have to place him in a private school where he *can* be educated. In other words, they reimburse you for the private schooling. We don't have to wait to enroll him, it's already October. If you have the money for this semester's tuition, we can notify Grayson that we're placing him in private school, then we place him, sue the district, and go to a hearing for reimbursement. If we win, you don't have to pay my fees, either. The school district does."

"Great!" Edward smiled, and the deep lines in his forehead smoothed briefly. "Do you work on a retainer basis?"

"No, but my fee is $300 an hour." Mary hated the size of her fee, but as a partner, she was making herself get over it, especially since Edward could get reimbursed if she won.

"Okay, you're hired." Edward smiled again.

"Terrific. I'll send you a representation agreement." Mary patted his hand. "Don't worry. We can do this. We'll help him." She rose. "Let's get started. I'll go call the lawyer and be right back. I'd like you to call the doctor and see if you can take Patrick today, to get a look at that bruise on his face. See if the doc can determine how it happened and when. Tell him the situation."

"Ok. I'll go get Patrick in school now, because they are keeping him in the office until I can get back." Edward reached in his jacket pocket for his cell phone, and Mary picked up the Complaint. She left the conference room and headed for her office, mentally rearranging her calendar. She had other cases to work, but none of them involved a little boy being used as a punching bag, so this got top priority.

It wasn't about Machiavelli anymore, it was about Patrick.

CHAPTER THREE

Mary got back to her office, closed the door behind her, and called Machiavelli, whose number she knew because it was plastered on every bus in the city, namely 1-800-DRK-PRNC.

"The Machiavelli Organization," said the receptionist, picking up Mary's call.

"This is Mary DiNunzio, is he in?"

"Please hold, Ms. DiNunzio."

"Thank you." Mary held her cell phone to her ear, trying to calm down. It wouldn't serve Edward or Patrick's interests if she was angry before she even started the phone call. She reminded herself that as an attorney, she worked in a representative capacity, for someone else. If she were representing herself right now, she might've fired a bullet through the telephone line.

She glanced around her office, getting her bearings. It was boxy, the same size as the other lawyers, since Rosato & DiNunzio kept it real. Sunshine streamed from the window behind her, casting a glowing shaft of light on her uncluttered pine desk, neat bookshelves containing bound treatises and black practice notebooks, and green copies of the Federal and State Rules of Civil and Criminal Procedure, since she preferred the hard copies to looking up the rules online. The office was furnished simply but in a way that suited her, with bar admissions certificates and diplomas lining one wall, and hanging opposite them her prized possession, a handmade quilt in pastel hues, stitched in a traditional Amish wedding-ring pattern.

Mary's eyes traveled over the lovely quilt, taking in its antique scraps of cloth and tiny batted stitching. It was funny to think that she had bought the quilt long before she had thought about getting remarried. She had been widowed so young, and it had taken her years to get used to the idea of falling in love again and re-committing to someone, but a college professor named Anthony Rotunno had come along, and after some ups and downs, he had won her over.

Her gaze fell to her engagement ring, a beautiful diamond solitaire that Anthony had had to save for, and she turned her hand this way and that, watching its sparkly facets cast prisms on the wall, like miniature rainbows. She remembered that the point of the engagement ring, the caterer, the hair-and-makeup trial, the save-the-date cards, and all the other tasks wasn't the wedding, but the marriage. True love, forever. The thought gave her a moment of peace and happiness, until the phone clicked in her hand.

"Hello?" Mary said, confused, but the call had failed. Suddenly, her laptop came to life with a FaceTime call from an unknown number. The only person she'd ever FaceTimed with was Anthony, so she pressed ACCEPT on reflex.

Machiavelli's massive face appeared on her laptop screen. "DiNunzio, *come stai?*"

Mary took a minute to process what was happening. Machiavelli's face was only inches away from her, which made her feel oddly invaded, and he was the last person she'd ever want to FaceTime with. He was handsome in a vaguely disturbing way, like Satan. He wore his black hair slicked back, like a throwback Dracula, and his eyes were narrow slits, with dark brown irises that were the exact color of baking chocolate, and Mary would know. She was a total chocoholic, and when she was out of chocolate, she had been known to nibble in desperation on baking chocolate, a cruel trick because it looked normal on the outside but tasted horrible, so it was an apt analogy. Machiavelli's nose was straight and aquiline, but Mary was pretty sure that he had had a nose job, and maybe even a chin implant because his jawline was unusually pugnacious, like Mussolini. All in all, the man was a disgrace to Italian-Americans, lawyers, and men in general, and she could barely set her hatred aside to talk to him.

"Why didn't you answer my phone call?" Mary asked him. "I don't want to FaceTime with you."

"I want to FaceTime with *you*! Ha!" Machiavelli laughed, throwing back his serpentine head. "How have you been? I haven't seen you since high school."

"I'm fine," Mary answered simply.

"Aren't you going to ask me how I am?"

"I already know. You press-release constantly. If you fart, you make sure the entire legal community knows."

"Mary, Mary, Mary. That sense of humor! That gorgeous face! I miss you!" Machiavelli burst into laughter again, which Mary knew was completely manipulative, designed to make her lower her guard.

"You don't miss me. We don't even know each other."

"But, Mary, I like you."

"How can you like me if you don't even know me?" Mary suppressed an eye-roll.

"Why are you being so hard on me when you already broke my heart?"

"What are you talking about?"

"I heard you're getting married!" Machiavelli mock-frowned. "Boo-hoo. How can you do that to me? And really, Anthony Rotunno? You can do better than that nerd. Plus you make ten times what he does. You really want a man you have to support the rest of your life?"

"That's enough of that." Mary swallowed hard, hiding her emotions. Machiavelli was better than he knew at putting his finger on a soft spot. The disparity between her income and Anthony's had been a problem in their relationship, if only because Anthony felt so bad about it. But there was no way Machiavelli could have known that, oddly.

"If you were my wife, I wouldn't let you support me. I wouldn't even let you buy me lunch. A woman like you deserves to be treated better than that—"

"I'm calling you about a case. I have neither the time nor the inclination to discuss my personal life."

"Oh, strictly business. Boring. Zzzz." Machiavelli rolled his eyes. "I heard you made partner, too. Somebody's crushing it."

"Evidently, you're representing Steven Robertson, who's suing—"

"Mary, tell me the truth. You can't stand Rosato, can you? The woman has an ego the size of City Hall. You're twice the lawyer she is, you just don't know it."

"As I was saying, you filed a completely frivolous complaint against my client, Edward O'Brien, and the school district—"

"How long did Rosato make you wait for that partnership? Six years, seven? Criminal! I *know* that you bill more than she does."

"That's not true," Mary shot back, though it was.

"Come on. You and I have the same client base. I poach clients from you daily."

"The hell you do!" Mary took the bait, against her own better judgment.

"You know I do. You only have the clients I let you have. I play catch-and-release with those mom-and-pop stores in the neighborhood. I throw back the little ones to keep you alive."

"Oh shut up, Nick." Mary sounded like a teenager, and it was all his fault. Or hers. She felt her face redden.

"*That's* why I FaceTimed you, Mary! To see you blush! That used to happen to you at the dances, too! Remember? Do you still get those blotches on your neck when you're nervous? Open your shirt! Let me see!" Machiavelli laughed again.

"Listen, you filed a completely meritless lawsuit against my client. I have your demand letter, and you can stick it."

"Oooh! Ouch! Talk dirty to me, Mary DiNunzio!"

"You know that none of those allegations is true." Mary considered telling him that Robertson had punched Patrick in the face, but she didn't want to show her hand. With any other lawyer, she could have been direct, hashed out the facts on the phone, and probably agreed to disagree, but Machiavelli wasn't any other lawyer. She'd heard he was ruthless in pursuit of whatever he wanted and she would have to outmaneuver him to beat him. In fact, she already had a strategy in mind.

"Aw, don't be that way." Machiavelli stopped laughing abruptly, eyeing her. "I'm sorry. I was being rude. That was sexist of me. Or maybe sexy of me. Either way, I'm sorry. Do you accept my apology?"

"Now, to get back to the case—"

"Are you really going through with that wedding? I'm still single. We're perfect for each other. We've been circling each other since high school. Why don't you give me a shot?"

"I'm hanging up if we don't talk about the case—"

"You can be the Dark Princess to my Dark Prince! Can you imagine the two of us together? We'd be the ultimate power couple. Today it's South Philly, tomorrow the world. Ha!"

"That's it, I'm hanging up." Mary reached for the button.

"No, don't, wait. I'll be good. You want me to let your client out of the case?"

Mary's ears pricked up. "Yes. The allegations are false and they won't survive a motion to dismiss. You don't have enough to prove assault or battery, and even if the facts in the Complaint were taken as true, they don't rise to the level of intentional infliction."

"Beg to differ, darling. I absolutely will survive a motion to dismiss. The counts for assault and battery raise a question of fact that has to go to the jury."

"Wrong," Mary shot back, sure of the law. "It doesn't go to the jury if it's just your client's word against mine. Evidence in equipoise does not get to the jury. It takes more than that."

"True." Machiavelli lifted an eyebrow, his mouth suddenly an unsmiling line. "But what makes you so sure the evidence is in equipoise? How do you know I don't have enough to prove assault?"

"Because it didn't happen."

"It's the aide's word against the little psycho's. The Duke of Puke. Who would you believe? A teacher's aide with a spotless record or Up-Chucky?"

Mary felt her temper bubble up on Patrick's behalf, or maybe on behalf of bullied kids everywhere, including her. "Don't you think it's completely juvenile to nickname everything? The Dark Prince? The Duke of Puke? Do you realize you're functioning on a fifth-grade level?"

"Mary, you can't fight human nature. Everybody has a dark side. People like to laugh at other people. Besides, nicknames are fun. Most of South Philly has a nickname. Your dad's friend, Tony 'Two Feet' Pensiera? Everybody calls him 'Feet,' so even his nickname has a nickname—"

"Whoa, buddy," Mary interrupted. "Leave my family out of this. Don't even go there."

"You want me to wipe that smile off my face?"

"Yes, and while you're at it, can we drop the Machiavelli bit? Do you really expect people to believe that you're related to the real Machiavelli?"

"I'm not only related to the real Machiavelli, I *am* the real Machiavelli." Machiavelli smiled, but Mary thought she saw it falter, so she dug in.

"Don't start believing your own press releases, Nick. And I wish you luck convincing anybody that my skinny little fifth-grader attacked your big strong teacher's aide."

"Oh really?" Machiavelli snorted. "I don't know what grandpa is telling you, but he's wrong. You're defending the demon seed. That kid's a school-shooter in the making. I can prove it."

"That's not true," Mary said, though a warning note in Machiavelli's tone worried her.

"I'll give you some free discovery, since you and me go back." Machiavelli shuffled some papers on his desk, and in the next moment, held up a sheet of white paper, showing only the blank side. "Do you want to know what I have in my hand?"

"A hacky trick? We both know it's your client's word against my client's word. There are no witnesses, no cameras, and no videos. Your assault story is bull, and the emotional distress claim doesn't rise to the level on any planet we know of."

"Oh, honey," Machiavelli said, his tone turning singsong. "I can convince a jury that your little freak tried to stab my client, so I have intentional infliction, too. I'm going to put that brat on trial and break him in two. If you want to prevent that, you'd better tell grandpa to settle. From what I hear, the old man has the coin. They say he lives like a miser, and he's got it stowed away."

Mary felt her gut tense. She didn't know where Machiavelli got his information about Edward's finances, but she suspected it was accurate. She shuddered to think of Patrick on trial, a kid with an anxiety disorder being cross-examined. She could try to fight it, but any judge would rule against her. She decided that there was no point to being on the call any longer. She reached for the hang-up button again. "I have to go—"

"Check it." Machiavelli turned the sheet of paper around, showing the front. "Ta-da!"

Mary hid her surprise as the white paper filled her laptop screen. It was a drawing in Sharpie, fairly detailed, of a little boy stabbing a large man in the chest. Red blood squirted from the cartoon wound in all directions, and the little boy's face had a bizarre smile. She hit the button on the laptop and took a screenshot before Machiavelli moved the drawing away.

Suddenly Machiavelli's face reappeared, his dark eyes glittering in satisfaction, and he set the drawing aside with a grin. "What an *artiste*! Am I right or what?"

"So what?" Mary asked, with bravado. "There's no proof those drawings are his."

"Believe me, that's your little client's artwork. I have a complete series of his wacko drawings. Collect them all! You don't have to be a shrink to know that he's a child of the corn. Does he see dead people, too?"

"Very funny." Mary felt her heart sink, but couldn't let it show on her expression, and Machiavelli eased back in his chair, gloating.

"Mary, we both know the probative value of evidence like that. I think the jury will be much more inclined to believe that little Poopyface was running with scissors, since he's obviously been planning it for some time."

"There's no identification for the drawings, so they won't come into evidence."

"I'll put them in front of little Poindexter on the stand. I'll have him authenticate them. I'll ask him if he drew them. He won't lie, not about this. From what I hear, he's very proud of his drawings. He wants to be a comic book artist someday." Machiavelli chuckled. "Except that he can't read. Oops!"

Mary felt her fists clench. She knew that Machiavelli was low, but she hadn't thought he was low enough to make fun of a disabled child. He was no better than the bullies in the schoolyard, then it occurred to her that maybe schoolyard bullies grew up to be lawyers.

Machiavelli was still smiling. "So the evidence will come in. I'll put him on the stand after my favorite psychiatric experts, who will testify that the kid is a danger to the school, the community, and Western civilization." Machiavelli folded his arms. "Now. You want to consider meeting my settlement demand? A hundred grand would do it, but you must act now. Supply limited!"

"I'll see you in court," Mary said, hitting the button to end the call, shaken. She remained motionless a moment, her chest tight. Her neck felt aflame, and she knew there were blotches underneath her shirt, blossoming like poisoned roses. She eyed the Amish quilt, but her moment of Zen had vanished into thin air. Dust motes whirled around in the shaft of sunlight, disturbed by unseen currents.

Mary hit a button to print the drawing and collected her thoughts. The drawings were what lawyers call "bad facts," but she still doubted that Patrick had attacked Robertson. That said, she wondered if there was other evidence she didn't know about.

Mary rose, reminding herself that it took more than one punch to knock her down.

CHAPTER FOUR

Mary grabbed Patrick's drawing from the printer, left her office, and was heading back to the conference room when she was flagged down in the hallway by Anne Murphy, one of the other lawyers. Anne was the office fashionista, having been a catalog model before she went to law school, and she had long red hair, bright green eyes, and a dazzling smile. She was naturally slim, and today she had on a white pique dress, which proved that everybody but Mary could wear white and not look like a Beluga whale.

"Mary!" Anne said with an excited, if glossy, smile, grabbing her arm with a manicured hand. "Tonight is the night! We get to see our dresses! I can't wait!"

"But we saw them already, it's only the final fitting." Mary tried to switch mental gears. Edward was waiting for her in the conference room.

"Mary, the proper fit is *everything*." Anne looked at Mary like she was nuts. "We all needed tailoring, and they have to get it perfect. Don't forget to bring the shoes you're going to wear and the right bra."

"What's the *right* bra?"

"Anything but the one you're wearing."

"Thanks." Mary turned toward the conference room. "Plus I might be late tonight, I have a new case. You two go without me."

"But this is your *dress* we're talking about! You can't be late!" Anne's lipsticked lips parted, in girl shock.

"We'll talk later," Mary called over her shoulder, then she reached the conference-room door and opened it to find Edward looking at her expectantly, cell phone in hand.

"The pediatrician said she'd see Patrick right away."

"Well done." Mary crossed to the conference-room table with the drawing. "I told opposing counsel we weren't settling."

"Things are really moving quickly." Edward's gray eyebrows flew upward, as before.

"Yes, and I did learn something I need to share with you." Mary sat down and placed the drawing on the table in front of Edward. "Did Patrick draw this, do you know?"

"My God!" Edward recoiled.

"Do you think he drew it?"

"It looks like it. Where did you get this?"

"From opposing counsel. Are you sure Patrick drew it? That's the threshold question."

"I have to admit, it does look like it's his but I had no idea he could draw something so . . . violent."

"Have you ever seen him draw anything like this before?"

"No, not at all. He does his drawing in his room. He hasn't shown it to me in a long time." Edward kept shaking his head at the drawing.

"Is there any doubt in your mind that he drew it? Could it have been another little kid?" Mary was no expert, but a lot of kiddie artwork looked alike to her.

"No, he did it." Edward lifted his gaze to her, his aged eyes stricken. "I don't know what to say about this."

"Don't worry, we'll figure it out." Mary kept her tone reassuring. "In the drawing, does the man being stabbed look like Robertson?"

"I don't know. I never met Robertson."

"Hold on a second." Mary turned to her laptop and logged on to the website for the Philadelphia School District, then drilled down to find Grayson Elementary School. She hit a button for

FACULTY AND STAFF, then navigated to teacher's aides, where she found a thumbnail photo of Steven Robertson. He wore wire-rimmed glasses and he looked about thirty-five years old, with a dense thatch of dark hair, round brown eyes, and a round and fleshy face, with a wide nose and brushy mustache.

Edward looked over, squinting. "Is that him? My eyes aren't so good."

"That's him." Mary clicked on VIEW and enlarged the page. "Did you ever see him before?"

"No."

"That doesn't look like the man that Patrick is drawing. For one thing, he has a mustache. So that's good news." Mary slid the laptop aside. "Is there any other male figure in Patrick's life?"

"No."

"What about your friends?"

"Not really." Edward thought a minute. "I only have one friend. My stockbroker, Dave Kather, and he's more like a business acquaintance. He comes by sometimes or we meet for lunch. I like to keep an eye on my investments and we talk about the market and such."

"Does Patrick know Dave?"

"Sure, but they're not ever alone or anything like that."

Mary was getting the picture of an insular family life. "What about in the neighborhood? Is there any man he knows, a next-door neighbor? The UPS guy?"

"No. I don't get much from UPS."

"How about the father of any of his friends?"

"He doesn't have any friends."

Mary felt terrible for Patrick, though the gruesome drawing made her wonder if he was more troubled than she'd originally believed. "Does he have any male teachers?"

"No."

"Has Patrick ever complained to you about Robertson or anybody else at school? Saying that he wanted to hurt them?"

"No, not really."

Another question popped into Mary's mind, and it gave her pause, but she asked it anyway. "What's your relationship to Patrick like? Does he ever get this angry at you? Do you fight?"

"No, not really."

Mary blinked. "Edward, it would be normal for you to fight. I wouldn't think less of you, and it's okay to admit. I adore my parents, but we fight sometimes."

"No, we *don't* fight." Edward shook his head, his mouth setting firmly. "I never raise my voice, I don't have to. He's a gentle, nervous boy. He's very obedient. He's fearful, if anything. Why are you asking me that?" Edward's hooded eyes flared. "Are you thinking that it's a picture of *me* that he drew? You think Patrick wants to stab *me*?"

"I didn't think it, but I do have to ask." Mary hated ruining the rapport they had built so far. "Edward, as a technical matter, my client is Patrick. I always have to put his interests paramount, even as against your own. Do you understand that?"

"Yes, but I never, ever raise a hand to him. I love him. He's all I have, I'm all he has."

"Okay." Mary picked up the drawing, trying to move past the touchy subject. "So you didn't know that he had such violent drawings?"

"No, not at all." Edward's tone turned unmistakably defensive.

"He used to draw trucks and cars and animals. He liked jungle animals. Tigers. But now he draws a lot of superheroes, and he imagines he's a superhero. He used to show me his drawings when he was younger. I hung them on the refrigerator." Edward smiled briefly. "He liked that. It made him proud of himself, and he's a very good artist."

Mary found herself wishing Patrick wasn't such a good artist. "You say his father left before he was born?"

"Yes."

"Does Patrick ask about his father?"

"No, not anymore. He used to when he was little, but not anymore."

"What did he ask?"

Edward shrugged. "Only a few questions, like what was his name and what did he do. And why did he leave. He asked his mother."

"What did she answer, do you know?"

"She told him the truth." Edward frowned. "Are you thinking that the man in the picture could be his father?"

"Possibly. We're going to have to get Patrick a psychological evaluation, not for the lawsuit, but for his own sake. If he's feeling angry, we need to know that, don't you agree?"

"Yes, of course."

"Does Patrick take art in school?"

"Yes."

"Is his art teacher male or female?"

"A female, I think. Yes, she is. Ms. Gilam." Edward ran his hand over his bald head, and Mary could see his fingers were trembling slightly, so she wanted to wrap this up.

"And he never told you that he wanted to hurt anybody at school, or anyone at all?"

"No." Edward shook his head. "It's just not like him. He never said anything like that to me. This drawing, it's completely out of character."

"And you've never sent him to a psychiatrist or anything like that?"

"I never thought I had any reason to, before."

"Okay, we can deal with this." Mary tried to get back on an even keel. "If the pediatrician will take Patrick now, let's get going."

"Are you coming with us?" Edward rose, slowly.

"No, I've got to get busy."

CHAPTER FIVE

Mary drove north out of Center City, heading for the police station. The Hunting Park neighborhood was older, congested, and raggedy, owing to the mix of commercial traffic interspersed with the residential areas. Heavy-duty trucks and tractor-trailers muscled her car out of the way, and she passed auto body shops, empty lots mounded with crushed and abandoned vehicles, then a vast open lot topped by ugly concertina wire, with cyclone fencing that held a sign, CITY OF PHILADELPHIA FLEET MANAGEMENT SHOP. The streets widened the farther north she went, opening up to a blue sky that would've been pretty but for the heavy wires and cables strung across the streets, overhead.

Mary turned the corner that held the city's Highway Services Garage, a grim building of corrugated metal with a flat roof that emitted wiggly waves of heat in the sun. Up ahead she spotted the police station next to a massive lumberyard with more cyclone fencing and concertina wire, and because she knew she wouldn't be able to park in the police parking lot, she grabbed a parking space behind a pallet of building supplies, wrapped with dirty plastic. She parked, grabbed her bag, and climbed out of the car, stepping into air that felt even more humid than before, which she hadn't thought was possible. She flashed forward to her wedding day, when she would be married in pea soup and her hair would explode, especially since it looked like she might have to cancel her hair trial.

The police station was a grimy and utilitarian redbrick box flanked by two boxy smaller buildings, behind a set of broad concrete steps. Standing in front of it was an American flag, and tiny metal lettering over its door read, 25TH PRECINCT. The parking lot encircled the building in a U-shape, full to the brim with white police cruisers with the city's distinctive blue-and-yellow striping.

She passed a pair of patrolmen in their summer uniforms, short-sleeve, cobalt blue shirts with dark pants. They carried their hats under their crooked arms and smiled at her, and she smiled back, though her gaze strayed to their waists, where thick black utility belts held a holstered revolver, a walkie-talkie with a stiff antenna, a collapsible nightstick of matte-black metal, and handcuffs, jangling like janitors' keys as they went by.

Mary pushed open the smudged-glass doors and entered the building, not completely surprised by how dirty it smelled inside. She had handled criminal cases and had been in her share of police stations, but she never failed to be dismayed at how filthy they were, especially compared with their sanitized depiction in the movies or television. Not only did fiction get the dirt-level wrong, but the fake police precincts were always atmospherically dark, when in fact the opposite was true. Every police station she'd been in, including this one, was lit by fluorescent lighting so bright it required sunglasses.

The entrance hall was small and covered with grimy gray tile and peeling signs—INTERPRETERS AVAILABLE IN THE FOLLOWING LANGUAGES, PLEASE KEEP FEET OFF WALLS, and PHILADELPHIA POLICE SOCIAL MEDIA, announcing the department's Facebook, Twitter, and YouTube sites. The left wall was dominated by a bulletproof window that looked into an office lined with tan file cabinets, black plastic in-and-out boxes stacked one on top of the other, and a warren of gray cubicles bearing laptops with official screensavers. At the bottom of the window was a black counter with the metal tray and a little sign that read, touchingly, PEACE in blue capital letters.

Mary went to the window, where a female uniformed officer was just hanging up the phone. "Excuse me," she said.

"Yes, how may I help you?" the officer asked, her black nametag read CRUZAN.

Mary introduced herself, then said, "I'm here representing a ten-year-old boy who goes to Grayson Elementary and he was assaulted by a teacher's aide, three weeks ago. I'd like to file a complaint on his behalf."

"He was assaulted by a staff member?" Officer Cruzan's brown eyes flared.

"Yes."

"Did this take place on school grounds?"

"Yes."

"The procedure is for Grayson to call us. That's the way it works."

"I'm sure, but they weren't told about it, which is the only reason they didn't call you." Mary hadn't expected this to be easy, but she wanted to get the ball rolling. "I'm the child's lawyer and I'm here to tell you what happened, so that you can open a file and begin investigating."

Officer Cruzan frowned. "Is the complainant here?"

"My client? No, he's a ten-year-old boy, and he has anxiety. I think I can do that on his behalf."

Officer Cruzan thought a moment. "I hear you. You say this happened when?"

"Wednesday, September 16, but I just found out today. I'm assuming that I can file the papers to get a complaint started on his behalf."

"You mean, *in loco parentis*?"

"Yes, I'm his lawyer. Otherwise, I'd be happy to take the forms and have him fill them out at home. I'd like to avoid having to bring him in. Coming here would scare him."

"I don't know if this is procedure. Hold on, let me go ask my supervisor, please." Officer Cruzan frowned again.

"Great, please take my card and ID." Mary dug in her purse, extracted her wallet, and slid out her driver's license and a business card, passing them under the window.

"Fine, thank you." Officer Cruzan glanced at Mary's ID. "Be right back."

"Thanks." Mary watched the officer disappear into the office-like warren of cubicles behind the Plexiglas window, then turn right out of the room and disappear. It wasn't long until Officer Cruzan returned with an African-American officer wearing a white shirt instead of blue, which Mary knew meant he was a higher-up, though she never understood police rankings. His nametag read DIAMOND, and he had gold aviator glasses, a scar on his nose, and a head of salt-and-pepper hair, and he was smiling as he walked to the Plexiglas window.

"The famous Ms. DiNunzio!" he said, resting his hands on the desk on the other side of the window, and Mary tried not to act surprised, but she couldn't help herself.

"I didn't know I was famous. Wait, is your mom Rita Diamond?" Mary asked, pulling the name out of nowhere.

"Sure is!" Officer Diamond beamed. "She bought that new stove but the gas line was defective. She never stops singing your praises. You got her a replacement, for nothing!"

"I remember, she was afraid she was going to blow up the block." Mary smiled, cheered. It was about time some of her good karma followed her around, and she hoped it would work in Patrick's favor.

"That's her!" Officer Diamond chuckled. "She always imagines the worst thing that could happen. She goes right to disaster zone, zero to sixty. It was like, five, six years ago, wasn't it, that you fixed her up? I can't believe you remember that."

"She was unforgettable. All mothers are unforgettable." Mary thought instantly of Patrick, motherless.

"She sees your name in the paper and she says, 'I knew her when.' You're off the reservation today, aren't you?"

"Ha! Only in Philadelphia does three miles out of Center City qualify as off the reservation."

"Right!" Officer Diamond laughed, and Mary could see Officer Cruzan edge away with a relieved smile, letting him handle the situation.

"So Officer, as I'm sure Officer Cruzan told you, I'd like to file a complaint on behalf of a little boy without bringing him here and scaring him half to death. How do I accomplish that?"

"You're in loco parentis, so here's what we're going to do, to start out." Officer Diamond rummaged under the ledge and produced a complaint form, which he slid under the window along with her ID and business card. "You're going to fill out this 75-48, a general complaint. You know the relevant information, don't you? Date and time of incident, name of perpetrator, witnesses, if any."

"Yes, absolutely." Mary put away her card and ID, then looked over the form, which was straightforward.

"This can get us started investigating, but we're going to have to interview the boy, as soon as possible. We get the nuts and bolts, then you have to take him to PCA, the Philadelphia Children's Alliance, on Front Street." Officer Diamond gestured to his right, but Mary had a more immediate concern.

"Yes, but can you do your interview at the boy's house? He's—"

"I know, I heard the story. The answer is yes, considering he's a minor. Matter of fact, we might be able to squeeze him in this afternoon. We don't have that many jobs yet."

"That would be great, thanks." Mary smiled, and Officer Diamond smiled back, then it faded.

"Was the boy seriously injured?"

"I don't know, but I don't think so. He lives with his grandfather, and the grandfather said his face was swollen and bruised. They're getting him checked at St. Chris, as we speak."

"Good. That's just what we would have done." Officer Diamond nodded. "Did the grandfather seek medical attention for the boy at the time of the incident?"

"No, the boy didn't tell anyone about it, so he didn't. He said it was an accident."

"What about the school nurse? Did the boy see her?"

"Not her either," Mary assumed, though she had forgotten to ask Edward that question.

"Usually if there's any violence at Grayson, it's student-on-student and they call us. Is that why they didn't call us when it happened, do you know?"

"Yes, exactly."

"But you have since notified Grayson, haven't you?"

"The boy's grandfather has, and they're investigating the matter."

Mary didn't want to hide the ball about the lawsuit, and he'd find out anyway, when he went to the school and started asking questions. "I got involved today because the grandfather came to me. They're being sued. Believe it or not, this teacher's aide is now claiming that the kid came after him with the scissors."

"Really." Officer Diamond lifted an eyebrow.

"I don't believe that for a minute, but I wanted you to know the facts, going in. After all, if that was what happened, why didn't the teacher's aide tell the school or call you? The first time anybody heard of it was yesterday, when he filed the lawsuit against my client and the school district, for half a million dollars."

"Hmph. I hear that." Officer Diamond nodded, noncommittally, gesturing at the form. "Okay, you fill this out, and we'll get started. Let me get your contact info about what time I can get a uniform over to the house. Hopefully, in a couple hours or so." Officer Diamond winked. "My mom would kill me if I didn't take good care of you."

"Thanks," Mary said, grateful.

CHAPTER SIX

Mary cruised down Moretone Street, eyeing the houses for number 637, the O'Briens. Edward had called her after he'd taken Patrick to the pediatrician, but hadn't wanted to speak in front of Patrick about what the pediatrician had said. They'd set a time to meet at the house, with the police due whenever they got there, hopefully sooner rather than later.

Mary scanned the street, which seemed to be typical for Juniata, the neighborhood where the O'Briens lived, adjacent to Hunting Park. It was almost all residential, with long blocks of rowhouses, different from the rowhouses in South Philly. Typical South Philly rowhouses had varied façades but the rowhouses on Moretone Street were one long connected building of rowhouses, all the same red brick. Each house had a door on one side with a double-set of windows, with another double-set of windows on the second floor and a flat roof. The only variations were small elevated patios in front, paved with flagstone, brick, or concrete; some had railings, others not. Circling the block, Mary realized that Juniata did have one thing in common with South Philly—it took forever to find a parking space.

She finally spotted a space up the street, parked, got her stuff, and walked back to the O'Briens' past the houses. Air conditioners rumbled in the windows, dripping water, and a woman smoking a cigarette swept her front patio, which held a row of children's bicycles locked with a heavy chain. Other patios contained rusting barbecue grills, plastic sliding boards, and picnic tables. Tall oak trees lined the block, their limbs giving some relief from the sun, but none from the humidity, which was too much to ask of a tree.

As Mary approached the O'Briens' house, she glanced around for any police cruisers, but there were none. So she had arrived before the cops, which was good because she wanted to meet Patrick. She reached the O'Briens' and climbed up the front steps, glancing over at the concrete patio, which was completely empty of anything, like children's toys or bikes. She went to the front door and rang the buzzer.

The door was opened by Edward. "Mary, come in," he said, motioning her inside. "Patrick is upstairs."

"Thanks. What a nice home you have." Mary stepped inside, glancing around the small living room, which was neatly furnished with a mint-green padded couch under a long wall mirror, across from a wood coffee table that held a newspaper and some pencils, an older television on a table. It was somewhat dark, owing to the fact that an air conditioner filled one of the windows, but it must've been set on low because it was warm inside. Again, the room was devoid of any children's toys.

"Thank you. My wife and I bought it in the eighties." Edward shut the door behind her.

"Where does Patrick keep his toys and things? Where does he do his drawing?"

"Upstairs in his room. I don't like clutter."

"I'd like to see that later, if I may."

"Sure, right." Edward glanced over her shoulder, with a slight frown. "While Patrick is upstairs, I need to tell you what the pediatrician said. Patrick was listening when I called you, that's why I couldn't tell you before."

"Okay, what?"

"She said Patrick is healing nicely and he has no broken bones, or even cracked. She said he was lucky, he could have broken his orbital bone. That's the bone that goes around your eye sockets." Edward demonstrated by touching his gaunt cheekbone with a gnarled index finger.

"What did she say about the cause of the injury?"

"She couldn't tell how it happened. It was too late. She said it was a bruise that could've happened by Patrick hitting his face on a desk or by getting hit in the face."

"Understood." Mary had expected that would be the result, which put them back at square one, a credibility contest.

"I know that's not good for our case. I'm sorry I didn't take him in when it happened. I should have." Edward's frown deepened, but Mary patted him on the arm.

"Don't worry, you did fine. What did you tell Patrick about today?"

"What you told me to say, that a policeman was going to come and ask him a few questions about what happened in school."

"Was he nervous?"

"A little, but okay." Edward glanced over his shoulder again. "Should I tell him to come down?"

"Yes, please. I'd like to talk with him before the cops get here."

"Okay." Edward called upstairs. "Patrick, can you come down, please?"

"Coming!" Patrick called back, and in the next moment, a little shadow appeared at the top of the stairs, an adorably undersized silhouette.

Edward called out, "Patrick, come meet this nice lady! Her name is Mary!"

"Hi, Patrick!" Mary called up to him, smiling, but he didn't make eye contact with her or his grandfather, concentrating mightily on his feet as he bopped down the stairs, dragging his fingers along the wall. He had on a faded Phillies T-shirt that was too big for his frame, with plain gray gym shorts and oversized white tube socks that wrinkled like an accordion at the top of his no-name black sneakers.

When Patrick came into the light, Mary could see his features more clearly. He had very short reddish-brown hair and an inch-long fringe of bangs that framed a long, thin face, like his grandfather's. His ears stuck out and his two front teeth were oversized. Freckles dotted his longish nose, his eyes were set close together, and his right cheek bore the faint yellowish traces of a bruise, which got Mary's blood boiling all over again.

Patrick reached the ground floor, still without looking up, and Edward placed a hand on the boy's knobby shoulder. "Patrick, say hello to Mary."

"Hi," Patrick answered. He kept his face tilted down.

Edward frowned. "Patrick, you have better manners than that. Say hello to our guest—"

"No, that's okay," Mary interrupted, not wanting to press him. She looked up at Edward. "Why don't we all sit down?"

"Right." Edward motioned to the couch. "Can I get you something to drink, Mary? Some water?"

"No thanks." Mary sat down in the chair, sensing Edward looked more tired than earlier this morning. He moved slower, vaguely ill at ease, undoubtedly due to the stress of the day.

"Patrick. Go sit down." Edward prodded Patrick with a hand in his skinny little back, then sat down on the couch. "Mary wants to talk to you."

Patrick walked around the coffee table and sat in the middle of the couch. He still wasn't looking up, but Mary understood.

"Patrick, I want to tell you what's happening, so you'll understand. Your grandfather told me how smart you are, and I can see that, just from looking at you."

"Thank you," Patrick said politely, but still looking down.

"The police are going to come here and talk to you, but that doesn't mean you did anything wrong. They'll be wearing uniforms, and I'm not sure if there is going to be one or two of them, and they're going to ask you about what happened at school. Do you understand?"

"Yes. They're *investigating*. Like on *Law & Order*." Patrick looked up suddenly, and his brown eyes flashed with pride in himself, at knowing a correct answer.

"Right, exactly." Mary smiled. "All you have to do is answer their questions and tell them the truth. Do you understand?"

Patrick nodded, sucking on his lower lip, which disappeared

under his two front teeth, and Mary remembered that she had teeth like that when she was little, which they used to call buck teeth. Or at least the bullies did. Mary's nickname had been Bucky Beaver, a laugh riot.

"Patrick, if you don't understand anything the police ask you, you can ask them what they mean. Don't be afraid of them, they're here to help us and to understand what happened. Got it?"

Patrick nodded, still sucking away on his lip, and Mary wondered if it was a way of comforting himself, almost like a pacifier.

"It will be easy and it won't take very long." Mary paused. "Do you have any questions you want to ask me?"

Patrick didn't reply but shook his head, in the exaggerated way that Mary had seen little kids do.

"If you think of anything you want to ask me, you can say so later." Mary figured she had some time before the police arrived. "Your grandfather tells me you're very good at drawing."

Patrick brightened and stopped sucking his lip.

"Do you like to draw?"

"Yes!"

"What do you like about it?"

"It's fun!" Patrick smiled for the first time, showing missing teeth on the upper deck.

"What do you like to draw?"

"Oh I draw a lot of things, I can draw anything!" Patrick's voice sounded a new note of excitement, and Mary followed his enthusiasm.

"Like what?"

"Like *everything!*"

"Where do you do your drawings?"

"In my room." Patrick nodded in his exaggerated way.

"Would you like to show me your drawings, right now, while we're waiting?"

"Okay!" Patrick popped up from the couch like a jack-in-the-box and scampered around the coffee table to the steps.

"Great!" Mary rose, catching Edward's eye. She wanted to go upstairs alone with Patrick, but she didn't have to tell that twice to

Edward, who looked just as happy to stay behind, sinking backwards into the couch.

"Patrick," Edward said, calling after him. "Take Mary up to your room and show her your drawings. I'll call you when the police get here."

Patrick was already climbing the steps two at a time, trailing his finger pads on the wall, and Mary ascended behind him, keeping pace. He turned left at the top of the stairwell and ran down a short hallway until he got to the last room on the left, and Mary followed him inside, where it was uncomfortably warm.

"This is my room!" Patrick shouted, making a megaphone of his hands in a comical way, and Mary found herself liking him. He had a bright little spirit, with a surprising sense of humor, though it was hard to reconcile with his gruesome drawings.

"This place is great!" Mary said, glancing around the tiny room, which was remarkably orderly, and she was guessing that was how Edward ran the household. On the right side was a single bed, which had been made, the sheets folded over and a plaid coverlet at its foot. Next to the bed was a bookshelf of plain wood, its shelves filled with transparent containers of crayons, markers, pens, and pencils, and only a few thin children's books, a bunch of wrinkled comics, and a white copy of the Bible, with Patrick's name stamped on the spine. Posters of Spider-Man, Superman, and Ant-Man covered the walls, and there was a window that held a white plastic fan, but no air conditioner. Underneath the window was a blue Little Tykes table, its tabletop blanketed with drawings.

"This is my headquarters!" Patrick scooted to the table and began arranging the drawings into piles.

"Very cool!" Mary tried to catch sight of the drawings as he shuffled them around.

"Which do you want to see first?" Patrick looked up at her, directly, his brown eyes alive with animation, and Mary could see that his demeanor had changed completely from downstairs. He was freer, happier, more talkative, and even more confident.

"What are my choices? It looks like you made three piles."

"So this pile, the first one, is nature scenes, and the second pile is window scenes." Patrick pointed out the window to the row-houses across the street. "See? Those are new people that moved in, and I drew pictures of them with their moving van. It was *big*! And they had two cats. Two! One gray and one black and white."

"I heard you like comic books."

"That's *this* pile! *Bam!*" Patrick smacked his palm down on the third pile. The drawing on top was of a Transformer with shoulders like NFL shoulder pads, drawn in black Sharpie like the gruesome drawing had been.

"I want to see the third pile. I like comic books, too."

"Which comic books?" Patrick looked up, interested, his head still thrown back.

"Betty and Veronica." Mary didn't add that she was Betty. Every woman she knew was Betty. Or maybe Anne Murphy, from work, was Veronica.

"They're for girls." Patrick rolled his eyes, goofing around.

"Probably." Mary smiled, then glimpsed the bright red color from some bloody drawings at the bottom of the third pile. "What's that one? Is that blood?"

"Yes." Patrick yanked out one drawing, which was of a boy, just like the one on the drawing Machiavelli had shown her. The boy was stabbing the air, and in the distance was a large male figure.

"What's that?" Mary asked, keeping her tone light.

"That's Knife Boy killing a bad guy."

"Knife Boy?" Mary hid her concern. The drawing looked so much like the one Machiavelli had shown her, it could've come from the same series.

"Knife Boy is a superhero and he stabs bad guys with a knife, and sometimes he can turn himself *into* a knife." Patrick spoke more rapidly, with growing excitement, and he shuffled the drawings to show her another one, a boy shaped like a bullet, flying through the air. "This is Bullet Boy and he's like a bullet that gets shot out of a gun but sometimes he *has* a gun. He can either *be* a gun or be a bullet, whenever he wants to be. He can do whatever he wants to, to fight the bad guys. Same with Fog Boy, he is a poison fog like a ghost but a hero. He's like a hero ghost. I make up lots of stories about him."

"I see." Mary kept her tone noncommittal to keep him talking. "Is he a good guy or a bad guy?"

"Oh, he's a good guy, definitely! My superheroes are good guys and they fight bad guys." Patrick nodded, flipping through his drawings, and Mary could see him becoming absorbed in the fantasy world he had created, almost forgetting that she was there.

"And these are all superheroes that you invented?"

"Yes, and they are heroes like Spider-man and Superman and Iron Man and Ant-Man, he's my favorite because he's so funny and little and he can disappear *inside* pipes and motors and no one can see him, none of the bad guys."

"Ant-Man sounds cool." Mary guessed that Patrick identified with Ant-Man, probably the same way she identified with Betty.

"I love Ant-Man and Captain Merica, those are my favorites."

Mary realized that Patrick meant Captain America, but didn't correct him. Children who had dyslexia sometimes missed the beginning and endings of words.

"Those are the Marvel heroes but I make my own heroes and I am going to put them in comic books and be a comic-book artist when I grow up—oh, look at *this* one!" Patrick yanked out one of the drawings from the middle of the pack, which showed a boy as round as a bowling ball, with a cartoony string fuse coming out of his head. "This is Bomb Boy!"

"Wow! What does he do?"

"He rolls himself into the bad guys and he blows them up! But he doesn't die, he never dies, he lives forever, he just keeps coming back and back to fight bad guys."

"I see." Mary eyed the drawing, then the other ones. "Who are the bad guys?"

"Just bad guys," Patrick answered, as he looked at one drawing, then the next, lost in his imaginary world.

"Are they ever real people, in your life?"

"No, they're jus', like, they're evil terroris' or robbers or killers on *CSI*. They're just *bad*."

"What about the bad kids at school? There are bad kids at your school, aren't there?"

"Yes, but these are real bad guys, like, in the *world*."

"Are they ever real adults, you know? Like a neighbor or somebody else?"

"No, no, no." Patrick shook his head over the drawings. "They're bad guys, you know how there's bad guys everywhere? And you never know why bad guys are bad, they just are. That's why my Pops won't let me watch the news or go on the Internet by myself. Bad guys are there. You have to be careful."

"I agree." Mary thought it over. "How long have you been drawing these superheroes?"

"I don't know." Patrick shrugged his knobby shoulders.

"Would you say it was years ago or months ago?"

"Since I was little."

Mary hid her smile. "Who was the first superhero you invented?"

"Bullet Boy, then Knife Boy, they were the first two. I did them when I was really little."

Mary got an idea. "If I wanted to see one of those early Knife Man drawings, could you do that?"

"Yes, they're not in my headquarters because my Pops saves them in the office. He doesn't like me to keep a lot of papers in here. He says it's a fire hazard."

"He's right." Mary's mood lifted. If she could produce early drawings of Knife Boy that would predate Patrick's meeting Robertson, then that would suggest that the bad guy in the drawing wasn't Robertson. The more she thought about the drawings, the better she felt. Even though they depicted bloody scenes, Patrick wasn't angry when he talked about them and not all of his drawings were violent. Mary was no psychologist, but if she could argue to a jury that it was normal for a boy who generally felt powerless to imagine alter-egos who could defeat bad guys, then the drawing that Machiavelli had shown her, in context, no longer tended to prove that Patrick had tried to stab Robertson. The only place that Patrick felt empowered was in the imagined world of his artwork.

Mary tried to get him to open up. "So you want to make comic books someday?"

"Yes." Patrick looked over with a smile. "My Pops says I have a gift from God."

"That's true." Mary smiled back. "Talk to me about reading. That's a little bit harder for you, isn't it?"

"I can read," Patrick shot back, defensively.

"I see." Mary didn't want to challenge him directly, but she wanted him to be able to open up with her. Patrick was keeping his illiteracy secret, because he felt so ashamed, which was needless. "You know, Patrick, there are kids your age who can't read."

"That's not true." Patrick blinked. "Not in my class."

"I'm talking about kids that are in other schools." Mary had seen that dyslexic children could feel terribly alone. "Can you imagine a whole school full of children your age, but they can't read?"

"Why can't they?" Patrick eyed her directly, listening with a newly grave expression.

"Because everybody has a different brain and everybody learns differently. They go to a really great school where the teachers teach them differently and that's how they're learning to read. They're very smart, just like you, but they haven't been taught the way they need to be taught."

Patrick turned to the window. "They're here."

"The police? How do you know?"

"I hear them, don't you?" Patrick set down the drawings and went to the window, peeking through the blades.

Mary hadn't heard anything, but she looked out the window to see a police cruiser pulling up in front of the house, double-parking. She remembered that hyper-vigilance could be a symptom of dyslexia and also PTSD, but she didn't want to go there yet with Patrick.

"We'd better go downstairs." Patrick scooted around her, heading for the bedroom door. "My Pops says it's rude to be late."

CHAPTER SEVEN

Mary introduced herself to Officer Cindy Lee and Officer Jorge Muniz after Edward had introduced himself and Patrick, who had grown instantly quiet, looking up with wide eyes at the uniformed officers. Officer Lee was in her early thirties, with pretty features, an easy smile, and a shiny low ponytail, and she seemed to take the lead over her heavyset partner, perhaps because she was a woman.

Edward pulled in two wooden chairs from the kitchen, and the police officers sat down in them, their knees bumping the coffee table. Edward steered Patrick to the couch and sat down next to him, and Mary took the chair catty-corner to the couch, placing a notepad discreetly on her lap. She wanted to hear the story from Patrick's lips and resolved to listen objectively, even critically, to see what kind of a witness he would make, as well as resolve any doubts about the truth of what had happened.

The police officers slid skinny notepads from their back pockets, located some pens, and got settled, but Mary noticed that Patrick's demeanor had reverted back to his quieter, anxious self. He seemed to take in their every movement and he had resumed sucking his lower lip. He sat still on the couch cushion, neither bouncing nor swinging his legs, and he seemed to telescope down, roaching his back and hunching over, so that he seemed somehow smaller.

Officer Lee began by looking from Edward to Mary. "Folks, right now we're just going to get the bare-bones of what happened from Patrick. You'll need to take him to PCA, the Philadelphia Children's Alliance, after this for further questioning. We will give them a call that you're coming over and it shouldn't be a problem. They take walk-ins."

"I understand," Mary answered for her and Edward, because she could see him leaning forward, as if he hadn't heard. She remembered that Officer Diamond had mentioned PCA, too.

"Ms. DiNunzio and Mr. O'Brien, we ask you not to talk with Patrick about the incident between now and the time he's interviewed at PCA. It's procedure to keep the number of times he's interviewed to a minimum, for obvious reasons. That's why my interview now will be just enough to complete our file and begin our investigation." Officer Lee turned to Patrick with a reassuring smile. "So, Patrick, we want to hear from you. How did you get that bruise on your face?"

Patrick didn't say anything.

"What happened to you? I know it was a while ago, but do you remember what happened?"

Patrick nodded, but didn't say anything, then looked down.

"Okay. Let's just start at the beginning." Officer Lee consulted her notes. "You just started the fifth grade, right? I have a son in fourth grade, and his name is Adam."

Patrick didn't reply, and Mary felt pained on Patrick's behalf. It couldn't have felt good to hear about another boy about his age, lucky enough to have a pretty mom who also happened to be a cop.

Edward nudged Patrick. "Patrick, tell them what happened. They don't have all day. They're very busy."

Officer Lee pursed her lips. "Mr. O'Brien, thank you, but we have time. He can take his time."

"Take your time, Patrick," Officer Muniz added.

Patrick looked over at Mary, and on impulse, she winked at him. He flashed her a brief smile, which touched her.

Edward frowned. "Patrick, don't be rude. Tell her how you got hit at school, will you?"

Mary knew Edward was trying to speed things up, but he had put words in Patrick's mouth.

Officer Lee pursed her lips again. "Patrick, your grandfather means, tell us how you got the bruise."

Patrick stopped sucking his lip. "The teacher's aide hit me. Mr. Robertson."

"How did that come about, that Mr. Robertson hit you?" Officer Lee softened her tone.

"I was going to the assembly, and I started to get really, upset in my stomach, and I knew I was going to throw up, because sometimes I throw up in school and I get nervous." Patrick started working his lips again, looking down, and Mary and Officer Lee exchanged sympathetic glances.

"I know how that is," Officer Lee said, again modulating her tone. "I used to be very nervous in school. I didn't speak English that well, I had an accent, and the other kids teased me."

Patrick listened, but didn't say anything.

"I get nervous sometimes on my job, too."

Patrick nodded, his eyes flaring suddenly. "Because of terrorists."

"Right!" Officer Lee smiled.

"Terrorists, they try to shoot police, I saw on the news."

"Yes, that's very true." Office Lee nodded. "So everybody gets scared and nervous, sometimes. It's okay to be scared sometimes and to get sick. So what happened, you threw up?"

Patrick nodded, blinking, meeting Officer Lee's gentle gaze.

"And then what happened?"

"Mr. Robertson got really mad, like, really mad. He said, 'you better clean that out, you have to clean that up!'" Patrick's voice sped up, the story rushing out like a dam opening. "But it was on the floor and it has like a rug and it's like a blue rug and I didn't know how to clean it up, so I said to Mr. Robertson, 'What do I clean it up with?' I didn't see any paper towels or anything that I could pick it up with and he said, 'You have to lick it up.'"

Officer Lee blinked. "That's not very nice, is it?"

Mary masked her reaction. The very notion revolted her, and she also felt confused, in that this wasn't the story that Edward had told her. She didn't know if Edward had known this, he had just forgotten, or if Patrick was just telling it anew. She would have to clarify the time and location of the incident, but that was for another day. She looked over at Edward, whose expression had fallen into sorrowful lines.

Patrick shook his head no, in his exaggerated way. "I mean, it's my fault because I threw up but I didn't *want* to throw up, it came out of me, my cereal for breakfast. It was Special K."

Mary's heart went out to Patrick, thinking it was his fault, but she didn't want to interrupt him. Officer Muniz's lip curled in distaste, and he leaned away.

Officer Lee nodded in a sympathetic way. "So then what happened, Patrick?"

"So I tried to lick it up but I couldn't swallow it again, I tried to, it tasted gross." Patrick flushed under his freckles. "But then when I tried to eat it again, I started to throw up again, and then all of a sudden, Mr. Robertson picked me up and I started to cry and he hit me in the face with his hand."

Mary swallowed hard because it was awful to hear, and she had no doubt watching Patrick tell it, that every word was true. She wondered what the reference to "again" was, but kept her own counsel, leaving it to Officer Lee to continue the questioning.

"Patrick, when he hit you, did he use his fist or was it a slap?"

"I don't know, his hand, and it hurt a lot and I don't know what happened, like it's not that I don't remember, but it happened all at once, and I went across the room, like I *flew* across the room." Patrick's eyes flared with the memory. "And then when I looked up, I was on the floor and my face hurt really bad and I started to cry. I couldn't help it."

Mary could visualize the scene, which turned her stomach. She noticed Edward blinking wetness from his hooded eyes behind his glasses.

Officer Lee nodded. "I understand, I would cry too. That's a terrible thing to have happen. Did he hit you once or more than once?"

"One time, this time. But, like, before . . ." Patrick stopped abruptly.

Mary held her breath, waiting for him to finish. She realized she hadn't taken any notes while he spoke, but she wouldn't forget what he'd said.

Officer Lee asked, "Had this happened before, that Mr. Robertson hit you?"

Patrick swallowed hard. "He didn't hit me before, but he pushed me and I hurt myself."

"What happened that time?"

"I never used to throw up in school, like last year I didn't, but this year it's different, the teacher, Mrs. Krantz yells a lot and I feel more nervous, and I threw up the first day of school and that's when they said I was the Duke of Puke and then everybody started calling me that."

"The kids were teasing you?"

"Yes, and they thought that name was so funny and so they call me that and they make noises whenever they see me, like they pretend they're gonna puke." Patrick blinked, and his lower lip trembled, but he didn't cry. "Mr. Robertson got me another time, like before the last time, and he didn't hit me but he shoved me, like, pushed me into the wall and I hurt my shoulder."

"Which shoulder was that?"

"This one." Patrick pointed to his left shoulder.

"Did you tell your grandfather about that?"

Patrick shook his head, no. Mary glanced at Edward, whose eyes were still wet. He must not have known about the earlier incident, and she knew he would be feeling terrible.

Officer Lee continued, "The first time, did Mr. Robertson say anything to you?"

"He was saying I was the Duke of Puke, that I was a big baby and I should be ashamed of myself for being such a baby and so stupid."

Mary wanted to wring Robertson's neck. It killed her to hear about Patrick being victimized, and he wasn't even hers. She wondered how she would ever be a mother.

Office Lee frowned. "Was there anybody else around the time that he hit you in the face?"

Patrick shook his head, no.

"Was anyone else around the time that he pushed you against the wall?"

Patrick shook his head, no, again.

"Where did this take place, the first time?"

"In a room near the classroom at school."

"And the second time, was it the same place or a different place?"

"The same place."

"What room was this?"

"I don't know. It had cleaning machines."

Officer Lee consulted her notepad. "Now, I understand that the time he hit you in the face, that was on Wednesday, on September the 16. Does that sound like the right day to you?"

Patrick shrugged. "I don't know."

Officer Lee continued, "Well, let's try and figure it out. How many days were between the first time and the second time Mr. Robertson hurt you?"

"Like a few days." Patrick flushed again. "He doesn't like me. He says I'm stupid and retarded and I don't know how to read."

Officer Lee frowned. "That's not very nice. It's mean to call people names, and I'm sure you know how to read."

Mary bit her tongue. Before she practiced special-education law, she would have assumed that all fifth-graders could read, too. Edward looked down, linking his hands in his lap.

Officer Lee cleared her throat, in a final way. "Well, that's all the questions I have for you, Patrick. You're a very brave boy and you did the right thing, talking to us today."

Patrick flushed. "Mr. Robertson told me not to say anything. He told me if I told anybody what he did that he would kill me. He said he would kill me and he would kill my grandfather. He would kill my whole family."

Officer Lee frowned. "You don't have to worry about that. We're not going to let him do that. He's just being a bully."

"Would you guard our house? I don't want him to kill us."

"We'll keep an eye on you both. You don't have to worry about that."

"My Pops says, 'don't be a tattle-tale.' "

At that, Edward looked up. "That's only something I say, that's what my mother always said. I told him that when he was little."

Officer Lee nodded. "Of course, Mr. O'Brien, we understand. There's a generational difference here, and times have changed, especially with respect to school violence." She turned to face Patrick and leaned over toward him. "Patrick, that is not the way things are anymore."

"The sixth-graders say, 'snitches get stitches.' "

"I know, but they're wrong," Officer Lee said, in a new Mom-tone. "You mentioned the terrorists before, remember? Did you ever hear people say, 'If you see something, say something?' "

Patrick nodded, yes.

"Well, *that's* the right thing. Saying something is the right thing, always. If a bad thing happens, or if you see a bad thing, you have to tell the teacher. Or your grandfather."

Patrick nodded, yes, but started sucking his lip again.

"Good, thank you, Patrick." Officer Lee flipped her notebook closed and stood up, returning it to her back pocket. "Mr. O'Brien and Ms. DiNunzio, thanks."

"Folks, thank you very much." Officer Muniz rose, putting his notebook away. "Patrick, you did the right thing today. I'm proud of you."

"Thank you," Patrick said in his polite way, looking up at Edward for approval, but Edward was already rising and walking stiffly to the door.

"Officers, let me show you out, and thank you very much for your time." Edward reached the door and opened it wide.

Mary got up, but stayed with Patrick. "Thank you, Officers," she called to them.

"You're welcome." Officer Lee stopped at the door. "Call the

Philadelphia Children's Alliance. They conduct a forensic interview, which is videotaped and admissible in court. Give them the heads-up that you're taking him over."

"Thanks. Will do." Mary nodded, sliding her phone from her pocket.

CHAPTER EIGHT

The modern gray complex of low-rise buildings on Hunting Park Avenue housed all of children's welfare services under one roof: PCA, or the Philadelphia Children's Alliance, DHS, or the Department of Human Services, and the Police Department's SVU, or Special Victims Unit. The striking architecture of the buildings stood out in this gritty industrial section of Hunting Park.

"The building looks nice," Mary chirped, trying to lighten the mood. She was driving the O'Briens in her car, with Edward in the front seat and Patrick in the back, and on the ride over, both of them had looked out of their respective windows, saying nothing the entire time. Mary understood that not all families were as talkative as hers, that men talked less than women, and that nobody talked as much as Italian-American women, so she didn't take it personally even if it was a culture shock.

Mary pulled into the lower lot and parked, but left the engine running for the air-conditioning. She glanced in the rearview mirror at Patrick. "Hey, pal, how you doing back there?"

"Okay." Patrick didn't look away from the window.

"Let me explain to you what's going to happen inside." Mary had gotten the basics from the receptionist when she'd called to say they were coming in. "This is no big deal. There's going to be a nice lady and she's going to ask you what happened, just like with the police, and you should just tell her the truth. There's nothing to worry about or be nervous about. Okay?"

"Okay." Patrick still didn't look away from the window, so Mary turned around to face him, and in the daylight, she could see that his bruise was larger than she'd thought, though it was faint.

"You're not worried, are you?"

"No."

"Do you have any questions before we go in?"

"No." Patrick kept turned to the window.

"You sure? You can ask me anything, you know that."

"I know." Patrick shrugged.

Edward turned, emitting a low grunt as he twisted around in the seat. "Patrick, look at Mary when she's talking to you. She's trying to help you."

Mary said, "Edward, it's okay—"

"Wait, I have a question." Patrick turned to Mary. "How do you get the air-conditioning in your car to be so good?"

Mary smiled. "I keep it on high."

"I like it." Patrick smiled back, which Mary thought was adorable.

"Good. Any other questions?"

"Is this place we're going air-conditioned?"

"Yes, I'm sure it is." Mary chuckled.

"Do they keep it on high?"

"I'm sure they do."

Edward shook his head. "Patrick—"

"Let's go," Mary interrupted, preempting what she sensed was going to be a reprimand. She liked Edward, but she could see that he was getting crankier as the day went on, and though she understood his reaction, her focus was Patrick. The boy was the one who had been beaten up and now had to answer questions about it, twice in a row. The three of them got out of the car, and Mary led the way through the parking lot. She noticed that Patrick bopped along at Edward's side, but they didn't hold hands, which must have been another cultural difference. Mary's mother didn't let go of Mary's hand in parking lots until sometime last year.

They reached the Philadelphia Children's Alliance entrance, which was of frosted glass with a transparent single door. Patrick scooted forward to open the door for them, glancing up at Edward for approval, but Edward was already walking through the door with Mary, who stepped into a waiting room that struck her immediately as an oasis for children. The room was large, with every square inch made for kids. The reception desk was on the left, painted on three sides with a mural of a fantastical garden, and on the right were green-padded chairs, with lots of smaller chairs for kids. Two little girls were watching a new flat-screen TV that hung on the wall, playing a *Shrek* DVD, a little boy and a girl were playing in a brown Little Tykes kitchen stocked with molded pork chops, fake fruits, and a pretend roasted chicken, and next to a kiddie-height table covered with construction paper, Magic Markers, and crayons.

Patrick's gaze went immediately to the art table, then he looked up at Edward. "Can I?"

"No," Edward answered, and Mary kept her own counsel. She would have said yes, but she kept that to herself and crossed to the reception desk.

"How can I help you?" asked the receptionist, a young girl with a long ponytail.

"I'm Mary DiNunzio, I called for a walk-in for Patrick?" Mary intentionally didn't use his last name, which was standard practice in any case involving a minor.

"Please, sit down. That will just be a minute."

"Thank you." Mary went to the seating area and took a chair next to Edward, with Patrick on the other side.

Mary sat down, getting her bearings. The waiting room was almost full, with men and women reading their phones in the chairs, amid a noise level predictable for children, and fortunately, the air-conditioning on full blast. Mary watched the little girls mesmerized by *Shrek* on DVD, then the little boy cutting the pretend pork chop with a toy knife, then slowly, it dawned on her that the happy scene wasn't so happy, at all. This was the intake for all of the child abuse cases in the city, and that meant that all of these children had been abused and that these parents were here in their worst moments, just like Edward.

Mary's mouth went dry at the thought, and she kicked herself for not realizing it when she had first entered the waiting room. It was really too awful to contemplate, not only that anybody could harm an innocent child, but that there were so many of them, and they all looked so adorable at play, little girls in their flowery sundresses and pink sandals, with their hair in barrettes, and little boys in tank tops with skinny arms and crumbling wash-off tattoos.

The children were of all ethnicities: white, black, Hispanic, and Asian, and the adults showed the same mix, though when Mary looked closer at their faces, she realized that they all shared the same expression, the controlled anger and unbearable strain of adults whose children had been abused—the same pursed lips, subtle frown, out-of-proportion concentration on a phone screen— masking the pain, anger, and hurt they must be feeling for their children.

"Ms. DiNunzio, Mr. O'Brien, and Patrick?" a young African-American woman called out, as she came through a door on the other side of the room, carrying a manila folder. She had a round, pretty face dominated by lively brown eyes and framed with dark, oiled curls. She smiled broadly when she spotted Mary, Edward, and Patrick, standing up.

"Here, we are." Mary brightened as she walked forward with Edward and Patrick.

"I'm Cassandra Porter," said the woman, shaking Mary's hand, then Edward's, and smiling down at Patrick. "Hi, Patrick, come on in."

"Thanks," Mary said, and they passed through the door into a large open space that led to a long hallway of closed doors, with a blue-patterned carpet. The walls were a soft creamy hue, clean and freshly painted, and appealing, large-scale cityscapes painted by children lined the walls on both sides. Yellow signs outside the doors read QUIET ZONE, SENSITIVE RECORDING IN PROGRESS.

"Welcome, folks." Cassandra smiled again, down at Patrick. "Patrick, nice to see you."

Patrick didn't reply except to nod, looking around.

"I'm Edward O'Brien, Patrick's grandfather." Edward extended a hand to Cassandra, and she shook it.

"Good to meet you, Mr. O'Brien. Thank you for bringing him in."

"Are you sure this is necessary?" Edward asked, his tone unmistakably cranky.

Mary looked over at him, surprised at his question. She had explained the reason for the forensic interview at the house, out of Patrick's earshot.

"Yes, it is, and it's standard procedure," Cassandra answered pleasantly, then returned her attention to Patrick. "Patrick, I'm going to be speaking with you today and asking you a few questions. But first, will you do me a favor and step into this room for a moment, so I can talk to your grandfather and Ms. DiNunzio?"

Patrick nodded, yes.

"Here we go." Cassandra opened the first door in the hallway, and it swung open onto a white room the size of a cubicle, with purple-and-orange bubbles painted on the walls. There was nothing in the room but a round white table with two kiddie-sized blue stools, and on the table was a small box of Kleenex and a tray of Magic Markers and some white paper. Patrick spotted the art supplies immediately, though Mary's gaze found the box of Kleenex, knowing what it was for, sadly.

"Can I go draw?" Patrick asked, looking up at Edward.

Cassandra answered, "Go right ahead, Patrick."

Patrick took off, already in motion when Edward called after him, "Patrick?"

Cassandra shut the door, closing Patrick inside, then looked to Edward and Mary. "Folks," she said, lowering her voice. "Follow me, so we can chat about this without disturbing the other interviews." She turned on her heels and led them two doors down, where she opened the door with a red triangle that said CONSULTATION ROOM.

Mary stepped inside to find a larger room than the cubicle, containing a round conference table of wood veneer, and around the table sat four adult-sized padded chairs. On the near wall hung another child's cityscape, but opposite that was a large LG flat screen.

Cassandra shut the door behind them. "Mr. O'Brien, it's standard operating procedure in a child abuse case for a forensic interview."

"But why do you need another interview?" Edward frowned. "He just talked to the police. Why don't you just use that one?"

Mary still didn't understand why he was asking. She had explained to him that this would be a videotaped interview, but she let Cassandra answer.

"Mr. O'Brien, a forensic interview is a fuller investigation of the facts than the police do, especially with a minor. In addition, we videotape the interview and audiotape it as well—"

Edward interrupted, "I didn't see a camera."

"The camera is hidden, and that's by design. We don't want the child to feel inhibited by the fact that he or she is being filmed, nor do we want them to perform for the camera." Cassandra kept her tone reasonable, though firm. "The camera lens is mounted in the corner near the ceiling, so it's not in the child's view, and if you notice the metal plate next to the table, that's where the audio feed comes in."

Mary blinked, surprised. She hadn't gotten these details over the phone when she made the appointment. She hadn't realized the camera would be hidden and just now, she hadn't even noticed the metal plate, too distracted by the Kleenex box.

Cassandra gestured at the LG screen. "This is actually the monitor where we can watch the videotape of the interview. The audiotape comes through over there, at that metal plaque on the wall."

Edward and Mary both looked over at a piece of metal no larger than an electrical plate, but with a grate.

Cassandra continued, "This is where the team meets, and we liaise with the D.A., the SVU detective, and DHS, if applicable, for children in foster care."

"And what happens here?" Mary said, wanting to know more.

"This is where, for example, a district attorney will watch the testimony and decide whether to bring charges and which charges to bring." Cassandra returned her attention to Edward. "But let's go back to your question about why the forensic interview is necessary. In addition to there being a different physical setup than a police interview, I am a trained forensic investigator, specializing in child abuse cases. I have a master's degree and I've been doing this for almost eight years now. I know how to establish a rapport with children in Patrick's position. As a result, I am going to be able to get more information out of Patrick, and the details in an abuse case can make the difference between an acquittal and a conviction."

"Good," Mary said, brightening. "Because during the police interview, Patrick recounted a second incidence of abuse by the teacher's aide—"

"Please, stop." Cassandra held up her palm. "I know you're trying to be helpful, but let me explain something to you, about getting testimony from children in abuse cases. May I?"

"Please, do," Mary answered.

"Briefly put, PCA is what is also called a CAC, or children's advocacy center. The concept was started decades ago by a lawyer in Huntsville, Alabama, who represented children in sexual abuse cases. He found that he was losing cases because clever defense lawyers could pick apart the inconsistencies in the child's story." Cassandra's brown eyes flashed with a passion for her subject. "Research has shown that children, when they are asked the same question repeatedly, will automatically begin to change the answer in some ways. Small ways. They somehow get the idea that they are not pleasing the adult and they are not giving the right answer, so they begin to change the answer."

"Okay," Mary said, following along.

"In addition, the more people who interview a child, the more likely it is that the child's testimony will become tainted or contaminated. Words the child didn't know before get introduced, and suddenly the interviewer begins to influence the story that the child is telling, even if the story starts out being true."

"I can see that," Mary said glancing over at Edward, who remained quiet while Cassandra continued.

"The purpose of a children's advocacy center like PCA is to preserve the integrity of the child's testimony. We limit the number of times a child is interviewed to this one time, and the police have been trained *not* to elicit detailed information during their inter-view or to contaminate any testimony that comes in. They are simply supposed to get the facts enough to begin the investiga-tion, then refer the child to us. Isn't that what happened for you folks, today?"

"Yes," Mary answered for them both.

"Okay." Cassandra's expression softened. "Sorry about the lec-ture, but I wanted you both to understand our process, and Mary, I wanted you to understand why I *don't* want to hear any facts you heard during the police investigation. In other words, I don't want *you* to taint *me*."

"Sorry," Mary said, kicking herself. "This is all new to me. I've handled special-education cases, but never a child abuse case."

"They're related, and sometimes they go hand-in-hand, but wel-come to my world." Cassandra smiled, grimly. "We served almost three thousand five hundred children at this center last year, most of them abused sexually, but some physical abuse only. About 225 of those children were from this very zip code, which was the high-est number of anywhere in the city."

Edward recoiled.

Mary blinked.

Cassandra walked to the door. "We know what we're doing. If Patrick was abused, we'll find out how, when, and by whom. We'll get the evidence the D.A. needs to charge the offender. We'll refer Patrick to therapy. Most children who suffer from abuse exhibit symptoms of PTSD and they need treatment to heal." Cassandra put her hand on the doorknob. "So now, if you have no further questions, please return to the waiting room and wait there. I'll call you when Patrick and I are finished."

Edward's mouth dropped open. "Hold on a minute. You mean we're not going to be in the room with him, when you talk to him, or interview him, or whatever?"

Mary didn't get it, either. "Wait, what? I understand why we're not allowed in the interview room, but I thought that we would be sitting here in the consultation room, so we can watch and listen to the interview."

"No, neither is going to happen. That's not how it works." Cassandra shook her head, her hand on the doorknob. "You both wait in the waiting room. You don't get to listen to the interview or watch it."

"That's not right." Edward shook his head. "I'm family, his only family."

"And I'm his lawyer," Mary added, confused. It went against all of her instincts to allow a client to go unrepresented in any proceeding with legal ramifications. "It's weird enough that I'm not sitting at his side, but there's no reason I can't just stay in this room and watch. He won't know."

Cassandra shook her head again. "That's not the law. If you need the legal cite, I'll go find it. The law furthers our goal to preserve the integrity of Patrick's testimony and find out the truth. If he is aware that either of you are watching him from this room, he may try to please you. He may leave out parts of the story or fabricate other parts, in order to make you happy." Cassandra looked from Mary to Edward. "So I hope you understand and I have to ask you both to wait in the waiting room. The forensic interview may take an hour or longer. If you leave to get coffee or something to eat, then let the receptionist know."

Edward scoffed. "This is ridiculous! There's no reason in the world why I can't be with my grandson, or at least stay here and listen to what he says on TV. I have half a mind to get him out of here!"

Mary touched his arm. "Edward, don't. If this is the way they do it, this is the way they do it. I'll look up the law and double-check, but they're just trying to help Patrick." Mary turned to Cassandra. "Do you create a DVD or an audiotape of his testimony?"

"Yes, but you can't obtain it without a subpoena or court order."

"Really?" Mary asked, surprised. Then she realized that Cassandra and PCA were just good people trying to protect children from a world that abused them, exploited them, and stole their innocence. The entire legal procedure was designed to find out the truth, and ultimately, to do justice for children.

"Yes, of course, it would be different if this came to us as a typical abuse case and if you, Mary, were a Child Advocate. If you were a Child Advocate, you would be permitted to observe the forensic interview in this room. But you're not a Child Advocate *per se*. You're representing both the caregiver and the child."

"Yes, that's true." Mary understood the distinction. Cassandra couldn't be certain that there wasn't a conflict of interests between Edward's interests and Patrick's, and she had to operate under the assumption that Edward might have abused Patrick, but she was too diplomatic to say so.

"Are we all on the same page?" Cassandra twisted the doorknob.

Edward asked, "How do we find out what he said?"

"I will call you in when we're finished."

"Mary?" Edward turned to her, his gray eyebrows flying upward in outrage. "Am I supposed to take this lying down?"

"Yes." Mary took his arm. "Let's go, and I'll explain outside."

CHAPTER NINE

Mary steered Edward by his elbow through the busy waiting room and then the exit door, to the PCA entrance, which was of elevated concrete bordered by a gray metal fence. To the left was the Police SVU building, and to the right was DHS, but there were no benches anywhere in sight, and she could see Edward sagging almost visibly, his back characteristically stooped.

"I can't believe this, I just can't believe this," Edward said under his breath, shaking his head, and Mary held on to his arm and got him to the railing.

"Would you like to go sit in the car? I can turn on the air-conditioning, we can talk. You can be comfortable."

"No, I don't want to go far." Edward leaned on the railing, bending over and looking out over the parking lot, his hooded eyes flitting over the cars broiling in the sun.

"You'll be more comfortable, really."

"No, I'm fine, I'm tired, it's a lot of activity for one day."

"Of course, I understand that," Mary said, though she guessed it was the stress, not the activity level, that was getting to him. "Or if you want, we could go get a soda and relax. You heard Cassandra, it's going to be awhile."

"No, I don't want to leave him. It's that—" Edward stopped abruptly, still shaking his head. He kept looking out over the parking lot, but Mary could see that he wasn't really focusing on anything. In fact there was nothing to focus on, since nobody was in the parking lot or on the sidewalk, and the only scenery was two water towers to the left and a crappy brick warehouse across the street to the right.

"PCA is a good place, Edward. A great place." Mary patted his back, and the cottony cloth of his sportcoat felt worn under her finger pads. "Try not to worry about him, they know what they're doing."

"I know, I know, it's just that this whole thing . . . this whole thing is shameful, just shameful . . ." Edward's sentence trailed off.

"Yes it is, but we're going to make it right. She'll get the information she needs, and we'll go forward." Mary wanted to focus him, because she had some questions she wanted answers to, as well. "Edward, let me ask you, did you hear what I heard during the police interview? Like that there were some differences between the story that you told me in my office and that Patrick told the police?"

"Yes, I did, I can't remember now." Edward rubbed his forehead with trembling hands, leaving pinkish marks on his lined skin.

"There were a few. Did you hear Patrick say there was a previous incident with Steve Robertson?"

"Yes, I did," Edward answered, miserably. "I heard him say that, too."

"Did you know that before?"

"No, no." Edward's tone went soft with pain.

"And did you hear Patrick tell the police that Steve told him to 'lick up' the vomit?"

"Yes, yes, I heard him say that too." Edward rounded his tongue over dry lips. "I heard him say that, and it's disgusting. It's *disgusting.*"

"Did you know about that?"

"No, no." Edward bent over farther, slumping on the railing and looking down. "God in heaven, God in heaven. That poor boy, that little boy."

"I know, it's awful. We'll set it right, Edward."

"You heard what she said. PTSD, therapy, that's the life he's going to have from now on. Not a normal life, not the life he deserves."

"He can have a normal life, Edward. We can get the help he needs." Mary tried to find a bright note. "But I'm not as worried about his artwork as before. He showed it to me upstairs and I think he's just drawing bad guys, not any guy in particular, much less Mr. Robertson."

Edward sighed. "My poor boy. He was so cute, what a happy little boy. My daughter, Suzanne, she adored him. The sun rose and set on that child. His feet never touched the ground the first year." Edward's voice coarsened, choked with emotion. "She read to him, she did everything. She would never forgive me."

"You haven't done anything, Edward." Mary patted his back again. "This isn't your fault."

"Yes, it is, it really is. You don't know." Edward looked out at the parking lot again, and Mary could see the wetness in his eyes.

"What don't I know?"

"You asked me if I knew, and I'm going to tell you something now, something awful."

"What?" Mary asked, hearing the anguish in his voice.

"I know. In fact, I *knew*." Edward looked up at her, his eyes brimming. "When Patrick came home with that bruise on his face, I knew someone had hit him. I didn't believe his story about falling down, not for a minute. I've been around the block. I know what it looks like when you get hit in the face. I figured one of the other kids in the schoolyard got into it with him."

Mary masked her shock. "Why didn't you do anything about it?"

"Truth is, I pretended not to know because I didn't *want* to do anything about it. I thought to myself, 'okay, he can take a punch, maybe it'll toughen him up. He'll learn to hit back.' Can you imagine a grandfather thinking such an awful thing?" Edward blinked, and a tear rolled his cheek, but he wiped it away quickly, tucking a knuckle under his glasses.

"You can't blame yourself," Mary said, her tone softer. She wasn't sure that she believed her own words, but it was the best that could be done now.

"You want the whole truth?" Edward wiped his eyes again, meeting her gaze. "I wouldn't have done anything if Robertson hadn't filed his lawsuit. It was a *lawsuit* that got me to you, not that my *grandson* got punched in the face. I couldn't ignore the lawsuit like I could ignore that little boy, my precious grandson."

Mary said nothing, and Edward's lower lip started to tremble as he wiped another tear from his eyes.

"I wonder what my daughter can be thinking now, looking down on me, I pray to her to forgive me. I've done such a terrible job with that little boy—"

"No, you haven't." Mary rubbed his back.

"I have, you don't know, and sometimes I'm so tired, I send him upstairs because I'm too tired to deal with him. His chatter, his questions, his homework, his worksheets. I don't even help him anymore. He helps me more than I help him. I used to have my diabetes under control with the pills, but not anymore. I have to check my blood sugar and inject myself four times a day now. He does it for me sometimes if I get the shakes. So who takes care of who?" Edward stifled a sob. "The truth is by dinner time, I'm so damn tired I think to myself, 'God didn't make a seventy-two-year-old to be a parent.' Then as I tired as I am, I can't sleep all the way through the night. I wake up to go to the bathroom, then I can't get back to sleep, worrying. I take Ambien, it knocks me out." Edward shook his head, trying not to cry. "I can't do it. I can be a grandpop, yes, but a father, no. I'm an accountant, I'm good with numbers, and I read somewhere that 10 percent of the kids in America, they're raised by grandparents. We love our grandkids, but it's hard, so hard, and sometimes I'm afraid I can't do it another day."

"I'm sure, that's natural." Mary heard the door opening behind them, and two young women left PCA, looking pointedly away, but Edward was too distraught to notice, continuing.

"If my daughter were alive, she would've done so much more, and she wouldn't have let his reading go the way I did. I see the commercials on TV, lots of things that can be done for dyslexia, but I didn't do any of them." Edward looked down, shaking his head. "I let him down, I failed him, he can't even read a sentence and he's terrible with math, he can barely add. *That's* what happened on my watch, that's who he has for a parent, a tired old man who was willing to look the other way when some bastard hit him in the face—" Edward finally broke down in tears, his forehead dropping onto the fist made by his hands, his shoulders shuddering.

"Oh, Edward, let's go to the car." Mary put an arm around his shaking shoulders, then helped him down the steps and toward the car. She fished a Kleenex out of her purse, passed it to him, and he held it to his nose, his tears dripping inside his glasses. They reached the car, where she installed them in the passenger seat and closed the door behind him. She hurried around the front of the car, climbing inside and turning on the air-conditioning, and by then, his sobbing was subsiding and he was blowing his nose.

"Mary, I'm . . . so sorry, I'm so ashamed . . ."

"No apologies are necessary."

"God help me."

"Just rest, Edward. Put your head back and rest."

"I will, I need to, thank you." Edward blew his nose again, making his cheeks flush a violent red, then he let his bald head fall back against the headrest. "I'll just rest my eyes, only for a second."

"Sure, please do." Mary stayed quiet as he closed his eyes, his glasses awry and the fissures of his cheeks stained with tears, and in the next moment, she realized that he was falling asleep. His shoulders let down and palms fell open on his lap, one hand still clutching the soggy Kleenex. His jaw went slack, and his head rolled slightly to the side.

Mary felt touched at the sight, feeling for him. He had stepped up, borne an impossible burden, and done the best that he could. She didn't judge him, and what was past was past. She glanced at the dashboard clock and she realized she had other work to do. She wanted to wrap up as many matters as she could before the wedding.

Mary picked up her purse, eased out of the seat, and stepped outside the car. She leaned on the car, scrolling through her phone, then pressed in the number of her first client, watching the traffic idly while the phone call rang. Front Street was lined with parked cars, and she happened to look at the cars parked across the street. They were all empty, but a brown sedan parked across from the PCA entrance idled with a driver inside.

Mary got a good look at the driver because the sedan had a sun-roof. She blinked. He looked familiar. He had a mustache. The driver looked a lot like Robertson.

Mary's mouth went dry. Was it Robertson? Could he be follow-ing them? Had he followed them here? Patrick said he had threat-ened to kill him and Edward. She felt a tingle of fear. She hung up the phone but kept it to her ear, walking toward the brown sedan, but in the next moment, the driver took off.

Quickly Mary scrolled to the photo function on her phone to try to take a picture of the car or the license plate, but it was too late. The sedan had joined the traffic going in the opposite direction. She watched, stricken, as it disappeared down the street.

An hour later, Mary had sweated through her suit and Edward was still asleep, but she figured it had to be almost time for Patrick to be finished. She woke Edward up, and they crossed back through the parking lot, climbed the steps to the entrance, and went inside. She would tell him about the brown sedan when she had the chance, later.

Mary took one look at Cassandra's face and knew there was trouble.

CHAPTER TEN

Cassandra ushered Mary and Edward to another white cubicle that was the same as the others except for a bookshelf containing toys and art around adult-sized table and chairs, and two large posters on the wall, which were impossible not to read. The one said at the top: HOW ARE YOU FEELING TODAY? *COMO TE TIENES HOY?* Underneath were cartoon kid faces in an array of expressions, labeled in English and Spanish: HAPPY, FELIZ. AFRAID, CON MIEDO. SAD, TRISTE. CONFUSED, CONFUNDIDO. ANGRY, ENOJADO. Next to that hung a rectangular poster that read at the top, FEELINGS THERMOMETER, next to a picture of a thermometer. Number 10 was at the top of the thermometer, with the feeling I'M FREAKING OUT!!!! Number 9 was VERY BAD, Number 8 was BAD, Number 7 was DIFFICULT, Number 6 was NOT GOOD, NOT TERRIBLE, and the numbers went down to Number 1, which was GOOD.

Mary sat down in the chair across from Cassandra, wondering what it must be like to be a child who was freaked out, angry, confused, and sad. She knew that there were abused children in the world but it had been an abstract matter until now, when she had met Patrick and saw the bruise on his little face, and until she had come to PCA and was staring face-to-face with a "Feelings Thermometer," undoubtedly invented to help little kids express how horrible they were feeling at the hands of the adults who were supposed to love and protect them. It hurt her heart, and she glanced at the Feelings Thermometer to realize that her own feelings were probably at a Number 9, VERY BAD.

Cassandra looked up from a white page of notes, her expression professional, if grim. She glanced from Edward to Mary and back again to Edward. "I'd like to speak with you both briefly about the results of our investigation, but first I have to caution you. You in particular, Edward."

"Yes?" Edward blinked, coming to full alertness. His lined mouth was already turning down at the corners, he lifted his chin, trying to be strong.

"Edward, what I am about to tell you will be difficult for you, as Patrick's grandfather, to hear. It would be difficult for anyone to hear, but especially family. It is our policy to share information with family and other caregivers regarding what a child tells us during the forensic interview. There are a few exceptions to this, which don't apply in this case, but the one that does apply is that we will not give you the information if you cannot emotionally handle the information." Cassandra blinked. "Edward, if you don't feel that you can handle the information, then you should feel free to step out of the room. I would not appreciate a replay of your earlier reaction. We could be overheard by other children."

"I'll be fine," Edward answered with such finality that even Mary believed him. "Where is Patrick?"

"He's playing in one of the other rooms. I gave him some watercolors and he went to town." Cassandra smiled briefly.

"That would be Patrick." Edward managed to smile back, but Mary could see that it was an effort.

Cassandra consulted her notes. "Okay, folks, I'll keep this brief. As an overview, the forensic interview with Patrick went well. After a slow start, he was able to express himself and open up to me. He cried, which is completely normal. In fact, I worry when children *don't* cry."

Edward nodded but didn't say anything.

Mary swallowed hard.

Cassandra continued. "In my opinion, Patrick's account of what happened is completely credible. My experience tells me that he is telling the truth. He's an intelligent and brave little boy, and he isn't doing this for attention. On the contrary, he avoids attention and has anxiety, which he will require treatment to overcome."

Edward nodded. "I told Mary that. He doesn't do it for attention. And he doesn't lie."

Cassandra glanced at her notes. "My findings are that Patrick was not only physically abused by the teacher's aide, a Mr. Robertson, but Patrick was also sexually abused by Mr. Robertson. Robertson fondled Patrick on three occasions."

"My God," Edward said, choked.

Mary felt shocked, reaching out for Edward's elbow to steady him.

Cassandra looked sympathetically at Edward. "I know this is terrible news for you. The only comfort I can offer you is that we will do our level best to get justice for Patrick and to get him the therapy he needs."

Edward nodded, his eyes suddenly brimming.

Cassandra pushed a blue box of tissues toward Edward. "In terms of the facts, the first incident of fondling occurred on September 9, the day after school started. The assault took place in a closet or small room off a hallway near the classroom. Patrick said it had a 'floor machine' in it, and the police will follow up. Robertson managed to get Patrick alone and fondled him by touching his genitals on both the inside and the outside of his pants."

"No." Edward took a Kleenex and wiped his eyes under his glasses, and Mary felt outrage tightening her chest, that such a thing could happen at school. Where were the teachers? Where were the other kids? Questions raced through her mind, and she knew Edward must have them, too.

Cassandra glanced again at her notes. "Patrick had never been touched that way by anyone else and told me that he was confused and frightened. Robertson threatened him not to tell anybody or he would kill him—and you, Edward."

Edward grimaced, and Mary thought of the brown sedan outside.

"Cassandra, not to interrupt, but I think I saw Robertson, or a man who looked a lot like him, parked in a car out front across the street."

Edward looked over. "When?"

"When you were asleep."

Cassandra frowned, in alarm. "Are you sure it was him?"

"No," Mary had to answer, "but it looked like him. He had a mustache, dark hair. The car was a brown sedan."

Cassandra took notes. "Did you get the make or model?"

"No, I tried but it drove away."

"I'd admonish you both to keep an eye out for him. It's not uncommon for predators to stalk their victims and intimidate them to keep them silent. We can't rule out the possibility that Robertson is violent and may try to carry through on his threat. I'll report this sighting to the police, but if you see him again, either of you, call 911. Do not engage with him yourself in any way, shape, or form."

Mary nodded. "Okay."

Edward stiffened. "I'll keep an eye out at the house. I don't know where Robertson lives, but it probably is in the neighborhood. It's not hard to find out where we live, either."

Cassandra nodded gravely. "Keep an eye out, and as I say, do not engage. If you see him, call 911 immediately. It's not only safer for you and Patrick, but it's better for our record."

Mary felt concerned. "If it was Robertson in the sedan, he knows we're here. He knows we reported him to you. What effect do you think that will have on him, in your experience?"

"He's not going away since you came here, if that's what you're asking. I think the danger still exists. If it was him, he's not going away, and the fact is, he'd still want to prevent you from taking this further. There's a trial left, after all. Be on guard." Cassandra paused. "Before I go on to the other two incidents, you should know that children in special education programming are often targeted by sexual offenders because they are the most vulnerable. Depending on the nature and extent of their disabilities, they are often out of the classroom for pullout sessions or to cool down, giving ample opportunity to offenders. Sadly, they are not always believed when they inform on any such incidents of abuse, and their reports are often dismissed as difficulties with perception, if not outright fabrication. Neither of these things is true with Patrick. He has anxiety issues, and simply put, Patrick is afraid of Robertson."

Edward nodded, taking a Kleenex from the box and wiping his eyes under his glasses.

Mary interjected, "By the way, Robertson no longer works at the school. Evidently, he quit a few days ago, and I don't expect that Patrick will be at Grayson much longer. They're not programming for him and I'm hoping to place him at Fairmount Prep."

"Great. That can help his recovery, if he doesn't have to go back to the school where he was abused." Cassandra glanced again at her notes. "Now, as I was saying, the second such incident of fondling and physical abuse occurred on Friday, September 11, in the same room. Again, same situation, same fondling, on top and in the pants. Patrick told me that he was frightened, but because it had happened before, he knew what was happening and he told Robertson to stop. Robertson did not stop. Patrick threw up, and Robertson, evidently in anger, grabbed Patrick and forced him to lick up the vomit, and the incident ended."

Edward sniffled, and Mary knew it was hard to hear the graphic details of the abuse, but it was necessary going forward, for her lawsuit. She credited Cassandra for presenting the information in such a professional manner. It had to help Edward to deal with it, like being at a doctor's office and hearing a diagnosis of terminal cancer.

Cassandra looked up from her notes, pausing. "The third incident of physical and sexual abuse occurred in the morning of Wednesday, September 16. The incident took place in the same room, but the activity escalated." Cassandra paused, then kept going. "To stay on track, on the morning of the sixteenth at Grayson, there was an assembly. Patrick was walking with his class to the assembly, and Mr. Robertson managed to get him away from the others, which went unnoticed."

Edward wiped his eyes, and Mary could see that he was using every ounce of strength to maintain his composure. She wondered again if Machiavelli knew what scum he was representing. She had to believe he didn't, that even he couldn't be that low.

Cassandra cleared her throat. "On this third incident, Patrick tells me that Robertson led him into the closet, fondled him, and this time, tried to force Patrick's hand on Robertson's own genitals. Patrick refused and vomited, so Robertson struck him in the face in anger."

Edward's eyes brimmed again, and Mary's heart broke for him.

Cassandra continued, "We have a pediatrician on our premises, and she examined Patrick. She found no evidence of damage to his genital or anal area, though she did find faint bruises on his face consistent with his account. We made photographs of the bruise for evidentiary purposes." Cassandra exhaled, sliding her notepad away from her. "Let me explain what our procedures are. I'll make recommendations to you for a therapist for Patrick and I'll write up a report about my forensic interview for the team here, which includes a caseworker from DHS and a detective from Special Victims Unit. They will read my report, view Patrick's DVD, review our medical report and photographic evidence and also review the police investigation report, when that is sent from the Twenty-fifth Precinct. We will then make a recommendation to the District Attorney's Office about whether charges will be filed."

Mary asked, "What will you recommend?"

Cassandra turned to Mary, her dark gaze steady. "The district attorney makes the charging decisions, but I would recommend that Robertson be charged with sexual assault, statutory sexual assault, sexual abuse of children, endangering the welfare of a child, corrupting the morals of a minor, simple assault and battery, and unlawful restraint."

"Amen," Edward said hoarsely, wiping his eyes. His parchment-thin skin looked mottled again, and his shoulders sagged, letting down now that the worst was over.

"I agree," Mary said, patting his arm.

"Edward," Cassandra said softening her tone. "I think Patrick is a very special boy. I'm aware that he has challenges, and I saw evidence of his dyslexia and reading issues myself. But I truly believe that he's got some fight inside him. He's going to get through this."

"Thank you." Edward managed a shaky smile. "God bless you."

"You're welcome." Cassandra smiled back at Edward, brighter than before. "And I will tell you one thing, that boy sure does *love* his 'Pops.' He couldn't stop talking about you. He loves taking care of you, making soup and helping with your meds. That gives him a lot of self-esteem, that he helps with your insulin. You're everything to him, and he loves you very much."

"I love him too," Edward said, his eyes spilling over. "Very much."

Mary felt her own eyes brimming and grabbed a Kleenex from the box, which was definitely unlawyerlike, but she didn't care.

Cassandra straightened up, in a back-to-business way. "Okay, folks. Unless you have any questions, I think we should go get Patrick."

"No questions." Edward rose slowly, pushing himself up by leaning on the table.

"I have a question," Mary said. "During his interview, did Patrick mention anything about a scissors? About Robertson threatening him with a scissors, or him attacking Robertson with a scissors?"

Cassandra frowned. "No, why?"

"That's the allegation in Robertson's suit against Patrick. I think what happened was that when Robertson's 'attempt' failed, he started to worry. He knew that sooner or later, Patrick would tell somebody, so he filed the suit to preempt Patrick."

Cassandra nodded. "He shouldn't have done anything."

"He didn't want to take a chance and he thinks that Edward has money. Robertson saw his opportunity and took it, killing two birds with one stone."

Cassandra glowered. "Well, now I've heard it all."

Mary stood up. "Thank you so much, for all you did for Patrick and all you do for children in Philly. It's really admirable."

"You're welcome." Cassandra smiled at Mary, rising and picking up her pad. "In terms of timing, this will proceed fairly quickly, and in the next few days, somebody will get back to you about charges and the like." Cassandra turned to Edward, as she walked them to the door. "Edward, in the meantime, I would advise you not to open a discussion with Patrick about this. If he initiates discussion, answer his questions. If he brings it up, let him say what he needs to say."

"I understand." Edward nodded, drained.

"Be supportive, but don't question him further. We want you to support him, but not position yourself in a way that might hinder or compromise the investigation." Cassandra flashed Edward a final smile. "I know this is difficult."

"Thanks." Edward heaved a heavy sigh, then stood tall. "Now. Let's go get my boy."

CHAPTER ELEVEN

Mary hurried past the antique shops and artsy jewelry stores to the bridal salon, troubled after her meeting at PCA. She couldn't shake what she had heard about Patrick being abused, and Edward and Patrick had remained silent the entire ride home, during which she had kept a watchful eye out for the brown sedan. After she'd dropped them off at home, she'd emailed their firm investigator, Lou Jacobs, a former cop with plenty of contacts on the force, asking him to see if a brown sedan was registered to a Steven Robertson and to find out where Robertson lived. She knew that Lou's Blue Mafia would come up with an answer, ASAP.

Cars and buses clogged Pine Street, which was only wide enough for colonial traffic, and she plowed down the sidewalk through the businesspeople thumbing their phones as they walked. Ahead she spotted the sign for the bridal salon in curlicue script, POUR LES BRIDES. Mary got the gist of the French translation; a bride who bought her dress here would end up poor. She made a beeline for the faux French Provincial door, opened it, and entered the air-conditioned salon, which was like walking into a cumulus cloud, with dove-white cushiness everywhere and no harsh reality in sight.

White wedding dresses hung on padded hangers around the perimeter of the room, and the walls were of raw white silk. A white shag rug covered the floor, and a matching curved couch sat at the center of the room, embracing a dramatically lit elevated pedestal with a trifold floor-to-ceiling mirror. On the far side of the room, next to a pickled-white French Provincial desk and a completely American cash register, sat a circular glass display case of veils, tiaras, and more grandiose bridal headpieces, which Judy and Anne were gawking at, plastic champagne flutes in hand.

"Mary, Mary!" Anne and Judy squealed, almost in unison, spotting her. They rushed toward Mary, hoisting their flutes so they didn't spill their champagne.

"Hey guys," she called back, rallying at the sight of her friends, though the two women couldn't have been more different: Judy in her funky yellow hair, multicolored outfit, and Mario-Batali crocs, and Anne exquisitely dressed in her sleek Lilly Pulitzer sheath with tan Manolo mules, so that together they looked like a punk-rock star and her chic stylist.

"I'm so glad you didn't cancel!" Anne said, hugging Mary in her bony way.

"Me, too!" Judy said, throwing her arms around Mary like a bear. "How else would we get to drink champagne on a school night?"

Mary smiled, coming around. "Sorry I'm late. This special ed case is such a tough one."

"Why?" Judy asked, frowning.

"It's so—"

"Stop!" Anne said, raising her manicured hand. "No shop talk tonight, bitches. This is a lawyer-free zone, and we're here tonight for love, marriage, and most importantly, clothes."

Judy grinned. "Good point, except for the 'bitches' part. I'm not your bitch. You're *my* bitch."

Anne snorted. "We're both Mary's bitches, since she's a partner and almost a wife."

Mary rolled her eyes. "Don't start. Now, where's my dress?"

Judy giggled. "Natalia the Slavic Saleswoman will materialize at any minute. You won't see her coming. She's stealthy, from years of training with the KGB."

Mary smiled at the nickname, which she herself had thought up.

She wondered uncomfortably if Machiavelli had been right; that it was a South Philly thing, or if she was being mean at someone else's expense.

Anne smiled at Judy. "Girl, didn't you ever work retail? They have a buzzer that sounds in the back when a customer comes in, and they can look on the security camera and see who it is. Natalia will be here in three, two, one . . ."

As if on cue, Natalia the Slavic Saleswoman flagged them down as she approached, carrying a fake silver tray with a plastic flute of champagne. Natalia was a middle-aged woman with a blonde chignon, dressed in a fashionable black shirt, straight skirt, and worn mules with flattened backs, which she scuffed around in like bedroom slippers. Natalia's Russian accent and imperious demeanor inspired confidence as well as obedience, and Mary was happy to have help, even if Natalia could occasionally be Stalinesque.

"Hi, Natalia." Mary smiled. "I'm sorry I'm late, I had to—"

"Not a problem, Mary." Natalia handed her the champagne flute. "But we have only two hours until closing time. You are the bride, so you must go first. Then Judy, then Anne."

"Okay." Mary sipped the champagne, which was free, if you didn't count the cost of the dress, the veil, the new shoes, the "good" bra, and the alterations, which were going to be revealed tonight.

"Mary, come with me." Natalia took off, scuffing toward the fitting room. "Judy and Anne, sit on couch. Judy, touch nothing."

"Aww, Mom," Judy whined, and Mary followed Natalia like a baby duckling, if ducklings drank champagne.

The two women passed through the door to the fitting rooms, which led to an all-white hallway with louvered doors on either side. The setup reminded Mary unhappily of the interview rooms at PCA, but she took another sip of champagne to chase those memories away. Natalia unlocked the door to the first room on the right, using a key ring as full as a corrections officer's.

"Come," Natalia said, ushering Mary inside the small fitting room.

"Is my dress here?" Mary glanced around excitedly, but the white fitting room was bare except for a white chair against the wall, next to a row of grimy white pumps you could borrow to try dresses on with, collapsed in a loopy heap, like drunks at an orgy.

"I will bring. You have bra and shoes?"

"Yes." Mary hoisted the Bloomie's bag that held the bra and shoes, then set it on the floor with her purse.

"Handbag does not belong on floor." Natalia picked up Mary's purse and put it on the chair. "Change into underwear, but not shoes. I will return momentarily."

"*Da,*" Mary said, since it was the only Russian she knew.

Natalia winked in a good-humored way, left the fitting room, and closed the louvered door, and Mary drained the champagne flute and set it down on the chair, beginning to relax. She took off her dark suit and white silk shirt, which she practically had to unpeel from her armpits, then kicked off her shoes. She changed quickly into the fancy bra, which had cost a fortune, and as soon as she looked in the mirror, she understood why. It came with its own breasts. There were two white lacy mounds on either side of her chest, exactly where her breasts would have been, if they filled the cups.

Mary peeked inside the bra, surprised to see that her nipple was looking back at her. She looked at her body in the mirror, equally surprised to see that she was kind of thin, for her. Her waist went in on the sides, which was a new thing, and her tummy was so flat she could see her crotch, also a first. She had struggled with weight most of her life and was delighted to see that she might have lost a few pounds without even trying, or getting that intestinal flu that every girl prays for before her wedding.

Mary did a little happy dance, wiggling her butt in her cottony bikini underwear, having gotten over thongs a long time ago. She heard a swishing in the hall, and the next moment, the keys jingled as the door was unlocked and Natalia appeared with a massive mound of pure whiteness in an overlong garment bag of clear plastic.

"My dress!" Mary clapped, jumping up and down, but Natalia frowned, eyeing her up and down.

"Your body. What happen?"

"Let me have my dress!" Mary reached for her dress, but Natalia didn't let go.

"Mary, you lose weight."

"Let's put on the dress!" Mary squealed, the alcohol beginning to take effect. She couldn't remember the last time she'd eaten. Maybe last week. "I'm so excited, and Judy and Anne are waiting!"

"Allow me." Natalia hung the dress on a high hook, and Mary's gaze drank in every detail of the dress, which was perfect. It had a lovely sweetheart neckline, short cap sleeves, with a simple, dropped waist. It was cotton lace all over, with only the lightest beading, which gave it just a hint of sparkle.

Mary clapped again, in delight. "Isn't it pretty?"

"Very pretty. I like very much this dress." Natalia held the hanger and slid the garment bag off expertly, then unzipped the back of the dress while Mary tried to contain her excitement.

"I can't even believe it, it's so beautiful!"

"Very beautiful." Natalia's accent made it sound like *byutiful*, which to Mary's ear sounded even more *byutiful* than *beautiful*.

"I love it! It is *classic!*"

"Very classic. Arms up."

Mary reached up as Natalia guided the dress over her hands, down her arms, and onto her shoulders. "This is so exciting, isn't it?"

"Yes," Natalia answered, though she didn't sound excited.

Mary's head popped through the top of the dress like a baby being born, then she whirled around to face the mirror, the voluminous skirt swirling around her like vanilla softserve. She practically gasped in delight. "It looks so beautiful, I couldn't be happier! Thank you so much, Natalia, for all of your help!"

"Stand still, and I zip." Natalia went around the back of the dress and zipped it up.

Mary obeyed, surveying her reflection, her heart soaring. She could never have imagined that it would feel this wonderful to be in her wedding dress, though she had been happily married before. But her life was beginning anew, starting over again with

Anthony, and she knew that they would be happy together, forever. They would be perfect, just like this dress. They were *classic*.

"Hmmm," Natalia said, without elaboration.

"Are you going to zip it up?" Mary asked, glancing behind her.

"Is zipped." Natalia stepped aside, eyeing Mary's reflection in the mirror.

"It can't be." Mary looked down, confused. She was swimming in the dress. She peeked inside the top and she could see her bra, her nipple, and all the way down to the elastic waistband of her Hanes. She looked like a small child standing in a sparkly white barrel.

"You have los' much weight."

"Not *that* much."

"Yes. Dress is too big."

"That can't be!"

"Is true."

"What?" Mary deflated, crestfallen and bewildered, then she heard the door open in the hallway and giggling outside the fitting room.

"Mare, what's taking so long?" Judy asked, knocking on the louvered door.

"We don't wanna wait anymore!" Anne chimed in.

"Guys!" Mary reached for the doorknob and flung open the door. "Look!"

"Oh no!" Anne said, horrified. Her glossy mouth dropped open.

"Yikes!" Judy grimaced. "It's way too big."

"I lost weight!" Mary wailed. "It doesn't fit!"

Anne stepped into the fitting room, her lovely green eyes scrutinizing the dress like a garment surgeon. "Nobody freak out. I'm excellent in a fashion emergency."

"What am I gonna do?" Mary wailed again.

"Eat something?" Judy offered. "Like, a pizza? Or two?"

"Hush, Judy." Anne grabbed the clip from her hair, stepped around the back of the dress, and used it to gather up the fabric. "See, this is no problem. This is nothing. Natalia, you can have the tailor take it in, back here. You just hide the seam in the zipper and move the darts in the front, on the bust."

"I lost my boobs," Mary said, trying not to whine. "Only my nipples are left."

Natalia shook her head in disapproval. "Ladies. Problem is, time."

Anne scoffed. "The wedding is two weeks away, that's enough time."

"Tailoring, so much as that, take time."

"How much will it cost to rush it?" Anne shot back.

Natalia folded her meaty arms. "Many dresses before this. Is busy now. We make no promises."

"How *much*?" Anne repeated, her eyes glittering.

Mary sighed inwardly. She hadn't known she was a sad drunk, until now. Maybe the horrible day was catching up with her. "Natalia, can I get more champagne?"

CHAPTER TWELVE

It was dark by the time Mary got home, because they'd gone out drinking to celebrate the fact that the bridesmaids' dresses fit Judy and Anne perfectly. It was going to cost Mary $500 in rush charges to get her dress tailored in time for the wedding, with no guarantees from Natalia, who'd been harder to negotiate with than Vladimir Putin.

Mary juggled her purse and messenger bag to unlock the front door to her townhouse. The door swung open into the dark hallway, and she shut the door behind her. She didn't turn on the light or bother to pick up the mail that lay scattered all over the floor, because it got delivered through the mail slot in the door. She was in no mood for dealing with bills or anything else tonight.

She dropped her purse and messenger bag on the floor, twisted the deadbolt locked, and walked down the hallway, her heels clacking on the hardwood floor until she kicked them off and sent them skidding into the darkened living room. The house was cool, thanks to central air, though it felt large and vaguely hollow without Anthony. Still, it wasn't the worst thing, to have it all to herself. The place was large by Center City standards, a full-sized three-bedroom, two-and-a-half-bath townhome that she had bought after she made partner, and that had been a struggle, with Anthony feeling terrible that he hadn't been able to pay half of the mortgage payment, much less the down payment. Finally, they had resolved the problem, and he paid what he could, which was fine with her.

She walked upstairs in the darkness, sliding her phone from her jacket pocket to see if Anthony had called. She checked the glowing home screen for a text or call alert, but there were none. He was on the West Coast, three hours behind her, so it would be about dinnertime in Los Angeles, now. They usually spoke once or twice a day, but it was for the best that he hadn't called, since she'd had her hands full with Edward and Patrick.

She reached the top of the stairs, using the phone screen to light her way, and turned on the hall light, then headed into the bedroom. She didn't bother going into the bathroom, she didn't need to use the toilet and she wasn't even going to bother to wash her face. She trundled into the bedroom, fighting off low-level depression that she knew had nothing to do with her wedding dress issues, as aggravating as those were. She kept thinking about Patrick and Edward, and the sadness of their situation was settling into her bones, making all of her personal problems trivial by comparison.

Mary leaned over and turned on the lamp on the nightstand, then she wandered over to the chair, shedding her jacket, taking her blouse off over her head, and snapping off her bra, which shot in the air like a slingshot. She didn't know where it landed and she didn't care. She shimmied out of her skirt, dumped it on the chair, and went to bed in her good old Hanes, taking off her glasses and slipping under the covers holding the phone.

Mary took a moment to exhale, looking around the cozy bedroom, a sight that usually gave her so much comfort, but not now. Tonight she was acutely aware of how very lucky she was to have the house she had, the life she had, and the neighborhood where she lived, having been given all of the advantages as a child. Not money certainly, but two remarkable parents, Vita and Mariano DiNunzio, who loved her to the very marrow. When she was a child, they hovered over her and her twin sister Angie, cheered them on, and defended them from anyone. Her mother made novenas so they would do well on their SATs and cast colorful folkloric curses on anyone who even thought about doing them wrong. Mary didn't want to judge Edward, but she knew her father would have cut off his right arm before he'd let her take a punch.

She shifted onto her right side, her head full of Edward's family and her family, then the Machiavellis. The DiNunzios had always disliked them for their phoniness, and her mother called them *spacone*, or "show off." Mary shuddered to think what they would say if they knew that Machiavelli was defending a man capable not only of abusing a child, but of trying to profit from his disgusting crime.

Mary sighed and tried to quiet her mind. She checked the phone, but Anthony still hadn't called. She felt drowsy and tired, so she set the phone on his pillow on his side of the bed, which was farther from the bathroom, only fair because he was the guy. He and Mary had shared equally in decorating their bedroom, making all the decisions together, and it had turned out beautiful.

Byutiful.

Moonlight poured through the window, making a shimmering shaft on the foot of her bed and illuminating the entire bedroom. She could see all of the familiar shapes in the moonshine; the pine dressers on the other side of the room, his and hers, which they bought from an antique store in Lambertville, and an almost-matching pine armoire on the right side of the room, since the house was of colonial vintage, a time when nobody was prioritizing closet space.

Mary shifted onto her back and above her was a lovely dotted Swiss canopy, another find when they were scouring for antique bedding; the canopy looked so fitting on their canopy bed, which was made of tiger maple, a wood that Anthony had fallen in love with. They were both homebodies, with him developing an interest in woodworking, and Mary surprised to find that she loved making an herb garden in their kitchen and the tiny patch of yard, in the back of the house.

All of these thoughts made Mary miss him, so she reached for the phone, scrolled to FAVORITES, and pressed the first name. When the call connected, she said, "Hey, honey—"

"Babe! I was just about to call you!" Anthony sounded alert, happy, and loud, owing to some background chatter, so Mary held the phone away from her ear.

"I figured, but I'm going to bed early. I'm so beat. I've had the day from hell—"

"Things are great here! I'm about to go out to dinner with a bunch of my colleagues from the department."

"Oh, really?"

"Yes, they're great! I'm helping them with some research, too. They might even credit me on their paper."

"Wow." Mary felt happy for him. He was an academic, and he was at UCLA doing research for his book on Carlo Tresca and American anarchism in the 1920s. He'd gotten a book contract from an academic press, which was wonderful. "Right up your alley."

"I know, right? And you're not going to believe this, but I went to the beach today."

Mary chuckled. "UCLA is near a beach?"

"Everywhere in California is near a beach. The whole damn state is a beach! It's unreal! I might learn how to surf!"

"Really?"

"Why not, huh? I tried it and it was awesome! We had a great time!"

"We?" Mary couldn't help but wonder if there were women in the group, but she wasn't the jealous type, and Anthony would never cheat on her.

"You know, the grad students and the faculty."

"That sounds great. You know, I tried on my dress—"

"Babe, I have to go. They're waiting for me, for dinner."

"Okay, sure. Great. Have fun. Love you," Mary said, but Anthony had already hung up.

Mary set the phone down, stewing. The final draft of Anthony's manuscript was due in a month, and she didn't know how he'd get his book done if he was surfing. But that was his look-out. Still she thought of him at a beach with a balmy sea breeze, but with no humidity. California was a mythical place, and she'd never been, though Anthony kept telling her it was beautiful.

Byutiful.

Mary realized she hadn't gotten a chance to tell him about the crabmeat appetizer, which she wanted to run by him. She'd also wanted to tell him about the dress, too, but mostly she wanted to vent about Patrick's case, how awful it was, how emotional. He would have understood that, and she'd wanted to hear his voice. It wasn't like him to practically hang up on her.

And he'd forgotten to say, I love you.

CHAPTER THIRTEEN

Every Friday morning, the lawyers of Rosato & DiNunzio held a staff meeting to update each other on their cases, and though Mary usually enjoyed going, she didn't today. She felt completely preoccupied when she entered conference room C, where everybody was making small talk, grabbing fresh coffee and muffins. She went to the credenza, where the cityscape outside the window looked sunny, bright, and metallic.

Last night she had lost sleep worrying about Patrick, and Lou Jacobs, their firm investigator, had emailed her Robertson's address, which was only three miles from Edward's house in Juniata. Lou had learned that the only car registered to Robertson was a 2006 red VW Passat, not a brown sedan, but Mary figured he could have borrowed the sedan, in case he was spotted.

She placed a blueberry muffin on a paper plate, although now that she could afford the calories, she wasn't hungry. She felt unusually separate from everyone around her, a half-step behind. Maybe it was because she'd been late to the office again, because she'd worked on Patrick's case.

"Let's sit down and get started," Bennie Rosato said, clutching a coffee and taking her seat at the head of the conference table, as founding partner of the firm. The fact that Mary had made partner didn't mean that the firm's seating order would reshuffle, and Mary was fine with that, disliking change in general. Bennie was the same way, never changing anything, not even her look; she was a six-foot tall, athletic blonde, and she always wore her hair in a messy topknot and dressed in a white oxford shirt and plain khaki suit, like a legal uniform.

Mary sat down catty-corner to Bennie, and Judy sat down next to Mary, shooting her a quick smile. Across the table sat Anne Murphy and John Foxman, their new associate, and the only male lawyer in the firm. John was good-looking in a preppy way, with a congenitally serious expression, pale blue eyes, costly rimless glasses, and precisely layered red hair. John worked for Judy on her asbestos cases, which was fine with Mary because he reminded her of the white-shoe litigators at her old law firm, Grun & Stalling. To her mind, there was nothing a snob deserved more than the flaming hell of asbestos cases.

"Okay, gang," Bennie began, "since last week, my news is that we filed a motion for summary judgment in that massive arbitration dispute over oil and gas leases with landowners in northeastern Pennsylvania. The leases had a ridiculously ambiguous arbitration provision that read, something like, 'in the event of a disagreement between lessor and lessee concerning this lease, performance thereunder, or damages . . .' "

Mary found herself zoning out, as she sometimes did with Bennie, who was interested in all types of litigation and joked that she loved being a trial lawyer so much that she was born standing up. Mary admired her, but didn't feel the same way. She had often wondered if being a lawyer was for her, until she started taking special education cases, like Patrick's. She could only imagine how Edward was feeling today and she wondered if Patrick had asked him any questions last night. Then she wondered how Patrick felt, having had to relive his assaults yesterday.

"DiNunzio?" Bennie was saying, cocking her head. "You with us? What's new with your cases?"

"Uh, nothing," Mary answered, coming out of her reverie.

"Nothing?" Bennie repeated, surprised. "What about that matter for Paxton Butler? I'm dying to know."

"Uh, nothing new." Mary couldn't remember the case at the

moment, then it came to her. Paxton Butler was an independent stock brokerage company she'd been referred, which was suing a former vice-president for breach of the confidentiality provision of his golden parachute. The stakes were high, in that the contract was worth $2 million, but it was hard to get excited about a fight between rich people.

"You know, that's going to be a very big case." Bennie's blue eyes glittered with interest. "The law on employment contracts in Pennsylvania is changing every day. There are a lot of eyes on you. Did you schedule the defendant's deposition yet?"

"Uh, no." Mary realized she was supposed to send out a Notice of Deposition yesterday, but had forgotten.

"It's already Friday, and Monday is Columbus Day." Bennie frowned slightly. "I'm not criticizing, I'm just confused. You told me you wanted to get the discovery finished by the end of the year."

"Uh, well, I got busy."

"With what, that new case? I heard from Marshall that one came in yesterday."

"Uh, yes."

"Is it another referral? As big as Paxton Butler?"

"Well, no—"

Judy interjected, "Bennie, everyone! I have major news this week, other than my awesome new hair color."

"More awesome than that?" Bennie chuckled, turning her attention to Judy, and they all laughed except for Mary, who realized that her best friend was trying to save her ass.

"Yes, if you can believe that." Judy grinned, comically fluffing up her hot-pink hair. "We won big this week! We defeated a motion to dismiss in that sex discrimination case, *Adelman v. United Group*. If you remember, Bonnie Adelman is the insurance agent who was denied a promotion, and her boss made a number of outrageous comments to her, like he said that 'her pregnancy hormones were driving her crazy' and . . ."

Mary zoned out as Judy regaled everyone with stories about the supervisor's comments, and she would usually have found them outrageous, too. But after meeting with Cassandra about Patrick, Mary couldn't share the same level of outrage. What had happened to Patrick was truly outrageous, and to add insult to the most griev- ous of injuries, he *also* had to endure verbal bullying, day after day. And he was a *child*, a little boy.

Mary barely listened to the rest of Judy's case presentation, then it was Anne's turn to talk about some environmental matters, say- ing, ". . . and we're going to file an amicus brief *pro bono* under the Clean Air Act against a coal manufacturing and byproducts re- covery facility in Allegheny County. If you have ever done environ- mental work, you know that the EPA sets NAAQs, or National Ambient Air Quality Standards, and that Pennsylvania is required to create a SIP, or a state implementation plan, detailing how it will attain and maintain the NAAQS . . ."

Mary tried to pay attention, but she couldn't. Ugly images popped into her mind, and she couldn't stop them. She pictured Robert- son with Patrick, upsetting him so much that he vomited. Suddenly she noticed that her hands, which had been resting on the table, were clenching into fists.

"DiNunzio, are you okay?" Bennie asked, returning her atten- tion to her.

"Sure, yes, fine."

"So tell us about the new matter. We didn't get to hear."

"It's nothing major," Mary answered, simply. She knew the facts were upsetting and she wanted to protect Patrick's privacy, even though everyone around the table was bound to keep the matter confidential. Even so, she didn't want to discuss it over coffee and muffins.

Bennie leaned back in her chair. "I heard that your opposing counsel is that jerk Machiavelli. Is that right?"

"Yes."

"Good. Kick his ass. What type of matter is it, now?"

"Special education."

"Oh." Bennie nodded, satisfied. "Out of my bailiwick. Kick his ass anyway."

"Mary, I can help you, if you want." John raised his hand in a way that looked as if he were summoning the waiter at a country club.

"Thank you, but I don't need the help."

"In fact, I can take the case off your hands." John blinked behind his fancy glasses. "You said you were too busy to do Paxton Butler, and if I took the special education case from you, that would free you up."

"That's okay, I can handle both."

"Frankly, you'd be doing me a favor. I could use a break from the asbestos cases." John smiled, showing perfect teeth, undoubtedly straightened by orthodonture that Mary's parents couldn't afford until she was in high school, which was why she was Bucky Beaver.

"Sorry, but no thanks."

"And with your wedding coming up, does it really make sense for you to start a new matter?"

"John, enough," Mary snapped. "I can manage my own schedule."

Judy and Anne exchanged glances.

Bennie turned to Mary, lifting an eyebrow. "He's trying to help."

John interjected again, "Exactly, and I have a window of time."

"I understand that, but I don't need the help. I know the case and I'm working the case."

John shrugged. "If it came in yesterday, you've only been working it a day. It's not like there's a big file I have to catch up on. Why don't you let me lighten your load?"

"John, have you ever handled a special education case?"

"No, but how hard can it be?" John chuckled, uncomfortably. "It's *special*, right?"

"What's *that* supposed to mean? Are you making fun of the disabled?"

"No, I didn't mean it that way." John's eyes flared behind his glasses. "It came out wrong, I'm sorry."

"John, for your information, special education law is a very complex practice. It's governed by the Individuals with Disabilities Education Act, a federal law just like the Civil Rights Act or the

Clean Air Act. If you've never worked on a special education case, you can't just *wing it*. A child's life is at stake, and a child's education. And their future, their safety. Their psyche. And their very *soul*." Mary spoke with passion that came from deep within, and she wasn't about to stop, though she'd made her point. "It matters at least as much as a broken contract, or a sexist comment, or polluted air. To me, it matters *more* because you're talking about an innocent, sweet, funny, adorable little boy who has been dealt every lousy card that life has to offer and has faced every single one of his challenges with more bravery than any adult I've ever met—"

"Mare?" Judy touched Mary's hand.

"—and John, you can never take this case from me, and furthermore, I'm a named partner at this law firm and you're an associate, so when I say back off, *back off*."

Bennie and Anne exchanged glances, and Mary couldn't see Judy's reaction, but she knew what it was, that Mary was getting too emotionally involved in this case, which was undoubtedly correct. She realized there was nothing left to say, and she had tons of things to do for Patrick.

Mary rose, turned on her heel, and left the conference room.

CHAPTER FOURTEEN

Mary left her outburst behind and started to feel better and stronger, doing what she needed to be doing. The sun warmed her shoulders, and she caught sight of her reflection in a shop window. She had on a fresh new outfit, a tan shirtdress with a light white sweater, and her makeup concealed the dark circles under her eyes. Her hair was freshly blown-dry, her contacts were back in, and her heels were back on, the girl trifecta that made her feel like she could take on the world.

Mary pulled her phone from her purse, pressed in the number for Kevin Reynolds, who was one of the lawyers who handled special ed cases for the Philadelphia School District. She listened to the call ring as she threaded her way through people on the sidewalk. Everybody else was on their phones while they drank Starbucks iced-venti-somethings through green straws, or smoked cigarettes, leaving acrid clouds in the air, which probably improved Philadelphia's general air quality.

"Philadelphia School District, Office of General Counsel," said the receptionist.

"Hi, this is Mary DiNunzio. Can you put me through to Kevin Reynolds?" Mary powered forward, hustling down the street toward the parking garage.

"Hey, Mary, how you doing?" Kevin asked, in his typically resonant bass. He was widely respected as one of the best lawyers working for the school district: smart, fair, and easy to deal with because he always had the students' best interests at heart.

"I found out some shocking news late yesterday afternoon about my client Patrick O'Brien, a dyslexic fifth-grader at Grayson Elementary." Mary picked up the pace, since the garage was in sight.

"I heard about that case. The whole office is talking about it. Do you believe Machiavelli?" Kevin snorted. "He's suing the district because we didn't train him correctly? We're responsible for the fact that he's terrible at his job? Machiavelli's creative, I'll give him that."

"No, he's manipulative." Mary walked into the garage and headed for the elevator.

"So the boy attacked a teacher's aide?"

"No, that entire story is a fabrication. The aide has been assaulting the boy since the beginning of school, both physically and sexually."

"Oh no," Kevin said, his tone horrified. "Okay, just so we're clear, I'm not conceding as true the facts you're telling me right now."

"Understood, I'll have plenty of proof. I've already had the boy seen by PCA and filed a report with the police. I fully expect Robertson to be charged. Given the assault, I think we need an emergency meeting up at Grayson."

"When?"

"Today, in about an hour and a half. I would have given you more notice, but I didn't have any." Mary got into the elevator and pressed the button for the roof level, where she always parked so she didn't have to remember the level number. "I want to meet with you and the Special Ed Director, Ms. Latimer. The programming for the boy's dyslexia is insufficient and I'm thinking about taking him out of Grayson, placing him at Fairmount Prep, and asking you guys to foot the bill."

"Can you prove that his programming is insufficient?"

"I don't think that will be a problem. He's a ten-year-old who can't read a sentence." Mary sensed that Kevin was sussing out the possibility of settlement. He had worked with her long enough to know that she didn't make claims she couldn't back up, and the district wouldn't want allegations of sexual assault in an elementary school to come to light.

"What about the ten-day letter?" Kevin asked, referring to the requirement that in order to be considered for tuition reimbursement, a parent had to notify the school district in writing, ten days prior to moving the child.

"Really, Kevin? You're going to stand on a technicality in a horrible case like this?" Mary stepped out of the elevator and hustled toward her car. "If I find out this morning that the programming for the boy is as bad as I think it is, I'm going to want to move him as soon as possible, maybe even over the weekend."

"Before the ten days?"

"Yes, and I'm going to ask you to waive the ten-day requirement, given the circumstances." Mary got her keys out of her purse and chirped the car unlocked. "The boy is already exhibiting anxiety and symptoms of PTSD, and I want to get him started at Fairmount Prep and the treatment they offer."

"Why take him out of Grayson? Robertson doesn't work there anymore. The Complaint alleges he quit."

"As I say, I think they haven't programmed for him, and it's not just the aide, it's the location. It has to have an effect on my client." Mary would play hardball, if she had to. "Besides, how is it possible that students at Grayson are so unsupervised that one can be assaulted three times—and nobody notices? I don't want my client at Grayson anymore."

"You're killing me, Mary. I can't waive the ten days. I don't have authority."

"Ask your boss to waive it. I'll get you the ten-day letter today, and that has to be good enough. If not, you and I are not going to be able to come to terms in this matter, at all." Mary reached the car and climbed inside, turning on the ignition to get the air-conditioning going.

"All right, all right, I'll see what I can do."

"Thanks." Mary reversed out of the parking space. "Can you meet me at Grayson in an hour and a half?"

"No problem, see you there."

"Thanks." Mary was giving herself a little extra time to do some investigating herself, but Kevin didn't need to know that. She drove down the exit, corkscrewing to the ground level. "On a related point, I don't think I have to invite Machiavelli to our meeting. He has filed a Complaint against my client and the school district in Common Pleas Court, sounding in tort and contract. But the way I see it, there are two separate causes of action on behalf of my client. The first is a special education matter, and that's between my client and you, the school district, over his programming. You have to be present for any meeting on that matter."

"Agreed, and I won't permit you to talk to school staff without me present."

"Understood, and the second matter I have would be in Common Pleas Court, against Robertson for assaulting my client and against the school district for negligent supervision of students under its care." Mary tried not to make it sound hostile. "I'm not saying I'm going to sue the district in Common Pleas Court, I'm just saying that's what the second cause of action would be."

"I'm following you," Kevin said, warily.

"My point is, I'm going up to Grayson to talk about the special education matter, which is why I called you. I'm *not* going up to Grayson to talk about the Common Pleas Court matter, because in that event, I'd have to invite Machiavelli."

"Fine with me. There's no reason for Machiavelli to come. I can't stand the guy." Kevin harrumphed. "And I would just as soon *not* discuss any Common Pleas Court action with you, yet. It's way premature. I have to get up to speed, and you have to get your ducks in a row."

"Okay, so I'm not calling Machiavelli."

"Don't. I'm out of cootie spray."

"Ha!" Mary smiled. "You've been working with kids too long, Kevin."

"Ain't that the truth. See you later."

"Bye now." Mary hung up the phone as she descended, then reached the ground level, found her monthly pass, and used it to get out of the lot. Traffic was busy on Locust Street, so while she waited, she pressed in Edward's number. She wanted to see how he and Patrick were doing, and she would need Edward's signature on the ten-day letter and on the papers to place Patrick at Fairmount Prep, which she had downloaded and printed this morning.

The phone rang and rang, and while Mary listened, she entered traffic on Locust Street, which was bumper-to-bumper. The phone stopped ringing, and the call went to voicemail, so she left a message, asking Edward to call her, then hung up. She drove through Center City on autopilot, maneuvering around City Hall, the Gothic building with the statue of William Penn on top, then headed north on Broad Street, where traffic freed up.

The phone rang on the passenger seat, and Mary glanced down to see that it was Judy, so she picked up. Otherwise she didn't drive and talk on the phone unless it was absolutely necessary, because she knew it wasn't safe. Plus if she ever died in a car crash because she was on the phone, her father would kill her.

"Girl, what got into you?" Judy asked, concerned. "Are you okay?"

"I'm fine, I just don't like your boy's attitude."

"He's not my boy."

"He's your old friend from school, right? That's why you hired him."

"Well, that and he has a stellar record."

"Okay, fine." Mary drove up Broad Street, unhappily. She didn't like fighting with Judy, which had only happened once or twice, both times over cases. "I'm not doubting his stellar record. In fact, that's my problem with him. He's too full of himself."

"What makes you say that? He was offering to help you."

"That he was offering to help me, that's exactly what makes me say that." Mary switched lanes, her crankiness returning. "He just assumes that he can step in and do what I'm doing, and doesn't it just figure?"

"What?"

"Like, men always figure they can just *do things*. They just start *doing things*. But women like me, we never do that. I would never jump into anything unprepared."

"You might be right, but that's not his fault. That's to his credit, and are you turning into a man-hater? Because if you are, it doesn't bode well for your marriage."

"It's not that he's a man, it's that he is an arrogant man. And what about that snarky comment about special education law? What a jerk!"

"He was trying to make a joke."

"I don't joke about that. You don't either. You didn't think it was funny, did you?" Mary switched lanes to go faster, sensing that her heavy foot on the gas had something to do with the conversation.

"No, but I know him and he didn't mean anything by it. He just felt ill at ease."

"Gimme a break. If it were a racist or a sexist joke, we wouldn't laugh at it. It's no different. If he knew what I was dealing with, if he could see how this little boy I'm representing, Patrick, gets made fun of . . ." Mary couldn't even finish the sentence, she was so bothered. "That kind of joking is bullying. It ruins kids' lives. We have to stop thinking of it as a joke."

"Okay, but I don't think he meant it that way. You came down pretty hard on him." Judy chuckled. "You got class-warfare on his heinie."

"I don't like how snotty he is." Mary smiled at the reference, reflecting that no matter how cranky she was, Judy could cheer her up.

"He's not snotty. You never worked with him. I don't think that's what's bothering you anyway. I think it's the wedding, after what happened with your dress. Don't be bridezilla."

"I'm not bridezilla. I'm lawyerzilla."

Judy chuckled. "Look, don't get too wrapped up in this special ed case. Be careful. Don't get crazy."

"I won't," Mary said, but she already was. "Okay, let me go, I'm driving."

"You gonna apologize to John?"

"Hell, no."

Judy snorted. "Drive safe. See you."

"Bye." Mary hung up, set the phone aside, and checked her rearview mirror, where William Penn was disappearing into the haze.

CHAPTER FIFTEEN

Mary reached Grayson Elementary and parked on the street across from the school, cutting the ignition. She scanned the scene reflexively for the brown sedan or a red Passat, but saw neither. The rowhouses in this neighborhood were more run-down than those in Edward's neighborhood, and paint peeled off the front doors. Broken windows remained unrepaired, and some of the houses stood vacant, boarded shut by graffitied plywood. The cars parked along the curb were older, and she realized that hers was the nicest car on the street, which made her feel both guilty and nervous. She grabbed her purse and got out of the car.

She crossed the street to the school, which was situated behind a forbidding fence of pointed black bars and surrounded by asphalt, with no trees or bushes in sight. The playground was an asphalt side yard that had a basketball backboard, but no hoop or net, and nobody could've played basketball anyway, because cars were parked randomly on the court. Worst of all, the school building itself looked run-down and ancient, a fact confirmed by a glance at its keystone, which read, almost unbelievably, 1927.

Mary had known that the Philadelphia city schools were in a sorry state, but she hadn't thought it was this bad. The building's design was vintage, an institutional block of dark brown brick, four stories tall. Its windows were narrow and in a state of disrepair; cracks in some of them had been covered with duct tape, and one

window was even boarded up with plywood. She couldn't imagine going to school every day in such a decrepit and grim place, but she realized that most inner-city kids did, every day.

Mary made a beeline for the entrance, marked by a marble plaque engraved with GRAYSON ELEMENTARY SCHOOL. It would have been charming but for the fact that it was mounted over two window-less metal doors painted battleship gray, rusting where they'd been dented. An industrial-sized intercom had been retrofitted into the brick wall beside the door, and Mary assumed it connected to the office.

She pressed the buzzer, but nothing happened. She had arrived ahead of Kevin, intentionally early because she wanted to learn and record as much as she could about the layout of the school, to sup-port Patrick's story. She pressed the buzzer again, and finally it crackled to life. Nobody said anything, so she said, "I'm Mary Di-Nunzio, a lawyer representing Patrick O'Brien, and I have a meet-ing with Kevin Reynolds, the lawyer from the school district."

There was silence, and Mary waited, then pressed the button and repeated what she'd said, but still no one spoke and the door didn't click open. She wondered if it was broken and, in the next moment, the door was opened by a heavyset janitor in a hoodie and jeans, coming out of the door dragging a filthy plastic tub of trash, so she held the door open for him and ducked inside, saying, "Thanks so much."

Mary found herself on a dimly lit stairway landing, with grimy gray stairs that had metal crosshatching and walls with real rose-marble wainscoting. The staircases ran downstairs, to some sort of basement, and upstairs. Offices were usually upstairs, so she climbed the steps. The air smelled dirty and felt stifling; she realized that the age of the building prohibited central air-conditioning and there were no windows in the common areas in which to install a win-dow unit. She didn't know how the teachers stood it, much less the children.

She reached the top of the stairwell, where a poster put up by the school district read in bold letters: WEAPONS ARE PROHIBITED, and underneath, PENNSYLVANIA LAW REQUIRES THAT ANY STUDENTS,

REGARDLESS OF AGE OR GRADE LEVEL, FOUND TO POSSESS A WEAPON ON SCHOOL PREMISES OR AT EVENTS, OR WHILE TRAVELING TO AND FROM A SCHOOL OR SCHOOL PROGRAM OR EVENT (INCLUDING SCHOOL BUSES AND PUBLIC TRANSPORTATION) BE ARRESTED AND EXPELLED FROM THE SCHOOL DISTRICT FOR AT LEAST ONE YEAR. THE LAW DEFINES A WEAPON AS "ANY KNIFE, CUTTING INSTRUMENT, CUTTING TOOL, FIREARM, SHOTGUN . . ."

Mary knew this was the school rule that Patrick was supposed to have broken by supposedly attacking Robertson with the scissors. She knew that city schools had no tolerance for weapons of any kind, and she'd been in schools much worse than Grayson, where she'd had to go through a metal detector to enter. She kept going, through an old-fashioned set of French doors with varnish peeling off the dark wood, and found herself in a short hallway with a floor of polished concrete.

At the beginning of the hallway was an old wooden desk, staffed by an older woman with a sign-in log in front of her, a spiral-bound notebook, and she looked up at Mary pleasantly, from behind thick glasses. "May I help you?"

"Yes, I have a meeting with a lawyer from the school district."

"If you'll show me your identification and sign in here, the office is down the hall to the right."

"Thank you." Mary extracted her wallet from her purse, showed her ID, then signed in. "Is there a ladies' room on this floor?"

"Yes, near the office."

Mary had figured as much. "By the way, does this school have an auditorium?"

"Yes, it's after the office. If you take a right out of the office, you'll see it at the end of the hall. Have a good day."

"Thanks." Mary walked down the hall, sliding her phone from her pocket to take photos. She walked down the hallway, taking photos of the classrooms on both sides. She could see kids through the windows in the old wooden doors, and she assumed that Patrick's classroom wasn't on this floor because kids looked younger, like first- and second-graders. Still she took a few pictures, noticing there were no surveillance cameras, then she passed another

poster put up by the school district: BULLYING POLICY, it read at the top and underneath: WHAT IS BULLYING? BULLYING IS CHARAC-TERIZED BY THE FOLLOWING THREE (3) CRITERIA. IT IS AGGRESSIVE BEHAVIOR OR INTENTIONAL HARM-DOING, IT IS CARRIED OUT RE-PEATEDLY OVER TIME, AND IT OCCURS WITHIN AN INTERPERSONAL RELATIONSHIP WHERE THERE IS AN IMBALANCE OF POWER . . ."

She resumed going down the hallway, cheered by a bulletin board decorated with multicolored happy faces drawn by the students, under a poster-painted banner CELEBRATE UNIQUENESS, NO PLACE FOR HATE. The board was filled with yellow construction paper on which each student had inked his thumbprint; it looked as if every classroom in the school was included, and penciled beside each thumbprint was the student's name.

Mary scanned the classroom names—*Ms. Sandoval 201, Ms. Swanson 405, Ms. Chickowski 106*—then spotted Patrick's classroom teacher, *Ms. Krantz 504*. Mary counted thirty-one thumbprints on the construction paper, so the class was very large, and she found Patrick's thumbprint easily, because his lettering was poor. She felt a pang and found herself putting her thumb over his thumbprint. She hoped he was okay at home, but Edward still hadn't called her back. She'd follow up later.

She turned right down another hallway and noticed instantly that the classrooms had disappeared, replaced by a row of old wooden doors that no longer had any windows, though they were all closed and their purpose wasn't clear. It was apparently a series of administrative offices and closets because in the middle on the right was the school office, denoted by an Art Deco sign above another set of French doors, which sat propped open.

Mary walked forward, taking pictures surreptitiously in case there were any surveillance cameras she hadn't detected. She reached the office, but didn't go in. Instead, she glanced in on the fly, finding that it looked much as she had expected, but even older; it actually had wooden floorboards and a paneled counter that had been retrofitted to accommodate a printer and computer, and behind the counter, a young woman looked up curiously.

"Going to the bathroom, be right back," Mary said to her, making the I-Have-to-Pee face that every woman had made at one time or another. She kept going, snapping photos of the wooden doors on either side of the hallway. On her right was a wooden door that read Ladies' Room in old-fashioned gold script, and beyond that at the end of the hallway were double doors with another Art Deco sign, AUDITORIUM.

Mary wanted to find the room in which Patrick was assaulted and she sensed she was getting closer. She hurried past the auditorium and encountered another right turn, which she took, finding herself on another hallway lined with classrooms. She picked up the pace, snapping a few pictures on the run, and noticed that the children in the classrooms seemed older, and she passed classroom 501, so she knew she had reached the fifth-grade classrooms.

She walked past 502, and 503, on alternating sides of the hallway, and finally reached Patrick's classroom, which was on her left. She stole a glance inside to see a young, blonde teacher, but then kept going, trying to find the room. The classrooms ended, and on the far left, near another stairwell, she spotted a wooden door similar to the administrative doors, unmarked and without any window. It was wider than a conventional door, and Mary remembered that Patrick had said something about floor machines being in the room. It could be that the door was wide enough to permit floor polishers and the like to be stored there.

Mary crossed to the door, turned its brass knob, and opened it. At first she couldn't see anything because it was windowless and dark inside, but she closed the door behind her, used her phone as a flashlight, located the light switch, and turned it on. Ancient fluorescent lighting flickered overhead, illuminating a long, rectangular utility room lined with a few old stainless-steel floor polishers with oversized orbital brushes, then a bunch of mops in scuffed yellow rolling buckets, and at the farthest side, away from the door, was a wide washbasin.

Mary took pictures of the room, snapping as many as she could to examine them later. Her chest felt tight the entire time, and she was afraid of being discovered, so she finished quickly, turned off the light, then slipped out of the room. She headed back toward the office, mentally retracing Patrick steps, now that she understood the school layout. She could imagine exactly how what Patrick had described had taken place. If Patrick was heading toward the auditorium and straggling at the end of the line, which was likely considering he didn't have any friends in class, it would have been easy for Robertson to pick him off from the crowd. Then all Robertson would have to do would be to steer Patrick in the opposite direction, head back toward the utility room, and close them both inside. The utility room was off the beaten path near the stairwell, and since all of the students and staff were at the assembly, nobody would've heard or seen anything amiss.

Mary had gotten part of what she had come for, now it was time to get the rest. She went back down the corridor that ended in the auditorium, then took a left and headed for the office, surprised to see that coming toward her in the opposite direction was the lawyer for the school district, Kevin Reynolds, striding toward the office in a suit and tie, and cool aviator sunglasses. A former power forward at Villanova, Kevin was hard to miss because he was so tall, plus he liked to wear his hair in a bushy Afro that added two inches to his height. He was biracial, with light skin, gorgeous features, and a confident smile. None of the female lawyers minded when he appeared for the district.

"Hey, Kevin!" Mary called out to him, putting on her game face. "You're here early."

"You're here earlier." Kevin grinned, hooking his sunglasses with a finger and looking over them, his hazel eyes knowing. "What have you been up to?"

"Uh, I had to go to the bathroom." Mary gestured vaguely behind her, but Kevin only chuckled.

"Please. You think I'm stupid just 'cause I'm pretty?"

CHAPTER SIXTEEN

Mary spent the next hour presenting Patrick's case to Kevin and Julie Latimer, the Special Education Director, who greeted them with a nervous smile. Julie was in her early thirties, with light brown eyes, a long nose, and a heart-shaped face framed by short brown hair that was cut in a wedge, with one side higher than the other. She had on a light blue tank top with white Capri pants and matching sandals, and even so, looked uncomfortable in the stifling air of her tiny office, which lacked not only a window, but oxygen.

The three of them huddled around Julie's clunky wooden desk, which was cluttered with newsletters, workbooks, an old Mac laptop, and a Week-At-A-Glance spiral calendar, as well as a pink Play-Doh cup, a multicolored array of old Silly Bandz around a Phillies mug, photos of a chubby ginger cat and kittens, and a stack of confiscated cell phones. Mismatched file cabinets lined the walls, covering the rose-marble wainscoting, and above that were an array of motivational posters, a green sign that read COLLEGE BOUND HIGHWAY, and PRACTICE RANDOM ACTS OF KINDNESS in rainbow letters.

Mary showed Kevin and Julie that Patrick was identified in first grade as having a reading disability, but since then Grayson had not programmed him for reading support in any meaningful way. She presented Patrick's case, that he was still at first-grade reading level, hadn't been reevaluated within three years, and needed intensive remediation for his dyslexia. She moved on to his anxiety issues, arguing that they went hand-in-hand with his untreated dyslexia. The connection between stress, anxiety, and dyslexia was well-known, in that dyslexic children experience an inordinate amount of stress arising from the fact that no matter how hard they try in school, they fail. Combined with the bullying from classmates, it resulted in them shutting down and destroyed a child's self-esteem, which was happening with Patrick.

"Okay, we hear you," Kevin said when she was finished. He leaned away from the table, glancing at Julie. "What has Grayson done to program for Patrick? Would you like to explain your side of the story?"

"Yes." Julie flashed her nervous smile. "Well, Mary, we know what we're doing. We do guided reading."

Mary knew that wasn't enough. That just meant that the teacher stood at the front of the classroom, reading aloud while thirty students watched. That would be like showing someone a set of weights and expecting them to get in shape without lifting them.

"Our teachers work hard, and they know what they're doing. That's balanced literacy."

"But that is not a research-based reading intervention program. Patrick needs intensive interventions. He is only going to get further and further behind. The longer you wait, the harder it is to catch up, so the gap between him and his peers widens. That's why you start to see the behaviors, the shutting down and the vomiting. We're losing this kid."

"Look, I get it, I wish we could do more, but we don't have a special ed teacher to pull him out into a small group. I requested for this building to have an additional teacher and to have teachers trained in a research-based program, but I got turned down. The budget isn't there for it. I don't have the staff or the teachers to give him what he needs."

Mary turned to Kevin. "So that's an utter failure to program for him—"

"You made your point, Mary." Kevin raised his hand gently, so Mary moved to the next issue.

"What are you doing about his anxiety? He's school-phobic, he gets bullied by the other kids because he can't read and now he's throwing up. Has anybody made the connection between his anxiety and his dyslexia? Doesn't anybody care?"

Julie leaned over. "Mary, you have to understand our position. It's not like we don't care about Patrick. We do. We care about all of the children here."

"I'm sorry, I don't mean to criticize you. I'm trying to get his needs met."

"I know." Julie nodded, meeting Mary's eye directly. "And I wish I had a counselor here. We do the best we can with the resources we have."

Mary appreciated her frankness. "I get it, you're doing the best you can with the support you have."

"Exactly." Julie nodded, frowning in a plaintive way, her eyebrows sloping down unhappily. "You know, I agree with you that his anxiety, the vomiting, all of those behaviors, are getting worse. The kids tease him, Up-Chucky, all that. And to be completely honest with you, it is very disruptive to class when he vomits. Ms. Krantz, who couldn't leave class or she would be here, says it's disgusting to clean up and the smell never leaves the classroom. You could meet with our guidance counselor, but she's only here one day a week because of the budget cuts. She'd tell you the same thing."

"I'm sure." Mary was getting the hint that although Julie had compassion for Patrick, nobody would mind overmuch if he went to school elsewhere, so he could smell up *their* classroom.

"As far as psychological help for him, granted, somebody should be connecting the dots." Julie spread her delicate hands, palm up in appeal. "Believe me, I'd appreciate whatever you can do to get this school more resources. You know what it's like in the district, thanks to the politics in Harrisburg. They're starving us. We've gone through years of budget cutbacks and over three thousand layoffs. Do you know that there are 173 teacher vacancies in the district— that's classrooms that don't even have a *teacher*? There are 123 schools without full-time nurses and 50 without full-time counselors."

Mary knew it was true. Philadelphia's was the eighth-largest school district in the country, with 14 percent of students in special education, but state government had slashed the city's education budget by a billion dollars. Tragically, children all over the district were underserved, and two children had even died last year in elementary schools without nurses, one due to an asthma attack that should not have been fatal and another due to unspecified causes.

"Mary, I'm truly sorry we missed him, and I guess we did because, well, I have so many students and the initiative for counseling often comes from the parent. Or in Patrick's case, his grandfather."

Mary moaned. "But it's not fair to blame his grandfather. It's not his job to provide the services, it's yours. It's the school's responsibility under the law."

"I'm not making excuses, but I'm only one person. I look to our Grayson parents to partner with me and to raise issues they feel are important. You can't imagine how many parents—and *grandparents*—call me on the phone, asking for counseling. I checked, and Patrick's grandfather has never made any such request."

"But again"—Mary couldn't let it go, or maybe she just felt defensive on Edward's behalf—"under the law, it's not his responsibility, it's the school's."

Kevin interjected, "Mary, in the ideal world, you're right."

Mary frowned. "No, it's not the ideal, it's the *law*."

Kevin held up his big hand, like a stop sign. "Be real. The squeaky wheel gets the grease. You can understand why Julie has to deal first with the parents requesting help, and she's swamped. Patrick fell through the cracks. It's not impossible to miss the student who needs psychological services but whose caregiver doesn't request any."

Mary couldn't hide her pique. "Is it easy to miss when he's throwing up in front of you? Because nobody misses him when it's time to send him to a cooling-off room."

Kevin frowned. "What's got into you today? You're not usually so caffeinated."

"This is a tough case, Kevin." Mary softened her tone. "You can't program for him, you don't have the staff or the resources. A school like Fairmount Prep uses research-based reading programs, and with respect to anxiety, they have an in-house psychologist who offers counseling services in what they call a STEPS program."

Kevin chuckled under his breath. "Fairmount Prep is private and at thirty-five grand a year, they can offer Paradise. We can't."

"I know that." Mary met his eye evenly. "That's why he should be placed there, it's perfect for him. We have to put him where he can get help before it's too late. We're losing this kid. He's not just falling through the cracks, he's *disintegrating.* Please consider settling this for tuition." Mary tried to dial it back. "I'll prepare a settlement proposal and detail my position."

"Send me a letter," Kevin answered, meeting her eye.

By this time the meeting was over and Mary left Grayson. She looked around for the brown sedan or the red Passat but again, saw neither. She chirped her car unlocked and hurried across the street. She reached her car, got inside, and started the engine and AC. She checked her phone, but Edward still hadn't called back.

She pressed in Edward's number, but the phone rang and rang, and the call went to mechanical voicemail again. She wondered if Edward had taken Patrick to the zoo or someplace fun, as Cassandra had suggested, but there was only one way to find out. Mary decided to drop in at the house, since they lived so close.

She pulled out of the space, drove down the street, took a right, and in no time, was driving down Moretone Street. All the time she was scanning the street for the brown sedan or a red Passat, but they weren't in sight. She questioned whether that had been Robertson in the sedan yesterday or if she had made a mistake, but she stayed on alert. She spotted a parking space directly across the street from the O'Briens', so she pulled in, parked, and got out of the car, crossing to the house. She glanced up at Patrick's bedroom window but it was too dark to see inside.

She hustled up the few steps to the front door and pressed the buzzer, waiting. There was no answer, so she pressed it again, then called out, "Edward? Patrick?" She waited a minute, listening, but there was still no answer, and after a few minutes had passed, she tried one more time. The house sounded still, and she figured they had gone out, which made her happy.

Mary turned away from the front door, checking the time on her phone. It was just after two o'clock, and she scrolled through her email as she walked down the front walk, spotting the one she'd been waiting for, from the Admissions Director at Fairmount Prep, Kate Sand Ridolfi. Mary had written Kate this morning, inquiring about placing Patrick immediately.

The email read: **Mary, You're in luck! We have an opening for Patrick O'Brien. Please call ASAP and we can talk. Best, Kate.**

"Yes!" Mary breathed a happy sigh. Everything was falling into place, and Patrick was one step closer to getting back on track. She wished that Edward was home, so she could tell him the wonderful news.

Cheered, she looked up from her phone and suddenly noticed a brown sedan driving away. It was a Subaru and it was about to turn the corner.

Her heart stopped. The sedan was too far away to tell for sure, but she was pretty sure it was the same car. The sedan must have passed while she was reading her email. She didn't know if it was Robertson, but it couldn't have been a coincidence that she'd seen the same brown Subaru two days in a row.

She ran across the street to her car, chirping it unlocked just as the brown Subaru turned the corner and disappeared from view.

Mary jumped in her car, started the ignition, and zoomed out of the space.

She was going after him.

CHAPTER SEVENTEEN

Mary raced to the end of the street and turned right, but abruptly slammed on her brakes. A massive garbage truck was reversing onto the street from the side street, beeping in warning. The garbage truck blocked her way. There was no room to go around him. The street was too narrow. Parked cars lined both sides. She honked but the truck ignored her, taking up the entire street.

She thought fast, putting her car in reverse to back out of the street and go down another block before the Subaru got away. But a black SUV pulled up behind her, blocking her from behind as well.

Mary put her car in park, hopped out of the driver's seat with her phone, and tried to catch sight of the brown Subaru or get a picture of its license plate, but the Subaru was nowhere in sight.

Damn! Mary got back in the car, slammed the door shut, and got another idea. She scrolled through her phone, found the email from Lou Jacobs that had Robertson's home address, and pressed the link. Google Maps popped onto her screen, showing that his house was in the neighborhood, less than ten minutes away.

She pressed the button to get driving directions, and the garbage truck finally moved out of the way, driving forward down the street. She followed the phone's directions, scanning the passing traffic for the brown Subaru, but she didn't see it. The neighborhood changed as she got closer to Robertson's house, and the brick rowhouses turned into larger brick twins, with driveways on either side.

She turned right, then left, forming a plan. She knew not to confront Robertson because he could've been dangerous and she had
been warned against that by Cassandra. But if Mary went to his
house, she could check out his driveway and see what cars he had.
If there was a brown Subaru in addition to the red Passat that Lou
had told her about, it would beef up her case against Robertson, as
well as protect Edward and Patrick.

Mary felt her heart pound a little quicker the closer she got to
Robertson's block. She scanned the parked cars on the way for the
brown Subaru, just in case Robertson had seen her and tried to
hide the car. There were a lot of older-model cars parked along
the streets, but none of them was the Subaru.

After a few blocks, she found herself driving slowly down Robertson's street, Grove Street, toward his house—495. The odd-number
houses were on the left side of the street, and she looked ahead to see
that 495 was in the middle of the block. She cruised slowly toward it,
keeping an eye out for the brown Subaru among the parked cars,
but so far hadn't seen it. Robertson's house was a redbrick twin, three
stories tall and in decent repair, but its driveway was on the far side
of the house. Mary had to get closer to see if it held any cars.

She drove ahead, glancing over as she passed 495, and she spotted the red Passat parked in the driveway, but no Subaru.

Mary felt disappointed but kept driving, circling the block to see
if the brown Subaru had been parked elsewhere. She didn't see
it, but she couldn't give up so easily. She went to Plan B. She drove
back to Grove Street, turned onto Robertson's block, and steered
into the first empty parking spot, which was on the right. It gave
her an excellent view of Robertson's house and driveway, and if she
waited a little, she could see if the brown Subaru appeared.

She cut the ignition and checked the dashboard clock—3:45. She
would sit here for an hour or two and see what happened. She kept
her window closed and set the air-conditioning so the interior would
stay cool for a while. She remembered that she was supposed to
meet her mother and mother-in-law tonight, but she could cancel
that if she had to. This was more important, and she felt like she
was really onto something.

She kept an eye on the house, trying to analyze the situation. There weren't that many old brown Subarus in the world, and it seemed too coincidental to see one, two days in a row, especially if it was the same brown Subaru. It was always possible that the brown Subaru was owned by somebody in Edward's neighborhood, but the Philadelphia Children's Alliance, where she had seen the car yesterday, was a different neighborhood, Hunting Park, and there was nothing else around it except industry.

Mary had a hunch that it was the same brown Subaru, and she wanted to get to the bottom of it. She picked up her phone and took a few pictures of the house, just for reference.

Bam! Suddenly someone slammed a hand on her car window.

Mary jumped, terrified to see that it was Robertson, his eyes popping with anger. He held his phone in his hand, filming a video of her.

"Why are you spying on me and my family?" he yelled, loud enough to be heard through the glass. "What are you doing parked on my street? You have no business being here! You're watching my house! You're stalking me!"

Mary dropped her phone. Fear bolted through her system. She didn't know what Robertson was capable of. She had never seen such a crazy glint in anyone's eyes, ever before. She had to get away. She twisted on the ignition as Robertson kept filming, inches from her window.

"You're harassing me and my family! You're not going to get away with this!"

Mary slammed her foot on the gas. Her car lurched forward as Robertson stepped back, still filming. She tore out of the space and raced down the street, her heart hammering.

"This is harassment! This is illegal!" Robertson shouted after her car, making such a scene that drivers craned their necks to see what was going on and passersby on the sidewalk turned to watch.

Mary caught a green light, drove forward, and took the first turn she could off Grove Street, trying to recover her composure. She didn't know where Robertson had come from. But he knew who she was, which told her something. She was too panicky to figure out what.

She decreased her rate of speed and looked around, not knowing how to get back to the city. Her phone had fallen to the floor on the passenger side and when she stopped at a red light, she undid her seatbelt, reached over, and picked it up. It started ringing almost immediately, and she didn't have to check the screen to know that it was Machiavelli calling.

Mary answered the call, driving ahead. "Your client the child molester has major anger issues, you know that, don't you?"

Machiavelli chuckled. "Now, is that a nice thing to say about a warm and fuzzy teacher's aide?"

"He's a child molester. He physically and sexually assaulted my client, a ten-year-old boy. That's who you're representing. That's who Robertson is."

"I have no idea what you're talking about."

"Oh please." Mary could barely keep a civil tongue. "Are you trying to tell me that you believed his story about a scrawny little fifth-grader attacking him with a scissors? A man as big and scary as Robertson? Don't tell me you don't know what happened. Robertson physically and sexually assaulted my client three times, and I can prove it. And I will."

"That's completely untrue, and I'm surprised that *you* would believe the fabrications of a deeply troubled child. You will recall he draws pictures of himself killing people."

"I always knew you were low, but I never thought you were that low. You've got clients out the wazoo. You couldn't let a child molester go? You couldn't let somebody else represent the absolute dregs of humanity? Don't you have any heart at all?"

"Look who's talking about low." Machiavelli snorted. "I would've FaceTimed you, but I happen to know you're driving around, harassing my client. How'd that work out for you? I hear not so good."

"Robertson has been following my clients, and you'd better make him stop. The fact that he borrowed a car doesn't fool anybody. I've already reported it to PCA, and they're going to report it to the police. If Robertson thinks he can intimidate my clients, he's gonna have to get through me."

"That's tough talk, Mary. All I know is, my client has a video of you sitting in a car on his street, taking pictures of his house. Would you like to explain to me who was following whom? Or do I have to get a TRO against you?"

"Not before I get one against Robertson," Mary said, because she was getting the picture. "In addition to assaulting children, Robertson is one of those jerks who pushes people around by suing them. He's suing my clients because he thought that would preempt a criminal prosecution, but it didn't work. He followed us to PCA and figured out that the train left the station, so now he's going to try to sue me."

"Don't be silly." Machiavelli's tone turned sarcastic. "Nobody's suing you. Peace is better than war. You really should settle this case, Mary. You're losing your damn mind over it. Stalking plaintiffs is so unlike you. What would the nuns say?"

"We're never settling, ever. Robertson's going to jail." Mary hung up the phone and tossed it aside, exhaling. It took her the entire drive back to the city for her heartbeat to return to normal.

She just hoped it was normal enough to pass inspection by her mother.

CHAPTER EIGHTEEN

Mary hurried up Walnut Street, late to her hair-and-makeup trial. Her mother was waiting for her at the salon and so was her future mother-in-law, Elvira "El Virus" Rotunno. Mary hated leaving her mother alone with El Virus, who was mouthy, brassy, and pushy. El Virus was in her seventies, but acted like she was in her twenties and dressed like she was in the eighties, the Crazy-Mother-In-Law Trifecta.

Mary picked up the pace. Her mother couldn't have been more different from El Virus. Her mother was quiet and stereotypically loving, though she ruled her house with an iron fist and her kitchen with a wooden spoon. Because she was born in Italy, her mother's English wasn't perfect, but her meatballs were. Mary's mother was also ten years senior to El Virus, having become a mother late in life; her doctor had told her that she couldn't have children, then one day she became pregnant with Mary and her twin sister Angie, which she called a special gift from God. Everybody else called it malpractice.

Mary spotted the sign for The Cutting Edge, two doors up. She had never been here before, but Anne had told her it was the best salon in the city.

She ran to the door and hurried inside, looking for her mother. The salon was long and narrow, with black-lacquered styling stations in rows down both sides, and customers filled the black swivel chairs, their heads wet or covered with folded tinfoil while they chatted with their hairstylists over the expensive whoosh of ionic blow-dryers. The walls were a stark black, and piped music filled the air, which smelled like hydrocarbons.

She spotted her mother across the room, sitting in a swivel chair in one of the styling stations. Her mother wasn't wearing her thick trifocals, so she couldn't see anything, and her warm brown eyes, milky gray at the rims, looked vaguely terrified. A black plastic logo smock covered her entire body, but since she was barely five feet tall, the only thing that showed were her swollen feet in her flesh-tone knee stockings and brown orthopedic shoes, dangling above the polished parquet floor.

Mary hurried toward her, confused. Her mother was alone, and El Virus was nowhere in sight. Neither was Courtney, the hair-stylist who was supposed to be doing her mother's hair. Mary had anticipated that her mother might be intimidated by the upscale salon, but that didn't explain why she looked so upset.

"Ma, it's me," Mary said, when she reached her mother, then leaned over and kissed her soft cheek. "I'm sorry I'm late, what's the matter?"

"*Maria?*" Her mother looked up, her sparse gray eyebrows lift-ing, then she grabbed Mary's hand and squeezed hard. "Is Elvira, she say they fix my hair."

"Don't worry, Ma. That's why we're here. They're going to fix your hair. Mine too, and Elvira's, for the wedding." Mary stroked her mother's short gray curls, which look freshly trimmed and smelled like mangoes. "Did they already do you? Did I miss every-thing? And where's Courtney?"

"No, no, no, you no understand, Courtn', she wash alla, she cut alla, but is Elvira." Her mother shook her head, agitated.

"What did Elvira do?"

"Elvira—" Her mother started to answer, but clammed up when El Virus came clacking toward them, in a black V-neck showing major cleavage bedazzled with I STILL GOT IT, which she had on with her black stirrup pants and black half-boots with stiletto heels. She believed that bedazzling improved everything, including the wedding dress she'd wanted Mary to marry Anthony in, but that was another story. She piled on the makeup and wore her hair in a tight black perm, which was truly permanent.

"Hey, Mare!" El Virus gave them a manicured wave hello as she approached with a tattooed-and-pierced Goth stylist. " 'Bout time you got here!"

"Sorry," Mary said, when El Virus got closer. "What's going on? Where's Courtney?"

"Courtney cut your mom's hair, but she felt sick and had to go home. I got a better stylist anyway, one who knows what to do with your mother." El Virus jerked her thumb at a skinny twenty-five-year-old with heavy black eyeliner, black lipstick, and short matte black hair, which matched her black tank dress, black belt with studs, and black Roman sandals. Mary assumed she liked black, or had been to a funeral.

"I'm Lucretia." Lucretia smiled, revealing a silvery grille that reminded Mary of the braces she never had, and in Lucretia's hands was a silver tray that held a number of hair products Mary had never seen before.

"What's that stuff?"

"It's for your mother," El Virus interjected, then took Mary's arm and tugged her toward the empty hair station next to her mother. "And look what I got for you!"

"What?" Mary asked, increasingly bewildered.

"Check this!" El Virus waved in front of the black-lacquered counter, and on its top sat round brushes, big-tooth combs, and bottles of pump hairspray, but next to them were long strands of hair, ranging from dark blonde to light blonde, hanging from a thin plastic string that looked like fishing wire.

"Extensions!" called out a young girl from behind her, and Mary turned around to see a second stylist, who looked and dressed like Lucretia except that her grille was gold, not silver, and suddenly nothing was making any sense.

"Where's Ellen?" Mary wanted Ellen, the hairstylist Anne had recommended for her. "And I don't want extensions."

The second stylist answered, "Mary, I'm Teegan, and Ellen had to drive Courtney home. Ellen said I should take over, so I'm here to do your hair. I think your mother-in-law is right. You totally need extensions. Here, sit down, please."

"No, wait—" Mary said, though she allowed Teegan to press her into the black swivel chair beside her mother while she tried to figure out what was going on.

El Virus stood between the two workstations, cracking her gum. "Mary, the extensions were my idea, and you totally need them. Nobody in Hollywood has their real hair. Take it from me."

Mary bit her tongue, as Elvira had never been west of Eighth Street. "Elvira, I don't want extensions. I'm not going to wear extensions."

"But it makes your hair fuller."

"I know what they are."

"Give it a try, you'll like it."

"I don't want them."

"Anthony will love them."

"Then let *him* wear them."

Lucretia picked up the extensions and plopped them in Mary's lap, like a small dog that needed grooming. "She's right, give it a try. We use only one hundred percent human hair at this salon. You need to pick some that are highlights, some that are lowlights, and some that match your exact color. We'll do that while your hair is dry, then we'll get you a smock, get you shampooed, and we're good to—"

"No, no, no!" Mary said, at the same moment that she heard her mother, next to her, saying:

"No, no, no!"

"Ma, what is it?" Mary turned to see her mother covering her head with her hands while Lucretia was trying to spray something onto her hair. "Lucretia, what are you doing?"

El Virus dismissed Mary with an airy wave. "Don't worry about it, Mare. Lucretia's takin' care of your mother's bald spot."

"*What?*" Mary cringed. Her mother was supersensitive about the bald spot at her crown, which was why she got her hair teased every week at her corner beauty salon.

Lucretia raised the shiny black can. "This is a scalp concealer, and it hides her bald spot. Wait 'til you see. Let me just spray this, then it turns to powder. The chemicals make, like, fibers, and you can't even see the bald spot, and we follow it with a finishing spray—"

"No, no, no!" her mother said, cowering under her hands.

"She doesn't have a bald spot," Mary said, to save face for her mother. Her mother had never acknowledged the existence of her bald spot, and both Mary and her father supported her denial, which was how they did things in the DiNunzio family. Because they loved each other.

El Virus snorted. "Oh, your mother's bald! She's *really bald*. I remember when I first met her, her bald spot was about the size of a fig, then a plum, but *then* it got to be the size of an orange, and pretty soon it's gonna be as big as a *cantaloupe*—"

"—Ma, don't listen to her, you're not bald—"

"—and Mare," El Virus continued, "you're gonna be bald too, it's hereditary. That's why you need the extensions, on account of the fact that your hair is so thin, and nobody wants thin hair on her wedding day. You gotta have *volume*, a lotta volume, like me—"

Mary stopped listening, stood up, put the extensions on the counter, and crossed to her mother. "Ma, you okay?"

"*Maria, no.*" Her mother's cloudy eyes began to glisten, which broke Mary's heart.

"I don't like it here. Do you, Ma?"

"No, no, *Maria*. I no like." Her mother lowered her hands, blinking.

"Let's go home." Mary picked up her mother's glasses from the counter, unfolded the acetate stems, and slid them onto her mother's lined face, kissing her on the forehead.

"*Andiamo!*" Her mother blinked her tears away and hopped out of the swivel chair like a much younger woman.

"I love you, Ma." Mary unsnapped her mother's plastic smock, helped her out of it, and left it bunched on the chair. Underneath she had on her flowered housedress, which smelled of mothballs and oregano, which was perfect.

"Ti amo, Maria." Her mother smiled again, then picked up her handbag.

El Virus looked at them like they were crazy. "Ladies, what're ya doin'? Where ya goin'? This place is great! And Mare, wait, I tol' Teegan to get you false eyelashes because your eyelashes are real thin, too—"

"Elvira, thanks, but no thanks." Mary turned to Lucretia and Teegan. "Ladies, we appreciate it, but this isn't our style."

"Whatever," Lucretia and Teegan said in unison.

"Hmph, I'm staying!" El Virus folded her arms over her bedazzled breasts.

"Please do, you're welcome to, Elvira." Mary managed a smile, only to maintain relations. "Let me treat you to it, they have my credit card info. Feel free. Get a manicure or a pedicure, whatever you like, but I'm going to take my mother home."

"Suit yourself, Mare." Elvira shrugged. "Thanks. Bye."

"Ciao, Elvira."

"Bye, Elvira." Mary took her mother by the arm, and as they turned and headed for the door, she realized this was the second time she was walking out of a room today, which was a personal best. Or worst.

El Virus called after her, "Hey, Mare, can I get a Brazilian, too?"

Her mother looked up at her, not understanding. *"Che?"*

CHAPTER NINETEEN

It took Mary a long time to calm her mother down, and Mary didn't succeed until her mother started cooking, making her a big bowl of spaghetti, which she ate, and then Mary's father had gotten home, so she stayed while her mother made him a big bowl of spaghetti and he ate it, at which point, world order was restored in the DiNunzio household, through carbohydrates.

It was late by the time Mary left her parents' house, and the sun had tarnished to a coppery hue, sliding like a penny on a wall behind the flat tar roofs, ugly satellite dishes, and sagging cables that marked the South Philadelphia sky. She drove past the rowhouses with their brick, stucco, or stone façades, the front windows bay or single-paned, plugged with rattling air conditioners. Raucous boys played in front of the houses, shouting to each other as they hopped on skateboards, flying with their arms extended, sending them into whoops of excited laughter.

It made Mary think of Patrick, who never got to play like that, and she had second thoughts about going back to the office or even home. She'd called Edward again, but he still hadn't replied, and she needed to get his signature on admission papers to keep Patrick on track at Fairmount Prep. She glanced at the dashboard clock, which read 7:17, and she took a right toward Broad Street, heading north.

Traffic was light, since rush hour was finished and everybody was home, which meant that when Mary finally reached Juniata, she had to circle the O'Briens' block of Moretone Street again and again to find a parking space. She kept an eye out for the brown Subaru or a red Passat, but she didn't expect to see either after what had happened today.

She found a parking space around the corner, on Bird Street. She got out of the car, chirped it locked, and walked down Bird, feeling the air cool now that twilight had fallen, darkening the sky. Lights went on inside the houses, and big TVs flickered in the living rooms, flashing on the front windows like electronic lightning. Women came outside to water potted plants, and men smoked cigarettes on their front step.

Mary turned onto Moretone Street. The O'Briens' house was on the right side of the street and she was on the left, and she saw immediately that lights were on in the house, so they'd gotten back. She glanced up at Patrick's room, also lit, and just behind his window fan, she made out the outline of Patrick's head, bent down, presumably over his artwork. The sight did her heart good, and she hoped he wasn't too traumatized by yesterday's events.

She crossed the street, smiled at the neighbors she passed, then reached the O'Briens' and on impulse, stopped and called up to Patrick's window. "Hey Patrick, it's Mary!" she called out, smiling. She expected his little head to pop into the window beside the fan, but in the next moment, his bedroom went dark.

She assumed he was coming downstairs to open the door so she climbed the front stoop and rang the buzzer. She waited, but nobody answered. She rang again, but nobody answered again.

"Patrick, Edward!" Mary called out, but there was still no answer, which left her nonplussed. She knew they were home; Patrick's light had been on, and the downstairs lights were still on. She leaned over and peeked in the living room, but she couldn't see through the curtains, except to confirm that the light was still on. But suddenly, in the next moment, the living room light blinked off.

"Patrick? Edward?" Mary didn't get it. She knew they were inside but they were turning the lights off. She flashed on her morning outside Grayson Elementary, ringing the buzzer and trying to get inside the school. If she didn't know better, she would think Edward and Patrick were avoiding her, too.

"Guys, it's Mary! Patrick! Edward?" Mary rang the buzzer, then pounded on the door. She stepped back from the doorstep, walked back down the front walk, and peered up at the house, which remained dark inside.

"Edward, Patrick!" Mary called out, making a megaphone of her hands, and in the next moment, the neighbor's door opened and a ponytailed woman popped her head out, holding a baby in a diaper on her hip.

"Yo, can I help you?" the neighbor called to Mary, with a frown.

"Sorry!" Mary called back. "I'm a friend of the O'Briens and I wanted to see them. I think they're home."

"I'm sure they are, they always are. But can you keep it down, please? I'm trying to put my baby down." The woman went inside the house, closing the door.

Mary took out her phone, pressed REDIAL for Edward, and went back up to the front door, listening for the ring of his cell phone. If she could hear it, that would mean he was in the living room. She couldn't hear it. She ended the call, then leaned on the buzzer, longer, and let off. She knew Patrick had seen her even if Edward was taking a nap, so she knocked on the door one last time.

"Patrick, let me in. It's really important. I need to see you and your grandfather." Mary waited at the doorway, listening, but no sound came from within.

"Patrick, please? It's really important, and I'm not going away unless you let me in." Mary waited at the door another moment, then sat on the front stoop. She didn't want to disturb the neighbors anymore, and she didn't know what was going on, but she would give it another minute. Her phone started ringing, and she looked down at the home screen, which showed it was Anne Murphy, from the office. Anne must have been calling to hear how the hair-and-makeup trial went, so Mary sent the call to voicemail. This wasn't the time or place for a conversation about extensions, plus she knew Anne would definitely be in favor.

Suddenly, the door opened behind her with a scraping sound, and Mary turned around to see Patrick frowning at her.

"My Pops is taking a nap. I'm not allowed to wake him up. Can you come back later?"

"No, and I'm sure he won't mind if I wake him up, because this is important." Mary tried the screen door, but it was locked. "Patrick, unlock the door and let me in."

"I can't. My Pops will be mad."

"No, he won't, I promise. Please?"

Patrick unlocked the screen door, then stepped back and let Mary into the living room, which was dim without the lights on.

"How're you doing?" Mary asked him, glancing around the living room, which was empty. So Edward wasn't sleeping on the couch, a time-honored tradition in the DiNunzio household, but Patrick was acting distant.

"Okay."

"You all right?"

"Yes." Patrick shrugged, looking down.

Mary crossed to the table lamp and turned it on, but Patrick was strangely subdued. He had on a faded black Transformers T-shirt with the same gym shorts as yesterday and bare feet. It felt warm inside, the window air conditioner barely making a difference. "What did you guys do today?"

"Nothing." Patrick shrugged again, still downcast.

"Really?" Mary glanced upstairs, reflexively. "But you weren't home, were you?"

Patrick didn't reply, but he started sucking his lip, and Mary wondered what was making him anxious.

"I called your grandfather but he didn't answer. Is he taking a nap upstairs?" Mary walked to the bottom of the stairwell and put a hand on the banister. She was starting to wonder if something was wrong.

"He's in bed." Patrick didn't turn around, just stood still, his head down and his arms hanging at his side.

"Okay, you wait here, and I'll be right back down." Mary went up the stairs, not understanding why Patrick was behaving so oddly.

She reached the top of the stairwell, which was too dark to see anything. She felt around for a switchplate and flipped on the light, illuminating the hallway. She knew that to the left was Patrick's bedroom, but to the right must have been Edward's. The hallway ended in a closed door, and she walked in that direction.

There was an open door on her right, a bathroom, and then she passed an open door to her left, which seemed to be a small den. She reached the end of the hall and knocked on the closed door.

"Edward, it's Mary."

Mary waited outside the door. She was getting a bad feeling, but then again, maybe it was nothing. Patrick was a little boy, and kids acted funny without reason.

"Edward?" Mary said more loudly, then knocked again. She waited, then opened the door. It was dark in the room, which had only one window, with a thick roll-up shade pulled down to the top of the window fan.

"Edward?" Mary's eyes adjusted to the dimness, and she saw Edward in the bed under a white sheet, lying still. Too still. Instinctively, she entered the room, went to his side, and touched his shoulder.

"Edward," Mary said, hushed.

Edward didn't move.

Mary turned on the lamp on the night table. She gasped in horror. She couldn't believe what she was seeing. Edward lay motionless in bed, his eyes closed and his head resting on a thin pillow. His mouth hung open grotesquely, his jaw had gone completely slack. His face was drained of color, and his skin ashen. A white sheet covered his body from the chest down. He had on lightweight blue pajamas.

Mary had to make sure. She touched Edward's shoulder again and felt the chill of his body through the thin cotton. She removed her hand and leaned over him, turning her head so that her ear faced him. She prayed to hear breathing, but there was no sound. She straightened up stiffly, trying to collect her thoughts. She considered trying to feel his neck for a pulse, but she couldn't bear it. She knew what she would find.

An unpleasant smell came from the bed, and she knew without looking that Edward had soiled the sheets. She made a mental note to strip the bed and wash the sheets before Patrick saw anything upsetting.

"Oh, no," Mary said under her breath. She didn't know when Edward had passed, but she assumed it had been in his sleep last night. She didn't know how much Patrick knew or understood. She realized that he had been here all day, even when she'd come knocking. Evidently Patrick had spent the day shut inside with Edward's body, keeping the world at bay.

Mary swallowed hard, choking her emotions down. She thought it was bizarre of Patrick, but he was just a kid and he must have been terrified. He hadn't known what to do. His grandfather was his world. He didn't want to lose Edward.

Her gaze flitted around the bedroom, and she took in its contents: a night table held his smartphone, a watch, a worn brown wallet, a rosary with opalescent beads, a bottle of Ambien, a silvery CVS glucose meter, a vial of insulin, and a used syringe. Across from the bed was a ladderback chair with a white Oxford shirt hanging from one side, and on the far wall, a simple wood dresser-and-mirror that held several framed photographs.

Mary walked over to the photographs. One was an old black-and-white eight-by-ten of four grinning GIs in sweaty T-shirts and Army-issue pants, their metal dog tags looped around their necks and their strong arms linked around each other. Mary recognized a younger Edward on the end, the only soldier with glasses. She assumed it had to be in Vietnam. She hadn't known that he'd served.

Next to that sat framed photos of a pretty young woman, grinning and holding a baby. It had to be Suzanne and Patrick. A laminated card from the funeral home showed another photo of Suzanne, propped up on a statue of the Virgin Mary, its plastic yellowed with age.

"Mary?" Patrick said quietly, from the door.

CHAPTER TWENTY

"Patrick, don't come in," Mary said gently, heading for the door, but Patrick was already entering the bedroom.

"That's a picture of my Pops in the war." Patrick walked past the bed without looking over. "He told me all about it. He was in a jungle and he was with his friends. I know all the names."

"Patrick, let's go." Mary tried to turn him around, but Patrick reached for the photograph on the dresser, picking it up.

"This guy is Tommy and he was from Maine. That's a state where it snows a lot." Patrick pointed at the second GI from the left. "And this guy is Shemp. That's not his real name, that's what they called him, and he was from Chicago. My Pops went there after the war was over and he visited Shemp. Shemp has a grandson too. His name is Bobby."

Mary wasn't completely sure what to do, so she let Patrick talk, resting a hand on his shoulder. She didn't want to alarm him by rushing him out of the room, making something so traumatic even worse.

"And this guy is Jacob and he was my Pops's best friend. My Pops says that Jacob was funny and smart and he was going to be a doctor, that's how smart he was. And he was from Cherry Hill, and my Pops says that it's near us, but it's not a hill and it doesn't have any cherries. It has a mall."

Mary listened as Patrick moved his finger to Edward.

"This is my Pops, and he was the *captain*, that means he was the *best* one of all of the soldiers. He rode in tanks and *choppers*." Patrick's tone changed, echoing a note of a child's pride, and the very sound of it seemed to reach deep inside Mary, striking a chord she didn't even know she had. She blinked her eyes clear as Patrick nodded, still looking down at the photograph, his finger on his grandfather's face, back when Edward had been smiling, young, alive, and at war. "My Pops told me about the war, and we watch the History Channel and he tells me about the battles, about Anzio, Normandy, and D-day. He knows where the cities are, it's far away, not here. In Vietnam, where he was a soldier, they have jungles and tigers."

Mary thought of something Edward had told her, that Patrick drew tigers when he was younger. She wondered how long Edward had been telling Patrick his war stories from Vietnam.

"My Pops said one time they were in the jungle and they were eating their lunch, and a bad guy was hiding in the bushes but they didn't know it, and all of a sudden, the bad guy started to shoot them so they were ambushed. That's when the bad guy shot Jacob and killed him, and then the bad guy was going to shoot Pops, too."

Mary let Patrick continue, thinking about the bad guys and the good guys that he talked about so much.

"And then what happened was that the bad guy's gun stopped working, like, his gun *jammed*, that means it didn't work, and so then the bad guy got his *bayonet,* that's like a knife, and he came after Pops to kill him with his bayonet."

"Oh no." Mary thought of Patrick's artwork, of the good guy killing the bad guy with a knife.

"Pops didn't have his gun because he was eating, so he got his knife, and just when the bad guy was going to kill him with the bayonet, Pops killed the bad guy with his knife and so he was saved and he didn't die and he came home."

Mary felt a realization come over her, drenching her in a warm wave of sadness. The good guy in Patrick's drawings wasn't Patrick, imagining himself as a superhero. It was *Edward*. Edward was Patrick's ultimate good guy. His own personal captain. His hero. His grandfather.

"The Army gave my Pops a medal because he did that and he was so brave and he did such a good job, but he doesn't have the medal because he gave it to Jacob's mom in Cherry Hill, so I never got to see it. He said he would take me to see the medal but we never went."

Mary nodded, mute with emotion, and Patrick put the photograph back on the dresser.

"My Pops has a lot of stories, and he knows a lot about war, and every night he prays the rosary for Jacob and for his other friends. He says they didn't come home from the war but that really means that they got killed by the bad guys"—Patrick kept talking as he turned to the other photographs—"he used to kneel by his bed while he prayed, but then he got older and he has to do it in his bed, but he says Jacob and all of his friends are in heaven now and they're happy."

"I'm sure they are." Mary was raised in the Catholic Church, but she had fallen away. Still she found herself wishing that Edward had had Last Rites, a wish she couldn't quite explain. "So you never met any of his buddies from the war?"

"No."

"Does he have any other friends?"

"Dave. He likes Dave. They talk about money and stocks."

Mary remembered that Edward had mentioned him.

"My Pops said my grandmother was his best friend, but after she died, he didn't get any new best friends."

Mary felt a pang. "Did he have any uncles or anything like that? Like any family?"

"No." Patrick shook his head.

"Do you? Do you know any uncles or aunts or cousins?"

"No."

Mary wondered if he could be right. "What about Thanksgiving? Does anyone ever come over?"

"No."

"Do you ever go to anyone else's house for the holidays?"

"No. We stay home. We get a special turkey that doesn't have any legs or arms because that's what we like. White meat. We cook it in the oven. I help make the stuffing. Stove Top." Patrick pointed to a photo of him with his mother. "That's me when I was little. That's my mom. She's in heaven too. Her name was Suzanne." Patrick looked up at Mary with a slight frown, his brown eyes troubled. "What's your mom's name?"

"Vita," Mary answered, her throat thick. She felt strange talking to Patrick with Edward lying in bed only a few feet away. She sensed that the boy was in some sort of denial.

"Do you have a daddy?"

"Yes." Mary realized that Patrick didn't have a daddy, so he didn't naturally assume that everyone had a daddy.

"What's his name?"

"His name is Mariano, but he goes by Matty. People call him Matty."

"There's a kid in my class named Matt. He talks a lot." Patrick turned to the bed. "Pops is still asleep. The diabetes makes him tired and shaky. He needs his sleep."

Mary wasn't sure what to do or say, but she couldn't let this go on. "Patrick, I have some very bad news for you. Your grandfather, he's not asleep."

"Yes he is." Patrick nodded, matter-of-factly. "That's how he sleeps. His mouth always looks like that. He sleeps with his mouth open. Sometimes he snores."

Mary patted Patrick's shoulder. "Maybe that's true, but this time, I don't think he's asleep, I think that—"

"He always says he sleeps like a log. Sometimes he sleeps so long he misses dinner. He doesn't even wake up if I push him. He needs to sleep. That's why I'm not allowed to wake him up."

Mary wondered if Edward's diabetes had been worse than she thought or if he'd had heart problems. It would explain why he'd been so tired yesterday and why he seemed so much older than his years. She felt awful, wondering if the stress had been too much for him.

"Be right back." Patrick started walking to the door.

"Wait, what? Patrick?" Mary went after him, confused, but he went down the stairs, trailing his hand on the wall, with her following.

"Patrick?"

"I have to do something." Patrick took a left through the living room, and Mary followed him to the back of the house, into a small, square kitchen lined with white refaced cabinets and white countertops. In the center of the room was a rectangular wooden table with two chairs, one at the head and one catty-corner. An uneaten bologna sandwich sat on a flowered plate at one seat, which had been set with a folded napkin and a full glass of milk, untouched.

"He likes soup." Patrick grabbed a chair, dragged it across the floor, pulled it up to the counter, and climbed up on top.

"What are you doing?"

"My Pops likes soup. I know how to make it." Patrick opened the cabinet, slid out a can of Progresso soup, and showed it to Mary. "He *loves* this soup. This is his favorite. Pea soup. Once I called it peepee soup and he laughed. Now we call it peepee soup."

"Patrick, why do you want to make him soup?"

"Because he likes it." Patrick climbed down off the chair, leaving it in place against the counter, as well as the cabinet hanging open, then he started to pull off the tab on top of the can.

"Don't do that, you'll hurt yourself." Mary came over.

"No I won't. Watch. It's only hard to get it started." Patrick stuck his index finger in the tab and yanked it. "See? I do it all the time." He moved the chair one cabinet over, then climbed up on it again, opened the next cabinet, and retrieved an oversized mug. He climbed down again, saying, "I make him soup if he doesn't feel good, and he loves it."

"I see." Mary watched him, heartsick, but didn't stop him. She sensed that he knew the truth and she didn't see the harm in letting him make soup.

"He didn't wake up for his bologna sandwich but he doesn't like sandwiches as much as he likes soup. I help him all the time because of the diabetes. He says the soup helps him." Patrick went back to the can, poured the green glop into the mug, then leaned over the sink, turned on the faucet, and poured some water into the mug. "Pops says to add water because it makes it last longer. They don't tell you to do that because the company wants you to use up all your money and buy more soup."

"Patrick, you make the soup, I'm going to go make a phone call, okay?"

"Okay." Patrick hoisted the mug into the microwave.

"Don't burn yourself."

"I never do. I put it on two-and-a-half minutes. He says it gets too hot if you put it on three."

"Good job." Mary slipped out of the kitchen, went back to the living room, got her purse from the chair, and reached inside for her phone. She would have to call the police, and they would bring the city medical examiner. Edward's death was unattended, so by law, that meant an autopsy would have to be performed, since he wasn't in hospice. The only open question was what would happen to Patrick.

Mary's gut twisted. Patrick was now an orphan. The very thought was heartbreaking enough, and she dreaded to think of what would happen to him now. She assumed that the police would call DHS and he would be placed in the foster care system.

Mary sank into the chair, holding her phone. She didn't know much about foster care, but what she knew wasn't good. There wasn't a month that went by in Philadelphia when the newspaper didn't have some awful story about the foster care system. Maybe the stories weren't a fair representation, and there were undoubtedly wonderful foster parents who took great care of foster children. But that couldn't be guaranteed, especially for a child with special needs like Patrick.

Mary stared at her phone, frozen. She couldn't bring herself to call the police yet. As soon as she did, she would set in motion a series of events that would remove Patrick from the only home he knew and place him in the foster system. The authorities would take him, this very night, and he would go to sleep in a strange bed, in a stranger's house. On the other hand, Mary couldn't *not* call the police. It was grotesque that Edward's body lay upstairs in bed, where it had been all night and all day.

Mary couldn't wrap her mind around how quickly the boy's life had turned upside down and her hopes for his future scuttled. He'd been about to enter Fairmount Prep; she had it all rigged. But now all of that hung in jeopardy, and she could only imagine how losing his grandfather would hurt him. Coming on the heels of his assault, it might plunge him into depression.

Mary heard the microwave *ping* in the kitchen. If she could convince the police to wait until tomorrow to call DHS, she could stay at the house tonight with Patrick. Officer Diamond owed her a favor, and it was the best thing for Patrick. Officers Lee and Muniz had been here only yesterday, and they knew Patrick's situation.

Mary pressed in the number for the Twenty-fifth Precinct.

CHAPTER TWENTY-ONE

Mary hung up the phone. It had taken her longer than she'd expected, but the police were on the way to take Edward's body and so was the medical examiner, since they happened to be at a "job" nearby. She hadn't been able to get through to Officers Diamond, Lee, or Muniz but she'd dropped their names, as well as Bennie Rosato's, then made her request to hold off DHS until morning. The police weren't making any promises, except that they'd come without sirens.

Mary went back to the kitchen, where Patrick was sitting at the table in front of a glass of water. He seemed more nervous than before, resting his forearms on the table and playing a game with his right hand, tapping each finger on the table, like a slow-motion drumming. An oversized mug of pea soup sat in front of Edward's empty seat, next to a napkin with a tablespoon. She didn't know what had happened to the bologna sandwich. The glass of milk had been replaced with a glass of water.

"The soup is ready for him," Patrick said, with a grimly satisfied set to his mouth that made him look older. "I think he'll be down pretty soon. He doesn't mind if it's cold, he likes it that way."

"I see." Mary sat down in the empty chair next to him. She knew she had to say something, but she wasn't sure exactly what to say. She didn't know how to prepare a child for what was to come and she hadn't yet figured out all of the implications. She could only view it from his perspective, which was that his beloved grandfather was about to be taken from their house, never to be seen again. The random thought popped into her head that she could call a priest. It was too late for Last Rites, but it might help Patrick to see his priest right now.

"Patrick, do you go to church?"

Patrick nodded. "Every Saturday, we go to four o'clock Mass and then we go to Lee's Hoagies and eat Swiss cheese hoagies. He gets peppers and onions but I don't get that. We used to go to Mass on Sunday morning, but he likes to sleep in."

"Who's your priest?"

"Father Pep. Our church is St. Catherine's. I go to CCD every Wednesday at the school."

"Would you like me to call Father Pep and have him come over?"

"No." Patrick shook his head emphatically. "We don't know him. He shakes my hand when we leave, that's all."

"So you're not very involved with the church?"

Patrick shook his head. "I wrapped up the milk and the bologna sandwich and I put them back in the refrigerator. My Pops says it's a sin to waste food."

Mary ignored the *non sequitur* and braced herself. "Patrick, I want you to understand what's going to happen next. The police are coming and they're going to go upstairs—"

"I already talked to the police. I told them about Mr. Robertson. You were there." Patrick kept playing with his fingers, and Mary moved her hand lightly on top of his hand, so the drumming stopped.

"This will be different police, and they're here about your grandfather."

"They're not going to be able to wake him up. It's hard to wake him up when he's asleep. He knows how much he sleeps every day. He writes it down."

"He does?" Mary asked, surprised.

"Yep." Patrick shook his head again, and though his fingers had stopped drumming, his foot started wiggling. "He has an office and he has a big calendar on his desk and every day he writes down in the boxes how much money he spent, what he ate, and how much he slept."

"Really." Mary made a mental note. "Is his office where he keeps his papers? Like, his important papers?"

"Yes." Patrick wiggled his foot.

"Is his office the room upstairs next to his bedroom?"

Patrick nodded. "That's where he keeps everything and that's where he pays the bills. He told me that I could go in there but I'm not allowed to touch anything on the desk because I'll mess it up."

"I see." Mary guessed that was probably where Edward had kept his will. Hopefully there would be a lawyer she could contact about probate, as well as maybe tracking down any relatives who could take Patrick in. Edward was such a methodical man, and he must have made some provision for where Patrick could live.

"I wouldn't mess it up, I *never* would mess it up, but once I was drawing in there on the calendar, and he didn't like that, so I don't do that anymore." Patrick turned his head toward the window, and Mary heard the slamming of heavy car doors in front of the house and rose quickly.

"Patrick, you stay here. Let me answer the door."

"I have to tell them not to wake him up." Patrick jumped out of his chair, but Mary tried to stop him.

"Patrick, no, I can tell them—"

"*I* have to tell them!" Patrick scooted past her into the living room, and she hustled after him, taking his arm gently as she opened the front door. She tried to put him behind her, but he peeked out.

Two uniformed officers, the medical examiner, and several of his uniformed assistants filled the step, their official presence jarring even to her.

A collapsible metal gurney with a flat body bag took up the front walk, and double-parked in front of the house were two police cruisers and the somber black Econoline van of the medical examiner, bearing his official emblem. Neighbors were already coming out of their houses and looking from their windows, so Mary let the officers inside quickly.

"Officers, I'm Mary DiNunzio, and you can go straight upstairs and go right toward the end of the hall."

"Thanks, Ms. DiNunzio," one of the cops said, stepping forward. He seemed older than the others, and he took charge of the situation. "I'm Officer Agabe-Diaz, a friend of Officer Diamond's. He said to tell you that he's trying to make that call but he doesn't think he'll get through 'til tomorrow morning."

"Please thank him for me." Mary felt a wave of relief. So Officer Diamond had unofficially granted her request not to take Patrick into DHS custody until tomorrow morning.

"No problem." Officer Agabe-Diaz looked down at Patrick and ruffled up his head. "Hey buddy, you do me a favor? Go wait in the kitchen while we go upstairs?"

Patrick shook his head. "Don't wake up my Pops. I'm not allowed to wake up my Pops."

"Buddy, you go back to the kitchen now," Officer Agabe-Diaz repeated, gesturing Mary and Patrick out of the way, while behind him, the other uniformed officer, the medical examiner, and his assistants climbed the stairs, their heavy shoes pounding on the steps.

Mary put a firm hand on Patrick's shoulder. She didn't want him to see the gurney come into the house. "Patrick, let's go in the kitchen and wait there. Come on."

"No!" Patrick broke free and ran over to the couch, where he sat down. "I want to wait here. I want to tell him about his soup. His soup is ready."

"Patrick, please, no." Mary hurried around the coffee table to the couch. "Please, come with me."

"Patrick," Officer Agabe-Diaz said, his tone newly firm. "Do what Mary says. Go in the kitchen with her. She's going to stay with you in the kitchen."

Patrick permitted Mary to take him by the hand and lead him, but he stopped as soon as they got into the kitchen. He stood still, his hands at his side and his head cocked, listening to the mortuary assistants talking to each other in Spanish as they hoisted the gurney over the threshold on a three-count then carried it upstairs.

Mary put an arm around his narrow shoulders, holding him to her hip. "It's okay, honey. It's all right."

"He sleeps like a log."

"I understand. Everything is going to be all right, you'll see." Mary could hear the noises upstairs, the heavy tread and the wheels of the stainless-steel gurney rolling down the hall.

"Ms. DiNunzio?" Officer Agabe-Diaz lumbered toward the kitchen with a clipboard. "I will need some information and a signature."

"I gave the information over the phone, about how he was found."

"I know, just to confirm. Decedent's name is Edward O'Brien?"

"Yes."

"Middle name?"

"Uh, I don't know," Mary answered. "Can I find out and let you know later?"

"Fitzgerald," Patrick interjected, clinging to Mary's hip and looking up at Officer Agabe-Diaz. "My Pops's name is Edward Fitzgerald O'Brien and my name is Patrick Neil O'Brien. He's seventy-two years old and I'm ten years old. I'm in fifth grade."

"Wow." Officer Agabe-Diaz smiled down at him, making a note on the form on his clipboard. "Your grandfather is seventy-two? Do you know when his birthday is?"

Patrick nodded. "November 8. He can't kneel anymore. In church, he sits on the pew when you're supposed to kneel on the pad. He says Jesus doesn't mind."

"I'm getting pretty old myself." Officer Agabe-Diaz made another note, subtracting to get Edward's date of birth, then glanced at Mary. "Any next of kin we should notify?"

"Not that I know of," Mary answered quietly.

"Will you be following up?"

"Yes." Mary assumed that the question was about funeral arrangements but she wasn't about to clarify it in front of Patrick.

"Okay then, if you would sign here." Officer Agabe-Diaz showed her the form on the clipboard.

"Sure." Mary signed it quickly for Patrick's sake.

"Thank you." Officer Agabe-Diaz put the clipboard discreetly behind his back, bending down to Patrick. "So you're in the fifth grade, buddy?"

Patrick nodded, his head still cocked, listening to the noises upstairs, the Spanish muffled now. Edward's bedroom must have been overhead because the ceiling creaked.

"Do you like school?" Officer Agabe-Diaz asked, in a conversational tone.

Patrick shook his head, no. Mary cringed inwardly, realizing that all the school questions that came so easily to grown-ups were a minefield for Patrick. Still she was grateful because she could tell that Officer Agabe-Diaz was trying to distract Patrick from what they were doing upstairs.

"How about recess, buddy? I bet you like recess."

Patrick shook his head no, and Mary felt his arm tighten around her. She realized he was hugging her, which caught her in the throat. Upstairs she could hear the men's voices, then the gurney being rolled back down the second-floor hallway toward the stair. She knew that Patrick could hear it, too.

Officer Agabe-Diaz asked him, "What sports do you play?"

Patrick shook his head no.

Officer Agabe-Diaz blinked. "Do you like video games? I like Xbox. I play with my son, Dave. He's older than you are. We like Madden. Do you like Madden?"

Patrick shook his head no, again. Mary found herself listening to Officer Agabe-Diaz's questions from Patrick's perspective, dispatches from a strange and unusual world where sons and fathers shared video games, a world that was never his own.

"Patrick, I know, I bet you like *Goosebumps*. Do you like *Goosebumps* books? They're scary, right? Bloody hands playing the piano! Cool, right?"

Patrick shook his head, while upstairs, the men's Spanish grew louder and they descended the staircase heavily.

Officer Agabe-Diaz asked, "Patrick, what *do* you like to do? You like to watch TV?"

Patrick nodded yes, and Mary knew they were about to carry Edward out, so she patted Patrick's back, trying to soothe him.

Officer Agabe-Diaz smiled. "Patrick, what's your favorite show? Tell me about your favorite TV show. *Modern Family? The Big Bang?*"

"The History Channel." Patrick craned his neck, trying to peek past Officer Agabe-Diaz. "What are they doing? Did they wake up my Pops? I made the soup. I have to go tell him."

"No, you stay right here. They're taking very good care of your grandfather."

"Patrick, it's okay." Mary hugged him closer.

"No, no! He needs *me!*" Patrick let go of Mary, shoved past Officer Agabe-Diaz, and bolted out of the kitchen. Officer Agabe-Diaz went after him, and so did Mary.

"Patrick!" Mary called to him, but Officer Agabe-Diaz reached him first, then everything seemed to happen at once:

The mortuary assistants bumped the gurney against the doorjamb, jostling the black vinyl body bag. The uniformed officers rushed to help them as Patrick came running toward the stretcher, bursting into tears. Officer Agabe-Diaz scooped Patrick up just before he got there, then turned and handed him screaming and crying to Mary, who hugged him as tightly as she could, almost falling onto the couch with him, so he would have a soft place to land as Officer Agabe-Diaz hustled the other police officers, the mortuary assistants, and the gurney out of the house and slammed the door closed behind them.

"Pops, Pops, Pops!" Patrick screamed at the top of his lungs, blasting Mary's eardrums, but she held him tightly, trying to soothe him, telling him it would be okay and holding him on the couch, making him stay so that he didn't run back to the door and pull it open.

She couldn't hear anything outside over his screaming, but she could see headlights flash outside the window, so she knew the police cruisers were starting their engines and the mortuary assistants were loading the gurney inside the black van. Mary prayed that if she could just hold Patrick on the couch and hug him through the worst thing that had ever happened to him, then he would finally cry himself into a heartbroken sleep.

Which was exactly what happened.

CHAPTER TWENTY-TWO

Mary waited until Patrick had fallen asleep, extricated herself quietly, and stood up. Mary had a lot to do. Patrick had to be taken care of now that Edward was gone, and DHS would be here in the morning. She had to pack Patrick's things and find Edward's will.

She went upstairs, glancing down the hall at Edward's bedroom, which stood ajar. It was so hard to believe that he was gone, just like that, but Mary knew that was how death struck. She had lost her husband Mike, just like that. Death was such a coward, offering no warning. Striking by ambush. Just like that.

Mary went to Patrick's room and looked under the bed for a suitcase, but there wasn't one. She checked the closet but there wasn't one there, either. Edward had to have one, so she went back down the hallway to his room, noting that the room smelled even more unpleasant. She stripped the bed quickly, balled up the sheets, and went back down the hallway until she found the laundry room, tossed the sheets inside, and got them going.

She went back to Edward's room and looked under his bed, but there was no suitcase. She crossed to his closet, and at the bottom was an old tan suitcase with no rollers. She pulled it out and was leaving the room when she stopped at the photographs of Edward, Suzanne, and Patrick on the dresser. Mary packed them for Patrick and on the way out of the bedroom, stopped at the night table. She picked up Edward's wallet and slid out the credit cards and ATM cards, so they could be canceled, then flipped through, seeing the only thing that remained were wallet-sized school pictures of Patrick, a high-school graduation photo of Suzanne, and Edward's faded wedding photo. There were only a few dollars in the billfold so she left it. She picked up Edward's watch, phone, and rosary then cleaned up, tossing the Ambien and diabetes paraphernalia in the wastebasket.

Quickly she went to Patrick's room and packed his clothes from the dresser and closet, which took no time because he had so little. She even had room for his drawings and art supplies in the zipper flaps, and when she was finished, she set the suitcase by the bedroom door.

Mary took a last look around the room, checking to see that she hadn't missed anything, but she hadn't. Her gaze returned to the suitcase, and it struck her as somehow sad that everything that Patrick owned could fit into a single suitcase. She thought back to her own childhood and reflected that that never would have been possible.

Mary found herself sinking onto Patrick's bed, thinking back to her own childhood. The DiNunzios didn't have much money either, but Mary had so many things—books, records, stuffed animals, toys, scrapbooks, clothes, earrings, drugstore makeup. She had so many prized possessions—a stuffed bunny named Pinky, an "autograph dog" shaped like a dachshund, signed by all of her friends, and a brag book she had made with her friends, with all of their pictures inside.

She'd realized then that she had so much stuff because her life was so full, and she'd been given so much by her parents and by her friends. She owed everything she had become in life to that head start, which she'd been given by the sheer grace of God.

Mary looked again at the suitcase and realized that in her haste to perform all of the tasks necessary to take care of Patrick, she had lost sight of the little boy, himself. She had been avoiding thinking about placing him in foster care, but the suitcase made that reality visible. And when she projected forward and imagined herself handing Patrick a suitcase and telling him good-bye, she couldn't conceive of that happening. Somewhere along the line, Patrick had become much more than a case to her, and she couldn't deny that she cared about him.

Mary felt her eyes moisten, but blinked them clear. She looked at the suitcase without really seeing it anymore. She felt herself going inward and listening to her own heart. She was so close to changing Patrick's future and she had to make sure that her plans came to fruition. She couldn't do that if she were going to hand him off to foster care because she couldn't be sure that he'd get the support he'd need at a foster home.

Mary knew from her clients that parents of dyslexic kids had to put in hours and hours at home, drilling them, but deep inside, she knew it wasn't about dyslexia at all. She wanted to make sure that Patrick got the same head start that she'd had and she couldn't let him go to foster care. She couldn't turn a blind eye to what she read in the papers about the broken foster care system.

She couldn't imagine Patrick being shuttled from house to house, and she doubted that any of them could offer him what she could. The whole idea behind the foster system was to get children permanently adopted, and Mary knew she could fulfill that function far better, improving Patrick's prospects for permanent adoption. She knew she would never sleep at night, worrying that he wasn't getting the help, attention, and even love that he needed. Mary realized that she simply couldn't let Patrick go, not yet. She made a decision. She was going to step up for him and become his guardian.

Mary straightened up, confirming in her mind that her decision was sound. Even if it were temporary guardianship, only until Patrick could be permanently adopted, then she would feel better. If she had him for a year or two, she could get him through the rough patch of his new school as well as his grieving Edward. She could help him improve to reading at grade level and help him with his anxiety, ease the transition, all of which would make him a better candidate for permanent adoption.

The more Mary thought about it, the more she liked the idea. She had plenty of money and she could find the time. She was a partner now and she could arrange her own schedule. She could turn down referrals that came her way and she could work from home. She could make it work, if she had to. She took one last look at the suitcase and realized that she had to. She was going to try to become Patrick's temporary guardian.

But there was only one problem. Anthony. She was to be getting married in two weeks and she had to talk to him, to see if he agreed. She got her phone and called him, but the call rang a few times, then went to voicemail. She hung up and tried again, pressing REDIAL. She listened to the call ring and ring, then it went to voicemail, too.

Mary tried one last time and left a message: "Honey, I know it's late but it's important. I need to talk to you. Please call me as soon as you can. Love you." She hung up, then scrolled to the text function and texted him: **know it's late but need to talk. please call me ASAP xoxox**

She thought about calling Judy to talk it over, but decided against it. Mary knew what she wanted to do and she knew how she felt. Her decision was made. She was about to change her life, and Patrick's.

Mary was about to become a temporary guardian.

CHAPTER TWENTY-THREE

Mary still had to find Edward's will, so she went into his office, which was small, well-organized, and neat, containing only a white bookshelf filled with old accounting journals, a gray file cabinet, and a computer workstation that held an old IBM desktop with a thick monitor. A keyboard and a wired mouse rested on top of a large desk calendar, which she remembered Patrick telling her about.

Mary crossed to the desk, nudged the mouse over, and scanned Edward's shaky notations for yesterday, written in ink:

9.2 hours sleep (up early for lawyer)
sunny, 82
blood sugar 125
two egg whites, wheat toast, butter
blood sugar 115
sandwich in car
parking lot in Center City $25/2 hrs (RIP OFF!!)
tip $2
legal fee (will be invoiced)($300 per hour!)(No retainer!)
blood sugar 117
dinner—chicken soup, peas, Tater Tots
vanilla ice cream (Good!)

Mary realized she was looking at the last day of Edward's life, but she pressed the thought to the back of her mind. She wanted to find his will, and most people who had wills knew to leave them someplace easy to find. She went to the file cabinet, and the first drawer was labeled *Bills.*

She confirmed it by opening the drawer, and inside was a rack of Pendaflex file folders, one for each of Edward's bills, labeled in his shaky hand, starting with *AAA (American Automobile Association).* After the bills was a divider that read *Patrick,* so Mary thumbed through those folders to find Patrick's old report cards and artwork. She remembered that Patrick had said something about Edward saving his artwork, and this must have been what he meant. She didn't have time to look through it now, so she took it out of the drawer and set it aside to go through later.

She went to the second drawer, labeled *Documents*, and hit paydirt. The first folder was the deed to the house and the second was the will. She slid out a thick booklet with a cover that read: **Last Will and Testament of Edward F. O'Brien**. Underneath that was the attorney's name, **James R. Geltz, Esq.**, with an office address nearby.

Mary read Edward's will, which named Geltz as the executor, so she would have to notify him of Edward's death, as soon as possible. She read on to find that Edward hadn't named a godparent or guardian for Patrick, which was what she had expected since no one else was in the picture. Patrick was Edward's sole beneficiary, and Edward had bequeathed him the house, a life insurance policy for $50,000, a 2009 Ford Fiesta, Edward's bank accounts at PNC Bank, and investments in a brokerage account at Cornerstone Financial. The will didn't specify the balances in any of those accounts.

Mary turned to the appendices and found PNC Bank and Cornerstone statements from the time the will was executed, four years ago. Edward had $1,092 in checking, $9,927 in savings in the bank and $201,928 in stocks and bonds at Cornerstone Financial. There was another appendix that showed a market value of the house at $71,000. Mary ballparked the estate value at $330,000, including the life insurance policy, so Patrick had enough money for a college fund, which was excellent news.

Mary wondered if the investment portfolio had grown, so she set the will aside to take with her, and went to the second drawer, labeled *Financial*. The first few folders were old computer statements from Schwab, Waterstone, and E*TRADE. Behind them was the Cornerstone Financial folder, and Mary pulled it out and looked inside. The most recent statement showed that Dave Kather was the broker, and she skimmed to the balance, which was $225,928. So the inheritance had increased, and Mary assumed that if it stayed properly invested, it would do even better, but the decisions about finances would be Geltz's, as executor. God knew how much college tuition would be by the time Patrick was ready to enroll.

She checked the time on her phone, and it was not too late to call Geltz in a situation like this. She navigated online on her phone, checking him out before they spoke. Geltz's website popped onto the screen, with only one small picture of him. Geltz looked almost as old as Edward, a short, gray-haired lawyer with thick glasses and a professional smile, posed at his desk with his fingers linked in front of him.

Mary scrolled to the phone function, pressed in his cell-phone number, and the call was answered on the third ring. "Hello, is this James Geltz?"

"Why, yes," Geltz answered in a thin voice. "It's rather late. Who is this?"

"I'm sorry to be calling you at this hour. My name's Mary DiNunzio and I'm a special education lawyer who was hired by Edward O'Brien, a client of yours. I'm sorry to tell you that Edward has passed away."

"Oh my. How? Was he ill?"

"No, he passed away in his sleep last night. I'm at his house and I found his will, which you prepared."

"Ah, yes, I recall preparing Edward's will. That was about four years ago, now. I don't recall much else about it, I'm sorry to say."

"His grandson, Patrick, is his sole beneficiary."

"Oh, yes, I seem to recall that. How old is the grandson?"

"Ten."

"Oh my. Young. How is he?"

"He's very upset, he adored his grandfather." Mary hesitated. "I gather you didn't know Edward and Patrick that well."

"No, not well at all. Edward came in for his will, and we had one meeting to plan his estate with a stockbroker, as I recall. I forget his name."

"Dave Kather, Cornerstone Financial?"

"Yes, that sounds right. I drafted Edward's will and finalized it by email. Edward came in to sign it because it had to be witnessed and notarized, but I haven't seen him since then."

"I noticed that the will doesn't name a guardian for Patrick. I was wondering if there's a more recent version."

James *tsk-tsked*. "No, that's it, to the best of my knowledge. I must tell you, I advised him to name a guardian. He said he would but he never did. That's not uncommon in my practice. No man is eager to face his own mortality. We estate lawyers have to nag our clients, and I did, via email. I'm sure you will find my emails if you look."

Mary sensed he was covering his butt, but she let it go. "I'm going to become Patrick's temporary guardian. He doesn't have any other family, and I have him set up for a private school admission, at Fairmount Prep. It specializes in children with dyslexia, which Patrick has. I'm hoping to obtain tuition reimbursement for him, but I will need to have tuition money to get him admitted. Can you authorize that, as executor?"

"Yes. How much will you need?"

"Thirty grand, but it will get reimbursed by law. From the looks of it, the estate has the money. I reviewed his portfolio statements from Cornerstone Financial, and it looks as if Edward's estate is worth about $350,000."

"That's sounds correct, as far as I recall. The estate was sizable. I'll file the will, get it probated, and authorize a disbursement for the tuition. When do you think you will need it by?"

"Within two weeks."

"Oh my. Well. In that case, I may have to file for an emergency disbursement, though I don't think that should be a problem. Probation generally takes longer than two weeks." James paused. "May

I ask, would you tell me about yourself and why you are stepping forward for Patrick? You do realize that Patrick doesn't receive his inheritance immediately, since he is under the age of majority. As executor, I manage the fund and authorize necessary and appropriate disbursements for his health, education, and welfare."

Mary realized that he was doubting her motives, which made sense considering that he didn't know her. "James, I am not becoming Patrick's guardian for his money and I understand that he doesn't inherit instantly. I'm becoming his temporary guardian because I've come to really like him, I know the care he needs, and I have the means to take care of him and help him get permanently adopted. I'm a partner at Rosato & DiNunzio in Center City. Do you know the firm?"

"I've heard of Ms. Rosato, but not you. Sorry to offend."

"None taken." Mary got that a lot.

"So what you're telling me is that you have means of your own. As far as suitability, you'll have to go to court to petition for temporary guardianship. Are you prepared to do so?"

"Yes, I'm getting ready to do that. I'm hoping to be in court on an emergency basis."

"Well, good for you. Once you're named temporary guardian, I'll set the process in motion and apply to the court. I'm glad to hear that Patrick will be in good hands."

"Thank you. What do we do about the particulars, like the funeral and such? I know they went to St. Catherine's. Their priest was a Father Pep."

"I know the church. Edward's remains should be sent to Topperton Memorial Funeral Home near his house, and I'll call the church and arrange a funeral Mass, if you like, once the remains are released."

"That would be wonderful."

"I'll take care of the house and the effects. You don't have to worry about any of that."

"Thanks." Mary thought a minute. "Will you leave the money at Cornerstone? I'm thinking ahead to college funds."

"I'll leave it there if they've grown it. I understand college is so expensive these days."

"Is there anyone else I should be getting in touch with to notify them of Edward's death? It seems like there's no one else, except Dave Kather at Cornerstone."

"I don't know anyone else but Dave. I met him when we had our meeting to set up Edward's estate. Please tell him I'll be in touch about the disbursement for tuition, after you're approved as guardian and I file with the court."

"I will, thanks."

"Well then, I'll be going back to bed. I'll call you about the funeral arrangements."

"Bye now," Mary said, hanging up. She took a moment to look up Dave Kather online before she called him, plugging his name into her phone. His website popped onto the screen, and it was more current. Dave looked younger, tall and thin, with dark hair and wire-rimmed glasses. He had an affable smile, and he posed in a gray suit and tie with his arms folded. Mary pressed in the cell phone number, which was on the business card in the file.

Dave answered on the first ring. "Dave Kather."

"Hello." Mary braced herself to give him the bad news. "Dave, I'm Mary DiNunzio, a special education lawyer representing Patrick O'Brien, Edward O'Brien's grandson. I believe you know Edward."

"Oh, yes, of course. How can I help you?" A dog yapped in the background.

"I'm calling you with some very bad news. I'm sorry to have to tell you that Edward passed away last night."

"Oh no," Dave said, dismayed. "How terrible. What happened?"

"He passed away in his sleep. Patrick was home alone and found him. By the time I got here, he had passed. I'm so sorry."

"Oh no," Dave said again. "Poor Patrick. That must have been tough on the kid. How sad. I just saw Edward."

"When was that?"

"Last week for lunch. Monday. He was fine. Tired, but he always said he was tired. I told him to exercise more. I'm a walker. It's because of the dog, always wants to go out."

"He did tell me that you and he had become friendly, and I know this must be a blow."

"Yes, we were friends, business acquaintances probably more like it. Edward was a lone wolf. What's going to happen to Patrick? How is he?"

Mary explained that she was becoming his guardian, as she had before. "I really think I can do right by him."

"It's wonderful that you're going to take Patrick. He really loved Edward and this is going to be hard on him." Dave paused. "It was just the two of them. They were close."

"I'm hoping that Patrick will do better once he gets into a private school. They'll get him reading on grade level and build his self-esteem, too. I think that will help him make friends."

"That's a great idea. The city schools are in deep trouble."

"Yes, and I already spoke with James Geltz, who drafted Edward's will, and he's going to be asking you for a disbursement to cover tuition. It will get reimbursed when the school district settles with me, which I think they will."

"The district reimburses for tuition? How does that work?"

Mary explained the law. "But we'll need the money in the short run."

"How much?"

"Thirty grand."

"Does Edward have it in the bank? I'm not privy to his bank accounts and I hate to liquidate anything in this market."

"No, there's only ten thousand dollars in the bank."

"Too bad, the market is down now. Tell you what makes financial sense." Dave morphed into salesman mode. "I suggest we wait a week, so we're not selling in a down market. You follow?"

"Yes." Mary did, though she was no investment expert. "That sounds fine with me if it's fine with James, the executor. I don't care where the money comes from, I only care that I get enough to pay for tuition, and as I say, the estate will be reimbursed."

"Not a problem, I was able to grow his portfolio significantly." Dave's dog barked again in the background. "You know, Edward was an accountant and he kept an eye on his investments. He was always asking questions, but I like an informed client. It's a challenge, but I'd rather have an informed client than someone who doesn't pay attention."

"I agree." Mary actually felt the same way.

"Edward managed his own money for a long time, and he did very well. It took years for me to get his account, but I convinced him that we were able to stay on top of the market. When he saw his return increase, he agreed." Dave chuckled. "I do everything I can to justify the fee we charge, which is actually standard, 1 percent. Edward bargained it down to .25 percent, since he didn't have much activity."

"Somehow that sounds like him." Mary smiled.

"I might've put him in more bonds at his age, but Edward was risk-tolerant. He picked some stocks on his own, and some we picked together."

Mary checked her watch. She wanted to get the sheets out of the washer and into the dryer.

"Edward was saving for Patrick. He loved that kid, and Patrick is quiet, but well-behaved. He would sit there drawing while Edward and I were talking. Take it from me, rebalancing portfolios is not the kind of talk that most kids will put up with. My kids would have interrupted a million times. But not Patrick. We never heard a peep."

"I'm sure," Mary said, though it made her sad.

"Thank you for stepping up for him. That's a class thing to do. When is the funeral? My wife and I would like to go." The dog started barking again.

"James is making arrangements, and I'll stay in touch with you."

"Do that. Thank you. I better go, gotta take the dog out. Good night."

"Good night." Mary hung up, mentally ticking the item off her list. She picked up the Cornerstone Financial statements, the will, and the Patrick folders, then left Edward's office. She wanted to finish the laundry and do some research about guardianship before DHS got here. She checked her phone but Anthony still hadn't called or texted back. She prayed he called her soon.

Or she was going to become a mother without him.

CHAPTER TWENTY-FOUR

Mary had finished her tasks, grabbed some sleep, and was in the kitchen, making eggs. She was going to serve breakfast because Patrick should have something in his stomach, presumably something he could hold down. She didn't feel much better herself, dreading DHS's coming.

She cracked an egg into a Pyrex bowl and found a wastebasket under the counter for the shell. Anthony hadn't called her yesterday, which was odd. He'd be flying all day and probably wouldn't get home until eight o'clock or so. She'd have to talk to him about taking Patrick, another item on her Things to Dread list.

Sunlight filtered into the kitchen through a small window, and Mary cracked another egg into the bowl, hearing Patrick stirring in the living room, which was good. She didn't know what time DHS would get here, but she needed to talk to him before then to see how he felt about living with her. She went into the refrigerator, found milk, mixed it in, and poured the eggs into the pan.

"What are you making?" Patrick appeared in the doorway, his eyes puffy. In his hands were Edward's wallet and watch, which Mary had left on the coffee table.

"Hi, honey." Mary went over and gave him a hug, rubbing his back. "I'm making scrambled eggs. Do you want some?"

"Yes." Patrick looked up at her. "Is my Pops in heaven?"

Mary felt caught off guard. She'd been hoping they could ease into it, but evidently Patrick wasn't an ease-into-it kind of kid. Or maybe no kid was, she didn't know. She stroked his cheek. "Yes, honey, I'm sorry. He is."

"Do you think he found my mom? She's in heaven."

"I'm sure he did." Mary felt her throat constrict. "Here, why don't you sit down? Let me get you some water."

"I can get it, I know how."

"I know, but let me—"

"I can." Patrick set the wallet and watch on the counter, then grabbed his chair and pulled it over, climbed up and retrieved the glass from the cabinet. "How is he going to find her? There are so many people. How do you know he'll find her?"

Mary tried to think of an answer. "There are a lot of nice people up there, and if he can't find her, he'll ask around. And they'll help him because they're nice."

"I think he'll just *know*. I'm pretty sure that's how it works." Patrick held the glass under the water, then took a sip.

"That, too." Mary turned the heat up so the eggs would cook faster. "Patrick, please go sit down. There's something we need to talk about."

"He'll like being with her. He'll like that a lot." Patrick picked up the wallet and watch, holding them against his chest with his glass of water. He went back to the table, set them down, and sat down.

"I'm sure he will." Mary stirred the eggs. "I want to explain to you what's going to happen."

"I already know. I'm going to a new school. Pops already told me. He said it's a good school and the kids are nicer."

"How do you feel about that?" Mary looked over her shoulder, and Patrick had a worried frown, two deep lines prematurely creasing his forehead.

"I don't want to go to a new school."

"Why? Do you like your old school that much?"

"No, but I know where it is and I know the kids. I know it."

"I understand." Mary saw that the eggs were finished, so she turned off the gas and brought the pan over to the table. "But this is a great school and the kids are much nicer."

"I don't want to go."

Mary let it go for the time being. She put some eggs on Patrick's plate, then her own. "Yes, but I mean where you're going to live."

"I live here. This is my house." Patrick picked up his glass and took a sip of water.

Mary left the pan on the table and sat down. She wanted to be face-to-face for this conversation. "But honey, now you have to live somewhere else."

"Why?"

"Because the law says that kids can't live in houses by themselves. The people who make the law don't think kids can take care of themselves."

"I can take care of myself." Patrick dug into his eggs.

"Careful, they're hot."

"I know." Patrick scooped up a forkful of eggs and ate them up so quickly that she worried about his stomach issues.

"Patrick, try not to eat so fast."

"I like to eat fast. My Pops likes to eat fast too. We like to see how fast we can eat." Patrick ate another forkful.

"But that's not so great for your tummy."

"I'm not going to puke. Are you worried I'm going to puke?"

"Yes," Mary answered, busted.

"Ms. Krantz says, 'if you're gonna puke, run to the trash can.' But I only puke when I'm afraid."

Mary felt for him. "Okay, then I won't worry."

"I can make sandwiches and soup." Patrick kept eating. "I know about the microwave and I know how to work the remote. I know how to work the shower so it's not too hot and I know how to give my Pops his medicine when he gets the shakes. I'm not stupid, I can do everything."

"I know you're not stupid. I think you're very smart." Mary smiled at him. "But it's just the rules that you can't live in this house by yourself."

"Can you live here with me?"

Mary hadn't seen that coming. "No, because I have a house of my own. It's a very nice house."

"Can you live in my house and go to your house on the weekend? There's a girl in my class, her parents are divorced and she goes to her daddy's house on the weekend."

"I can't do that. My house is near my work and I need my house close to my work."

"Can I live with you in your house?" Patrick finished his eggs and put the fork down.

"Is that what you would like to do?" Mary held her breath. "Because I would like that."

"Do you have good air-conditioning like in your car?"

"Yes." Mary laughed.

"Can I bring my comics?"

"Yes, of course, you would have your own room, just like here. I already packed your things. I'd like you to stay with me, but only if you want to."

"I do want to. I like you." Patrick nodded, with a new smile.

"I like you too." Mary smiled back, touched.

"My Pops says you're nice and smart and not too bossy."

"That would be me." Mary chuckled.

"He says you care about me and you're helping me."

"I do care about you."

"I want to go to your house." Patrick smiled again.

"Okay, but here's is the thing. You can stay with me, but not until after the weekend." Mary hoped she could explain to him.

"Why not?"

"It's the law, again. A lady will be coming here soon, and she's going to talk to you about where you are going to live. I'm not sure I can convince her to let you come stay with me today."

"Why not?" Patrick's frown returned.

"Because that's not the law. I'm going to try to convince her, but if I can't, I'm going to go to her boss after the weekend. So you'll probably have to go where she says this weekend, do you understand?"

"Where?"

"I'm not sure, but I'm sure it's a good place."

"I don't want to do that."

"I know, but you might have to."

"Go to her house? With strangers?" Patrick's frown deepened, and his foot started to wiggle. "I'm not allowed to talk to strangers."

"This isn't that kind of stranger, this is a nice person you don't know." Mary realized how ridiculous she sounded as soon as she'd finished the sentence. "What I mean is, it's not really a stranger. It's a nice family who wants to have a little boy stay at their house and they're called a foster family."

"Do they have other kids?" Patrick eyes flared with worry. "Other kids in the family?"

"I don't know yet. She's going to come and visit us this morning and tell us, and she'll answer all of your questions."

Suddenly, the doorbell buzzed, and they both looked over. Mary checked her watch, which read 7:58, so DHS had come early. "Patrick, I'll get the door—" she said, getting up, but he was already in motion, scooting out of the kitchen.

"I got it!"

CHAPTER TWENTY-FIVE

After the introductions were made, Mary sat down next to Patrick on the couch, offering the chair to the DHS caseworker, Olivia Solo, a slim, petite woman who was much younger than Mary had expected, probably in her mid-twenties, with her long black hair slicked back into a supertight ponytail. She had a round, fleshy face and her large features looked even larger because her makeup was heavy. Her round brown eyes were thickly lined, her eyebrows were penciled over, and even her lips were outlined, covered with a purplish red lipstick. Mary caught Patrick staring at all the lines and colors in Olivia's face, as if he were drawing.

"So how are you, Patrick?" Olivia flashed him a pat smile as she set her oversized black leather handbag and black nylon messenger bag beside her chair. She crossed her legs in her tight jeans, which she had on with a lightweight white cotton sweater and heeled sandals. Around her neck was a gold chain, and her perfume was strong and floral.

Patrick didn't reply, wiggling his foot.

"I'm sorry about your loss," Olivia said, making quick eye contact with Patrick, then pulling a pad from her messenger bag and placing it on her thighs.

Patrick didn't reply, and Mary doubted he knew what she was talking about. Mary couldn't help but wonder how much experience with children a twenty-something could have. Olivia wasn't wearing a wedding ring, so Mary assumed she didn't have children of her own.

"Patrick, I know this is a very hard thing for you to go through. We're here to help you. I work for the city, and my job is with the Department of Human Services. That's a place that takes care of kids like you. You heard my name, it's Olivia, and I'm going to be the person who takes care of you—"

"I don't want to go to your house. I want to go to Mary's house."

Mary patted Patrick's leg. "She doesn't mean you'll live with her, she means—"

"Mary, I can explain it to him," Olivia said, politely. "Patrick, my job is to find the best place for you until we can find you a forever home, and I've found a wonderful family that would love to have you stay in their home for a few days, until we can find you another home."

Mary asked, "So this is just temporary?"

Olivia nodded. "Yes, we maintain a roster of foster parents who are willing to take children on an emergency basis for a few days to a week." She consulted the notepad on her lap. "We're going to place him with Jill and Peter Canides, and they have three other foster children, all boys, so he can have fun. They're a very active family."

Mary cringed inwardly, knowing how Patrick would feel. "Where do they live?"

"An apartment in Belle North."

"Belle North?" Mary shuddered. It was a rough neighborhood on the other side of the city.

Patrick shook his head, vigorously. "I don't want to go to strangers. I want to live with Mary."

Mary saw an opening. "Olivia, you heard him, and if you're only offering him a temporary placement, I can offer that as well. He and I discussed it, and he wants to stay with me. In fact, I'm going to—"

"Excuse me." Olivia held up her hand like a traffic cop, if a traffic cop had fake diamonds embedded in her fingernails. "Mary, you're the family's attorney, isn't that right?"

"Yes." Mary went into her purse, pulled out a business card, and handed it across the coffee table. "I'm representing Patrick in his special education case and we've made great progress, and there's other litigation down the road—"

"Are you a *guardian ad litem*?" Olivia glanced at the card, then put it down.

Mary couldn't say yes, since a *guardian ad litem* was a lawyer appointed to represent a child's interest in a court proceeding. "No."

Olivia lifted a penciled eyebrow. "You're not Patrick's legal guardian, are you?"

"No, he doesn't have one, and none was designated in his grandfather's will, but I intend to apply for temporary legal guardianship in Family Court. I'm going to schedule an emergency dependency hearing." Mary had done her research online last night to get the procedure right. "I'd like to request kinship care today, with you, so that I can take both legal and physical custody of him this weekend. I thought that might be agreeable to DHS, because I know DHS prefers to place a child in kinship care whenever possible, rather than into the foster system."

"But you're not a relative."

"No, he has no living relatives, and from what I read, kinship care extends beyond blood relatives, to individuals who are close to the child and are willing and able to step forward and take responsibility for him."

"Have you known Patrick a long time?"

"Not really, but we've grown close in a short time."

"How long have you known him?" Olivia's eyes narrowed, but Mary couldn't bring herself to answer, *two days*. It seemed like longer, but she doubted that counted.

"We met only recently, but I know a lot about him and I've met with his special education teacher, and I am completely familiar with him, his school record, and his personal history."

"Kinship care is for blood relatives or those who have a *significant* relationship to the child."

"I have a significant relationship to the child."

Olivia turned to Patrick. "Patrick, how long have you known Mary?"

Mary interjected, "It's not about length of time. It's about the quality of the time."

Patrick shrugged. "I want to live with Mary. She has a nice house and a nice car and she has *great* air-conditioning. The best ever!"

Olivia smiled at Patrick. "That sounds pretty great to me! Is that why you want to go live with Mary?"

"Yes!" Patrick nodded emphatically.

Mary's heart sank. "Patrick, that's not the only reason, is it?"

"Mary, please." Olivia frowned, rising from her chair. "Patrick, excuse us, the adults have to talk in the other room. You stay here and watch TV. What do you like to watch on TV?"

"Not *Modern Family* and not *Big Bang*." Patrick picked up the remote and turned on the TV. The History Channel came on with black-and-white footage of a loud tank battle from World War II. Patrick raised the remote. "See? I know how to work it. I can work the shower too. I want to go to Mary's house. I want—"

"Patrick," Olivia interrupted, frowning, "the house I have for you is wonderful and—"

"I don't want to go to them, I don't know them." Patrick's eyes widened with anxiety. "I want to go to Mary!"

"Patrick, that's enough. Stay here. Mary and I are going to talk about this." Olivia flared her eyes at Mary.

"Olivia, okay, let's go into the kitchen." Mary led her into the kitchen, and Olivia followed on her heels and ended up standing uncomfortably close to her in front of the kitchen sink.

"Mary, you're not taking him just because you're a lawyer with a nice house and a fancy car."

"That's not the reason, and we get along very well. We like each other. He told me that."

"You mean you coached him to say that." Olivia frowned, her penciled eyebrows coming close together, and Mary could see they had gotten off on the wrong foot.

"That's not true. He offered it."

"You should know better as an attorney. Patrick doesn't determine what's in his best interest. DHS does. If we let every ten-year-old decide where he wanted to live, they'd be following home whoever buys them cotton candy."

"That's not what's happening here." Mary softened her tone, to make peace. "What's happening here is that this is a little boy who has an anxiety disorder that requires being sensitive to the disruption and changes in his life."

"My file didn't say anything about an anxiety disorder. Has he been diagnosed with that? Do you have that report?"

"He hasn't been diagnosed with that as yet, and I can offer him more than any foster home you place him in this weekend, which will only require moving again when I get guardianship."

Olivia folded her arms. "This isn't our procedure at all. We have him in our legal custody and we take that commitment very seriously. To enter our kinship care program, you have to qualify, the same as any other foster parent, even a blood relative."

"Obviously, I do qualify."

"We don't just take your say-so, and again, you should know that as an attorney. You can't ignore our procedures. To qualify for kinship care, you have to make a proper application and undergo orientation and training. It takes three or four months before you're certified. We have to conduct an in-home interview, covering why you want to be a foster parent, your family background, your employment, income, medical history and the like—"

Mary knew all this, though she didn't interrupt Olivia. It was covered in the DHS Handbook on Foster Care she had read online last night.

"—and you need to undergo a medical exam yourself, a check for a criminal history, and child abuse clearances. You have to attend an orientation session and complete two full days of training sessions. Just because it's kinship care doesn't mean it's a lesser standard."

"You're offering him a foster family with three other kids, in a lousy neighborhood. Can't you see that I can do better than that right now, at a critical time for him? Can't common sense prevail?"

Olivia bristled. "I *am* using common sense. We provide a safe, stable, and nurturing family experience when a child is in crisis. We can't be certain you provide that to him until you qualify."

"Be real, Olivia. He just lost his grandfather, whom he adored, and you don't know this, but he was assaulted a few weeks ago at school. He's still suffering the effects of that, he's confused and scared, and he's changing schools at the same time. Plus in the next few weeks, criminal charges will be brought against the man who assaulted him and—"

"I don't need to be lectured to." Olivia scowled. "This is what happens every time a lawyer gets involved. You're all alike. You throw your weight around and expect everybody to jump to your tune. You don't respect any rules at all."

Mary masked her anger. "No, Olivia, what I expect is for you to use your brain and your heart to understand what that little boy is going through, and try to make his life easier, not harder."

"It's not about the easy answer, it's about the *correct* answer. Any kinship home must be in full compliance with DHS foster requirements."

"Let me just keep him until I go to court and make it all legal. It's the least disruptive for him."

"Sorry, that's not our procedures and that's not going to happen." Olivia stiffened. "If you need me to call the police, I'll do that."

"No, don't." Mary felt resigned. She had expected to lose today because she knew the law wasn't on her side, even though she was in the right. Justice didn't always matter as much as the law, which was ironic.

Suddenly, Patrick yelled from the living room, "I don't want to go to strangers! I don't want to go to strangers! I'm not going! I'm not going!"

Olivia glowered at Mary. "This is *your* fault. You encouraged him to resist our placement."

"No I didn't, I swear. He's telling you what he honestly wants."

"He doesn't get to call the tune, and neither do you."

Mary took one last shot. "You're ignoring him in favor of your procedures. You're placing form over substance."

"This conversation is *over*. We're going back in that living room and when we do, you'd better get on board. You'd better tell him that coming with me is the only choice."

"Then it's not a choice."

Olivia ignored the statement. "If you don't get with the program, I'm going to make you leave the premises. Don't think I don't have the authority to do that."

"I'M NOT GOING!" Patrick hollered at the top of his lungs, his tone turning angrier. In the background, the TV blared the tank battle.

Olivia gritted her teeth. "Mary, you'd *better* tell him to come with me."

"Fine, I will." Mary resigned herself to the fact that she had lost the battle, but she knew she'd win the war. She followed Olivia out of the kitchen but when they reached the living room, they both froze, shocked.

Patrick was standing in front of the coffee table, tears filling his eyes.

And in his hand was a gun, aimed at them.

CHAPTER TWENTY-SIX

"I want to go with Mary!" Patrick hollered, over the blaring TV. A tear rolled down his cheek. His skinny body trembled, and the gun barrel wavered as he held it in a double-grip, arms outstretched.

"Patrick, please put the gun down," Mary said quietly. She had to defuse the situation. She didn't think he would shoot. She didn't think he had it in him. She had no idea where he'd gotten the gun. She didn't know if it was loaded. It looked old and clunky, and she wondered if it was Edward's from the war.

"No, please!" Olivia screamed, putting her hands up. "Please, don't shoot! Oh my God!"

"I want to go with Mary!" Patrick's eyes spilled over, but he held on to the gun. "I'm not going to strangers! *I don't play ball!*"

"I know, honey." Mary took a careful step toward him. "I understand. Please put the gun down."

"Patrick, listen to her!" Olivia shrieked. Hands still up, she edged backwards toward the kitchen. "Put it down! Put it down this instant!"

Mary took another step toward him. "Honey, look on the coffee table. There's your Pops's wallet and watch. Pick them up, and put the gun down. You don't want to forget about the wallet and watch, do you?"

"I'm not going to strangers!" Patrick swung the gun in Olivia's direction. "I'M NOT GOING WITH YOU!"

"Help!" Olivia shrieked, then bolted into the kitchen.

"Honey, put the gun down."

"I want *you*." Patrick lowered the gun, then put it on the table, bursting into tears as he gathered up the wallet and watch. "I want my Pops . . ."

"I know, sweetheart." Mary rushed forward and gave him a big hug as he collapsed into her arms, trying to speak while sobs wracked his small frame.

"I want my Pops back . . . I want my Pops back . . . I want to go with you . . . I want to go with you . . ."

"I understand, honey." Mary scooped him up and sat with him on the couch, pulling him onto her lap, and Patrick cuddled up, burying his tear-stained face into her neck and clutching Edward's wallet and watch to his chest.

"I'm sorry, I'm sorry . . . my Pops told me not to touch his gun . . . I don't want him to be mad . . . I wasn't going to shoot it . . . I don't know how . . ."

"It's okay, sweetie. I know you wouldn't have shot anybody." Mary heard Olivia talking in the kitchen, but between the hoarse, choking sound of Patrick's sobs and the *rat-a-tat* of the tank battle on the TV, Mary couldn't make out what Olivia was saying.

"Don't let her take me . . . Don't let her take me . . ."

Mary rubbed his back, trying to soothe him. "Patrick, you have to go with her today, but it's just for the weekend, and after the weekend—"

"A *weekend* . . ."

"I have to go to court for you, and I can't do that until Monday." Mary heard Olivia talking in the kitchen, and when the TV tank battle stopped and a History Channel commentator came on, she heard what Olivia was saying:

"—637 Moretone Street, please, hurry, he has a gun. Yes, a gun! Don't hang up, stay with me—"

Olivia was calling 911. Mary thought it was the worst possible thing for Patrick, who started crying harder, so she couldn't get up and go in the kitchen to stop Olivia. "Olivia! Olivia! You don't need to do that, we're fine now!"

". . . I don't want to go with her . . . I want to go with you . . ."

Mary shouted again, "Olivia, call them off! We don't need any help! It's fine now! Come in and you'll see!"

"Noooo!" Patrick wailed, sobbing anew. "I don't want Olivia . . . I don't want Olivia . . . I don't want her . . ."

"Dispatch, don't hang up!" Olivia came barging into the room, still on the phone. She bolted for the coffee table, picked up the gun, and shoved it into her messenger bag, which she hoisted to her shoulder. "I have the gun! I have it, thank God! Yes, please hurry, please hurry!"

Mary felt Patrick cling tighter to her. "Olivia, call them off, please! Look, it's all over. It's fine. I have him."

". . . I don't want to go . . . I don't want . . . I don't want to go . . ."

"Mary, are you *kidding me right now*?" Olivia covered the phone with her hand, her lined eyes flaring with anger. "He had a gun! He tried to *kill* me! You saw it!"

". . . I don't want to go . . . I don't want to go . . . I don't want to . . ."

"Olivia, we don't need 911. They're just going to upset him more—"

"He shoulda thought of that when he tried to kill me!" Olivia grabbed her purse, and in the next moment, there was the sound of approaching police sirens. "The cops will be here any minute! They come fast when there's a gun!"

"We don't need the cops—"

"You're as crazy as he is!" Olivia headed for the door.

"He wasn't going to shoot!"

"The hell he wasn't!" Olivia flew out of the door and slammed it behind her.

Patrick sobbed. "I just want to go with you . . . I just want to go with you."

Mary had to prepare him. "Honey, you need to calm down. The

police are going to come, and you should be calm. They're going to take you for the weekend—"

"I don't want to go, I don't want to go!" Patrick cried, becoming hysterical. "I want my Pops . . . I want my Pops . . ."

Mary heard car doors slamming outside in the street, a commotion out front, then boots running up the sidewalk. She cuddled Patrick, shielding him with her body as a group of uniformed officers burst through the door, drawing their weapons.

"Officers, don't shoot, it's fine!" Mary called out, as Patrick cried loudly. "Everything's fine! There's no gun! There's no danger!"

"We have to take the child," one of the cops said, hurrying toward her as the others holstered their guns.

"Officer, there's no reason to do it by force. Let me calm him down, he just got upset—"

"Miss, the child has to come with me right now. He's in DHS custody." The police officer reached out his arms to take Patrick, but Mary stood up.

"No, wait, I have him, I can just carry him outside myself." Mary rose with the crying Patrick. "His luggage is upstairs, you could go get his luggage—"

"Miss, we have our orders. Give me the child."

"Just let me get him out, and I can calm him down, it doesn't have to be this way—"

"Miss, please." The officer wrenched Patrick from Mary's arms, and he started kicking and screaming.

"Mary! Mary! MARY!"

"Patrick, it's okay!" Mary called back to him, her heart responding to his cries, her arms suddenly empty. The police officer rushed to the door and hustled from the house with Patrick, followed by the other police officers.

Mary rushed to the door, but stopped there, stricken. It took every fiber of her being not to run after Patrick, but that would make it worse for him. She watched the awful scene from the doorway; the police loading Patrick kicking and screaming into one of the police cruisers, and Olivia was giving the gun to another uniformed police officer. The officers hustled around the front of the cruiser bearing Patrick, and Olivia left in a separate cruiser.

Mary stayed at the door until the police cruisers disappeared down the street, then realized that she heard her cell phone was ringing. It had to be Anthony. She looked wildly around, trying to remember where she had left her phone, but it was nowhere in sight. She raced into the kitchen, found it on the table, and grabbed it just as it stopped ringing.

"Anthony?" she said, breathless, but it was too late. The home screen showed a message from him, and she played the message: "Babe, sorry I missed you, I was out with my colleagues and I left my phone in the bar. I'm on the plane and I have to turn off my phone, but I'll see you tonight."

"Damn!" Mary didn't know why he hadn't called her before he boarded. It drove her crazy that she couldn't talk to him, but she couldn't let it stop her. She had set a course in motion and she had to follow through. She had to get into the office, do more legal research, and prepare and file her emergency petition, so she could get a hearing.

She hurried from the kitchen, making one more phone call on the fly. Every woman had a best friend she could call to sort out her thoughts, and better yet, to hear that she wasn't crazy.

For Mary, that person was Judy.

CHAPTER TWENTY-SEVEN

"You're crazy!" Judy said, throwing up her hands. She was sitting opposite Mary's desk in a white T-shirt and gym shorts, her standard outfit for working on the weekends.

"You don't really think that." Mary chewed the toasted bagel she'd grabbed on the way in. Sun spilled from the window behind her, filling her office with warm sunlight.

"But you're talking about a kid. You're effectively becoming a mother."

"A *foster* mother. It's temporary."

"How so? What's the plan?"

"Here's what I'm thinking. Patrick just went through hell, between the assault at school and Edward's passing. He has to deal with his grieving, while he's changing schools. I need to get him into Fairmount Prep and that's all set to go."

"It's hard to change schools. I know, I had ten different schools growing up."

"Right." Mary remembered that Judy's father had been in the military. "Not only that, but he's at the center of litigation. The criminal prosecution for his assault is about to start, and the Complaint that Machiavelli's bringing will go forward."

"You think Machiavelli will still sue, even though Edward died?"

"Of course. When he finds out that Edward died, he'll amend the Complaint to replace Edward with Edward's estate. Look, he sent me sixty pages of interrogatories for Edward and Patrick and he scheduled depositions for both of them." Mary picked up a massive stack of documents that had been on her desk when she'd come in this morning, hand-delivered by Machiavelli yesterday.

"Oh man." Judy picked up the top set of papers, flipping through them. "He's going to depose a ten-year-old?"

"Patrick is the soft spot, which makes him the target."

"Why is he doing this?" Judy tossed the papers back on the desk, in disgust.

"He's trying to pressure me into settling, using Patrick as leverage. He'll do whatever he can to hurt Patrick so I'll write a check to make it stop."

"Maybe he *is* related to Machiavelli."

"Now you see." Mary tried to set her emotions aside, hate-eating her bagel. "So I'm thinking that if Patrick came to live with me temporarily, I can help him through."

"How long is temporary?"

"Six months to a year. By then he'll be through the worst of his grief, he'll be set up at Fairmount Prep, have been in therapy, and his reading skills will have improved."

"But how do you have the time? You're too busy to even take a honeymoon."

"I'm going to have to change things around." Mary had been mentally rearranging her schedule. "I'm a partner now. I don't have to take cases from Bennie anymore, and I'll just say no to new cases and referrals. If we have to, we'll hire a contract lawyer or a paralegal."

"So you'll cut back on your hours?"

"Yes, and I'll work from home when I can. I'm sure I can hire somebody to get him after school and babysit him at the house. I have the money, he'll get the best of care. It's only temporary."

"But will you really be able to let him go, in the end?" Judy's Delft-blue eyes narrowed with skepticism.

"It won't be easy, but I will." Mary felt her chest tighten but pressed that away. "Right now, I need to get him. I can't let him stay in the foster system. Do you know what that's like?"

"What about his psychological issues?" Judy frowned in concern. "He pulled a gun on you."

"He wasn't going to shoot and he felt backed into a corner. He'd lost his grandfather the night before. Can you imagine, being forced to move the very next day, at that age?" Mary felt her gut twist and wondered if wolfing down a bagel and coffee was a good idea.

"Where'd he get the gun?"

"Edward must've had it somewhere."

Judy pursed her lips. "But what about the drawings, the bloody drawings?"

"I explained that to you. It's the same thing, the war stories that his grandfather told him about. His grandfather was his world, and the house was the only place he felt safe. That's why he pulled the gun."

Judy pursed her lips. "You're making excuses for him, Mare."

"No, not at all. I just understand him. I get him." Mary gulped some coffee, which was hot and perfect. "I'm not being naïve, I know he has issues, but they're not issues that can't be dealt with, and I have the resources. I have money, I have time, I have everything. And he has nothing."

"It sounds like you feel guilty about that."

"Of course I do. Have we met?" Mary smiled, but Judy didn't.

"But that's not a reason to take him. You can't feel responsible for the world. You're *not* responsible for the world."

"That's not the reason I'd be taking him. This isn't about me, it's about him, and I just think it's the right thing to do. In foster care, he's going to get shuffled from house to house, and he's not the kind of kid who can handle that." Mary felt herself getting emotional, but kept it in control. "I can't turn my back on him. I can't pretend not to know what I already know. He's an orphan."

"Edward didn't appoint a guardian for him in the will?"

"No. I think he just avoided the issue, but he took care of the financial end, just like you'd expect from an accountant. And believe it or not, Patrick inherits about $350,000."

"That's great." Judy perked up. "I wish *I* had that much."

"The estates lawyer is going to get the will probated, and I have to be named Patrick's legal guardian before I can use any funds for his expenses. I need to get into court. The law favors kinship care, which is what they call it when a family member or someone else steps up to be guardian." Mary thought it over. "You don't really think this is crazy, do you?"

"No, I get it," Judy answered, with a sad smile. "But it's such a major change in your life and it happened on a dime."

"Just like that." Mary had thought of that phrase before, when it came to death. But maybe it applied to life, as well. "You really don't know where life leads you. You just have to respond."

"Like falling in love."

"It kind of is." Mary felt a peace inside.

"Is he cute? I don't want a temporary nephew who's ugly."

Mary felt her heart lift. "My God, I didn't even think about that! You would be his aunt. Temporary Aunt Judy!"

"Yay!" Judy's eyes lit up. "We have a baby but we don't have to *have* a baby. I could teach him to draw!"

"There you go!" Mary smiled.

"But you haven't talked to Anthony yet." Judy made a funny face. "Ruh-roh. What's hubby going to say?"

"I don't think he'll love the idea initially, but I think he'll understand why it's the right thing to do. And once he meets Patrick, he'll be totally on board."

"Your parents will be over the moon." Judy grinned.

"Agree. They don't care where they get a grandkid, just so they get one." Mary switched mental gears. "So, do you know anything about guardianship law?"

"That's a trust-and-estates issue." A slow smile spread across Judy's face. "That was John's expertise before he came here."

"Our John? John Foxman?" Mary thought of her outburst the other day in the conference room.

"He's in. I noticed his door's closed down the hall."

"I guess I have to apologize to him." Mary rose, taking a last bite of her bagel.

"Say you're sorry like you mean it when you do, *Mom*."

"Thanks." Mary picked up her coffee, left her office, and went down the hall to John's, where she knocked on the door.

"Come in," he called from inside, and Mary opened the door, not surprised to see him in a white Lacoste shirt and khaki pants. Neat stacks of documents sat on his desk, and on his bookshelves were Bisel's Pennsylvania Orphans' Court Lawsource, *Trusts and Estates Magazine*, and *The Philadelphia Estate Practitioner Handbook*. Accordion files sat in alphabetical order atop his file cabinet, and his diplomas and certificates of admission hung on the walls. There was nothing personal about the office except for a signed photo of some tennis player.

"John, hi." Mary managed a smile.

"Oh, hi." John straightened at his laptop, blinking behind his glasses.

"Listen, I'm sorry that I snapped the other day."

"Not a problem." John smiled stiffly.

"Hey, do you know anything about guardianship law? The little boy in that special education case needs a guardian, and I want to be it."

"I can tell you exactly what to do. I know everything about guardianship in Pennsylvania."

"How is that? I thought you were a litigator before."

"I'm my brother's guardian. He has cerebral palsy."

"Oh, I didn't know." Mary's mouth went dry.

"No one does, here. So you see, I would *never* make fun of the disabled. I know better."

Mary felt like a total jerk. Obviously, there was more to John than she'd thought.

"So." John gestured to a chair opposite his desk. "Come in and tell me about your case."

CHAPTER TWENTY-EIGHT

"Mary, let me clarify where you stand now," John said, after she brought him up to speed. "You currently have three lawsuits pertaining to Patrick. Primary at this point is the dependency proceeding, during which you hope to be appointed his guardian. Second is the special education matter, under which you are hoping to transfer him into Fairmount Prep. Third is the Common Pleas Court matter, and you are defending the allegations of assault against the teacher's aide."

"Exactly." Mary realized the litigation had gotten suddenly very complicated.

"So do you have any questions for me?"

"Yes, what happens at a dependency hearing? Is the procedure different from a matter in Common Pleas Court or in federal court? It's a judge, not a master, right?"

"First, call it a 'shelter care hearing.' That's the term they use in Family Court." John folded his hands on his desk. "A shelter care hearing is held in front of a judge or a master, and the procedures are different than other courts. The rules that govern shelter care hearings and any subsequent hearings are the Pennsylvania Rules of Juvenile Court Procedure."

"Good to know." Mary assumed she could find the rules online. "So we go to the shelter care hearing, and basically, my job is to prove that I would be a good guardian for Patrick, is that right?"

"Roughly put, yes." John frowned. "But you don't represent your-self in the shelter care hearing. You understand that, don't you?"

"No." Mary blinked.

"A shelter care hearing is more like a trial than an oral argument. You have to present evidence."

"So testimony is taken through witnesses?"

John nodded. "You have to prove you're a good guardian. That won't be difficult because you easily qualify, but you're going to have to take the witness stand. You're going to be subject to direct examination by the City Solicitor and the Child Advocate."

"So I can't represent myself." Mary realized this was more com-plicated than she had thought. "So what do I do?"

"You need a lawyer."

Mary wondered when law got so complicated that even the lawyers needed lawyers. "Where am I going to get a lawyer, this quick? I wanted to go to court on Monday."

"I'll represent you," John answered without hesitation.

"Really?" Mary's face burned. "You don't have to do that."

"I want to. I'm happy to do it. Really." John smiled, genuinely. "I meant it at the staff meeting, I do want to work with you."

"Do you have the time?"

"I'll make the time. Family law is like that. Everything's an emer-gency, and you have to drop everything. Have you ever been to Family Court before?"

"Never."

"There's a new courthouse on Arch Street, and it was designed to combine all of the matters that encompass family law—divorce, cus-tody, protection from abuse, juvenile law, termination of parental rights, adoption, and dependency cases. When we go over there, you'll see what I mean. It's a courthouse unlike any other." John paused, his smile fading. "Family law makes and breaks families. It's the most important—and emotional—law there is. It has that in common with special education law, as you correctly pointed out."

"I'm sorry," Mary said again, but John dismissed her with a wave.

"I mention it only to say that family law is subject to all of the vagaries that make us human. My motto is, expect the unexpected."

"That worries me."

"It shouldn't." John smiled. "We can handle anything."

"What will be our argument for me to become his guardian? Just that I'm an upstanding citizen, no criminal record, care about him, stuff like that?"

"Again, roughly, that's true. Our main argument is that under Pennsylvania law, the judge must place the child consistent with the child's best interests in the *least restrictive setting.* It's been interpreted in case after case that kinship care is much less restrictive than foster care. In other words, you trump foster care."

"Thank God."

"It's true that you would nevertheless have to qualify and become a fully licensed foster parent within sixty days, but you won't have a problem with that. There's an adjudication hearing ten days after the shelter care hearing, but if we win at the shelter care hearing, you're home free."

"Do you think we'll win at the shelter care hearing?"

"Yes. The only argument they can make involves Patrick's pulling the gun."

"What's their argument, if I'm not worried about it? If I'm willing to assume the risk, why do they care?"

"This isn't tort law, so an assumption-of-risk analysis doesn't come into play. The City Solicitor will represent DHS and she'll argue that DHS should retain custody because of danger to you and others, but also exposes the City to liability. I think we can meet those arguments to the judge's satisfaction."

"How? My testimony?"

"That's not all." John turned to his laptop, hit a few keys, and started reading his screen, his sharp blue eyes darting back and forth as he read. "We're going to stack the deck."

"I don't know what you mean, but I like the sound of it." Mary leaned forward, intrigued.

"I over-prepare for every shelter care hearing. It's just my way. Some lawyers would walk into court with just one witness. You. That's not how I work. You may be the most important part of our case, but you're not the only part of our case." John spoke as he hit another key. "Take a look at this."

Mary rose, came around the side of the desk, and looked over his shoulder to see a list of attorneys' names on his laptop screen.

"Most of the shelter care cases are heard by Judge Green, and he's very good. He has a list of Child Advocates whom he appoints to advise him, and the Child Advocates are appointed in a rotating order."

"What's a 'Child Advocate?' "

"Excellent question." John looked up. " 'Child Advocate' is the term of art for lawyers trained to represent children in custody, termination, dependency, and adoption cases. The job of the Child Advocate is to speak for the child because the child doesn't generally come to court, not a ten-year-old. In other words, a Child Advocate will say what the child wants."

"Isn't that what a *guardian ad litem* does?" Mary knew the term from law school.

"No. A *guardian ad litem,* a GAL, is similar to a Child Advocate in that both are lawyers trained to represent children in these cases. But a GAL doesn't represent what the child *wants.* A GAL represents what the child *needs* and what is in the child's best legal interests." John looked up at her. "Take the case where the Child Advocate will testify that the child wants to reunite with his parents, after parental rights have been terminated. The GAL may testify that the parents have failed subsequent drug testing and the child should therefore not be reunited. Understand the difference?"

"Yes. So how does that apply to this case?"

"This is a list of the Child Advocates who are on rotation for Judge Green." John waved at his laptop screen. "A lot of lawyers would wait for Judge Green to appoint one and that would mean a second shelter care hearing. But that's not how I do it. I want *one* effective shelter care hearing that goes my way, not a series of hearings that may or may not result in the adjudication I want."

"I agree." Mary was loving how methodical and precise he

sounded, albeit still aggressive. "So bottom line, you're getting Patrick a lawyer?"

"Exactly. Look." John pointed to the first name on the list. "This is Abby Ortega, and she's up next in the rotation. I know her well. She's smart and she cares. I'm going to call her, give her the heads-up, and ask her to go see Patrick this weekend at his foster family's, interview him, and get to know him."

"She can do that?" Mary felt reassured to know that somebody would be checking on Patrick because she had been worrying about him.

"Family law is twenty-four/seven, Mary. Even the courthouse is open on Sundays."

"Really." Mary had never heard of a courthouse open on Sunday.

"Protection from abuse orders and child abuse cases are heard around the clock. There are custody orders that provide only supervised visits, and those are held in the courthouse on Sunday. If you're on the fifth floor of the courthouse on a Sunday, you might think you're at nursery school."

"That's sad."

"I know. To return to point, I'm going to call Abby and have her go see Patrick. Let's hope she agrees with us. That will shore up our case because it buttresses your testimony. It won't be only your word that Patrick wants to live with you."

"Terrific." Mary thought a minute. "What about a *guardian ad litem?* Are we going to call one of those, too?"

"No." John shook his head. "I don't think we'll need one. If Abby goes our way, a GAL will be cumulative. But I do want another witness. An expert." John returned to his laptop, opening files. "Patrick is having psychological issues, and I think we need an independent psychiatrist to meet with him."

"I have a list that I use as experts in special ed matters. Should I call one of them?"

"No, it's better if we use an expert known to Green and who testifies in Family Court all the time." John stopped hitting buttons. "This is a list of my go-to psychiatric experts. I can arrange one of them to visit Patrick this weekend, too. They won't be able to do a full evaluation, but they can give an expert opinion." John looked up, with a wink. "They'll help us win, if they agree with us."

"That's so great, John!" Mary threw her arms around him and gave him a big hug.

"Oh, you're a hugger." John chuckled, righting his glasses, which had gone awry. "Why am I not surprised."

"I really mean it, thank you so much!" Mary felt her throat thicken. "It's not that you're helping me, it's that you're helping Patrick."

"I get it. Go sit down." John returned to his computer. "We'll have to work this weekend. I want you to get started on the paperwork while I make the phone calls. Please, turn around, open that first accordion on the credenza, and grab the book in front."

"On it!" Mary grabbed the accordion and pulled out the contents, which turned out to be a Xeroxed *Bench Manual in Dependency Proceedings,* and she followed John's directions, reading the rules and making notes so they could prepare the papers they needed to file. John started making the phone calls, and the two lawyers worked together all day, drafting the papers and getting them ready for filing.

The sky began to change outside John's office window, and at the end of the day, Mary checked her watch—7:15, so it was time to go home. She and John walked out together, then they parted ways. She hurried to the garage to get her car, feeling her anxiety catch up with her. She was going to become a guardian of a child that Anthony didn't even know existed. She knew he would come around in time, but it would be a shock.

Mary got her car and steered home through the city, gripping the wheel tight.

CHAPTER TWENTY-NINE

Mary unlocked the front door to Anthony's roller bag and back-pack in the entrance hall. The mail had been stacked neatly on the console table, and she could hear him humming in the kitchen. She set her purse and messenger bag down on the floor, wishing she had time to shower and change before she saw him. Her contacts were probably fusing to her corneas, but blindness was a small price to pay to look good when she asked him to take in a child he'd never met.

"Hey honey!" Mary finger-combed her hair as she passed the dining room table, surprised to see that it had been set for a romantic dinner, including candles and a fragrant bouquet of red roses.

"Babe!" Anthony came out of the kitchen grinning, his long arms outstretched, and Mary felt her heart lift at the sight of him, so familiar in his white oxford shirt and Dockers.

"I'm so happy to see you!" Mary buried her face in his chest, feeling the familiar sensation of his body against hers. He wasn't that tall, just shy of six feet, but they fit each other like those stuffed toys sold on Valentine's Day, their arms wrapped around each other and their hands felt Velcroed together.

"I missed you, I missed *this,*" Anthony whispered into her ear, then kissed her forehead, her cheek, and her mouth, gently, and Mary kissed him back, matching his gentleness, feeling their love connecting them, at the most physical and elemental level between man and woman.

"I missed that too." Mary kissed him one last time, then looking up at him. "I can't believe you went to all this trouble, roses and everything? That's so sweet."

"Wait'll you see what's for dinner." Anthony took her hand and led her into the kitchen, which smelled deliciously of olive oil and garlic.

The kitchen was one of the reasons that Mary had wanted to buy the house, because it was large and newly renovated, ringed with white paneled cabinets and glistening black granite counters. An arched window over the sink overlooked a small flagstone backyard, and all of the appliances were top-of-the-line. Two wineglasses sat on the island next to a bottle of open Pinot Grigio, and on the stovetop rested a heavy skillet mounded with fresh broccoli rabe, ready to be sautéed, and on another burner was a skillet of chopped fresh tomatoes, fennel, capers, onions, and garlic, already cooking. Anthony was making their favorite topping for filleted bream, probably already in the oven.

"How did you get the time to do all this?" Mary asked, delighted.

"The plane got in early." Anthony grinned at her, and Mary smiled back, her gaze taking in his handsome features. He had large, dark brown eyes that were the exact hue of espresso and crow's-feet that crinkled when he smiled. His hair was thick, dark, and wavy, and his nose was long and Roman, on the large size for anybody but Italian-Americans.

"So did you have fun out there?" Mary didn't want to bring up the subject of Patrick yet. She would have to wait for the right moment, preferably after Anthony had downed a few glasses of wine.

"It was great!" Anthony turned the dial on the oven to get the fish cooking. "The people, the setting, the department. It was all great."

"That's wonderful."

"Wine?" Anthony asked, reading her mind. "I put yours in the fridge. I'm having the white."

"Yes, thanks." Mary started toward the refrigerator, but Anthony beat her to the punch, opening the refrigerator door and holding high a bottle of her favorite Lambrusco.

"Ta-da! We had one left."

Mary chuckled, amused at his high spirits. His nature was typically upbeat but tonight he seemed unusually energized. Or maybe she was just exhausted by comparison.

"My mother told me about the debacle at the hair salon." Anthony took a dish towel from the rack, wrapped it around the top of the Lambrusco bottle, then pried off the cork with a satisfying *pop*.

"She's not mad, is she?" Mary hadn't thought twice about the incident at the hair salon, and everything with Patrick had shooed it from her mind.

"No, not at all." Anthony poured the cold Lambrusco into a wineglass, where it bubbled, then slid the glass toward Mary. "Is your mother upset?"

"No, she's fine. I ate to calm her down."

"Ah." Anthony smiled, understanding what Mary meant without her having to explain, which was another thing that she loved about him. They came from the same neighborhood, both literally and figuratively.

"What did your mom say on the phone?"

"Just that your mom wanted to leave. I'm sorry if my mom terrorized her. We know she has the finesse of a blunt object."

Mary chuckled, but didn't comment. She always let Anthony criticize El Virus, but never did so herself. It was the first rule of Italian families. Nobody disses blood, but blood.

"Hold on, she sent a picture." Anthony poured more wine into his glass, then slipped his hand into his pocket, and pulled out his phone, thumbing the screen. "Didn't you see it? She copied you on the email."

"No, I haven't had a chance to check my email." Mary was woefully behind on her other cases, but she assumed she could catch up later. Photos from El Virus weren't among the priorities.

"Here we go." Anthony showed her the photo, and Mary tried not to laugh out loud. It was El Virus in full makeup, and her perm had gained ten pounds of curly extensions, which matched her new curly false eyelashes. She was making duck lips that looked better on Kim Kardashian. Or ducks.

"Gee, wow, uh, she looks . . ."

". . . certifiably insane?"

Mary chuckled. "Be grateful for small favors. She could have sent you a picture of her Brazilian."

"*What?*" Anthony's eyes flew open, and he laughed out loud, throwing back his head. "I don't want to know that!"

Mary joined him laughing. "Neither do I. See what you've been missing?"

Anthony picked up his wineglass. "I propose a toast."

"Great idea." Mary picked up her glass and held it up. The sooner she got Anthony drinking, the better. "To what?"

"To a long and happy marriage," Anthony said, looking at her, his dark eyes shining.

"Aww, I'll drink to that." Mary sipped her wine, which tasted chilly and deliciously fruity. "I love Lambrusco. It hits the spot, every time."

Anthony sipped his wine. "I had some great wines in LA."

"Fill me in. But don't make me feel bad about my humble Lambrusco."

"One of the guys in the department grew up in Sacramento, and he's an expert in California wines. He said we should take a vineyard tour in Sonoma. It sounds like fun. Would you like to do that?"

"Someday." Mary didn't see a lot of vineyard trips in their future, with Patrick.

Anthony eyed her, his expression suddenly serious over the delicate rim of his wineglass. "We could do it sooner rather than later, if we wanted to."

"I don't know about that, honey." Mary took another sip of wine, for liquid courage. She couldn't hold out much longer. The right moment was coming sooner than she would've liked, since neither of them was drunk.

"I know this sounds crazy, but we could do it as early as next week, if you could get free of work. And the airfare would be free."

"What are you talking about, free airfare?"

"There's something I need to talk to you about." Anthony's expression changed, his smile flattening. He set down his wineglass on the granite with a *clink*. "I have great news, but it's the kind of news that takes some getting used to."

"Really?" Mary thought he was kidding, since it was so coincidental. "Actually, I have great news too, but it's also the kind of news that takes getting used to."

"Really." Anthony lifted an eyebrow. "Let me go first. I may have a job offer at UCLA, and they're flying me back for more interviews, tomorrow."

"*What?*"

"It's an amazing offer for a full-time position, an assistant professor in the department on tenure track." Anthony met her gaze, his face alive with excitement. "It's what I've been waiting for, what I've been hoping for. I could finally earn a decent living, and it's a great department."

Mary's mouth went dry. "But it's at UCLA."

"Yes." Anthony pursed his lips. "We would have to move."

"From Philadelphia?" Mary heard the incredulous note in her own voice.

"There are other towns in the United States, honey."

"But not for us, not for me." Mary couldn't believe what he was saying. Suddenly she realized why he'd made the romantic dinner, brought the pretty roses, and cooked their favorite meal. "My family's here, my firm's here. We just bought this house."

"I know that." Anthony placed his hand over hers, his eyes pleading. "But people move away from where they grow up."

"Not us, not me." Mary didn't know how to explain it to him. She'd never thought she'd have to try. "I like Lambrusco."

"There are other wines in the world."

"I *am* Lambrusco."

"No you're not. Don't sell yourself short." Anthony touched her arm, leaning over with a new urgency. "You're an amazing person and an amazing lawyer. You can be anything you want to be."

"What about my client base? It's in South Philly."

"You got that client base because you're a great lawyer and you work hard. You'll get clients wherever you go, you'll attract new ones. They'll come to you because of your talent and your personality. And your dedication."

"But I love it here." Mary couldn't imagine moving away. "My parents are here, Judy is here. The Tonys. The city. This is my home. This is our home."

"No, it's just our hometown. It doesn't have to be our home, forever and ever." Anthony frowned, his desperation plain. "This is an opportunity I can't bring myself to turn down. I could have stayed the weekend but I came home to explain this all to you, to see how you felt, to try to work it out. I know it's a new idea, but if you come out with me this week, you can look around. UCLA sells itself. The sun, the beach, it's just a wonderful way to live, a healthy, clean, relaxed way to live—"

"I'm healthy and clean," Mary heard herself saying, bewildered. She felt vaguely disapproved of, by the man she loved most in the world. And then there was Patrick. "You know what *my* news is? A case came up this week, involving a ten-year-old boy. His grandfather died, and he has nobody else in the world. And I was going to ask you if we could have him come to live with us, only temporarily, because I'm going into court to become his guardian."

Anthony's eyes flared in shock. "Are you serious?"

"Yes." Mary realized this was her chance to pitch her case. "He's a wonderful little boy and I can't turn my back on him. I just can't bring myself to. I thought if I explained it to you, you would understand why we need to take him in. As I say, temporarily."

"How long are you talking about? A week, two weeks?"

"No, because we have to get him through a really tough time—"

"How long?"

"Like six months to a year? I just want to get him over the hump."

"Are you *kidding*? A *year*?" Anthony recoiled, aghast. His hand slipped from Mary's. "Why us?"

"His parents are dead and now his grandfather's dead."

"He must have somebody, some cousins to take him. Have you looked?"

"Even if there was some remote cousin or something, Patrick doesn't know him."

"*Patrick?*" Anthony edged away, shaking his head in disbelief.

"Patrick O'Brien. That's his name—"

"I don't want to know his name. I'm not responsible for him. You can't be responsible for him. You're not. How did you even get involved?"

"It was a special education case, and when the grandfather died, it turned into something else. I tried to call you, to tell you, but I couldn't reach you."

"Look, to tell you the truth, I was ducking your calls—"

"What?" Mary said, shocked.

"I knew I had to tell you about the job offer but I didn't want to tell you over the phone. I wanted to tell you in person. I'm sorry, but"—Anthony stopped speaking abruptly, then started again—"you *can't* be seriously considering this. I don't want a ten-year-old boy, not now. We're getting married. I want to move to California."

"I don't want to move to California."

"And I don't want a child right now, and not this way." Anthony looked at Mary like she was completely crazy. "And babe, if you think this is going to be temporary, even a year, you're not being realistic. You're kicking the can down the road. You're not going to take a kid into our house, live with him for a year, and then give him up. That's *so* not you."

"I'm going to make myself do it. I'm going to do it."

"No, you're not going to be able to. You don't do anything temporarily. You're going to fall in love with him and you're gonna fall hard." Anthony frowned. "And we're going to end up with *Patrick* as our child, our son, forever. You're asking me to change my whole life."

"You're asking me to change *my* whole life, by moving away."

"No, I'm not," Anthony shot back. "Moving isn't the same thing as taking on a child. You're talking about something that affects us as a couple, as a family."

"You're talking about me leaving my parents. They're my family.

How much longer do you think they have?" Mary didn't even want to think about her parents' passing.

"But now that we're getting married, *we're* the family."

"Our getting married doesn't mean we leave our families behind. That wasn't the deal. In fact, it was exactly the opposite." Mary couldn't believe she had to explain this to him. They were supposed to be from the same neighborhood, literally and figuratively. "Part of the reason we get along so well is that you love my family as much as I do. We fit together, all of us, even your mom."

"So take your family with us, I'd love it!" Anthony threw up his hands. "My mom would move to California if I asked her to. So would my brother."

"Well, mine wouldn't!" Mary shot back. "And I wouldn't ask them to. My parents are older than your mom, and my father's friends are here. They live here and they need me here. My mom doesn't feel that great from time to time, since her hysterectomy. And my father's knees act up. Now is when they need me the most."

"What about what *I* need? Where do I stand? Behind your parents? Behind Judy and The Tonys? Behind *Patrick, whoever he is*?" Anthony's lips parted, and his eyebrows slanted down, and he looked to Mary as if he was positively heartbroken, which was exactly how she felt. She hadn't really thought about it until this very moment, but she realized her parents did need her. The tables had turned in her life, and now she took care of the parents who used to take care of her. She flashed on Patrick, crying that Edward needed him. It struck her suddenly that the pull of being needed was just as strong as the pull of needing.

"Anthony, I love you, more than anybody. But I don't want to move away from my family and I want to take Patrick."

"Mary, I love *you*, more than anybody. But I want to move and I don't want to take Patrick."

Mary felt his words like a body blow. "So what do we do now?"

Anthony shook his head, sadly. "I don't know, but I'm leaving early tomorrow to go back to LA. The interviews are this week. I'll be back when I can, maybe Tuesday night."

Mary inhaled slowly, her wine souring on her tongue. "And by then I'll know if I'm Patrick's guardian."

"So we're at impasse."

"I guess so." Mary shrugged, crestfallen. She knew she was doing the right thing for Patrick, but maybe it was wrong for Anthony. She wondered if she *had* volunteered herself too fast, taking responsibility for a problem that wasn't hers.

"We'll have to figure this out, later."

"Will you at least think it over?"

"Yes, if you will." Anthony pursed his lips. "Unless the problem solves itself."

"How would it?"

"If they don't offer me the job." Anthony forced a smile.

"I guess I could always lose the hearing." Mary couldn't manage even a sarcastic smile. Too much was at stake. She didn't see how she won, either way. If she got Patrick, she could lose Anthony. She was supposed to be getting married in less than two weeks, now. Her next thought was unthinkable.

"So now we can wish the worst for each other."

"I don't wish the worst for you. Do you wish it for me?"

Anthony looked away, leaning on the island, his dark-eyed gaze focusing on a shaft of sunlight fading on the black granite. He didn't say anything, and Mary couldn't take the silence.

"Well?" she asked, her chest tight.

"I think the fish is burning," Anthony said, turning away.

CHAPTER THIRTY

"You can't go to California!" Judy wailed, sitting across from Mary's desk, dressed in her Sunday shorts and T-shirt, which was a lot like her Saturday shorts and T-shirt. Mary took another bite of her bagel, feeling like she was having a déjà vu of yesterday morning, except that most mornings at Rosato & DiNunzio started with her, Judy, and carbohydrates.

"I'm not going to California," Mary said, grateful that Judy had taken the time on Sunday morning to come in and talk it over.

"What did he say this morning before he left?"

"He left before I was up. I can't believe his flight was that early. I think he waited at the airport."

"Oh no." Judy grimaced. "Was it the gun that bothered him?"

"I didn't even get to tell him about that, it just went straight downhill. It makes me wonder if I'm doing the right thing with Patrick. When Anthony wasn't here, it was easy to put Patrick first, but last night when he came home, I could see how hurt he was and how much it meant to him."

"I get it. It made it real?"

"Exactly," Mary said, feeling validated, which was what best friends were for. "But on the other hand, I can't forget Patrick. I was thinking all morning, is there any way to compromise with Anthony? What if I take Patrick to California? Or what if Anthony takes the job for a year, and I take Patrick for a year? Isn't that what you're supposed to do when you get married, compromise?"

"I'm the last one to ask. I'm not only single, I'm in the dry spell of a lifetime. I think my hymen fused back together."

Mary smiled. "That can't happen."

"It happens with pierced ears. The holes close up."

"Anyway, it's a big thing to compromise over, not helping Patrick, and Anthony doesn't think it would be temporary."

Judy eyed her, knowingly. "I have to admit, Anthony might be right about that. I worried about it, too. You'll get attached to Patrick. You get attached to parking meters, pencils, anything. You even like my dog better than I do."

Mary took a gulp of her coffee. "So what should I do? I have to decide. We're going forward."

Judy shot her a sympathetic look. "Don't worry, you'll figure it out. You always do. It sounds corny, but just keep following your heart. Think about what you really want."

"I want everything. I want to help Patrick and I want to get married to Anthony and live in Philadelphia."

"Then you'll figure out a way to make that happen." Judy met her gaze directly. "I'll help you any way I can, you know that. And I'll love you no matter what you do, except if you move to California."

Mary turned to the door as Lou Jacobs, their firm investigator, appeared in the doorway. She'd asked him to come in to follow up on the brown Subaru and to satisfy Anthony's request that Patrick had no other family. Lou was a retired cop in his late sixties, his craggy face deeply sunburned after a summer spent crabbing in South Jersey. He was still trim, with piercing blue eyes, high cheekbones, and a strong nose with a tiny scar.

"Ladies, the cavalry is here." Lou flashed her a smile, stepped inside, and sat down next to Judy. "So our girl needs us again, eh?"

Judy smiled back. "Where would she be without us?"

"Up shit creek without a paddle."

Mary knew he was kidding. She and Lou had worked together since forever, and all of the lawyers at the firm loved him. She handed him a bag with breakfast. "Lou, I got you a bagel."

"Thanks, Mare."

"I told you about the case on the phone. I want to confirm that it was Robertson in the brown Subaru so if you could—"

"I don't want to talk about the case, I want to talk about your life." Lou unwrapped the bagel. "You're trying to become this kid's guardian? Do you know what you're getting into?"

"Yes." Mary didn't mind Lou asking, since everyone at the firm routinely invaded each other's privacy.

"Mare, I know your heart's in the right place but you can't rescue everybody."

"I know that," Mary said, defensively. "I'm just going to rescue this one kid."

"It's a big deal, having a kid."

"It's not forever, it's just for a year."

"Tell me another one. I know you, and *that* ain't happening." Lou parted the halves of his bagel, with approval. "This sandwich is a thing of beauty, is it not? Poppy seed, untoasted. Just the right amount of Nova, sliced thin. Plain cream cheese, not too much. Tomato sliced perfect. No onion. Just like I like. Thank you, Mary." Lou looked over at Judy. "You could take a lesson, you know. Mary always feeds me. With you, I'm lucky if I get a cuppa coffee. Now you know why I shave for Mary. For you, I don't shave."

Mary was running out of time. "Lou, what was your point about kids?"

"Mare, I got kids, so I know. I'm a kid expert. It changes your life, having a kid."

"*This* is your advice?"

"Don't make light. It's a true fact. Let it sink in. Think about it. You like your life? It's gonna change. You might not like it so much. That's what kids do." Lou took a massive bite of his bagel. "What does Anthony say?"

Mary hesitated. "I'm hoping he'll get on board."

Judy started laughing. "I'm hoping I'll meet Bradley Cooper."

Lou glanced at Judy, his cheek full. "Good one."

"Thank you."

Lou returned his attention to Mary. "So Anthony doesn't want the kid. I coulda told you that. You're gonna go ahead anyway? Is that any way to start marriage? Answer, no. I'm a marriage expert, too. I'm divorced twice."

"Before you side with Anthony, you should know that he wants me to move to California."

"No!" Lou's hooded eyes flared wide open. "You're not going anywhere. You're not allowed. Screw him!"

Mary smiled. "Lou, I forgot to mention, about the brown Subaru, please stay away from Grove Street. After what happened with Robertson, we have to give him a wide berth."

"I know, and I'll keep digging."

Just then John appeared in the threshold with an attractive woman, presumably Abby Ortega, the Child Advocate with whom they were supposed to meet. John said, "Good morning, Mary. This is Abby."

"Hi, John." Mary rose. "Abby, thanks for helping us."

"Hi, Mary. Nice to meet you." Abby smiled back warmly, and Mary liked her instantly. Abby had a big, friendly smile and a sweet, round face framed by glossy black hair cut in feathery layers. She had dark eyes, almond-shaped, with a tiny nose and a small mouth, and she was wearing a blue shirtdress hoisted up on one side by a heavy leather purse, messenger bag, and a cloth tote bag that rested on her shoulder.

"Good morning, everyone." John nodded at Judy and Lou, acknowledging them. He had on a blue-and-white checked shirt, jeans, and Gucci loafers.

Lou's mouth was too full to respond, so he nodded.

"Hi, guys." Judy smiled up at John. "Thanks for helping Mary. It's really nice of you."

"I'm happy to." John turned to Mary. "Good to go?"

"Sure," Mary answered, noticing a newly worrisome crease on John's forehead.

CHAPTER THIRTY-ONE

Mary settled into a chair next to Abby, and John took a seat at his desk, behind his laptop.

"So Abby," Mary began, "did you get to see Patrick?"

"Yes, he's a good kid, and it's so great that you're taking him." Abby's smile evaporated. "But I have bad news. The truth is, he's not doing well. DHS intends to move him into residential care for hard-to-place kids, if you don't win at the hearing."

"Why?" Mary asked, shocked. "What happened?"

John glanced over the top of his laptop, where he'd begun to tap out meeting notes, and Mary realized he already knew the bad news.

Abby continued, "Mary, I know you're not that familiar with the foster care system, so let me begin by putting Patrick's case in context. He comes from a very loving home where he was valued and taken good care of. That makes him highly unusual. The overwhelming majority of foster children enter the system from very challenging circumstances, physical or sexual abuse, neglect, of parents or single parents with drug and alcohol problems, things like that."

"Yes, but remember, Patrick was assaulted at school."

"I know, I don't mean to minimize that. But even as horrible as that was, the cases I see are worse. Of course, you understand that foster kids aren't 'bad kids.'" Abby made air quotes. "But children in foster care may have anger issues, poor impulse control, acting out, even violence."

John looked over. "Abby, you do know that Patrick brandished a gun at Mary and Olivia Solo, the caseworker from DHS."

Mary recoiled. "He didn't *brandish* it."

"I'm playing devil's advocate, Mary. You should want to hear what Abby says. You're taking Patrick into your home."

"I'm not worried," Mary said gently.

"Guys." Abby signaled for a referee's time-out. "You told me about the gun and the fact is, they didn't place Patrick in the foster home they were going to, because of it. They were concerned about the safety of the other foster children."

"So where is he?" Mary asked, surprised.

"Einstein Crisis Response Center. That's where DHS takes a child if they're concerned about his mental or emotional health, even physical health."

"The poor kid." Mary felt for him. "That was an overreaction."

"I agree, but DHS is taking no chances since the Kelly case. You probably read about the Kelly case, a fourteen-year-old with cerebral palsy who died of malnutrition in the home of a neglectful mother. Nine people, including a DHS caseworker, went to prison after that, and DHS reformed to make child safety paramount."

Mary remembered the Kelly case, which was all over the newspapers.

"DHS is in transition as we speak, and their reforms have resulted in more children being taken out of their homes, which burdens the foster care system. DHS is a fifteen-hundred-person agency that serves twelve thousand children. There are about six thousand children in Philly who live in foster care, group homes, or kinship care, which is what you want to do, Mary." Abby nodded in her direction. "Compare it with Montgomery and Delaware Counties in the suburbs. Montgomery County has only 277 kids in foster placement and Delaware County has 435."

"So why didn't DHS let me take Patrick, then?"

"They have to follow procedures." Abby frowned. "Anyway, I talked to Patrick about the gun at great length, and I'm not worried about his dangerousness. He doesn't even think it was loaded and he's sorry. It's his grandfather's gun from Vietnam."

"That's what I thought," Mary said, relieved. "So what happened this weekend?"

"He got into a fight with an older boy at the Crisis Center. Apparently Patrick had a wallet with him?"

"Yes, it's his grandfather's wallet and watch."

"The older boy took the wallet and scattered the pictures. There was a tussle, with Patrick trying to get the wallet back, then it turned into an altercation." Abby shook her head, the corners of her mouth turning unhappily down.

"Why did they allow this?" Mary could imagine how upset Patrick must've been. The wallet was all he had left of Edward.

"It happened before they could stop it. I went over at five o'clock, but they had already called DHS. Also Patrick started throwing up almost as soon as he got there. At first they thought he might have the flu, then they realized it was emotional."

"I could've taken him home with me this weekend. I could've saved him from all of this." Mary realized that she wasn't thinking about Anthony anymore. "He just lost his grandfather. Do they not understand that? Were they told that?"

"They knew and I reminded them. By the time I got there, they had reestablished order and taken the wallet and watch for safekeeping. But there is a silver lining." Abby smiled, bouncing back. "I interviewed Patrick and we had a very good conversation. He says hi."

"Awww." Mary swallowed hard. "Can I see him?"

"I think it would be better to wait, given the hearing. He really likes you. He understands that you're going to try to get him. He hopes that he can come and live with you. He wants to go to the new school, whatever you're setting up for him. He trusts you."

"That's wonderful." Mary felt a guilty twinge, torn in a way she hadn't been before.

"It is." Abby's smile broadened. "I'll testify that he wants to live with you and that he should. I do not believe he is dangerous in any way. I feel very confident about our chances in the shelter care hearing."

"Thanks, Abby." John looked up from his laptop. "Okay, ladies, moving right along, it's time to call Susan Bernardi, the child psychiatrist. I'll get her on FaceTime. Hang on."

"Thanks," Mary said, as John hit a few buttons on the laptop and she pulled her chair closer, to see better. Abby slid a legal pad and pen from her messenger bag and put it on her lap.

"Hi, Susan," John said, to the speaker on the laptop. "Susan, meet Mary, and you know Abby."

John turned the laptop around so they could see Dr. Susan Bernardi on the screen, and Mary thought she was a striking older woman, with a chic wedge of sterling-silver hair. Her dangling silver earrings emphasized a long face with high, elegant cheekbones and hooded gray-green eyes. She sat draped in a pinkish-gray pashmina in front of a bookshelf full of professional journals.

"Hi, all." Susan smiled, the movement blurring her image for a moment. "I'm running late, so I'll jump right in. I interviewed Patrick last evening. I learned enough to identify his issues and testify at the shelter care hearing. Time and circumstances didn't permit me to talk to all of the people involved or have a psychologist do testing that I would typically include in a comprehensive risk evaluation."

"We understand." John started taking notes on a legal pad. "Fill us in."

"Patrick struggles with anxiety and depression, understandable after having lost his grandfather. It's clear that he had a close relationship with his grandfather. To suddenly lose that anchor in his life presents a major challenge for him, considering his age." Susan took a sip from a flowered mug of coffee. "Also he lacks a support structure of siblings, extended family, or friends. He feels scared and vulnerable because he's alone, also understandable."

Mary nodded, knowing it was true.

"He worries about what's going to happen to him and where he's going to live, also normal in the circumstances. He wants to live with Mary, he's clear on that." Susan smiled at Mary. "He likes you. He especially liked the way you yelled at Olivia."

Mary smiled, but didn't interrupt.

"He's worried about losing the artwork that was in his bedroom at home. He has some special red pens that he doesn't want to lose. He kept talking about some photographs of his grandfather. He's worried he's not going to get them back. Mary, do you know where they are?"

"I have them," Mary answered. "I packed them with his clothes. I have his artwork too."

John interjected, "Susan, did you get a chance to look at the artwork I scanned for you? The one where the kid is stabbing somebody?"

Susan nodded. "Yes, I did, and you also told me Mary's explanation, and I asked him about the drawings and he explained that they were his superheroes, among them, his grandfather. I don't believe that the drawings demonstrate that he is a violent child. That's just not my take on him."

John made a note. "What about the gun that he pulled on the DHS caseworker and Mary?"

Susan nodded. "We talked about the gun a great deal as part of my safety evaluation. He did not know how to use it, he thought it was unloaded, and he did not know where the bullets were. He was not allowed to touch the gun, it was expressly forbidden by his grandfather. Patrick is very worried that he's going to get in trouble for even touching it. The gun was his grandfather's from the war, a souvenir."

Mary nodded, relieved, as Susan continued.

"One has to employ a more nuanced analysis, in my view. I have to look at questions like, why did he grab the gun? What was he afraid of or whom was he protecting? Did he not want to be taken out of the house? Did he view himself as the 'man of the house' and feel that he had to protect it? When I consider all of the circumstances, I don't see him as a dangerous child. He's a victim, not a perpetrator or aggressor. That will be my testimony at the hearing." Susan consulted her notes. "Apart from his grieving process, he has Generalized Anxiety Disorder. He worries about being bullied, making mistakes, and the like. He's fearful, he's nervous, and he's in a depressed mood. In addition, there was a fight yesterday at Einstein between Patrick and another foster child, who took his grandfather's wallet and watch."

John interjected, "Abby told us."

Abby nodded, looking up from her note-taking.

Mary said, "I would be interested to hear Susan's view, too."

Susan nodded. "Obviously, seeing his grandfather's personal effects mishandled and strewn around was very upsetting to him. Patrick didn't aggress on the boy, but wanted the wallet back. He withdrew after the altercation with the other foster child. He's shut down and probably has been for some time. Children who have experienced trauma get triggered by being in situations where they do not feel safe. They will only drive him deeper into his shell."

Mary had felt the same way about Patrick.

"Patrick is an intelligent and sensitive child and he feels every bump along the road. He would absolutely not benefit from being placed in residential care with hard-to-place kids. It's too rough-and-tumble for him."

Mary felt terrible, hearing the report. It was what she had expected, but it felt worse to hear it confirmed by a professional.

John looked up from his notes. "Susan, would that be your testimony?"

"Yes, John. There's no doubt in my mind that placement with Mary would be preferable. He needs quiet, he needs structure, and he would do best without other children around." Susan checked her notes. "Now, to his dyslexia. You understand that's not my expertise, but anxiety goes hand-in-hand with dyslexia. He's embarrassed that he can't read. He's worried that other foster children will find out and tease him. I problem-solved with him, and we came up with some things he could do to help himself calm down. I taught him how to take slow deep breaths, and he said he likes to draw, so I suggested he do that, too." Susan checked her notes again. "Next point. I got an earful about Patrick's vomiting. I explained to them that the vomiting is symptomatic of anxiety. I advised them to give Patrick some alone time during his stay. I prescribed him an anti-emetic and advised them to keep him hydrated."

"Thank you so much," Mary said, relieved.

"You're welcome. He's a skinny little guy, and we don't want him to end up in an emergency room for dehydration."

Mary hadn't even thought about dehydration. She was going to have to learn a lot if she was going to take him on.

John looked up from his notes. "Did you talk with him about the physical and sexual assault at school?"

"Just briefly, and that it wasn't the purpose of this evaluation. He did say that Mr. Robertson hit him in the face, and I didn't take it further. It was neither the time nor the place, and you had told me that criminal charges are pending. I didn't want to contaminate his testimony. This is not my first time evaluating a child who's been physically or sexually assaulted."

Mary thought that was sad, but didn't say so. It was awful to think that innocent children were horribly treated by those entrusted to love and care for them. She had always known it was true, but that was as an academic matter. Seeing it up close made it real, and if she could just save one of them, she should. Shouldn't she?

John asked, "Susan, do you have a diagnosis for him?"

"Yes, he has an Adjustment Disorder with a depressed mood arising out of the loss of his grandfather and Generalized Anxiety Disorder. I think he also has mild PTSD as a result of the assault at school. I would recommend psychotherapy. He would benefit from structured activities that involve a cognitive behavioral approach, that is, specific strategies to reduce his anxiety." Susan seemed to read from her notes, her tone turning more professional. "I would recommend role-playing to improve social interactions with other children and help him with bullying, shyness, avoidance, and social activities. I think it would be important to create opportunities to improve his flexibility and general social skills. He's never even been to a birthday party."

John looked up. "Do you think he needs medication?"

"No, not at this point. I think he would respond to talk therapy. I think his prognosis is excellent, given the right therapies, support, and placement." Susan's gaze shifted to Mary, her features softening. "I think Patrick will do very well with you. You'll be giving him a great head start and he's a wonderful candidate for permanent adoption. I have a list of referrals for therapy for him, and I wish you the best."

"Thank you," Mary said, grateful.

Abby called out, "Thanks, Susan!"

"Yes, thanks, Susan. Good-bye." John hit the button and the laptop went dark, leaving Mary to her own troubled thoughts.

"I'm going to go now." Abby put her pad away, with a happy sigh. "I feel so legit when Susan agrees with me, she's one of the best."

John rose. "I think we're all on the same page for the hearing. Let me walk you out."

"You don't have to." Abby turned to Mary, grinning. "He's such a gentleman, isn't he?"

"He is." Mary stood up. "Thank you so much."

"No worries." Abby hoisted her purse and messenger bag to her shoulder. "I hate carrying files."

"Let me help." John hustled over, lifted her tote bag, and handed it to Abby.

"Thanks." Abby went to the door. "I'll let you know if there are any changes or DHS moves him again."

"Thanks," John and Mary said, in unison, then Abby left the office.

"Mission accomplished." John went back to his desk with a satisfied smile, stretching his arms. "We're all set."

"Yes, we are." Mary sank into the chair, masking her mixed emotions.

"First, we finalize the paperwork for filing." John spoke as he typed. "Then we outline Abby and Susan's direct-examination. Next, we outline your testimony and rehearse you, then practice your cross. We're right on track."

"Great," Mary said, but she had never felt so confused. She wanted to take Patrick, but she was worried about taking him because of Anthony. For once in her life, she had no earthly idea what to do. She was running out of time to decide.

"Onward and upward!" John said, tapping away.

CHAPTER THIRTY-TWO

Mary and John worked through lunch, but all the time, her mind was racing. She couldn't stop thinking about Anthony's wounded expression last night or the pained tone of his voice when he asked her where he fit in her life. She knew in her heart that she put him first, but even she couldn't square that with her taking Patrick, against his express wishes.

She felt more nervous as the papers they needed to file got closer to final. Every time she thought that Anthony was right, she would remember Patrick. How lost and alone he was, and what a sweet child. She flashed on the horrible scene when the police had taken Edward's body from the house, and then, even worse, when they had taken Patrick.

The sun was falling in the sky outside John's window, and he was typing the cover letter to file their papers. Documents, Xerox cases, Family Court forms, and empty styrofoam cups of coffee cluttered his formerly neat desk. His hair had been finger-raked into rough layers, and his shirt sleeves had been folded up to the elbow.

Mary sat in the seat across from John's desk, staring at a draft of their papers without really seeing them. Everything had been set in motion. They were nearing the point of no return. She had to make a decision.

"Okay." John looked up at Mary with a weary smile. "I think we're good to go, don't you?"

"Um," Mary said, looking up from the draft.

"Is there a problem? Anything you want to correct or change?"

"No, it's perfect. You've done an amazing job. I couldn't be more grateful." Mary set the draft down, feeling a wave of guilt.

"But you're mad at me, aren't you?" John cocked his head. "Is it because I kept asking about the gun?"

"No, it's not that."

"Look, this is a tough situation, I know, I've been there."

"Is this what it was like for you, with your brother?" Mary realized that John had never returned to the subject of being his brother's guardian or given her any details.

"Yes," John answered, without elaborating. "But don't worry, we're in excellent shape. Abby and Susan's testimony will buttress yours in every particular. That means we hold three aces, including you."

Mary took the hint that he didn't want to talk about his brother, but she didn't feel like an ace.

"You don't seem very happy."

"I'm not." Mary had to come clean. "My fiancé, Anthony, isn't behind my taking Patrick. I didn't get to talk to him about it until last night because he was out of town, and I didn't think he would feel that way. He thinks it's going to be difficult for me to give Patrick up, when the time comes."

"It will be difficult to give Patrick up, but you can do it. I thought your plan to get him over the hump made sense. After he gets therapy and programming for his academic delays, he'll be a great candidate for permanent adoption."

"When I came in this morning, I was worrying that this wasn't the right thing to do, that my fiancé was right. But then, when I heard Abby and Susan, I knew I was doing the right thing." Mary felt a wave of shame, her neck flushing.

"You don't have to go forward if you don't want to." John's expression softened behind his glasses.

"But I want to, mostly."

"That's not good enough. Tell you what. Let's call it a day." John closed his laptop, stood up, and began rolling his left sleeve down, brushing it into place and buttoning it at the cuff.

"What about filing the papers?"

"We don't have to file today."

"When is the latest we can file?"

"Monday morning, it's an emergency hearing. I'll call chambers." John unrolled his right sleeve, brushed it down, and buttoned it at the cuff, too. "That gives you tonight to decide. Let me know if you want to keep going. Or stop now."

"How can I stop now?" Mary rose. "What about Patrick? And the experts we set in motion? And you, you've been working so hard. You gave up your whole weekend, you dropped everything. I don't want this all to have been for nothing."

"That's not what matters."

"I know. Patrick is what matters."

"So does your fiancé." John picked up his laptop, walked to a file cabinet near the door, and leaned against it. "Look, you have to make a very difficult choice. It's understandable to have reservations. It's not prudent to ignore them. I should've listened to my doubts more than I did."

Mary didn't say anything, not wanting to interrupt him, if he wanted to open up. She could see that the words didn't come easily to him, and neither did making himself so vulnerable.

"It's your decision, Mary. Make it carefully. I'll see you here at eight o'clock tomorrow morning. I'm coming in anyway."

"Thanks," Mary said, but John was leaving the office. She followed him out and watched him walk down the hall, his posture typically ramrod straight as he passed the empty offices. Judy and Lou had left a long time ago, and the firm had gone quiet and still, in the waning light of day.

Mary wondered what it was that he wished he had done differently with his brother. She heard a *ping* as the elevator cab arrived for John and still she remained motionless, alone with her decision. Then she realized she wasn't alone, and there was an opinion she hadn't sought yet. In fact, it was a veritable collection of opinions, and they wouldn't hesitate to let her know what they thought she should do. Truth to tell, she was pretty sure she wouldn't be able to shut them up.

The thought cheered her, and she hurried to her office for her purse.

CHAPTER THIRTY-THREE

Mercy Street was one of the skinniest streets in South Philly, lined with mismatched rowhouses and parked cars. The cars were longer than the rowhouses were wide, presenting a notorious parking problem that the residents solved in their own way, via self-help. Mary double-parked in front of her parents' house, the unwritten prerogative of every South Philly resident, all of whom knew each other well enough to be on a first-name basis not only with their parents, but with their automobiles.

Mary cut the ignition, took her purse, and got out of the car, but noticed that The Tonys, her father's three best friends, were carrying cardboard boxes away, down the street. The boxes looked heavy, so she hustled to catch up with them, catching Pigeon Tony Lucia, who was bringing up the rear like an antique caboose. He was in his eighties, and his lined skin was as brown as a nut because he spent so much time outdoors, tending his pigeon loft.

"*Come stai,*" Mary said, which was all the Italian she had energy for tonight.

"*Maria! Ciao bella!*" Pigeon Tony's face lit up. He always reminded Mary of a bird himself because his neat head was completely bald, his eyes were perfectly round and black, and his nose divided them in the middle, hooked as a beak.

"Please, let me help with that." Mary reached for the open box.

"No, *Maria,* is okay!" Pigeon Tony pulled the box away, but it fell to the ground. Round packs of red, white, and green streamers rolled down the sidewalk.

"Oh, sorry!" Mary scurried to pick up the packs before they rolled into the gutter.

"Alla good, *Maria*!" Pigeon Tony scrambled to pick up the other packs, then righted the box full of arts and craft supplies. Meanwhile the two other Tonys were turning, delighted to see Mary. On the left was Tony "From-Down-The-Block" LoMonaco and on the right was Tony "Two Feet" Pensiera, who went by Feet, since his nickname had a nickname. Mary remembered that Machiavelli had made some wisecrack about him, but she pushed that to the back of her mind.

"Mary, how you doin'?" Tony-From-Down-The-Block set down his box, then straightened up with a hand on his replacement hip. He had on a white T-shirt and plaid Bermuda shorts, which he always wore with black socks, rubbery brown sandals, and enough aftershave to bring Aqua Velva back.

"Good, how about you?" Mary tossed the streamers into the box, and Tony-From-Down-The-Block gave her a big hug.

"I can't believe you're getting married! You're too young!"

"I agree!" Mary grinned, having known The Tonys since she was little. In fact, all three were her godfathers, an octogenarian trifecta she considered her surrogate uncles and, sometimes, her crack investigative team.

"Don't get married, Mare! Play the field like me!"

Mary could only laugh. Tony-From-Down-The-Block had been married three times and was still actively dating. She guessed he had a new girlfriend since his remaining hair was a suspicious pitch black. The color was an improvement on his more recent orange, which looked better on orangutans.

Feet waddled over, his hooded eyes blinking behind his Mr. Potatohead trifocals. He had to walk slower than the others because he'd broken his foot working for her on a case. He also had on a white T-shirt, Bermuda shorts, and sandals, and Mary started to wonder if they were dressing alike after a lifetime of friendship. She wondered briefly if that would happen to her and Judy, and if so, which way that would cut.

"Mare, how's my baby girl?" Feet called out, raising his arms for a hug.

"Good!" Mary gave him a hug, breathing in his familiar scent of cigar smoke, onions, and BenGay. When he let her go, she gestured at the boxes sitting on the sidewalk. "What are you doing?"

"We're decoratin' the car. We're goin' to drive in the parade like big *mahafs*!" Feet gestured at his massive green Bonneville.

"What parade?" Mary asked, then remembered. "Oh, Columbus Day."

"Right, it's tomorrow!" Feet answered, pronouncing it *tammarah*.

"Mare, really?" Tony-From-Down-The-Block placed a gnarled hand on her shoulder. "Did you forget? Aren't you comin'?"

"I can't, I have to work." Mary knew that her father would be disappointed. He loved his drive down Broad Street in the Columbus Day Parade, a homegrown promenade of high-school bands, local dignitaries, and saturated fats. Her father and The Tonys belonged to the same Sons of Italy lodge, and tomorrow was their Super Bowl.

Feet added, "Mare, they got a rhyme to help you remember. 'In 1492, Columbus sailed the ocean blue.' So you can't forget. That's when Columbus discovered America!"

"Oh, right, of course." Mary had read there were going to be protestors at the parade, since not everybody worshipped Christopher Columbus, especially those with Wikipedia. "You know, there might be protests by people who don't think Columbus discovered America."

"Stupid!" said Tony-From-Down-The-Block.

"Dummies!" added Feet.

Pigeon Tony didn't reply, his beady eyes darting from one Tony to the other, and Mary suspected he knew more English, as well as world history, than he let on.

Mary tried again. "Guys, there are some people who say that the Vikings discovered America."

"What do they know?" Tony-From-Down-The-Block dismissed her with a wave. "The Vikings didn't discover nothin'!"

"The Vikings?" Feet snorted. "Ever see what they wear? Fred Flintstone clothes!"

Pigeon Tony looked away.

Mary took another swing. "Didn't you read in the paper, they say that Christopher Columbus did some bad things."

"Like what?" asked Tony-From-Down-The-Block.

"Yeah, like what?" added Feet.

Mary was about to answer, she hated to destroy the only idol they had left, now that Frank Sinatra and Dean Martin were both gone. Thank God for Tony Bennett. She took a deep breath. "Ah, you're right! What do *they* know? Happy Columbus Day!"

"Right!" Tony-From-Down-The-Block cheered.

"Yeah!" Feet joined in.

"*Bravo, Cristoforo!*" Pigeon Tony shook his little brown fist in the air, and Mary decided she had to get going. She said good-bye to each one, kissed them on the cheeks, and gave them each a hug big enough to last until she saw them again, which would probably be in fifteen minutes.

Mary headed toward the house, thinking about how she was going to break the news to her parents, which was when she realized that maybe she could take a lesson from what had just happened. She walked up her parents' front step, reached the screen door, and had an epiphany. She wouldn't tell them about Anthony's wish to move them to California. Her parents adored Anthony but they would never forgive him. And the decision she had to make by morning was about Patrick.

She stepped inside the house. "Ma! Pop!" she called out, happy to be home.

CHAPTER THIRTY-FOUR

Mary sat in the kitchen explaining the situation, and her parents sat across from her, listening. Tomato sauce, called gravy in the South Philly vernacular, bubbled away in the dented pot on the stove, and freshly percolated coffee sat cooling in cups near their hands. The air was scented with garlic and oregano, and the kitchen looked the way it had since forever: small, white, and clean, ringed by white wood cabinets, an ancient church calendar, and faded photos of Jesus Christ, John F. Kennedy, and Pope John. Evidently Pope Francis had joined the DiNunzios' All-Star Team, in the form of a newspaper photo of the Pontiff waving from his black Fiat during the Papal Visit.

Her mother didn't ask any questions, but her father turned into an assistant district attorney. His mind was still sharp as a tack, but his back had been deteriorating after a lifetime of setting tile. He was bald and adorably pudgy in his white T-shirt and Bermuda shorts, and he wore trifocals with black frames. His eyes were still good, though her mother's had worsened from a childhood spent sewing piecework in the basement of this very rowhouse. Being home only confirmed the correctness of Mary's decision not to tell them about Anthony's wish to move to California. It was a DiNunzio family tradition never to leave. The kitchen.

"So, what do you think?" Mary asked, when she was finished.

"Anthony doesn't want me to take Patrick, but I'm thinking that I should. What should I do?"

"MARE," her father shouted. He was hard of hearing and his hearing aid did nothing but plug his ears, so he spoke only in high decibels. "OF COURSE YOU SHOULD TAKE HIM! YOU GOTTA TAKE HIM. IF YOU DON'T TAKE HIM, YOUR MOTHER AND I WILL TAKE HIM." Her father looked over at her mother. "RIGHT, VEET?"

Her mother nodded but still didn't say anything, and Mary could see her mother's eyes glistening behind her thick glasses.

"THAT'S HOW WE RAISED YOU. THAT'S WHAT WE BELIEVE. THAT'S WHO WE ARE. YOU GIVE TO PEOPLE, 'SPECIALLY KIDS. YOU CAN'T LET HIM GO TO NO FOSTER HOME. HE'S AN *ORPHAN*."

Her mother nodded, blinking wetness from her eyes.

"WHAT ARE YOU GONNA DO WITH HIM WHEN YOU'RE AT WORK?"

"I'm going to cut back on my workload and work at home as much as I can. I could get a nanny to come to the house, too."

"PSSH!" Her father waved her off with a chubby hand. "I'LL PICK HIM UP AT SCHOOL. WHERE'S THAT SCHOOL YOU'RE TALKIN' ABOUT? IN FAIRMOUNT?"

"Yes," Mary answered. Fairmount Prep was in the upscale, tree-lined neighborhood where Bennie lived, around the Art Museum.

"IT'S ONLY FIFTEEN MINUTES AWAY. I'LL PICK HIM UP AND TAKE HIM HERE. THEN I'LL BRING HIM TO YOUR HOUSE WHEN YOU'RE DONE WORK."

"Pop, that's a lot of driving."

"SO WHAT? I LIKE TO DRIVE. WHAT ELSE I GOTTA DO? NO STRANGER'S GONNA BABYSIT MY GRANDSON."

Mary felt touched at the sound of the word. *Grandson.*

"EVERY DAY AFTER SCHOOL, YOUR MOTHER, SHE'LL FEED HIM HOMEMADES."

Mary knew he wasn't kidding. Nothing tasted better than cold spaghetti after school, and the DiNunzios had been known to pack spaghetti in a sandwich for school.

"YOU AND ANGIE, YOU'RE GIVERS LIKE YOUR MOTHER. YOU ALWAYS WERE. THE TWO OF YOU. PEAS IN A POD. TWINS."

Mary felt her chest tighten. She wished Angie could be at her wedding, but she knew it was impossible. Angie was half a world away on another mission, and Mary missed her twin every day.

"WE MISS ANGIE BUT WE KNOW SHE'S DOIN' THE RIGHT THING. SHE KNOWS IT INSIDE." Her father shrugged his heavy shoulders. "THAT'S JUST HOW IT IS. TO DO THE RIGHT THING, YOU GOTTA SACRIFICE."

Mary felt all of his words resonating deep within her chest, and she realized that she had grown up with these values. All of her instincts had been to take Patrick and she still felt the same way, deep inside. But there was still one problem. "What about Anthony?" Mary asked them.

"HE HAS TO SUCK IT UP. THAT'S HOW IT IS FOR THE HUSBAND. HAPPY WIFE, HAPPY LIFE. HE BETTER GET USED TO IT."

"Pop, don't you think I should consider what he says? We're about to get married. It's less than two weeks now."

"YOU DID CONSIDER IT. DON'T MEAN YOU HAVE TO AGREE. HE'S WRONG. HE KNOWS IT INSIDE. HE WAS RAISED THE SAME WAY YOU WERE. EVEN THAT CRAZY ELVIRA KNOWS BETTER. WANT ME TO CALL HER?" Her father gestured at the old tan wall phone. "I BET HE DIDN'T EVEN ASK HER. HE KNOWS WHAT SHE'D SAY."

Mary realized that her father was onto something, and Anthony would never tell El Virus about Patrick. Anthony would keep Patrick as secret as she did the idea of moving to California.

"ELVIRA WOULD BE VERY DISAPPOINTED IN HIM. IT'S NOT LIKE HIM. HE KNOWS BETTER. LET ME CALL HER. SHE'LL STRAIGHTEN HIM OUT." Her father was about to stand up, but Mary put her hand on his forearm.

"No, don't. Don't tell her. Don't say anything. This is a private conversation."

Her father looked at her mother. "VEET, WHADDAYA THINK? SHOULD I CALL?"

Her mother shook her head no, and her father resettled into his chair.

Mary breathed a relieved sigh, since she was now playing emotional chicken with her beloved fiancé.

"SO WE MADE A DECISION. RIGHT, MARE? WE'RE TAKIN' HIM? RIGHT?"

Mary still wanted to hear from her mother. "Ma? Do you think we should take him?"

"*Si, si.*" Her mother reached for her napkin, lifted up her acetate glasses, and wiped underneath her eyes.

"Aw, Ma." Mary leaned over and rubbed her soft back, soft in the cotton housedress. "Thank you both for being so wonderful. I think it's the right decision. I really do."

"*Si,* yes." Her mother nodded, holding back her tears.

"IT'S DEFINITELY THE RIGHT DECISION, MARE. WHEN DO WE GET HIM?" her father asked, his hooded eyes lighting up behind his trifocals. "CAN WE GET HIM IN TIME FOR THE PARADE?"

"No, that's why I can't go to the parade, I'm sorry. I have to go to court to get him, tomorrow."

"WHAT KINDA COURT'S OPEN ON COLUMBUS DAY? THAT SHOULD BE ILLEGAL! IT'S A NATIONAL HOLI-DAY!"

"Family Court never closes," Mary told him, without elaborating. "If we win, I can get him by the end of the day."

"AW, YOU'LL WIN, MARE. YOU WANT US TO COME TO COURT? WE CAN TELL THE JUDGE WE'LL TAKE GOOD CARE OF HIM."

"No, that's okay, Pop. You drive in the parade. The Tonys are excited."

"SO WHEN'S COURT OVER? WE GOTTA GET READY FOR HIM. YOUR MOTHER'S GOTTA GO FOOD SHOPPIN'. I GOTTA GO TO THE TOY STORE."

"Hold on." Mary held up her hand, but her parents were already revivified. Her father's eyes danced behind his glasses, and her mother gave a little shiver of excitement in her housedress.

"LET'S GO TELL THE BOYS. THEY'RE DECORATIN' FEET'S CAR." Her father started to get up, but Mary put a hand on his forearm.

"Ma, Pop, there's one important thing we all have to agree on. We don't get to keep Patrick forever. Like I said, we're only getting him over the hump, with his grandfather dying and his new school. Someday we'll have to let him go, so he can be permanently adopted."

"*Si*, yes," her mother answered, with a sly smile.

Her father snorted. "MARE, WHO ARE *YOU* KIDDING?"

CHAPTER THIRTY-FIVE

Monday morning was clear and sunny, perfect weather for the Columbus Day Parade, and Mary felt happy for her father, The Tonys, and their decorated Pontiac, which looked like the Italian flag on wheels. Instead, she was walking down the street to the courthouse next to John, trying to ignore the butterflies in her stomach.

Mary glanced over at John, and everything about him looked reassuring. His perfectly clean glasses, his fresh shave, his dark reddish hair layered into place, and his lightweight gray striped suit, with a rep tie. She had never been a witness before, but she couldn't be any more prepared than she was, and she had on a conservative navy-blue suit with low heels, trying to look worthy of being somebody's guardian.

Mary held her head high, hoisting her purse and messenger bag on her shoulder as they passed Love Park, so named for the iconic sculpture by Robert Indiana that spelled LOVE in red letters. It felt too ironic, given what she was doing today. She knew it was the right thing to step up for Patrick, even if it would make Anthony unhappy. He hadn't called her or texted last night, and she hadn't called or texted him. She gathered that they were both tabling their LOVE, hopefully only for the time being.

THE FAMILY COURT OF PHILADELPHIA, read the metal letters over the glistening steel-and-glass monolith that anchored the corner of seventeenth and Arch Street. The new, modern building didn't look that different from the other skyscrapers except for a handful of children, at its entrance, oblivious to the fact that they were entering a courthouse, where the biggest decisions in their young lives would be made, with or without their consultation.

Mary walked past a man on the corner handing out flyers, and he thrust one into her hands, which she glanced at on the fly, not completely surprised that it was from a lawyer. It read, **Don't go to Family Court without a lawyer! I listen, I fight, I make them hear you! I am here for you, so call now! My office is only minutes away!**

"Come," John said, gesturing her to the left. "The attorneys' entrance is around the side."

"Thanks." Mary tossed the flyer into a wastebasket and they walked along the shiny façade of the building, then took a right into a smoked-glass entrance hall that had only a few lawyers in line behind a massive bank of metal detectors.

"You need your bar card and ID. They improved the security measures here. Did you know that Family Court judges are the most threatened judges in the city?"

"No." Mary dug in her wallet and showed her credentials to a uniformed sheriff, then they went through security, finding themselves in a lobby with gray-marble floors and walls, which ended in a black-marble wall that held the Family Court of Philadelphia emblem, flanked by the American flag and the cobalt-blue flag of the Commonwealth of Pennsylvania.

"The escalator is this way." John led the way, but Mary heard someone call her name and turned around. It was Machiavelli. His black hair was slicked back and he had on a dark suit, expensively tailored with a silk tie, and in his hand was a black leather briefcase.

"Mary!" he said, with a grin. "What are *you* doing here?"

Mary's mouth went dry. She didn't want Machiavelli to know why they were here. John was ahead of her but he paused, waiting. She prayed John didn't blow their cover. "I have a case."

"I didn't know you did family law."

"You don't know everything about me."

"Aw." Machiavelli mock-pouted, taking a step closer. "Are you mad at me because I'm deposing Up-Chucky?"

"I don't care enough about you to be mad at you. I have to go." Mary turned to leave, but Machiavelli took her arm.

"You can still settle. It's the only way to save Dennis the Menace from his deposition."

Mary tugged her arm from his hand. "I'm going to object to your deposing him."

"Of course you are, but we both know you're going to lose. Settle while you can, for only two hundred grand." Machiavelli shrugged with an ironic smile. "Yes, my demand went up. I'm punishing you for saying no. I hate that."

"I have to go." Mary turned away and hurried toward John.

"You'll be sorry!" Machiavelli called after her.

Mary caught up with John. "That was him."

"The alleged Machiavelli?" John scoffed, and they fell into step together. "I see that guy here. He's the only lawyer left in Creation who carries a briefcase."

Mary tried to smile but couldn't. "You don't think he knows why we're here, do you?"

"Nah." John led her to the escalator and they traveled upstairs. "The courthouse is only a year or two old, and it was designed with the judges' help. You know what that means. The open space is pretty but the noise is worse because the voices echo off the walls, and this escalator switches direction later in the afternoon, which is always impossible to remember."

Mary knew he was making small talk to calm her down. "Thanks for doing this. I really appreciate it."

"You're welcome. Don't worry." They traveled upward, passing a floor that held vending machines and round white tables with black chairs, which were beginning to fill up with children and their families, getting snacks and watching large-screen televisions mounted on the wall.

They rode up to one of the courtroom floors, and got off to find it buzzing with activity. Four courtrooms ringed the massive lobby, and mounted above the entrances were large flat-screen TVs in front of chairs fixed to the floor, almost like a movie theater. Almost every seat was filled with families talking, reading phones, or quieting children, who squirmed in the seats or wandered over to the floor-to-ceiling glass window, pressing their hands to its surface. Court personnel circulated among the crowd, easy to spot in their blue logo polo shirts and red lanyards, and lawyers conferred with clients, standing out because they were in suits.

"Look, there's Abby and Susan." John led her down the center aisle, and Mary noticed that other women lawyers were checking John out, flashing him smiles and giving him friendly waves.

Mary realized that John was evidently quite the hit with the women, though he hadn't shared more about his personal life yesterday, so she didn't know if he had a girlfriend, though everybody at the office speculated he had a crush on Anne.

John reached Abby and Susan at the closed entrance to the courtroom. "Abby, Susan, thanks for coming," he said, shaking their hands, and they greeted each other.

"Hi, Mary! Hi, John!" Abby beamed, looking fresh in a print dress, still overburdened with bags.

"Hi, everyone. Nice to meet you in person, Mary." Susan smiled, elegant in a tan linen pantsuit with a silk paisley scarf.

"You too. Thanks for the help."

"Don't worry, we got this." Susan smiled.

"Hope so." Mary didn't say that Patrick's future hung in the balance. She told herself to stay calm and she put Machiavelli out of her mind.

It was showtime.

CHAPTER THIRTY-SIX

Mary took a seat at counsel table next to Abby and John, unaccustomed to sitting in the third chair like a client instead of first chair like a lawyer. She eyed opposing counsel, Assistant City Solicitor Hannah Chan-Willig, who sat reading her notes at counsel table. Chan-Willig was a ponytailed Asian woman, dressed in black statement-glasses and a suit with a bold black-and-white geometric pattern.

Mary glanced around the courtroom, noting that Olivia Solo from DHS hadn't arrived yet. The courtroom contained no gallery, since juvenile proceedings were confidential, and Susan sat behind counsel table, reading her phone. On the left side of the courtroom was a panel of windows, sending indirect light on a blue-patterned rug, and at the front stood a sleek wooden dais, flanked by a witness box on the left, and on the right, a desk for the administrative clerk, a heavyset man tapping away on a computer.

A phone rang on the clerk's desk, and he answered it, then hung up and rose, signaling that court was about to begin. John, Abby, and Mary stood up, as did Hannah Chan-Willig, and about the same time, the door opened in the back of the courtroom. Mary turned around to see Olivia entering, with her overly made-up face, long ponytail, and a black dress that was too tight, and she was with two middle-aged men; one was tall and well-built with trimmed, dark hair, a nice suit, and an authoritative air, and the other was shorter, an odd-looking man in a boxy suit with flyaway graying hair, carrying a thick red accordion file.

Mary had no clue who the men were, but she hoped they weren't witnesses because a surprise witness was never a good thing. If this had been a trial in Common Pleas or federal court, there would've been rules that prevented testimony by surprise witnesses, but there were no such rules for emergency shelter care hearings in Family Court. She remembered that John had told her that random people came to shelter care hearings, so maybe it was Olivia's boss or another higher-up at DHS. Mary didn't have time to ask John or Abby because the courtroom deputy was already rising.

"All rise for the Honorable Judge William R. Green. This Honorable Court is now in session!"

A pocket door opened, and Judge Green entered the courtroom. He was a short, African-American man who looked to be in his fifties, with warm brown eyes, chubby cheeks, and grayish patches throughout his short hair. He swept up the dais and looked around with a relaxed smile. "Good morning, people. Please, sit down, and let's get started. This is a shelter care hearing in the matter of P.O.B."

Everyone sat down except for Chan-Willig. "Your Honor, may it please the court, my name is Hannah Chan-Willig and I am here representing the Department of Human Services, DHS. I'd like to call my first witness, Detective Joseph Randolph."

Judge Green nodded. "Proceed, Ms. Chan-Willig. Detective Randolph, please come forward."

Mary looked over as the tall, authoritative man stood up, smoothed his striped tie, and strode to the stand, but she couldn't understand what was going on. She hadn't anticipated a detective being called as a witness, neither had Abby or John. She assumed it was in connection with the gun and she prayed that DHS wasn't considering weapons charges against Patrick. She couldn't catch Abby or John's attention because they were both turned away, watching the detective be sworn in and sit down in the witness box.

Chan-Willig stood in front of the witness stand. "Detective Randolph, would you please identify yourself for the court?"

"I'm Detective Joseph Randolph, and I've been assigned to the

Roundhouse, Philadelphia Police Headquarters, Sixth & Arch Streets, for the past twelve years." Detective Randolph gazed directly at Chan-Willig, his eyes brown and set close together. "Before that I was a uniformed patrol officer with the Philadelphia Police Department."

"Detective Randolph, have you ever testified in a shelter care hearing before?"

"No, I have not."

"Detective Randolph, do you understand that the purpose of a shelter care hearing is to determine the guardianship of Patrick O'Brien, a ten-year-old boy who is presently in DHS custody?"

"Yes, I do understand that."

Mary's mind raced, watching from counsel table. She couldn't imagine what Detective Randolph was going to testify about, but she was getting more and more worried. Still there was no basis to object to any of the questioning so far, and she could see that Judge Green was listening intently on the stand.

Chan-Willig stood straighter. "Detective Randolph, did there come a time when you were contacted in connection with this matter?"

"Yes."

"And who was it who contacted you in connection with this matter?"

"Dr. Amit Chopra contacted me last night at approximately 9:15 P.M. Dr. Chopra is one of the assistant medical examiners for the City of Philadelphia. He called me at night because he had to leave for a conference this morning and wanted to reach me before he left."

"Detective Randolph, why did Dr. Chopra contact you?"

"Dr. Chopra contacted me to tell me that the manner of Edward O'Brien's death is considered suspicious and that Patrick should be investigated as involved in his death."

Mary almost gasped, shocked to her very foundations. She couldn't believe what had just happened. It was a bombshell that would explode their case. There must have been some mistake. Edward's death wasn't suspicious. Patrick had nothing to do with his death. Edward had died in his sleep, and Patrick loved Edward. Patrick never would've done anything to hurt Edward, ever.

"Objection, Your Honor!" Abby and John said in unison, jumping to their feet.

Chan-Willig turned to Judge Green. "Your Honor, the question before this Court is whether DHS should retain physical custody of Patrick. There is absolutely no question that DHS should, given that the child may have been involved in the suspicious death of his grandfather. There is no possible reason for an objection."

Abby faced Judge Green, flustered. "Your Honor, uh, we were given no notice of this witness or this fact. I'm the Child Advocate of Patrick O'Brien and I should've been told about this."

John added, "Judge Green, my name is John Foxman and I represent Mary DiNunzio, who seeks guardianship of Patrick. We were not given notice of his witness, either. We object to the relevance and reliability of this testimony. What Dr. Chopra told the witness is rank hearsay."

"My goodness." Judge Green shook his head. "I've never before had a shelter care hearing in which the child involved was suspected of murder." He turned to Abby. "Ms. Ortega, I'm going to deny your objection. You know that notice procedures are more informal in shelter care proceedings, especially emergency proceedings. Please take your seat."

"Thank you, Your Honor." Abby wilted into her chair, glancing over at Mary, who met her gaze with equal shock. They both knew that Detective Randolph's testimony could be devastating to their case. Mary felt a bolt of fear that she was going to lose Patrick.

Judge Green turned to John. "Mr. Foxman, I decline to rule on your objection, since you have no standing to object to any testimony in this proceeding. I am aware that you filed papers on Ms. DiNunzio's behalf and I did review them before I came on the bench. However, the Child Advocate is usually lead attorney in these matters, and Ms. Ortega is capable of handling any objections."

John stood tall. "Thank you, Your Honor. But if it pleases the Court, Ms. Ortega and I have decided that because I am more familiar with the facts of Ms. DiNunzio's case, I will take the lead in presenting Ms. DiNunzio's case."

"That's not our procedure, Mr. Foxman, but at this moment, we have bigger fish to fry. As I have said, the procedural rules are informal in shelter care hearings, so I suppose if that's the way you and Ms. Ortega want to proceed, I'll grant your request. But I deny your objection for relevance and for hearsay. Our evidentiary rules are more relaxed in these proceedings, as well. Please sit down." Judge Green turned to Chan-Willig. "Ms. Chan-Willig, continue your questioning."

Chan-Willig faced the witness stand, where Detective Randolph sat unflustered. "Detective Randolph, what did Dr. Chopra tell you about his suspicions regarding the death of the grandfather Edward O'Brien?"

John rose. "Your Honor, I have a continuing objection to hearsay, for the record."

Judge Green frowned. "Mr. Foxman, please don't make me sorry that I agreed to this procedure. I'm going to deny your hearsay objection again, considering that the only cure would be bringing in Dr. Chopra himself to testify. That would turn a shelter care hearing into a murder trial, and I will not allow that."

"Thank you, Your Honor." John sat down, and Mary held her breath waiting for Detective Randolph's answer. She was still trying to get over the fact that they had said the word *murder* in connection with Edward's death. The word had a gravity all its own.

Chan-Willig said, "Detective Randolph, you may answer."

Detective Randolph looked at Judge Green. "Your Honor, before I do, I assume my testimony today is confidential, since it involves an ongoing police investigation."

Judge Green nodded. "Yes, Detective, these proceedings are non-public, and the records are sealed to protect the confidentiality of the minors involved."

"Thank you." Detective Randolph returned his attention to Chan-Willig. "Dr. Chopra performed the autopsy on Edward O'Brien and determined that Edward O'Brien had type 2 diabetes and that the cause of his death was hypoglycemia caused by an overdose of insulin, which eventually caused death. In addition, Dr. Chopra informed me that Mr. O'Brien most often injected himself in the abdomen, revealed by a physical examination of the body. However, Dr. Chopra observed that the most recent needlemark for insulin injection, that is, the injection that caused the death, had a point of entry on Mr. O'Brien's right arm, and Mr. O'Brien had never injected himself there previously. That raised the question in Dr. Chopra's mind that someone else had injected Edward O'Brien with insulin, causing his death."

Chan-Willig asked, "Detective Randolph, what does the fact that the site hadn't been previously used for insulin injection have to do with Patrick?"

"I'm in the preliminary stage of my investigation, but I have learned that Patrick was familiar with his grandfather's diabetes and his grandfather's routines regarding checking his blood sugar and injecting himself with insulin. Patrick also injected his grandfather with insulin from time to time, at his grandfather's request."

"Objection!" Mary found herself on her feet. "Your Honor, if Patrick injected Edward that night, he didn't know it would harm his grandfather. There must have been some mistake, maybe Edward forgot he had already injected himself and asked Patrick—"

"Ms. DiNunzio!" Judge Green snapped his head around to face Mary, his dark eyes flaring. "Sit down. You're out of order. I'll entertain objections from Mr. Foxman but that's as far as I'll go."

"Yes, Your Honor." Mary sat down, agitated. She looked over at John, who shot her a warning glance. She could see the strain in his expression and read his mind. They both knew their case was in real trouble.

Judge Green straightened in his tall chair, then swiveled to face Chan-Willig. "Please proceed with your line of questioning."

"Thank you, Your Honor." Chan-Willig turned back to the witness. "Detective Randolph, let's back up a minute. Is it your understanding that Patrick lived alone with his grandfather, Edward O'Brien?"

"Yes. Their residence was a house at 637 Moretone Street."

"Detective Randolph, is it also your understanding that prior to his death, Edward O'Brien was Patrick's sole caretaker?"

"Yes, that is my understanding."

"Detective Randolph, do you know when Edward O'Brien passed away?"

"Dr. Chopra had difficulty determining time of death because there was such a significant delay in notifying police of the death. In addition, Dr. Chopra tells me that death from hypoglycemia can take several hours. His tentative finding is that the last insulin injection was given at about eleven o'clock on the night of October 8, last Thursday. Dr. Chopra tentatively places the time of death as anywhere between the hours of five o'clock in the morning and nine o'clock in the morning on Friday, October 9."

"Detective Randolph, what did Dr. Chopra tell you about the status of his investigation?"

"Dr. Chopra told me that it was in its preliminary stages. He had finished his physical examination of the body, but he hadn't filed an autopsy report yet. He called me to let me know that, at the present time, the manner of Edward O'Brien's death was suspicious."

"Detective Randolph, upon hearing that information, what did you do?"

"I began my own investigation."

"Detective Randolph, what is the status of your investigation at this point?"

"It's very preliminary, too. That's what I wanted to explain to the court." Detective Randolph looked over at Judge Green. "Your Honor, I only received this call from Dr. Chopra late last night. Dr. Chopra would be here himself, if he hadn't had a previous commitment with the conference. This is not a murder case yet because Dr. Chopra has not officially determined that the manner of death was homicide. As you know, cause and manner of death are two different things."

Judge Green shook his head, his expression grim. "No, I wasn't aware of the difference. Please elaborate briefly, Detective Randolph. This is out of my wheelhouse."

Detective Randolph nodded. "Your Honor, the cause of death is the way a person died, which in Edward O'Brien's case was hypoglycemia. The manner of death is whether that death occurred by natural causes, accidental death, suicide, or homicide. Dr. Chopra has not yet determined that the manner of Edward O'Brien's death was a homicide. Dr. Chopra is waiting to file his official report and release the body until he consults with the Chief Medical Examiner, who is away on vacation for another week. Dr. Chopra called me to give me the heads-up, and I called DHS. That's when I learned that Patrick was in the Einstein Crisis Center and that this shelter care hearing was being held today. Then I called Assistant City Solicitor Ms. Chan-Willig, who asked me to testify. She also asked me if Dr. Chopra could testify, but he had already left for the conference."

Judge Green nodded. "Now I understand. Thank you."

Chan-Willig faced the witness stand. "Detective Randolph, did you interview Patrick in this case?"

"No, I have not."

Mary blinked, surprised. She had no idea how Detective Randolph learned that Patrick sometimes injected Edward with insulin. John glanced over, and she could see that he was surprised, too. Either way, she feared that their case was circling the drain.

Chan-Willig asked, "Detective Randolph, how did you discover that Patrick knew how to inject his grandfather with insulin and did so sometimes?"

"I learned that from Cassandra Porter of the Philadelphia Children's Alliance. She conducted a forensic interview of Patrick the day before Edward O'Brien died. She told me that Patrick told her that one of the ways in which he helped his grandfather was that he injected him with insulin when his hand was unsteady."

Mary took the news like a body blow. She tried to piece together what must have gone on behind the scenes. After Detective Randolph had spoken to DHS, DHS would have put him in contact with Cassandra. Cassandra would have had to cooperate with law enforcement, but Mary hoped that Cassandra had also told the detective that Patrick loved Edward and never would've hurt him intentionally.

Chan-Willig continued her questioning, "Detective Randolph, would you tell the court your theory of how Edward O'Brien died?"

Detective Randolph nodded. "It's too early to have a final theory of the case, but I'm investigating whether Patrick injected his grandfather with insulin, causing his death."

"Detective Randolph, do you have a theory, final or otherwise, about a motive that Patrick would have for intentionally injecting his grandfather with a lethal dose of insulin?"

Mary felt like objecting, but didn't dare. She looked over, but John's attention was riveted on the witness, as was Abby's.

Detective Randolph nodded. "Yes."

Chan-Willig stood tall. "Detective Randolph, what is your theory as regards to Patrick's motive?"

"That Patrick suffered physical and sexual abuse at the hands of his grandfather, which would provide motive."

Mary felt as if the wind had been knocked out of her. She couldn't imagine where Detective Randolph had gotten his theory of motive. Edward never would have abused Patrick. It couldn't have come from Cassandra. Robertson was the one who had abused Patrick, and Cassandra had known that. Mary felt utterly dumbfounded.

"Objection!" John leapt to his feet. "Your Honor, this is inadmissible. There are no facts in evidence to support this testimony, and even though procedural rules are informal in shelter care hearings, this is beyond the pale. It's plainly unreliable and speculative."

Chan-Willig turned to the judge. "Your Honor, it's insulting that Mr. Foxman would call Detective Randolph unreliable in any way. You have heard his years of expertise and service in law enforcement. Detective Randolph is more than qualified to explain to the Court his theory of motive in this case, even though it is in its formative stages."

Judge Green folded his arms, his mouth set grimly. "The objection is denied. Counsel, both of you, sit down. I will not allow this proceeding to get out of hand."

"Thank you, Your Honor." John sat down, as did Chan-Willig.

Judge Green glowered at John. "Mr. Foxman, we're not trying

to determine beyond a reasonable doubt whether Patrick is guilty of the murder of his grandfather. We're merely trying to determine where Patrick should live, and the standard for that is far lower. Detective Randolph's testimony is probative and extremely helpful to the Court in making that determination. In addition, I'm aware that his testimony comes as a surprise to you, but I'll advise you to limit your objections. I've had more objections today than I have all year. Are we clear, Mr. Foxman?"

"Yes, Your Honor." John nodded, and Mary tried to piece together her thoughts. Patrick's forensic interview with Cassandra was confidential, but not from law enforcement. Detective Randolph's theory of the case and the new suspicions about Edward's death pointed to Patrick's guilt, which was just plain wrong.

Judge Green sighed, his impatience plain. "Ms. Chan-Willig, please wrap this up. I have your point."

"Thank you, Your Honor." Chan-Willig faced Detective Randolph. "Detective Randolph, what have you done to further your investigation of Edward O'Brien's death?"

"I went to the residence on Moretone Street and conducted a walk-through myself, last night at about ten o'clock. I declared it a crime scene, established a perimeter, and called a mobile tech team to collect trace evidence, typically hair, fibers, and fingerprints. They arrived shortly thereafter."

"Detective Randolph, what has your or their investigation revealed that might be of interest to this Court?"

"As I testified, my investigation is in a preliminary stage, but we found a used syringe of insulin in the wastebasket of Edward O'Brien's bedroom, where his body was found in bed, it had a child's fingerprints."

"Detective Randolph, did you draw any relevant conclusion regarding the syringe used to inject Edward O'Brien for the last time, the lethal dose of insulin?"

"Yes. The fingerprints on the syringe match the child's fingerprints we also found in Patrick's bedroom, so we tentatively believe that the fingerprints on the syringe used last are Patrick's fingerprints."

Chan-Willig paused to let the testimony sink in. "Detective Randolph, moving on, what are the problems that you or Dr. Chopra are encountering in your investigation?"

"Yes, Edward O'Brien's death was reported by Ms. DiNunzio, who called 911 at around nine o'clock on Friday night, October 9. However, as I testified, there was a significant delay between the time of death and the time of report. Dr. Chopra told me that the delay between the time of death and the notification to police impedes his forensic investigation." Detective Randolph turned to Judge Green. "I'm no pathologist, so I won't speak to that in detail. For my part, the delay in reporting the death impedes my investigation because of the possibility of contamination of the crime scene."

Mary tried to remain composed, realizing the facts made Patrick look guilty when he wasn't. She was the only one who knew that Patrick had been in denial that Edward had died, not because Patrick had killed him but because he loved him so much. She wracked her brain for a way to counteract it when they put on their case, other than her testimony. She thought of calling Cassandra as a witness, but Cassandra was now in touch with Detective Randolph, so she couldn't testify for Patrick.

"Detective Randolph, was there any problem with contamination of the crime scene that you encountered in your investigation?"

"Yes, numerous problems. Specifically, the search for other trace evidence in the bedroom where Edward died has been impeded because someone cleaned up the scene. Edward's bedsheets had been washed and set folded on the bed, the top of his dresser was clear, and his night table had been swept clean, though we found the most recent syringe discarded in the wastebasket."

"Detective Randolph, do you have a theory as to who cleaned up Edward's bedroom?"

Detective Randolph glanced at Mary. "It's my understanding that Mary DiNunzio was the only one in the house with Patrick. We assume she is the one who cleaned it up. We do not currently know when she arrived at the house."

Mary kept her face rigidly forward and her expression impassive.

The testimony made it look as if she covered up Edward's death after the fact. When she took the stand, she would just have to explain that she hadn't done it to hide evidence of a murder, because there had been no murder. Patrick hadn't killed Edward, at least not on purpose. Maybe Edward had forgotten that he'd already injected himself and asked Patrick to inject him before bedtime. Mary couldn't explain why the needlemark was in a different location and she would have to ask Patrick why he did that. But he wasn't a killer.

"Detective Randolph, why wasn't the house declared a crime scene that very night when you were called, so that evidence wasn't lost or destroyed?"

"Ms. DiNunzio reported it as a natural death, which was confirmed by the assistant medical examiner on the scene because of the circumstances, a seventy-two-year-old man in ill health who had died in his sleep. It wasn't until the autopsy that the stray needlemark was found."

"Detective Randolph, given the information that you have at this point, have you formed an opinion as to Patrick's dangerousness that may be helpful to the Court in deciding where to place him?"

"Yes, I have an opinion as to Patrick's dangerousness."

"Detective Randolph, what is your opinion?"

"My opinion is that Patrick may have been involved in the death of his grandfather and is dangerous."

"Thank you, I have no further questions."

Judge Green swiveled his head to John, with a frown. "Mr. Foxman, any cross-examination?"

"Yes, Your Honor," John answered, standing up.

Mary prayed he'd repair the damage, but she had no idea how.

CHAPTER THIRTY-SEVEN

John stood a respectful distance from the witness stand. "Detective Randolph, you testified that your investigation is barely in the preliminary stages, isn't that correct?"

"Yes, that's correct."

"In fact, your investigation is only hours old, isn't that correct?"

"Yes."

"Detective Randolph, isn't it also true that it's not even a murder investigation yet, because there is officially no murder?"

"Yes, that's true."

"So it's a murder investigation without a murder?"

"Well, yes." Detective Randolph half-smiled.

"Detective Randolph, so isn't it fair to say that your theory isn't something you'd want to stake your reputation on, is it?"

"Yes, I absolutely wouldn't stake my reputation on it."

"Detective Randolph, isn't it true that as you learn new facts, your theory of the case may change?"

"Yes, that's true."

"For example, Detective Randolph, let's assume that Patrick injected his grandfather that night, but did so at his grandfather's request and with absolutely no intent to harm his grandfather. That's possible, isn't it?"

"Yes, that's possible."

"In fact, that's completely possible, isn't it?"

"Yes, that's completely possible."

"And Detective Randolph, if that were the case, wouldn't the manner of death be considered accidental, not homicide?"

"Yes, that's true."

"And Detective Randolph, isn't it also true that if that were the case, there would be no reason to believe that Patrick was dangerous, in terms of his custodial placement?"

"Yes, that's true, too," Detective Randolph admitted.

"Detective Randolph, if you were to find out that Patrick injected his grandfather at his grandfather's request and with no intent to harm him, you would have no opinion at all as to Patrick's custodial placement, would you?"

"True."

"Detective Randolph, you have testified about Patrick's alleged dangerousness, but you have never met Patrick, have you?"

"No, I have not."

"Detective Randolph, have you ever before given an opinion, in any court, about an adult or child without ever having met them?"

"No," Detective Randolph admitted, after a moment.

Watching, Mary thought that John was scoring some points, but Judge Green's expression remained stone-faced as he watched the testimony. There wasn't much else John could do to undermine Detective Randolph's testimony, but she knew he would try with all his might.

"Detective Randolph, isn't it true that you first learned that Patrick was the victim of alleged abuse when you spoke with Cassandra Porter at the Philadelphia Children's Alliance?"

"Yes."

"Detective Randolph, isn't it true that it was Patrick's grandfather and Ms. DiNunzio who took Patrick to the Philadelphia Children's Alliance to investigate his allegations of abuse?"

"Yes."

"Detective Randolph, isn't it true that Cassandra Porter told you that Patrick had never accused his grandfather of physical and sexual abuse?"

"Yes."

"Detective Randolph, isn't it also true that Cassandra Porter told you that Patrick made abuse allegations against someone other than Edward O'Brien?"

"Yes, that's true."

"So Detective Randolph, isn't it a fact that the basis for your assumption that Patrick was abused by his grandfather is merely the disbelief of his allegations that someone else abused him?"

Detective Randolph paused, frowning. "Yes, that is true. Cassandra told me that Patrick said that a teacher's aide abused him, but I began to question whether it was really his grandfather who abused him and he blamed it on the teacher's aide."

"Exactly my point." John squared his shoulders. "You have no facts on which to base a belief that Patrick was abused by his grandfather, isn't that correct?"

"Yes. At this point, that is correct."

"I have no further questions."

Judge Green said to Detective Randolph, "Thank you for your testimony. You may step down."

"Thank you." Detective Randolph stood up. "Your Honor, I assume I may leave the courtroom?"

"Yes, of course. Thank you for your time."

John returned to counsel table and sat down, as Mary wrote him a note, WELL DONE. He smiled, but they both knew that the testimony was so damaging they would have to fight extra hard to recover, if they even had a chance.

Chan-Willig was already on her feet, facing Judge Green. "Your Honor, may I call my next witness? I'd like to call Olivia Solo of DHS, Your Honor."

"Certainly." Judge Green nodded.

Mary sat back, bracing herself.

CHAPTER THIRTY-EIGHT

Mary watched with dread as Olivia was sworn in and sat down in the witness stand. She could feel John tense beside her, and Abby looked equally worried, biting her lip. Abby had told Mary that DHS was the heavyweight in a shelter care hearing, and Olivia's testimony would only reinforce Detective Randolph's.

Chan-Willig stood closer to the witness stand. "Ms. Solo, please tell the Court where you work."

"I'm a caseworker at Department of Human Services, DHS."

"How long have you worked at DHS?"

"Since I got out of college, so almost ten years."

"Ms. Solo, did there come a time when you met Patrick O'Brien?"

"Yes, on October 10. I was called to the house the morning after his grandfather died. I went to pick him up because I had arranged placement for him with one of the families on our emergency fosters list."

"Ms. Solo, what happened when you went to the house that morning?"

"I had a conversation in the living room with Ms. DiNunzio and I could see that Patrick was manipulating Ms. DiNunzio, so I asked her to come with me in the kitchen for a private conversation. There, I told Ms. DiNunzio that she was undermining my efforts to take Patrick into DHS custody and I told her that I would ask her to leave the premises if she would not cooperate."

Chan-Willig frowned. "So it is your testimony that Ms. DiNunzio was not cooperating with DHS's efforts?"

"Yes, that is exactly my testimony." Olivia shot Mary an unabashedly angry look, but Mary masked her reaction, which was vaguely homicidal.

Chan-Willig asked, "Ms. Solo, would you please tell the Court what happened when you and Ms. DiNunzio left the kitchen?"

Olivia readjusted to look up at the judge. "We came out of the kitchen and all of a sudden Patrick threatened to shoot us with a gun."

"A gun?" Judge Green blurted out, recoiling. "Did you say, a gun?"

"Yes, Your Honor," Olivia answered, indignant.

"But he's ten years old!"

"Just the same, he's very dangerous, Your Honor."

"Objection, Your Honor." John half-rose. "The testimony mischaracterizes what happened. Patrick didn't threaten them—"

"What?" Chan-Willig shook her head. "Your Honor, there's no basis for an objection. Mr. Foxman wasn't present. Patrick *did* threaten them. The witness was there. She can so testify."

Judge Green silenced the lawyers with a wave, focusing on Olivia. "Ms. Solo, where did the boy get the gun?"

Olivia answered, "It was in the home, Your Honor. It's in police custody at the present time. I took it and gave it to the police. They told me it was a .45 caliber pistol, a Colt semiautomatic from the Army. They said it was used during Vietnam, but it was in working order even though it was old."

"Mr. Foxman." Judge Green frowned, turning to John. "Do you dispute that Patrick threatened the DHS caseworker with a semiautomatic weapon?"

"Your Honor, Ms. DiNunzio was present, too, and she will testify that she did not feel threatened and the circumstances are not what Ms. Solo is describing—"

"Yes or no?" Judge Green frowned more deeply. "Do you dispute that Patrick pulled a gun on Ms. Solo and Ms. DiNunzio?"

"No." John had to answer.

"Please sit down, Mr. Foxman."

Mary felt her gut churn. She could see Judge Green's expression harden. Detective Randolph's theory that Patrick was guilty of murder seemed more reasonable than before. The case was slipping through their fingers, and so was Patrick.

Judge Green turned to the Assistant City Solicitor. "Ms. Chan-Willig, please continue with your questioning."

"Thank you, Your Honor." Chan-Willig turned to Olivia. "Ms. Solo, please continue telling the Court exactly what happened that morning, in detail."

Olivia nodded. "So we came out of the kitchen and there was Patrick, aiming the gun at us. By the way, he was aiming it more at me, not at Ms. DiNunzio, and he yelled at the top of his lungs, 'I'm not going anywhere with you!' so he was clearly talking to me. He was *threatening* me."

"Ms. Solo, can you describe for the court your state of mind at that time?"

"I have never in my life been so terrified." Olivia's eyes flew open in fear, and even Mary felt that it was genuine. "I have seen some rough-and-tumble things on this job but I have *never* been threatened with a gun pointed *right* at my chest. I was absolutely terrified to my very *soul*. I thought I was going to *die*. I prayed to God to let me live."

Chan-Willig paused, giving the testimony some hang time. "Ms. Solo, what did you do next?"

"I ran into the kitchen and called 911 and they told me what to do. Then Mary called me to come into the living room and said she had gotten the gun, so I picked the gun off the table and I ran out to the police and I gave it to them. My heart was beating out of my chest practically, and I swear to God, it didn't stop until, like, an hour later."

Mary watched Judge Green's reaction, his lips were pressed together, his disapproval obvious. She had lost cases before and seen judges look just like him. Their expression went from I'm-Listening to I've-Decided to Why-Are-You-Wasting-My-Time.

Chan-Willig asked, "Ms. Solo, what is your opinion about Patrick's dangerousness?"

"So I think it's obvious. I was in that room, I had a gun pointed at me, and I'm not going to make excuses for him, like Ms. DiNunzio." Olivia looked over at Judge Green. "Judge, this is a very dangerous little boy we're talking about and I think he would've shot me dead without a second thought. Ms. DiNunzio is in total denial about how dangerous he is, and he should stay in DHS custody because his anger issues are out of control. If you award temporary guardianship to Ms. DiNunzio, I think you would be making a very big mistake and I think you would come to regret it."

Chan-Willig continued, "Ms. Solo, have you seen any further evidence of his dangerousness during the emergency foster placement?"

"Absolutely. Because of the gun, we placed Patrick at Einstein Crisis Center, and he got into a fight within the first hour."

"With whom did he fight?"

"With another foster child, just because the other child wanted to see some belongings of his."

Mary simmered but didn't say anything, and John didn't object because it wasn't objectionable, just wrong.

Chan-Willig continued. "Ms. Solo, let me ask you, did you form an impression of Patrick when you first met him?"

"Yes." Olivia's lined lips set firmly together. "I got the impression that he was very used to getting what he wants and he becomes angry, aggressive, and violent when he doesn't get it."

"Ms. Solo, what were the facts that informed your opinion that Patrick had anger issues, even before he pulled a gun on you?"

"He told me from the beginning that he wanted to stay with Ms. DiNunzio and that he wasn't about to come with me. He refused to come with me and refused to leave the house. He does just what he pleases and only what he pleases."

"Ms. Solo, do you have a belief about why he wants to live with Ms. DiNunzio?"

"Yes, I doubt very much that he's so bonded to her, though that may be what she wants to believe." Olivia lifted an eyebrow. "He was certainly very excited about riding around in her fancy car and living at her fancy house, which he knew all about. He even told me later that she's going to put him into private school, which is supposedly better than public school. He's a manipulative child and he has completely manipulated Ms. DiNunzio."

Mary listened, incredulous, wondering how Olivia could have such a warped view of Patrick. John didn't object, since there was nothing legally objectionable. The testimony revealed more about Olivia's psychological problems than Patrick's, and Mary reflected that human beings became damaged in more ways than one. But Judge Green seemed to be taking it in, leaning on his hand.

Suddenly Mary got an idea. She slid the pad over and wrote to John. *The gun wasn't loaded. If it had been, she would've said so.*

Chan-Willig stepped away. "Your Honor, I have no further questions for Ms. Solo."

Judge Green looked over at John, who was already rising. "You have cross-examination, Mr. Foxman?"

"Just briefly, Your Honor." John approached the witness stand. "Ms. Solo, the gun that we have heard so much about wasn't loaded, was it?"

Olivia hesitated. "No, but I thought it was."

"Ms. Solo, I'm not asking you what you thought, I am asking you what is true. The gun that Patrick pointed at you was not loaded, was it?"

"No, it wasn't."

"And isn't it also true that because the gun was not loaded, you were never in any danger?"

Olivia hesitated again. "Yes."

"I have no further questions, Your Honor." John turned around, came back to counsel table, and sat down, and Mary couldn't help but think that it hadn't made much difference.

Judge Green turned to Olivia. "Ms. Solo, thank you for your testimony. You may step down."

"Thank you, Your Honor." Olivia left the witness stand and returned to her seat, and Judge Green leaned back in his tall leather chair, with a heavy sigh.

Chan-Willig rose. "Your Honor, may I call my next witness?"

"Yes, proceed." Judge Green nodded, and Mary turned to see

the odd-looking middle-aged man who had entered with Detective Randolph stand up and head toward the witness box.

Chan-Willig said, "Your Honor, I call Lawrence Harris, *guardian ad litem,* to the stand."

Mary's mouth dropped open. She had no idea what was going on. There was no *guardian ad litem* in this matter. She didn't know what Chan-Willig was talking about or where Harris had come from.

"Your Honor." John rose. "I was unaware that a *guardian ad litem,* a GAL, was appointed in this case. Mr. Harris didn't contact us or the Child Advocate, Abby Ortega."

Abby rose, too. "Your Honor, I agree with Mr. Foxman. I was never contacted by Lawrence Harris."

Judge Green frowned. "Counsel, a GAL need not coordinate his efforts with the Child Advocacy Center, though admittedly, that would have been preferable. I understand that Mr. Harris called my chambers and volunteered his services. His name was next on the list. You may know that the GAL list is posted online."

John said, "Yes, that's how we contacted the Child Advocate, but there is no need for a GAL in this matter."

Chan-Willig interjected, "Your Honor, evidently there is, since Mr. Harris is here to testify that Patrick is dangerous and should not be removed from DHS custody."

John frowned. "Your Honor, Abby interviewed Patrick this weekend and so did child psychologist, Dr. Susan Bernardi. Both are here today to recommend to the Court that Ms. DiNunzio be awarded guardianship."

Chan-Willig shook her head. "Your Honor, Mr. Harris interviewed the child, too."

"Please sit down, counsel. Both of you." Judge Green waved John into his seat. "We're wasting time. Mr. Harris has been before this Court many times and he's certainly qualified as GAL. I would like to hear his testimony."

Mary felt like crying. Their case had barely recovered from Detective Randolph's and Olivia's testimony, only to get hit again, out of the blue. And this time, she sensed she was seeing Machiavelli's handiwork, judging from the call to the judge's chambers. Machiavelli must have heard that Edward had died and found out about her going for guardianship, so Machiavelli must have done the same thing that she and John had—contacted the next lawyer on the GAL list, alerted him to Patrick's case, and suggested that he step forward. But Machiavelli would have told him what to say, too.

"Thank you, Your Honor." John sat down.

Judge Green motioned to Chan-Willig. "Ms. Chan-Willig, please have Mr. Harris come forward."

Suddenly Mary realized that her running into Machiavelli in the lobby was no chance encounter. He must have planned the whole thing. She doubted now that he even had a case in Family Court today.

She slumped in her chair, temporarily defeated.

CHAPTER THIRTY-NINE

Mary watched with dismay as Harris crossed to the witness stand, was sworn in, and sat down. He was such an odd bird, with oily graying hair and a mismatched suit that looked vaguely dirty. He kept pressing his eyeglasses up his greasy nose, almost like a tic, and he didn't make eye contact with anyone.

John picked up the pen, pulled over the legal pad, and wrote: *There are great lawyers on the GAL list—and also those who need the work. Harris is the latter, obv.* Mary nodded discreetly, wondering if Machiavelli was paying Harris.

Chan-Willig straightened up, facing the stand. "Mr. Harris, how long have you been on the active list of the GAL?"

"Twelve years."

"So is it fair to say you're experienced?"

"Yes." Harris moved his glasses up again.

"And Mr. Harris, during your twelve years of service on the active list, approximately how many children in foster care do you think you have interviewed?"

Judge Green gestured impatiently. "Ms. Chan-Willig, in the interest of saving time, please cut to the chase."

"Yes, Your Honor." Chan-Willig nodded. "Mr. Harris, please tell the Court when you visited Patrick at the Einstein Crisis Center."

"Sunday morning around ten o'clock."

"Did you have the opportunity to interview the child?"

"Yes."

"Mr. Harris, was Patrick alone or was anyone else present?"

"He was alone. He told me that he wants to be left alone."

Chan-Willig nodded. "Mr. Harris, could you please tell the Court what you observed at that time?"

"I observed that Patrick was withdrawn, hostile, and has major anger issues."

John half-rose. "Objection, your Honor. The witness is not qualified to give an expert psychological opinion."

Chan-Willig faced the judge. "Your Honor, the witness is not testifying in any psychological capacity. A layperson can observe how children act when they're angry and there's no basis for this objection."

Judge Green nodded. "I'll overrule the objection, but let me see if I can save us some time." He turned to Mr. Harris. "Sir, what is the testimony that you felt was important enough for this Court to hear, with regard to Patrick's custody?"

Harris cleared his throat. "Your Honor, as GAL, my concern is what is best for the child and what is in his legal interests. I am here to inform the Court that Ms. DiNunzio should not be awarded guardianship because it is my finding that this child is far more disturbed and dangerous than Ms. DiNunzio understands. I agree with Detective Randolph and Ms. Solo that Patrick should remain in DHS custody."

Mary listened, her heart sinking through the floor. Abby had taught her that GALs were accorded weight by the court, so now they would have the battle of the GALs, and even that wouldn't be enough to save their case. Patrick would be forced to stay in residential care with hard-to-place kids, and Mary could only imagine how that would affect him, in his already fragile state.

Chan-Willig asked, "Mr. Harris, what are the facts on which you base your opinion, apart from what Detective Randolph or Ms. Solo testified to?"

"When I interviewed Patrick, he told me that he had gotten into a fight with the other boy in the Crisis Center. He told me that he was angry at him and that he didn't like him. He also told me that he doesn't like the DHS caseworker, Olivia, and he was angry at her, too. He admitted to me that he threatened her with the gun. He didn't seem very sorry about it, which concerned me." Harris raked back his greasy hair. "Not only that, he showed me some drawings he was making, which were clearly violent in nature."

"What drawings?" Judge Green turned to Chan-Willig. "May I see them?"

"Yes, Your Honor. I was just about to move to admit them into evidence as Exhibits 1 through 8." Chan-Willig rose with papers in her hand, offered a set to John and Abby, and Mary could see that they were drawings of Patrick's, much like the others.

John rose. "Your Honor, I object to the admission of the drawings without their being interpreted by a child psychologist. Ms. Di-Nunzio is aware of the child's drawings and the reason he makes those drawings. When she testifies, she would be happy to explain to the court that those are in fact depictions of his grandfather at war in Vietnam."

Judge Green seemed not to hear John, scanning the drawings. The judge's eyes flared once or twice in alarm, then he set them aside. "Counsel, I'm going to grant Mr. Foxman's objection. Ms. Chan-Willig, we need not admit them into evidence. Please move on, your point is made."

"Thank you, Your Honor. I will move on then." Chan-Willig faced the witness stand. "Mr. Harris, did there come a time when you learned that a Complaint has recently been filed in Common Pleas Court, which alleges that in early September, Patrick attacked a teacher's aide at school with a scissors?"

"Yes."

"Objection." John jumped to his feet. "Your Honor, Ms. Di-Nunzio is defense counsel on that very litigation and she will testify that those allegations are false. The Complaint was brought by the man who physically and sexually abused Patrick, as a preemptive attempt to intimidate and silence him."

Chan-Willig took a step toward the dais. "Your Honor is perfectly capable of according the weight due allegations in the Complaint, and the weight of the evidence is overwhelming that DHS must retain custody of the child because of his dangerousness."

John interrupted, "Your Honor, Ms. DiNunzio does not believe he is dangerous."

Chan-Willig looked directly at the judge. "Your Honor, Patrick is under suspicion for murder, he threatened Ms. Solo and Ms. DiNunzio with a gun, he fought with another child at the Crisis Center, he has been sued for attacking a teacher's aide with a scissors, *and* he makes violent drawings. Ms. DiNunzio is *delusional*, in view of—"

John interrupted, "Your Honor, Ms. Chan-Willig is making a closing argument and an inappropriate slur against—"

Chan-Willig kept talking. "Your Honor, Patrick could easily become a danger to Ms. DiNunzio or to others during the course of her guardianship. DHS, the City, and even this Court could be exposed to substantial liability if he harmed Ms. DiNunzio or those around her while in her custody. The Court cannot place the City and DHS in such a vulnerable legal position. Patrick must remain in DHS custody, and Ms. DiNunzio must be saved from her own bad judgment."

John shook his head. "Your Honor, neither Abby nor Dr. Bernardi found that the child is dangerous, and after you hear them testify—"

"Counsel, both of you, silence!" Judge Green interrupted, his patience spent. He turned to Chan-Willig. "Ms. Chan-Willig, please wrap up Mr. Harris's testimony so we can break for a short recess."

Chan-Willig nodded. "Your Honor, I have no further questions for Mr. Harris and I have no further witnesses."

"Excellent." Judge Green swiveled his head to face John, with a deep frown. "Mr. Foxman, any cross-examination?"

John hesitated. "No, Your Honor."

"Well, that's good news!" Judge Green banged the gavel with vigor. "Court is in recess for fifteen minutes. When we return, Mr. Foxman will put on his first witness."

Mary glanced at her phone, which was sitting on counsel table on mute. Suddenly a banner popped onto her home screen with a text from Machiavelli:

Sorry yet?

CHAPTER FORTY

Mary, John, Abby, and Susan huddled with bottles of water around a white table in a windowless attorneys' conference room, and Mary felt as if she could finally let her emotions show. She covered her face with her hands, took a deep breath, and absorbed the testimony as if she'd been sucker-punched in the gut.

"That went terribly wrong," Mary said, then moved her hands from her face.

"I know." John looked equally distressed, his forehead creased with disappointment. "Mary, I'm not going to lie to you. We could've dealt with the gun, but I never dreamed that Edward's death would be considered suspicious and that Patrick would be a suspect. I mean, *what*? We couldn't have seen that coming. Detective Randolph destroys our case."

"You think?" Mary asked miserably, though she knew it was true.

"Yes. I tried to do what I could on cross, but if there's even a question that Patrick might have committed a murder and that you were involved to cover it up, it's just too much to overcome. Plus there was so much other support, all consistent with Patrick being dangerous. Judge Green is simply not going to ignore Detective Randolph, Solo, and the GAL, Harris, who came out of the blue."

"I bet that was Machiavelli's doing."

Abby looked over sharply. "Machiavelli? I hate that guy. He's in

Family Court all the time. He does divorce work. He represents all the rich husbands."

Susan Bernardi looked at them both like they were crazy. "Machiavelli who? *The* Machiavelli?"

Mary simmered. "He's a skeevy lawyer who claims he's descended from the real Machiavelli, and I'm starting to believe he might be. The guy is evil incarnate."

John opened his water bottle and took a sip. "I agree with you, but the bottom line is it didn't matter. Harris's testimony was cumulative, and Chan-Willig didn't need him. It all piled on top of Randolph. Suspicion of murder, pulling a gun"—John counted off on his fingers—"fighting with the other kid at Einstein, the violent drawings. It was a slow-motion train wreck." John met Mary's eyes, pained. "But here's the thing. We're not going to lie down. We're still going to put on a case. But you should think long-term. If we lose today, there's another hearing in ten days. It's called the adjudication hearing and it's much more formal. Do you remember I told you that?"

"Yes." Mary didn't remind him that her rehearsal dinner was in ten days, with her wedding on the very next day, assuming that Anthony was still willing to marry her. She thought back to the time when her biggest worry had been crabmeat appetizers.

John was saying, "Okay, so in ten days, things should be very different, in our favor. For one thing, the Medical Examiner will be back and he could have found that the manner of death was accidental. That helps us. Detective Randolph may have gone further in his investigation, too. Mary, you'll be all over that, if I know you."

Mary tried to take heart. "I'll shake his cage and get him to start investigating the death as accidental. I'll know more when I talk to Patrick, but if Patrick really injected Edward that night, any overdose was completely accidental. Patrick would never dream of hurting Edward. Patrick loved Edward."

"Of course." John scoffed. "It has to be next-to-impossible to prove that a ten-year-old boy had the requisite intent to kill, even if he did inject Edward. I don't think they'll ever have enough to charge Patrick with murder, given that hurdle."

"Or the fact that I evidently contaminated the crime scene." Mary felt defensive. "I just cleaned up, is all. I didn't think it was murder because it's *not* murder."

Abby chimed in, "I met Patrick, and I don't think Patrick would hurt Edward on purpose. It had to be accidental. And in ten days, we go to the adjudication and we can try all over again."

Mary gulped some water. "But ten days is a long time for Patrick to be in residential care, especially with hard-to-place kids. What's it like, Abby?"

"There are two options. A child who goes into DHS custody and has possible violent tendencies will be placed with a family that has training in dealing with violent children or in a residential center where they could get specialized treatment for their anger issues and the like."

"I assume the latter would be easier for Patrick, but not by much. Can we request that for him, if we lose?"

"Yes, and I already did, for when he leaves Einstein. They said they'd try, but no guarantees."

"Oh man." Mary rubbed her forehead. "Can you give me a phone number for him or an address?"

"Sure. I'll find out where he is and set up the visit, okay?"

"Yes." Mary realized that Abby was being tactful. "Oh, I can't do it myself, I have to go through you. Because if we lose today, I have no legal rights to even visit Patrick."

"Right." Abby nodded sadly. "Even as his lawyer, you have to go through me because he's a minor child in DHS custody."

Mary groaned. "This is a nightmare. I don't even want to think about how this impacts his schooling. He goes from hard-core residential care in the foster system to Fairmount Prep? How is that tenable? How long is it before he gets into trouble in the residential home and it undermines him at Fairmount Prep? Meantime, he falls further and further behind in school. Who's drilling him at home for his dyslexia? Nobody."

Susan sipped her soda. "Unfortunately, I share Mary's concern. I've seen cases where children like Patrick, with high levels of anxiety and depression, engage in self-harm and even become suicidal in foster care. In addition, Patrick is bereaved, so he's in crisis. He's at risk in foster care, even if it's only for ten more days."

"Oh no." Mary moaned.

John patted her back. "Hang in there. We took a blow to our bow, but we'll have to deal. Obviously, we should change our trial strategy. I don't think you should testify first anymore."

"I don't either," Mary said.

Abby shook her head. "Why? Mary makes the case. She can tell the judge our side of the story and say why Patrick did what he did. In my experience, he doesn't get a lot of people of her quality stepping up to be temporary guardians. As soon as he hears her, he'll see that she's terrific."

"Or delusional," Mary said, but nobody laughed.

"Nah." Abby met her eye with sympathy, and so did Dr. Bernardi, if more reserved.

John took a thoughtful sip of water. "I still think Mary shouldn't be the first witness. We need to offer Judge Green solid professional opinions, not ones that might be swayed by emotionality, from an alleged accomplice after the fact. Chan-Willig is arguing that Mary is overlooking Patrick's dangerousness, so we have to prove that Patrick is not dangerous, using an impartial expert opinion." John turned to Susan, sitting to his right. "Susan, that's where you come in. You have the psychiatric credentials. I think you should be our first witness and give the testimony that we discussed."

"Um, well, hold on, John." Susan hesitated, glancing around the table at everyone, with a new pursing of her lips. "Abby and Mary, I'm sorry, but I don't think that I can testify today, after what Detective Randolph testified to. I felt confident of my risk assessment of Patrick until now, but the points that Detective Randolph made gave me concern. I'm sure that you all are correct and that Patrick is harmless, but I simply cannot stake my professional reputation on my previous risk assessment, given that there's a question in my mind that Patrick might have administered that lethal dose to Edward."

"Really?" John recoiled, aghast. "I said in open court that we'd put you up."

"Susan, please, no," Mary begged. "You know Patrick would never kill Edward. You spoke to him about Edward's relationship to him."

"Sorry, John, and I know, Mary." Susan stood up to go, picking up her purse. "But now I have a *tiny* bit of reasonable doubt about Patrick's dangerousness. The fact is, you don't want me to take the stand when I have *any* doubt. I wouldn't be a very good witness for you, any longer. If Chan-Willig cross-examined me about my opinion, I couldn't say anymore that I held it to a reasonable certainty, given that Patrick is suspected of murder. I just couldn't. I'm very sorry."

"I understand, Susan." John rose and walked her to the door. "You wouldn't be a good witness for us if you had any doubt. Judge Green is too smart a judge not to detect that, and Chan-Willig is too worthy an adversary not to destroy you over it on cross-examination. We appreciate your honesty. Thank you for your time."

"Yes, thanks, Susan." Mary tried mightily to hide her disappointment. Their case was going down the tubes before her very eyes. "I'm sorry, but you're right not to testify if you're not one hundred percent sure. That would only hurt our case more."

"That's what I thought. Good-bye." Susan flashed them a final smile, then John opened the door, they all said good-bye, and she left, with John closing the door behind her.

"Mary, remain calm." John returned to his seat, talking.

"I'm trying." Mary turned to Abby. "You're still on board, Abby?"

"Yes, totally." Abby grinned. "I'm not going down without a fight."

"That's the spirit!" Mary said, thinking of her patron saint, St. Jude of Lost Causes.

John squared his shoulders. "We can adapt without Susan."

"I'll go first," Abby said, rallying. "Judge Green likes me, so there's that. I think that's why he went our way, on your doing the questioning."

"Good." John nodded. "Here's what I'm thinking, now. Judge Green believes that the safe decision is to leave Patrick where he is, but I want to move him off that position. I want to open his mind to the possibility, if not the likelihood, that Patrick is in danger if he stays in foster care. So, denying Mary's petition and leaving the status quo in place creates legal liability for DHS, the City, and perhaps even for the Court."

"Okay." Mary brightened. It was a sound legal strategy, turning the tables on Chan-Willig, and John was using all of his litigation skills in the family law context.

Abby looked over. "Okay, and in my testimony, I don't think I should emphasize how much Patrick really wants to be with Mary and that they like each other. That would be my usual testimony. As Child Advocate, I speak for Patrick. But that only reinforces Chan-Willig's position that because of her affection for Patrick, Mary might be blinded and Patrick is manipulating her."

Mary nodded. "Agree."

John asked, "So what will you say, Abby?"

"I would testify that I don't think Patrick is dangerous. He's the poor little runt who gets bullied, is all. Agree?"

"Yes," John answered. "Specifically, I'm going to question you about the gun and you can testify about Patrick's remorse. Also that he felt desperate and that's why he did it."

"Okay, and I think it was truly because he was leaving the only home that he's ever known, the morning after his grandfather died. It's horrible, and he felt powerless. The gun was an easy answer, but he never would've shot it, ever. I think he knew it wasn't loaded anyway."

John nodded. "Good. Then I'm going to ask you about the fight over the wallet in the Crisis Center and elicit from you that it was instigated by the other kid. Does that sound right?"

"Yes, totally."

"Perfect." John faced Mary, and his eyes met hers with concern. "You're up after Abby. Ready to testify? You're really going to have to sell it."

"I know." Mary felt her chest tighten. "Is there anything I should change about my testimony? Am I supposed to act like I don't care about Patrick? That I'm not emotionally invested in him?"

"No." John flashed her a reassuring smile. "Just be yourself and we'll do fine. Just speak from your heart. The judge will need to hear how much you really want to take Patrick."

"I can do that," Mary said, worried sick.

CHAPTER FORTY-ONE

John faced Judge Green. "Your Honor, I'd like to call my first witness, Child Advocate Abby Ortega."

"Good. She's one of my favorite people." Judge Green motioned Abby forward with a pleasant grin. "Ms. Ortega, it's always a pleasure to see you. You brighten my day."

Abby came forward, smiling. "That's why I make the big bucks, Your Honor."

"Ha!" The judge laughed, and everyone smiled, including the clerk. Mary realized that any form of humor was a welcome break in a dependency courtroom. John had told her that the only part of family law practice that he truly loved was adoptions, because it made everybody happy.

Abby was sworn in and sat down, and John began his direct examination, taking her methodically through her testimony and eliciting every point they had discussed, without objection. Abby's demeanor was so natural and winning on the stand that Judge Green listened carefully.

"Your Honor, I have no more questions." John returned to counsel table, and Mary smiled at him.

Chan-Willig rose. "Your Honor, I have cross-examination."

"Please proceed." Judge Green nodded.

"Thank you, Your Honor." Chan-Willig faced the witness box. "Ms. Ortega, we've worked together in many cases, haven't we?"

"Yes." Abby smiled. "Not that we always agree."

"Fair enough." Chan-Willig smiled back, and so did Judge Green, on the dais. "Ms. Ortega, I think it's fair to say that you are generally of an optimistic and positive nature, isn't that correct?"

"Yes." Abby's smile turned wary.

"Ms. Ortega, you testified, did you not, that you liked Patrick when you met him and interviewed him, isn't that correct?"

"Yes, I liked him very much. I thought he was a good kid."

"Ms. Ortega, you must have been surprised to hear Detective Randolph's testimony that Patrick is suspected of murdering his grandfather Edward, isn't that correct?"

"Yes."

"Ms. Ortega, isn't it correct that no matter what Detective Randolph testified, you don't think Patrick murdered his grandfather, is that correct?"

"Yes."

"And you were probably also surprised to hear that he pulled a gun on Ms. Solo and Ms. DiNunzio, isn't that correct?"

"Yes."

"Ms. Ortega, you testified that you did not believe that Patrick was going to fire the gun, is that correct?"

"Yes, that's my testimony."

"Ms. Ortega, isn't it correct that you based your belief that Patrick didn't kill his grandfather and that he wasn't going to fire the weapon on your subjective belief that he was a 'good kid'?"

Abby hesitated. "Well, yes. It was my assessment of him, of his nature. He is not aggressive. He's the kind of kid who gets bullied."

"But isn't it true in your experience that children who are bullied can become aggressive?"

"Well, yes, but not him."

"Ms. Ortega, isn't it true that it is objectively aggressive to pull a gun on another human being?"

Abby blinked. "He felt sorry he had done it and I'm sure he knew it wasn't loaded."

Chan-Willig frowned. "Ms. Ortega, as an attorney, aren't you aware that brandishing a handgun constitutes a terroristic threat in violation of Section 2706 of the Pennsylvania Crimes Code?"

"I guess so, but—"

"Yes or no?"

"Yes," Abby admitted.

"So now, Ms. Ortega, you *have* to agree, do you not, that it is objectively aggressive to pull a gun on another human being?"

"Well, it's not very nice," Abby answered slowly, but Judge Green wasn't smiling anymore.

Chan-Willig paused. "Ms. Ortega, in your time as a Child Advocate, have you ever been physically threatened with a weapon by any of the children you were interviewing?"

"No."

"Ms. Ortega, have you ever been threatened with a fist?"

"Yes." Abby pursed her lips.

"Ms. Ortega, when you were threatened with a fist, isn't it true that you felt aggressed upon?"

Abby paused. "Yes, but that case was different from Patrick's."

Chan-Willig frowned. "Ms. Ortega, isn't it correct that the only reason that that case is different is because you like Patrick?"

"Well, yes," Abby answered, flustered. "But it's hard to say which came first, the chicken or the egg. I like Patrick because he's a good kid and he would never do that."

Chan-Willig nodded. "Isn't it possible that *because* you like Patrick, you underestimate his dangerousness?"

Abby hesitated. "No, and I reiterate, I don't think he would have hurt anyone."

"Even though he is suspected of murder?"

"Yes."

"And even though he aimed a gun at two women, in violation of the criminal law of this Commonwealth?"

"Yes."

"I have no further questions, Your Honor." Chan-Willig returned to counsel table, making a show of giving up.

Mary felt a wave of abject despair. Abby's sweet and loving nature had just undercut her own credibility, and Judge Green's opinion about Patrick's dangerousness would remain unchanged. Mary looked over, heartened to see John rising for redirect examination, an attempt to rehabilitate Abby's testimony.

John rose. "Your Honor, I have redirect, if I may."

"Go ahead, Mr. Foxman." Judge Green pursed his lips. "But please, not too long."

"Certainly, Your Honor." John stayed at counsel table. "Ms. Ortega, you have obvious affection for Patrick, don't you?"

"Yes."

"Ms. Ortega, do you feel that the affection you may have for Patrick impairs your judgment about his putative dangerousness?"

"No." Abby shook her head, emphatically. "Not at all."

"So it is still your opinion that Patrick does not present any danger to the safety of Ms. DiNunzio or others?"

"Yes," Abby answered firmly.

"Thank you." John turned to Judge Green. "I have no further questions, Your Honor. I'm ready to call my final witness, Mary DiNunzio."

Chan-Willig looked over, arching an eyebrow. "What about Dr. Susan Bernardi? Isn't she testifying?"

John didn't miss a beat. "Dr. Bernardi had to go," he answered, without elaborating.

CHAPTER FORTY-TWO

Mary tried to relax as she took her seat in the witness box, but she felt nervous and disoriented. She'd stood in front of plenty of witness stands but never sat inside one, and it changed her perspective. The courtroom seemed intimidating with all the faces looking back at her, and she felt uncomfortably as if Judge Green were looking over her shoulder, instead of presiding.

She found her bearings while John took her through a string of preliminary questions, listing her background, education, and general worthiness as a guardian, then they segued into her testifying about how she had met Patrick, filed the complaint with Officer Diamond, and taken him to Cassandra Porter at the Philadelphia Children's Alliance, which was designed to explain to the judge the chronology of the case.

John stood before the witness stand. "Ms. DiNunzio, can you explain to the Court why you are stepping up to serve as a temporary guardian to Patrick?"

"Yes, Patrick deserves a chance to have a good life, just like any other kid. He has been dealt some terrible cards, the desertion of his father, the death of his mother, a terrifying assault at school, and now the death of the person closest to him, his grandfather, whom he loved very much." Mary continued, speaking from the heart. "I spend a lot of time in our city's elementary and middle schools, and I see child after child who's falling through the cracks. They are born into impossibly difficult circumstances and they can't succeed in school because they never get the helping hand they deserve. And I know that I can prevent that from happening for Patrick. I can give him a future, if I can just get him through this rough patch."

"Ms. DiNunzio, how exactly would you get Patrick through this 'rough patch'?"

"I already have him admitted to Fairmount Prep, where they can program for his dyslexia and give him therapy for his anxiety and depression. I also have referrals of child psychologists for independent counseling. He has money that can pay for counseling, and if I were his legal guardian, I could make those expenses for his benefit. If he gets what he needs, he will be a wonderful candidate for permanent adoption." Mary sensed she was speechifying, but there were no objections so she went with it. "But if he doesn't get that treatment, he could be forever damaged and forever lost. He's on the precipice now, and I would very much like to be his temporary guardian."

"Ms. DiNunzio, how do you feel about Patrick, as a personal matter?"

"I like him very much. He's smart, he's verbal, he's a talented artist. He forms bonds easily with people, he very much wants to be liked. He's just afraid and he's been bullied, and he will blossom if he is just given the chance. Even having the ability to read, something that we take for granted, will open his mind, broaden his horizons, and increase his self-esteem."

"Ms. DiNunzio, please explain to the Court how long you have known Patrick."

Mary swallowed hard. "I haven't known him long at all. In fact, I've known him only a few days. It's not a long-term relationship, but we bonded because I was with him through the hardest moment of his life."

"Ms. DiNunzio, what you mean by that?"

"As I testified, I was the one who discovered his grandfather dead and I was the one who told Patrick the worst news of his life. I held him that night and he cried himself to sleep, and I imagine that there will be many other nights when he will cry himself to sleep."

Mary felt wetness come to her eyes, but blinked it away. "Ms. DiNunzio, you heard Detective Randolph testify that Patrick is presently under suspicion for the murder of his grandfather, didn't you?"

"Yes, I did hear that."

"Ms. DiNunzio, you were surprised to hear that information, were you not?"

"Yes, completely. Actually I was shocked and it's completely wrong."

"Ms. DiNunzio, why were you shocked?"

"Because I know that Patrick loved and adored his grandfather. I'm the only one in this courtroom who has seen them together and spent time with them together. Patrick's grandfather meant everything to him and he was devastated by his death."

"Ms. DiNunzio, can you offer the Court an explanation for why Patrick did not call 911, the police, or even you upon his grandfather's death?'

"First of all, he's only ten years old and he reacted exactly as I would expect in the circumstances, especially for someone who was as devoted to his grandfather as Patrick was. He had nothing else in his life and he was probably terrified of what would happen. When I saw him that time, it is clear to me that he was completely in denial about his grandfather's death. He knew it, but he didn't want to know it. That's why he didn't call."

"Ms. DiNunzio, if what you're saying is true, then how can you explain to the Court the fact that Patrick's fingerprints may have been found on the syringe that was used to administer a lethal dose of insulin to his grandfather?"

"I'm not surprised by that at all, except for the fact that it was lethal. Patrick is very proud of the way he helped his grandfather, making him soup, reminding him of what medication was due, and things like that. He told me himself, as he told Cassandra and Abby that he helped his grandfather by injecting him with his insulin when he was asked to do so, because Edward got the shakes from time to time." Mary turned to Judge Green, hoping to drive her point home. "If Patrick administered that last dose, there is no doubt in my mind that the death was accidental. There is simply no grounds for murder here. There was at most an accidental death."

"Finally, Ms. DiNunzio, would you please explain to the Court your role in what Detective Randolph termed as contamination of the alleged crime scene?"

"Yes, I would be happy to." Mary turned to Judge Green again, avoiding Chan-Willig's cold gaze. "Judge Green, I would never participate in a cover-up of any crime, much less murder, and I was the one who found Edward in bed and I believed that he had passed away peacefully in his sleep. Frankly, he had soiled the bed and I didn't want Patrick to have to see that, because I knew it would upset him. That's why I cleaned up the sheets and the room. There was absolutely no nefarious intent, and I'm sure that Detective Randolph will determine that, once they've had a chance to interview me."

John nodded. "Ms. DiNunzio, you heard testimony that Patrick presents a physical danger to you and to others. Do you agree or disagree?"

"I absolutely disagree. I think Patrick is a gentle child who is terrified of a world that diminishes him for many reasons, among them the fact that he can't read, which is very difficult to hide and will only become more difficult as life goes on. That's the only reason he's lashed out and I don't think he'll ever lash out at me."

"Ms. DiNunzio, you have heard testimony that Patrick pulled a gun on Olivia from DHS. You were present when that occurred, were you not?"

"Yes I was. Patrick was so upset that day. He was being taken from his home the very next morning after his grandfather had died."

"Did Patrick point the gun at you?"

"In a sense, yes, because I was standing next to Olivia."

"Ms. DiNunzio, were you at any time in fear for your life or safety?"

"No."

"Ms. DiNunzio, how could you not be afraid when the gun was pointed at you?"

"Because I knew he wouldn't fire it and I understood the reason why he did it."

"Ms. DiNunzio, what was that reason, in your opinion?"

"It was because he was a scared little boy and he didn't want to leave the only home he's ever known, or his grandfather. He grew up listening to his grandfather's war stories in the Vietnam War. The same is true of his drawings, they're about his grandfather in war. Patrick would never, ever have harmed Olivia or me."

John took a deep breath, in a final way. "Thank you, Ms. DiNunzio. Your Honor, I have no further questions."

"Ms. Chan-Willig, do you have cross-examination?" Judge Green looked over at Chan-Willig, who was already on her feet, striding toward the witness stand.

"Ms. DiNunzio, isn't it correct that you have absolutely no training in child psychology?"

"Yes, that's true."

"And it is also correct that you have never interviewed a child to determine if he creates a risk to others?"

"That's true."

"Ms. DiNunzio, it's correct that you have no experience counseling children who present a danger to others, isn't it?"

"That's true."

"Ms. DiNunzio, you have no children of your own, isn't that also correct?"

"That's true." Mary thought this cross-examination was doing nothing for her self-esteem.

"Ms. DiNunzio, you have never served as a foster parent or guardian before, isn't that correct?"

"Yes, that's true."

Chan-Willig frowned. "Ms. DiNunzio, how is it possible that you have known Patrick only five days, have absolutely no experience with children, foster children, or child psychology, and yet could be so *completely* certain that Patrick didn't kill his grandfather and that he meant you and Ms. Solo no harm when he aimed a gun at you?"

Mary's mouth went dry. "I know him."

"Ms. DiNunzio, you have known him only five days, isn't that true?"

"I know who he is inside and I know what he was going through at the time."

"*Five days!*"

John half-rose. "Objection, Your Honor, this is argument."

Judge Green nodded. "I'll sustain the objection. Ms. Chan-Willig, you're entitled to explore the issue but not to argue with the witness."

"Thank you, Your Honor." Chan-Willig swiveled to face Mary. "So is it your position that this Court should transfer custody to you, though Patrick is under suspicion for murder and has demonstrated objectively dangerous behavior, because you met him only five days ago and think you *know him inside?*"

Mary didn't hesitate. "Yes."

Chan-Willig rolled her eyes, in a stagy way. "Moving on, Ms. DiNunzio, you are a partner at the law firm of Rosato & DiNunzio, is that true?"

"Yes."

"And as such, you're an experienced civil and criminal litigator, isn't that true?"

"Yes."

"Ms. DiNunzio, let's assume for the sake of argument that you are granted temporary guardianship today, but also the worst-case scenario happened, that is, Patrick ends up attempting to kill you or someone else. In your opinion as an experienced litigator, wouldn't you or that person have a colorable cause of action against DHS, the City, and even the Court?"

"Objection, Your Honor." John stood up. "That question obviously calls for speculation."

Mary turned to Judge Green. "Your Honor, I'd like to answer that question. I have no problem answering the question."

"Good, I intended to overrule the objection anyway. Please answer." Judge Green looked Mary directly in the eye, which told her that he was very concerned about this point.

"Your Honor, Ms. Chan-Willig is probably correct that if Patrick hurt someone, there would be a colorable cause of action. But the fact is, I would never take this child into my home if I thought that he would hurt me, anyone I love, or anyone at all. Granted, I haven't known Patrick that long, but I have known him longer than anyone else in this courtroom and I have known him *better* than anyone else in this courtroom, so I know *exactly* what I'm doing."

Mary kept going because this was her only shot. "And I quarrel with the premise of the question, which is the assumption that Patrick harming someone is the 'worst-case scenario.' Because to me, the worst-case scenario, and the *far more likely* worst-case scenario, is that Patrick will falter and drown in the foster care system, and he will never get the programming, treatment, or affection that he deserves, and he will have absolutely no chance at a future, only because we made the wrong decision today in fear of legal liability." Mary felt tears come but blinked them away again. "Your Honor, I am asking you, I'm begging you, to trust my judgment and let me help this child. I know it's the right thing to do and I promise you that you will never regret it, as long as you live."

Judge Green cleared his throat. "Thank you, Ms. DiNunzio," he said quietly.

Mary looked back at Chan-Willig, whose face was falling into concerned lines. They both knew that Mary had reached the judge's heart, so the prudent decision would be to get Mary off the stand.

"Your Honor, I have no further questions," Chan-Willig said, returning to counsel table.

"Your Honor, I have no redirect," John called out, from counsel table.

"Ms. DiNunzio, you may step down." Judge Green looked down at the papers on his desk. "Counsel, let's take a short break, fifteen minutes. When we reconvene, I'll have my ruling. Thank you very much."

"Thank you, Your Honor." Mary rose on shaky knees, stepped down, and made her way back to counsel table, where she sat down.

Bam! John had written on the pad.

CHAPTER FORTY-THREE

Mary, John, and Abby made their way through the crowd, which had diminished. All of the other proceedings were ending or had already ended, and there were fewer parents and children. Lawyers clustered in groups, their ties loosened or makeup worn off, trying to settle cases after a tough day, and courthouse employees laughed together, blowing off steam. Mary opened the door to the attorneys' conference room, and John and Abby piled inside, then sank into chairs around the table.

Mary closed the door behind them, then turned and leaned against it, facing them. "Gang, can I just say something? I want to say thank you, to both of you. No matter which way this turns out, I'm so grateful to you guys. John, you dropped everything and worked around the clock. Thank you very much."

"It was a pleasure, really." John smiled, warmly.

"And Abby, I know you're in there fighting with me and I know you feel the same way I do. Your dedication is incredible. Thank you very much."

"I'm happy to do it, and I'm really hoping we win, for Patrick's sake. I'm pitching for you, believe me." Abby grinned. "Fingers crossed."

"Right." Mary crossed her fingers.

John's smile faded. "Well, we left it on the field, as they say."

"Right." Mary felt the same way. "Does it mean anything that the judge is going to rule from the bench, so quickly?"

"No, it doesn't. Judges at shelter care hearings usually rule from the bench."

Abby nodded. "It's not like they have to go to chambers and get a clerk to research precedent."

Mary felt suddenly tired, taking an empty chair at the table. "So what do you think, folks? Do we have a shot? Is it slim to none?"

John shook his head. "We have a shot. But I would say it's slim, if I were a gambling man."

Abby rolled her eyes. "You, a gambling man? You're the most careful lawyer I know. I mean, do you even cross the street on a yellow light?"

"How dare you." John snorted. "But, no."

Abby shifted her animated gaze to Mary, when her smile vanished, too. "Mary, I wish I could make you feel better. I think we'll probably lose today but I think we will win in ten days. That said, you did great on the stand and if you do that in ten days, we'll win at the adjudication hearing. Patrick can make it ten days, if we both visit him and watch over him."

"I hope he can." Mary wanted to believe Abby was right, but just then she noticed John looking past her out the window, squinting.

"That's funny," he said, pointing. "Who are *they*? Those people look crazy."

Abby did the same thing, amused. "How did they get past security?"

Mary turned around and saw who they were talking about, and in one second, she was on her feet and running out of the room. She hustled forward as every head turned, watching the scene. Her father was hurrying toward the courtroom, still in his multicolored sash from the Columbus Day Parade, with her mother hanging onto his arm and hobbling along in her orthopedic shoes, followed by Feet in a KISS ME, I'M ITALIAN baseball cap and Tony-From-Down-The-Block in a T-shirt that read, LEIF WHO? Pigeon Tony brought up the rear, scurrying in his white shirt, green work pants, and jaunty red kerchief, which looked like his Columbus Day attire but was in fact what he wore every day.

"HIYA, MARE!" her father shouted, his lined face lighting up. "WE'RE HERE TO PICK UP PATRICK! WHERE IS HE? WE'RE GONNA HAVE A PARTY! YOUR MOTHER MADE GNOCCHI!"

"*Maria, Maria!*" her mother chimed in. "I'm a so happ', so happ'!"

"Hi, Ma, Pop, this is a surprise." Mary kissed her mother and father quickly, then Feet joined the huddle, smelling of pepper-and-egg sandwiches.

"Mare, we're so excited! We're gonna drive him home in the car! It's got the streamers on and all! He'll be ridin' in style!"

"Mare, look!" Tony-From-Down-The-Block waved a plastic bag. "I got him a Columbus Day T-shirt and a cap!"

"Ma, Pop, Tonys, listen." Mary tried to prepare them for bad news. "It's really nice of you to come downtown but—"

"WE LOOKED IT UP ON THE INTERNET, THAT'S HOW WE FOUND YOU. IT HAD YOUR NAME, RIGHT ON THE COMPUTER!"

Mary touched her father's arm. "Pop, but really, listen to me. The judge is deciding what to do now and he might not go our way. He may not give us Patrick. In fact, he probably won't."

"WHAT DO YOU MEAN?" Her father's milky eyes flared in outrage behind his bifocals. "WHY NOT, MARE? YOU'D BE A GREAT MOM! WE'D BE GREAT GRANDPARENTS!"

"*Maria, e vero?*" her mother said, her voice hushed with disappointment.

Feet scowled. "We want Patrick! I'll give that judge a piece of my mind!"

"Me too!" Tony-From-Down-The-Block lumbered toward the courtroom door.

"No, guys!" Mary hurried and stopped them. "Guys, you can't, please. Stay here and wait for me."

"BUT MARE, IF THE JUDGE MET US, HE'D GIVE PATRICK TO US. HE JUST DOESN'T KNOW US. HE NEEDS TO MEET OUR FAMILY."

"Pop, no." Mary didn't have time to explain. "It's not about you or me. It's about the law."

John hurried over with Abby, stepping into the breach. "Hello, Mr. DiNunzio, Mrs. DiNunzio, I'm John and this is Abby, we work with Mary. We have to go into the courtroom, right now. The judge is waiting—"

"GOOD, GREAT, PERFECT TIMING! LET'S GO!" Her father barreled ahead, but Mary blocked his path.

"Pop, no, you can't go in the courtroom. You're not allowed."

"WHY NOT? THIS IS A FREE COUNTRY."

"Pop, these proceedings are confidential." Mary backed up against the door to the courtroom, holding them off, then turned to her mother, usually the more sensible. "Ma, tell Pop and The Tonys, you have to wait there. I'll get in trouble if anybody tries to go in the courtroom."

"*Si, si, Maria.*" Her mother said, teary, which broke Mary's heart. Mary wished she had prepared them for the fact that she could lose, but as John said, she hadn't seen any of this coming.

"Mom, if we don't get Patrick today, we'll try again in ten days. Okay?"

"Mary, please?" John motioned to her toward the courtroom and held open the door.

Mary turned back to her mother. "Ma, now I have to do my job. Let me go inside and see what the judge decided, then I'll come out and tell you. Try not to be upset if I lose, okay?"

"*Si, si,*" her mother answered, her eyes glistening and her lower lip puckering.

"WE'LL WAIT HERE, DOLL." Her father hugged her mother close.

Tony-From-Down-The-Block nodded. "Whatever you want, Mare."

Feet shrugged. "You're the boss, Mare."

"Great, thanks. Stay here. Don't come in." Mary hustled into the courtroom behind John and Abby, just as the administrative clerk was hanging up the phone.

"Counsel, take your seats. The judge is on his way in."

"Sorry." Mary hustled to stand in front of her seat at counsel table next to John and Abby. Chan-Willig, Olivia, and Harris were already standing in place.

"Hear, hear! Please rise for the Honorable Judge William R. Green. This Honorable Court is now in session!"

Everyone stood up, the pocket door opened, and Judge Green entered the courtroom and swept up the steps of the dais. He glanced around without making eye contact, his expression solemn. "Please, sit down."

Mary took her seat, put her parents to the back of her mind, and focused on the judge, coming fully into the moment. She was always nervous when a judge came back with a ruling or a jury returned with a verdict, but she'd never felt like this before. Her heart pounded in her chest. She could feel blotches bursting into bloom onto her neck.

Judge Green said, "Folks, this was not an easy decision to make. However, I have made a decision, and as is my custom, I will deliver my ruling and then briefly explain my reasons. Ms. Chan-Willig and Mr. Foxman presented their cases in a very compelling fashion and I was able to consider the evidence as a totality. I took into account the testimony from professionals whose experience affords them ample basis for their opinions, Detective Randolph, Ms. Solo, Mr. Harris, and Ms. Ortega, as well as Ms. DiNunzio. It is clear to me that everyone who testified has the best interests of Patrick at heart, even though they differ on what his best interest may be."

Mary bit her lip, her mouth gone dry as paper. She wasn't thinking of herself or even her parents. If Judge Green went against her, they would live with the decision. The only one who couldn't live with that decision was Patrick.

Judge Green continued, "I am mindful that leaving Patrick in the custody of the foster care system may be as fraught with risk as transferring his custody to Ms. DiNunzio, given his challenges. I also applaud Ms. DiNunzio, who has unselfishly volunteered to help a child in need. Simply put, there is no perfect solution. But in consideration of the relevant facts and governing law, I have decided that Patrick O'Brien should remain in DHS custody at the present time. Therefore, I hereby grant DHS's Petition to Retain Custody in the Matter of P.O.B., and I hereby deny Ms. DiNunzio's Petition in Opposition." Judge Green banged the gavel. "So ordered."

Mary felt a wave of despair wash over her.

Judge Green banged the gavel, one last time. "Court is adjourned."

CHAPTER FORTY-FOUR

Mary gathered her purse and messenger bag and walked down the aisle of the courtroom ahead of Abby and John, letting them stop to shake Chan-Willig's hand. Mary wasn't here as a lawyer, but a client, and she would be damned if she'd shake Chan-Willig's hand. She felt heartbroken for Patrick, for herself, and for her family, and she couldn't bear to think of him in the foster system, unjustly suspected of murdering a grandfather he loved and sabotaged by the machinations of Machiavelli.

Mary reached the exit door to the courtroom and held her chin up, getting herself ready to see her parents. If she looked upset it would only upset them more and she had to keep it together for everybody's sake. She opened the door and stepped outside the courtroom, only to see her family clustered together on the seats, a forlorn little group of octogenarians in parade gear, trying to put on a brave face for her.

They rose as one sad little clump when Mary walked over, meeting her mother's glistening eyes. Her mother had already figured out that the judge had ruled against them, so Mary raised her arms and hugged her, enveloping her short little mother in an embrace fragrant with her familiar smells of Aquanet and mothballs.

"I'm sorry too." Mary managed not to cry. "I shouldn't have gotten you all excited."

"*Mi dispiace, Maria,*" her mother said, hugging her back.

"IT'S OKAY, HONEY. IT'S GONNA BE ALL RIGHT. EVERYTHING HAPPENS FOR A REASON." Her father came around Mary's other side, patting her back. "COME HOME AND HAVE DINNER WITH US, WILL YA?"

"Good idea," Mary said, grateful. She felt so touched that they had come all the way into Center City to stand up for her. She realized that it really did take a village, and she was grateful to her very marrow for hers. She felt terrible for letting them down, as well as Patrick.

Feet nodded. "Mare, don't let the bastards get you down. We'll give you a ride home with us. Cheer you right up."

Tony-From-Down-The-Block forced a smile. "Yeah, Mare, come with us. You'll feel like a million bucks in that car."

Only Pigeon Tony said nothing, his round dark eyes meeting Mary's with unusual seriousness, and she couldn't help but think he was reading her mind. In the next second, he shot her a wink, just like a bird.

John and Abby came out of the courtroom talking, and Abby waved a quick good-bye to Mary, who waved back while John came over, his heavy messenger bag on his shoulder, scrolling through his phone, then he looked up. "Sorry, Mr. and Mrs. DiNunzio. We gave it the old college try."

"IT ISN'T YOUR FAULT, JOHNNY BOY. YOU'RE A HELLUVA LAWYER. THANKS FOR EVERYTHING."

"John, you come to dinn'," Mary's mother said, taking John's arm and looking up at him through her thick glasses. "We have gnocchi, you come, eh?"

John smiled down at her, but shook his head. "Mrs. DiNunzio, thank you, and I would love to, but I have a lot to do."

"*D'ove?* Where?" Her mother's expression said that she couldn't imagine a better place than her kitchen, which was probably true.

"Ma." Mary put a gentle hand on her mother's arm. "Not everybody can be bribed with carbohydrates, like me. John has to go."

John waved his phone. "I have a lot of work to catch up on. Email, you know. I'm sorry."

"Ma, please. It's John's business." Mary put an arm around her mother. "Let's go downstairs. Come on."

"This way, everyone." John walked ahead, motioning to them as he read his phone on the fly.

"Thanks, John." Mary got her family on to the escalator, holding her mother's arm, then her father and The Tonys climbed on, yammering as they descended.

"MARE, YOU BELIEVE THIS BUILDING? IT DOESN'T LOOK LIKE A COURTHOUSE BECAUSE IT'S ALL GLASS."

"Also, no columns," Feet added, eyes agog.

Tony-From-Down-The-Block *tsk-tsk*ed with his dentures. "If it doesn't have columns, it's not a legit courthouse."

They reached the ground floor, where the black-marble lobby was emptying, lawyers, clients, and staff heading for the exits. John got off the escalator first, then looked up from his phone with an alarmed expression, but Mary didn't know why. She ushered her mother, father, and The Tonys off the escalator and shooed them in the direction of the exit.

"John, what's the matter?" Mary asked, concerned.

"Look at this." John showed her his phone and enlarged the image with his fingers. On the screen was a news story from the digital edition of their local tabloid, and the headline read: TEN-YEAR-OLD SUSPECTED OF GRANDPOP'S INSULIN MURDER.

"Oh my God!" Mary looked up at John, aghast. "Machiavelli must've leaked it to the newspaper."

John nodded, gravely. "Either Machiavelli or Harris, one or the other."

"If Harris leaked it, he did it on Machiavelli's behalf," Mary said, then read the article:

> Patrick O'Brien, 10, a fifth-grader at Grayson Elementary School in Juniata, is currently in DHS custody, suspected in the insulin murder of his grandfather and sole caretaker, Edward F. O'Brien, 72. Grandfather and grandson resided alone together at 637 Moretone Street in Juniata, and the grandfather was found dead on October 9. Police report that the investigation is in progress and criminal charges have not yet been

filed. The Office of the Medical Examiner declined comment.

Our investigation revealed that Patrick O'Brien was also named as a defendant in a Common Pleas Court action filed last week by Steven Robertson, a former teacher's aide at the elementary school, alleging that O'Brien attacked Robertson with a scissors. Robertson seeks $500,000 in damages against Patrick O'Brien, the deceased Edward O'Brien, and the School District of Philadelphia. The district declined comment except to say that the youngster has been suspended pending investigation . . .

"John, I cannot believe Machiavelli would do this! He's chewing this kid up, and for what? For what? I want to kill that guy!" Mary felt her temper rising, and all of the pain, frustration, and disappointment of losing the hearing rolled into a solid ball of fury, rising in her chest.

"Don't let him get to you."

"He wants me to settle the case with Robertson. This is extortion."

"Maybe you should think about settlement, purely for Patrick's sake. I know you hate the idea of settlement, but things are happening fast and you have to be flexible." John met her gaze directly, his blue eyes full of concern. "Can you imagine putting Patrick through a deposition, while you don't have him in your custody? How will you mitigate its effects?"

"Oh God." Mary fumed. "I won't settle. Edward didn't want to settle."

"Edward didn't foresee any of this. You told me the estate has money. Does it have enough to meet a demand? How much do they want?"

"The estate is $350,000 and Machiavelli wants most of it. It's supposed to be Patrick's college fund."

"Negotiate with Machiavelli. Patrick's not going to college if we can't help him now."

"I'm not settling." Mary noticed her mother and father looking over, worried that something was wrong. "Just tell me what we can do about this news story? Anything?"

"Honestly, nothing." John pursed his lips.

"There has to be something." Mary wracked her brain. "We could ask for a retraction, but it's not false. We could raise hell with the police, but they didn't comment. Same with the elementary school. Dammit!"

"Mary, they're waiting." John gestured at her parents. "Go home. You need to rest and recoup. You've been working twenty-four/seven, and the strain is getting to you. It was a bad day, and it needs to end."

"I can't let this go." Mary felt like she was going to explode.

"Please, do. Sleep on it. He just wants to jerk your chain."

"Then he's going to find out he's got a tiger by the tail. John, thanks so much for all of your help, but I have to go." Mary clapped his shoulder, then headed for her parents.

"Don't do it!" John called after her, but Mary was already kissing her mother and father good-bye.

"Ma, Pop, I have to go. I'm really sorry, but I can't come to dinner. I'll talk to you later, okay?"

"No, *Maria,* come 'ome." Her mother frowned, worried.

"MARY, COME HOME AND HAVE A NICE MEAL."

"No, thanks, I gotta go, Pop. Thanks for coming! Bye, everybody!" Mary waved good-bye to her parents and The Tonys, hustled across the marble lobby, and through the exit doors. She hurried out of the courthouse, pulling out her phone and pressing in Machiavelli's number on the fly. She was tired of playing games, of nasty texts and FaceTime calls. It was time for a face-to-face confrontation.

The sidewalk was crowded and traffic was congested on Arch Street but there was a Yellow Cab only a block away. Phone to her ear, she hurried toward it, flagging it down.

"The Machiavelli Organization," answered the receptionist.

"Is he in?" Mary asked, hustling for the cab.

"Yes. Whom may I say is—"

Mary hung up the phone, reached the cab, and hopped inside, giving the driver the address. "And hurry," she said, boiling mad.

.

CHAPTER FORTY-FIVE

Mary pulled up in the cab in front of Machiavelli's office, which was housed in a colonial mansion, with a bronze plaque signifying its listing on the National Register of Historic Places. His was the largest of the massive townhouses interspersed with the apartment buildings lining Rittenhouse Square, relics of a grander time, but it was still the ritziest address possible. Machiavelli owned the whole building, which must have cost millions to restore, since it was four stories of repointed red brick, layers of black-shuttered mullioned windows. Authentic gaslights flickered beside the double doors of black lacquer. But Mary wasn't interested in real estate porn today.

She glanced up at the mansion from the cab window, noticing that the second floor boasted a five-panel bay window that had a perfect view of the Square, so she knew that was Machiavelli's office. He would have chosen the God's eye view, but he was really the devil himself. "Keep the change," Mary said to the driver, handing him a twenty, climbing out of the cab, hurrying to the entrance, and blowing through the black-lacquered door.

"Hello?" A pretty blonde receptionist looked up, startled from an ornate reception desk. There was no one in the waiting area, and behind her desk was a grand carpeted staircase with a curved banister that wound around to the second floor. The walls were paneled walnut and wafer-thin Oriental rugs covered the floors, and Mary wasn't about to be delayed, much less denied.

"I'm Mary DiNunzio, here to see Machiavelli," Mary told the receptionist, but she didn't break stride, beelining for the staircase.

"Wait, Ms. DiNunzio? Ms. DiNunzio?"

Mary ignored her and hurried up to the second floor, where there were more Oriental rugs and walnut-paneled walls, but at the north side of the mansion, a flood of indirect light shone through a divider made of mullioned glass panels, revealing another reception area and another ornate desk staffed by another pretty brunette, who was just hanging up the phone, undoubtedly having been called by the downstairs blonde.

"I'm Mary DiNunzio, and I'm here to see Machiavelli."

"Ms. DiNunzio, he's in a meeting."

"I know. He's meeting with me." Mary headed for the heavy walnut door on the right and burst through to find Machiavelli grinning ear-to-ear, sitting at his ornate desk against the multi-paned window, his dark hair slicked back, his European-fit white shirt impeccable with a print silk tie, gray wool slacks perfectly unwrinkled, and Gucci loafers propped up on the desk, one crossed over the other.

"Mary, do you have any idea how predictable you are?" Machiavelli chuckled. "It's uncanny. I could have set my watch to you coming here."

"What the *hell* are you doing?" Mary stormed to the front of his desk, barely able to suppress her anger. "Do you know that you're destroying a child? Isn't there any part of you that understands that you are sacrificing a child for your own interests?"

Machiavelli shrugged. "I have no idea what you're talking about. I really don't. You're so emotional lately. It must be because of your wedding. Having doubts?"

"You know exactly what I'm talking about. You paid Harris to go to that shelter care hearing and testify against Patrick. You leaked the story to the newspaper. You're killing this child and you *know* he's not dangerous."

"Again, no clue what you're talking about." Machiavelli's grin never left his face, and he folded his arms. "But rant on, please do. I like that you came over. You've never been here before. It's nice, isn't it? Would you like a drink? A Scotch? Day is done, is it not?"

Mary ignored him. "You know that Patrick's not dangerous and you're willing to chew him up, for what? For money? Look around you!" She threw up her hands, looking around. "You have everything! This building, real Oriental rugs, nice art." She did a double-take at a watercolor of an austere fieldstone farmhouse, the style of which was unmistakable. "Is that a Wyeth? You even have an original Wyeth? What more can you want? What more can you buy? What's the difference to you, if you settle this case? If I settle the case, I practically bankrupt the child!"

"Keep talking. Get it out of your system. You'll feel better, I promise." Machiavelli cocked his head, plainly amused, and it struck Mary suddenly that he was enjoying every minute of her pain, almost sadistically so, which brought her up short.

"Who *did* this to you? Who turned you into such a monster?" Mary heard herself saying, her heart speaking for her. "I wish I knew your family, but I never met them. They should be ashamed of themselves, they did *such* a number on you. If you didn't cause so much harm, I'd feel sorry for you. You're killing this kid and you're enjoying it. Is that what gives you pleasure? Someone else's pain?"

"Oh come on, Mary." Machiavelli seemed to falter, his smile fading. "This is over-the-top, don't you think? You come here full of righteous indignation, blaming me for losing the shelter care hearing. Why don't you blame that brat? Why don't you wonder why Dennis the Menace murdered his beloved grandfather?"

"He didn't murder him! If he injected him, he didn't know it would kill him! He didn't do it on purpose and you know it!"

"No, I don't know it, and neither do you." Machiavelli's dark eyes flashed, and he swung his feet off the desk. "Whether I called Harris or not, you'll never be able to prove it. Whether I paid Harris or not, you'll never be able to prove it. Whether I messengered Harris a copy of the Complaint, or leaked the story to the newspapers, well, you get the idea. Your loss today makes Robertson's case stronger, and I love it!" Machiavelli met her eye, dead-on. "But I'll tell you one thing that I did *not* do. I did *not* inject that old man with a fatal dose of insulin. That's what the Duke of Puke did, and that's why you lost the hearing today. And that's why you'll never get him out of DHS custody. Because it's where he belongs. And he can rot there, for all I care."

"But that's the thing!" Mary shot back, agonized. "You say you don't care but you *do*! You care enough to ruin him! You care enough to make his life miserable! To make *my* life miserable!"

"Ah, now we're getting somewhere." Machiavelli nodded, smiling tightly. "That's why I care, that's *exactly* why I care."

"Why?" Mary demanded, nonplussed.

"Because you do. Because you care. Because of you." Machiavelli's dark eyes glittered. "You're absolutely right. You always were a smart girl. Number one in her class at Goretti. I used to see you at the dances. Nobody ever asked you to dance. But you got the last laugh, didn't you? Neighborhood Girl Who Made Good. The Sweetheart of South Philly."

"What's that supposed to mean? At least I don't call *myself* that. You call *yourself* the Dark Prince of South Philly, for God's sake."

"Oh, lighten up. That's just for fun. Did you see my Boxster? I got DRKPRNC. How great is that?" Machiavelli stood up, waving his hands with a flourish at his luxurious office. "And you're absolutely right, I have everything. I own this building, I own a lot of real estate in town and two homes. I make more money than I know what to do with. Every year I'm rated one of the top lawyers in Philadelphia and one of the top trial lawyers in the American Bar Association *and* the Trial Lawyers Association. Everything I want, I can have. All I have to do is snap my fingers." Machiavelli snapped his fingers.

"We get it."

"So it's in my nature to want what I can't have. It's in my blood. I can't help myself." Machiavelli walked around the side of the desk, slowly. "You want me to let this kid go, don't you?"

"Yes," Mary answered, edging backwards.

"You want me to settle with you? Aren't you gonna negotiate with me?" Machiavelli took a step toward her, and Mary found herself taking a step backwards. She didn't like the change that had come over Machiavelli's expression. His cocky smile had morphed into an ugly twist of his lips, like a wolf baring his teeth.

"All right, we'll settle it. Twenty-five grand."

"A hundred and fifty grand."

"Fifty grand."

"No, I changed my mind. I'm not negotiating anymore. That's not what I want anymore. Truth be told, it's not what I wanted, ever." Machiavelli kept walking toward Mary, and she edged backwards toward the bookcase, feeling a tingle of fear.

"Nick, if you're trying to scare me, it won't work."

"Scaring you is not my intent, my dear," Machiavelli answered, and suddenly he lunged at Mary, kissing her hard on the mouth, wrapping his arms around her, and grinding his hips against hers.

"No!" Mary shouted, yanking herself free. She stumbled backwards, falling against the bookcase, but Machiavelli kept coming, grabbing her shoulders, kissing her harder and trying to push her down to the floor. Mary felt a bolt of terror. Reflexively she smacked his face with all of her might, knocking him off-balance and sending him sprawling to the floor. Her engagement ring must have nicked his mouth because his lip sprouted blood.

"That's it!" Machiavelli shouted from the ground, his hand holding the bloody cut.

"You're insane!" Mary said, running for the door.

"I'll never let that brat go! Never!"

CHAPTER FORTY-SIX

Mary flew from Machiavelli's office and past the upstairs reception desk, now empty. She assumed the receptionist had fled to maintain deniability but she didn't stop to look for her. Mary felt shaken to the core, her knees weak as she hurried downstairs, running her fingers along the wooden banister to keep her balance.

Everything I want, I can have.

Her heart was still thundering when she reached the bottom of the staircase, noticing that the reception desk was empty there, too. She wondered fleetingly if she was the first woman to have been attacked in Machiavelli's office, but instinct told her no. She considered calling 911 and busting his ass, but that would only make things worse for Patrick.

I'm not negotiating anymore.

Mary burst through the front doors, hit the sidewalk, and took a left, heading toward home. She lived only fifteen minutes away and she walked through Rittenhouse Square every night on her way home, so the familiar route helped her feel vaguely normal. The sidewalk was filled with businessmen and women making their way to their apartments and houses after a long and busy day, lugging backpacks, messenger bags, and shopping totes.

The sun was setting behind the Dorchester, one of the taller of the apartment buildings on the west side of Rittenhouse Square, and the air was turning October crisp. She would be married soon. She hoped.

That's not what I want anymore.

Mary wished she could call Anthony, tell him what happened, and complain to him, but she had lost track of where he was and she knew that was the worst thing to do. She kept walking home, collecting her thoughts on the way. She couldn't begin to process what had happened with Machiavelli, but one thing was for certain. The pressure wasn't about to let up on Patrick, so she had to get busy.

Mary tried to rally. The sooner she cleared Patrick of any wrong-doing, the better it would be for him, and the sooner she could be named his guardian. She'd lost in court today, so she was down, but she was by no means out, especially after what happened with Machiavelli.

She pulled her phone from her purse and pressed in Abby Ortega's phone number, her fingers still trembling. "Hi, Abby," she said, when the call was answered.

"Hey, Mary," Abby said, her tone sympathetic. "How you doing? Are you taking it okay?"

"Sure, no problem," Mary answered, her chest tight. This wasn't the time to whine. She had to get in gear. "Abby, can you please get me in to see Patrick tonight?"

"Really?"

"Yes." Mary took a left on Twenty-second Street past the cool boutiques and storefront restaurants, heading for home. "I want to see Patrick as soon as possible and tell him what happened in court today, so he's not expecting me to take him home soon. I also want to talk to him about what happened the night Edward died. I have to get to the bottom of this thing with the insulin, if I want him clear of any suspicion."

"You're right. You sure you feel up to it?"

"Absolutely. I'm going to grab something to eat, grab my car, and I'll be good to go. I'm free anytime." Mary fell into step with a hipster carrying a bouquet of wildflowers.

Abby hesitated. "The problem is I have to go with you and I have other cases to deal with. I'm behind because I was in court all day."

Mary knew the feeling. She was pointedly ignoring her email. "I hate to put you out. Can't I go up without you? Could you call the foster family and make an appointment for me to go alone?"

"No, I think I should be there. I'll give you private time with him, but I'm erring on the side of caution, for the record. It makes sense when you're dealing with DHS, especially after today. They'll be watching our every move."

"Do you mind going with me tonight? I'll work around your schedule."

"Okay, I hear you. I'll call the foster family and get back to you. We can meet at the house, it's in the Juniata area."

"Thanks," Mary said, grateful. She crossed the street, passing a harried working mother who held a toddler by the hand, trying to move him along more quickly.

"I'll call or text you back the address. Okay?"

"Perfect. Thanks. Bye." Mary hung up, feeling stronger now that she was back in control of something, at least. She was just about to check her email when her phone started ringing again in her hand. She glanced at the screen, which read KATE SAND RIDOLFI, FAIRMOUNT PREP, so she took the call.

"Mary? It's Kate from Fairmount."

"Right, yes, hello." Mary's mind raced through the possibilities of why Kate would be calling, but none of them was very good. She turned onto Spruce Street, where the shops segued into a more residential neighborhood, with tall rowhomes divided into apartments.

"Mary, I have to ask you a question. Didn't you tell me that the name of the dyslexic fifth-grader you wanted to enroll was Patrick O'Brien?"

"Yes, that's him." Mary knew where this was going. Kate had read the newspaper story.

"He's not the same Patrick O'Brien that's suspected of killing his grandfather, is he? I assume it isn't and I know it's a very common name, so I wanted to check."

"Kate, he did nothing of the sort."

"Whew, I thought so. So it's not the same kid."

Mary couldn't mislead her. "Well, it is the same kid, but he did nothing like that."

"Mary, is it the same kid or not?"

"It's the same kid but he did *not* kill his grandfather—"

Kate gasped. "The police say he did. My assistant read it online."

"He hasn't been charged with a thing. It's a mix-up. Patrick sometimes administered insulin injections to his grandfather to help him out. It was completely unintentional, I swear to you."

"Mary, are you *serious*?" Kate asked, incredulous.

"Yes, trust me. I know what I'm talking about. He's a great kid, and I'm dying to get him in. Please, work with me on this. I swear to you, you'll see I'm right."

"Mary, I can't take him if he's under a cloud of suspicion about something as serious as *murder*. I have a Board of Directors to answer to, and parents."

"He has not been charged with murder, I promise you."

"Mary, when you called me, was the grandfather dead?"

"No, it just happened."

"So who's his guardian?"

"He's with DHS now, but I'll be his guardian, when we have an adjudication hearing. Just give me a few days and I promise, I'll have this confusion cleared up."

"I don't know." Kate paused. "You're asking me to go out on a limb here. We have a waiting list for admission, and I put you at the top, out of consideration for our friendship."

"I know, I appreciate that. I've never let you down before and I won't let you down now. Please, hold his space open, Kate. He'll be squeaky clean, I swear it."

"Okay, but you have to send me a deposit of $5,000, nonrefundable. I can't hold the space without a deposit in the circumstances."

"Fine, I'll make a phone call and get the deposit wired to you, tomorrow."

"Good. Email me when it's set up and I'll ask my assistant to send you the bank and routing information."

"I will. Thank you so much, Kate. I really appreciate it."

"Don't let me down, Mary."

"I won't. Good-bye now." Mary hung up quickly before Kate changed her mind, then she scrolled through her phone, found the cell-phone number for the executor, James Geltz, and pressed CALL.

The phone rang three times, then he picked up. "Hello?" James said vaguely, and Mary assumed he hadn't added her to his cell phone because he didn't know who was calling.

"James, hello, this is Mary DiNunzio, Patrick O'Brien's lawyer." Mary didn't get into the niceties of legal guardianship because she didn't want to delay. Until somebody stopped her, she was going to act as Patrick's lawyer, especially in the special education case.

"Oh yes. Mary, you caught me at a bad moment. I was just about to go out."

"Sorry, I'll make this fast. I'm calling to let you know that I need $5,000 to be wired to Fairmount Prep to reserve Patrick's spot for admission."

"I'm not sure where the funds are. I have to check."

"I can tell you that." Mary tried not to be impatient, though she got the impression that James hadn't followed up. "Did you call Dave Kather, the stockbroker?"

"No, not yet, but I will. As I say, I have to go."

"Wait, just to remind you, Edward doesn't have much in the bank and we still need to pay for the funeral, so we will have to sell some stock for the Fairmount tuition. Could you call Dave Kather and authorize that, then wire the $5,000 deposit to Fairmont Prep? I can email you the routing information tomorrow. Remember, it's ultimately reimbursable by the school district, so it's not as if I'm depleting the funds of the estate."

"Fine. I'll look into those accounts and get back to you. I really have to go."

Mary realized that James hadn't mentioned the news that Patrick was suspected of murdering Edward, so he must not have seen it online yet. She wanted to get ahead of the story, so she could explain to him it wasn't true. "James, one other thing, you're going to be seeing news about—"

"Mary, I really have to go. I'm late. I'll talk to you tomorrow, good-bye." James hung up the phone, leaving Mary annoyed. She hung up and slipped her phone back into her pocket. She'd email James about the newspaper story, but it concerned her that he wasn't paying the case enough attention. She doubted if he'd followed up on Edward's Mass and funeral, because if he had, he would've learned that Edward's body wasn't being released until next week, delaying any funeral arrangements.

Mary powered forward down the sidewalk, troubled. She needed James to give Patrick top priority or she would lose the space at school. She wished she could advance the $5,000 herself, but that was frowned upon. Lawyers paying debts for clients or otherwise commingling funds was considered bad practice, if not unethical.

Mary picked up the pace. She couldn't wait to talk to Patrick and figure out what had happened the night Edward died. It wouldn't be easy for Patrick to go back to that night, but she had no choice. The suspicion of murder could be as damaging to him as if charges were actually filed.

Scaring you is not my intent, my dear.

Mary picked up the pace, then broke into a light jog, not knowing whether she was running from something, or to something.

CHAPTER FORTY-SEVEN

It started to rain, so Mary parked in front of Patrick's foster home and waited in her car for Abby to arrive. Patrick had been placed with foster parents named Jane and Ray Stackpole, a couple who lived in Willow Park, a neighborhood fifteen minutes away from Juniata but considerably more run-down. The Stackpoles' rowhouse was one of the nicer ones on the block, but most of the rowhouses were in poor repair and some were vacant, their windows boarded up with graffitied plywood. Among the parked cars, two were stickered abandoned. The streetlights were all out, plunging the street into a gloomy rainfall. A plastic bag and other trash floated in water in the gutters, and broken glass glinted on the sidewalks.

Mary glanced around, feeling vaguely unsafe. She looked around reflexively for the brown Subaru, but she didn't see it. She glanced in the rearview mirror to see headlights approaching, though she couldn't tell the make or model of the car. She stiffened momentarily, but the car was white and small, a coupe. In the next moment, the coupe parked, and Abby emerged from the driver's seat, popping the hood of a yellow rain slicker over her head.

Mary flashed her high beams, and Abby hurried to meet her because they'd planned to touch base before they went inside. Mary leaned over and opened the passenger-side door, and Abby got in with her heavy bag, easing wetly into the seat and slipping her hood off her head.

"Yikes, what a downpour," she said, with a grin.

"I know, thanks for coming up."

"No worries."

"Can I say it's not that nice a neighborhood?"

"I hear you, but I asked some of my caseworker friends about the Stackpoles, and they have a pretty decent reputation. They're retired and the father, Ray, used to work in corrections."

"You mean the prison system?"

"Yes. He worked at Graterford."

"That's maximum-security," Mary said, surprised. It wasn't exactly warm and fuzzy, but she kept an open mind.

"The mother, Jane, was a stay-at-home mom, and their kids are grown up. They've been through DHS's program for troubled and violent children and they've been fostering for the past nine years. Their home environment is safe, which is the main thing."

Mary thought it was a low bar, but didn't say so. "Do they have any other foster children right now?"

"Yes, two brothers, age twelve and fifteen." Abby touched Mary on the arm. "Look, I know it's not ideal, but it's only temporary."

"Really." Mary didn't get one thing. "Can I just ask you one question? Why would a retired couple take potentially violent children into their home on a regular basis, for almost ten years?"

"Some foster families do it out of the goodness of their hearts, just like you. You stepped up for Patrick out of unselfishness, and most foster families do it for that reason. I don't want to take anything away from them."

"It sounds like there's a 'but' coming."

"But some people do it for the stipend." Abby pursed her lips.

"So, money. How much do they get?"

"About $300 or $400 a month per child, depending on a couple of factors, like they get more if the child has special needs." Abby shrugged. "But the way I look at it, even if their motive is money, that doesn't mean they won't do a good job. From what I hear, the Stackpoles do a very good job, and I have the impression that they do it as a kind of a home business. But that's not a bad thing, right?"

"Right." Mary tried to get back on track. "Did you see that the newspapers have the story about Patrick being suspected of his grandfather's murder?"

"Yes, how much does that suck?"

"Machiavelli leaked it."

"You're kidding me. What's that guy's deal?"

"You don't want to know." Mary didn't want to go into it now. She'd been trying to forget about it since it happened.

"I made the Stackpoles aware of it. We both agreed it was best to keep it from Patrick."

"I agree, but I'd also like to instruct them not to let Patrick talk to Detective Randolph or the police without me or you present."

"You're right, I should've thought of that. I'll talk to them about that tonight. I'll fill them in on school, too. He said we could stay for about an hour, and I asked him if I could talk to them separately and you can have private time with Patrick."

"Great, thanks. I have his suitcase." Mary looked out at the rain, coming down hard. Of course she had no umbrella. "I have to run for it."

"Okay let's go." Abby opened the car door, got out of the car, and hurried for the door, while Mary climbed out, went to the back door, grabbed Patrick's suitcase, then hurried toward the house behind Abby. The front door stood open, and an imposing silhouette of a man, presumably Ray Stackpole, stood behind the screen door waiting for them.

"Come on in, ladies." Ray opened the door. "You're late."

Abby stepped inside. "Sorry, the traffic was bad in this rain. I'm Abby Ortega and this is Mary DiNunzio."

"Welcome to our home."

"Thank you," Abby and Mary said, almost in unison.

Mary set down the suitcase, sizing Ray up while he shook Abby's hand. He was a huge man, about six-foot-three and weighing about 275 pounds, with the physique of a linebacker. He must've been in his mid-sixties, with thick, graying red hair, bright blue eyes, and large reddish-brown muttonchops. He had a loose plaid shirt and baggy cargo pants, but his sleeves were rolled up to show strong forearms covered with tattoos.

"The famous Mary DiNunzio," Ray said with a tight smile, extending his meaty hand toward Mary, and she shook it, trying to squeeze back. He had a manner that was polite, if not warm, and his size alone would have intimidated most felons.

"Ray, it's nice to meet you. Thank you for taking Patrick. He's a wonderful kid, he really is." Mary couldn't help but lobby on his behalf. It was all she could do not to beg him to be nice to Patrick.

"Happy to do it. Jane and I feel it's our calling. She's out food-shopping or she'd take you in the kitchen and bend your ear. She loves company."

"I'm sorry we missed her," Mary said, meaning it. She had been hoping to meet the foster mother, who would've been an important figure for Patrick, given that he didn't remember his mother. Mary gestured to the suitcase. "I brought Patrick's things from his bedroom and some personal pictures of his late grandfather and his mother, which I know he'll want to have."

"Fine." Ray nodded. "We can put that in his room. We require the kids to keep their personal items in their room at all times. That way it's under lock and key and there's no trouble. He's got that wallet and watch that he wanted to keep with him, but that's up there too. Safe and sound."

Mary hesitated. "The wallet and watch belonged to Patrick's late grandfather, Edward. That's why Patrick keeps them with him. It's like a security blanket for him."

"Maybe so, but we have house rules. A kid walking around with a wallet is a fight waiting to happen. Einstein Crisis Center found that out pretty damn quick, didn't they?"

Abby said, "You have a lovely home."

"Yes, you do," Mary chimed in, looking around the living room, which was clean and serviceable, with a plaid couch and chairs arranged around a coffee table. Across from that was a wooden entertainment center that held board games and office supplies, but no books or TV. There were no personal photos, knickknacks, or clutter, and on the walls hung inspirational posters with landscapes and motivational slogans, ATTITUDE, ACCOUNTABILITY, EXCELLENCE. Mary realized that there was no noise coming from any of the rooms, surprising given that the house contained three boys. She said, "You both must have your hands full, taking care of three boys."

"Not really," Ray answered matter-of-factly. "The key is maintaining order and having expectations. You see, a lot of these kids don't have expectations of them. That's not showing respect for a kid if you don't have expectations of them. We have expectations and we show these kids they can meet our expectations."

"That sounds great," Mary said, though she had grown up in the DiNunzio household, where the only expectation was love.

"We've been doing this so long, we have it down to a science. If the kids know our rules and expectations and follow them, we get along fine. The writing is on the wall, as they say." Ray gestured to a homemade sign on the back wall, titled **House Rules**, with a list: **No Profanity; No Fighting; Keep Your Property in Your Rooms; If It Isn't Your Property, Don't Touch It; Remove Earphones or Headphones When You Are Speaking or Being Spoken to**, and so on.

Mary couldn't bite her tongue. "Ray, you're aware that Patrick has dyslexia, aren't you? He won't be able to read that sign."

Ray shrugged. "Oh, right, DHS mentioned that. He can read a little, can't he?"

"No, he can't read at all, not even a sentence. He won't be able to read a word on that sign and he's ashamed about that, even though it's not his fault."

"Well, he'll get the idea."

Mary didn't want to argue, so she tried to be tactful. "He'll get the idea if you explain it to him, probably more than one time. A lot of families with dyslexic children put up pictures to help them remember things. For example, they put a picture of a pair of keys by the door, so the child won't forget to take his key when he leaves."

"He'll be fine," Ray said in a testy way, ending the conversation by his tone.

Abby jumped in, glossing over the awkward moment, "Ray, I'd love to talk with you privately and let Mary visit with Patrick. Is that okay with you?"

"Sure." Ray checked the clock on the wall. "Lights out is at eight o'clock, so you have about forty-five minutes. Wrap it up by five of eight, then I'll be able to get him in bed by eight."

"I will." Mary wanted to make a good first impression for future visits.

"I have to say, he's a sleepyhead. I think it's the medication they put him on at Einstein. The dosages might be off."

"What medication?"

Abby frowned. "They didn't tell me they put him on medication."

"Well, they did." Ray glanced at the clock again. "They have him on Xanax for anxiety, so he's sleepy, maybe even confused. We have kids on meds all the time, so I know the side effects. He took a nap in the afternoon but we woke him up for dinner at five. So he's good to go, now." Ray clapped his hands together. "Time's a-wasting. Mary, follow me into the kitchen. Patrick's waiting for you."

"Thank you." Mary felt surprised that Patrick hadn't come out to say hello, but her heart lightened at the prospect of seeing him again. She followed Ray through a small, darkened dining room into the kitchen at the back of the house.

"Patrick! Wake up buddy!" Ray clapped his hammy hands together, making a loud *smack,* and Mary came out from behind him, alarmed to see that Patrick was lying with his head on his arm, asleep at the kitchen table, sitting before a glass of water.

"Patrick?" Mary said, instinctively going around the table to his side and touching his head.

"Patrick, wake up. You have a guest. That's not how you act when you have a guest."

"Patrick? You okay, honey?" Mary said softly, and Patrick rolled his head slightly on his arm, blinking drowsily. A wan smile spread across his face when he recognized her.

"Mary?"

"Yes. Hi, honey." Mary reached out to him, stroking his cheek as he lay with his head resting on his arm. "I'm so happy to see you."

"Patrick, sit up!"

"Ray, it must be the medication." Mary suppressed the urge to back Ray down directly. She didn't want to antagonize Ray, but she didn't like the way he was talking to Patrick. "The dosage must be too high. This isn't how he acts normally. His energy level is better than this."

"I'll call the doctor about it tomorrow." Ray frowned. "Patrick!"

"Thank you, I'll take it from here," Mary said, as lightly as she could. If she had thought Edward was on the strict side, Ray was even stricter.

"All right, I'll leave you to it. Wrap it up at five to eight." Ray left the kitchen.

"How are you, honey?" Mary sat down in the chair next to Patrick, ruffling up his hair.

"Hi." Patrick raised himself to a sitting position, resting his head on his chin. He made eye contact with her, his blue eyes looking at her only briefly before his lids closed again.

Mary felt concerned. "Honey, I think it's the pills they gave you, they're making you sleepy."

"Yeah, I wish I could take a nap." Patrick's voice sounded wan, but the familiar timbre of his voice touched her heart.

"I miss you, honey."

"I miss you, too." Patrick met her eye, only momentarily. "Are we going home now?"

Mary felt her chest tighten. "No, and I'm so sorry about that. I wish I could take you home tonight, but I can't. It might be a little bit longer, maybe ten days."

"Okay," Patrick said, again wanly, and his affect seemed slack.

"How you doing?"

"Okay."

"I'm trying to arrange for you to go to your new school but that will be a few days, too. So you just have to hang in there, okay?"

"Okay."

"Guess what? I brought your clothes, your comics, and all of your art supplies. I have the pictures of your grandfather and your mom, too. All the things from your grandfather's room. I packed them in a suitcase and Ray will give them to you."

"Uh-huh." Patrick nodded, drowsily.

"I want you to know that I care about you very much and I'm always there for you, even if I can't take you home yet."

"Okay."

"The Stackpoles seem like very nice people." Mary lowered her voice. "Do you like it here?"

"It's okay." Patrick seemed blank, almost expressionless.

"Honey, want to drink some water?" Mary picked up his glass of water and gave it to him, and Patrick took it loosely, sipped some, and handed it back to her. She wondered if he was in any shape to talk to her about what happened the night Edward died, but she had to give it a try. "Patrick, can I talk to you about your grandfather, the night he died?"

"Okay."

"Remember you told me that sometimes you would give him his needle, like when his hand got the shakes?"

"Uh-huh," Patrick answered, and there was a change in his tone that suggested to Mary he understood the question.

"Did you give him his needle that last night, you know, the night before he passed away?"

"Uh-huh."

"Do you mean yes?" Mary asked, trying to clarify; he wasn't speaking clearly and his affect was absolutely unreadable.

"Uh-huh," Patrick said, and Mary took it as a yes.

"Patrick, try to wake up and listen to me, okay honey? Try to think back to that night. When you gave your grandfather his needle, do you remember where you gave it to him?"

"Uh-huh." Patrick nodded, still resting his chin on his hand.

"Okay, good. Where did you give it to him?"

"Okay."

Mary blinked. "Patrick, I'm asking you where you usually gave your Pops his needle?"

Patrick exhaled and inhaled, like a deep sigh. "In his belly. He likes soup."

"Right." Mary wasn't sure what to make of his answers, but kept going. "The night that your grandfather passed away, do you re-member him asking you to give him his needle?"

"Uh-huh?"

"So did you give him a needle the night that he passed away?"

"Uh-huh."

Mary fell silent, stroking his little fringe of bangs away from his forehead, and he closed his eyes, leaning against her hand. She could see that there wasn't much point in asking him questions tonight. She wanted to give him a little bit of comfort, in a world that had offered him so little of late. She reached over and hugged him, and Patrick leaned into her, resting his head on her chest and encircling her waist with his arms.

"Everything is going to be all right, honeybun," Mary said softly, but she didn't know if he heard her or not. She hoped he felt her comfort at some level, or at the very least, he had some respite. The house fell so quiet that the only sound was the rhythm of Patrick's breathing, and she realized that Ray and Abby must have gone out front to talk. In time, Mary found herself holding Patrick as he dozed, and it was the most peaceful she had felt all day.

She let her gaze wander around the kitchen, which was as clean, practical, and as generic as the living room, with white cabinets and a white Formica countertop. There was no residual aroma of food, which struck her as unusual, since she was used to kitchens smelling like oregano, basil, cigar smoke, or ecologically friendly counter cleanser.

The only item of interest in the room was a big chart taped to the refrigerator, which read EXPECTATIONS at the top, above the names Rashid, Amal, and after that, Patrick. Each boy had his own column, and there were gold stars in the boxes for Rashid and Amal, next to Make Bed; Clean Up Bathroom After You Use It, Seat Down; Rinse Bowls After Breakfast; Put Dishes in Dishwasher, Fac-ing Correctly, and so on.

Mary's heart sank. She couldn't bear that Patrick had to live here, among all the signs that he couldn't read. She had thought that Edward was strict, but Ray was stricter, and she didn't know how

Patrick could endure all that he had gone through. She would have to follow up about his meds, then she realized Abby might have to do it, since she had no legal status. There was so much to do to help Patrick, and Mary didn't know how she'd be able to do it without being his guardian, but she would have to try. She couldn't let him down and she would always be there for him, no matter what, and that was exactly what she told him, whispering into his ear as he slept. Until Ray returned, frowning, at five minutes to eight.

Later, Mary drove back toward the city, heartsick after leaving Patrick behind at the Stackpoles'. She had to get him out of there and she had to deal with the suspicion that he was involved with Edward's death. Abby had told her that Ray had believed the newspaper reports, which was natural since he'd been in law enforcement. Ray had also asked Abby about the Robertson Complaint brought by Machiavelli, so he had the same evidence as Judge Green, all of it consistent and damning. Mary prayed that Ray's attitude toward Patrick wasn't tainted by his mistaken beliefs, but Ray was only human.

Mary drove through the neighborhood without really seeing the traffic or the TV lights in the houses, flickering on either side of her as she passed. She made her way to I-95 because it was quicker, taking her directly into the city if she got off at Callowhill Street, which was only a block from the Roundhouse, Philadelphia's police headquarters. She had done her share of criminal work and handled more than a few murder cases. Homicide detectives, who worked around-the-clock, were even busier at night. In fact, she knew their unofficial slogan was Our Day Begins When Yours Ends.

Mary mulled it over, making her way to the highway. Detective Randolph might be at the Roundhouse right now, and even if he wasn't, she had to believe he would come in to meet with her. After all, he was considering her as an accomplice after the fact, a cover-up to Edward's murder. She had information he wanted. But if she called him, she could be walking into the lion's den. She would take her chances, for Patrick.

She reached for her cell phone.

CHAPTER FORTY-EIGHT

HOMICIDE DIVISION, read an old plaque on the wall outside the elevator, and Mary made her way down the narrow, filthy corridor, which curved around to the right because the building was shaped like three circles stuck together, which was why it was called the Roundhouse. It had been built in the sixties, when its design was space-age, but now it was dated and in horrible condition. Every year or so, the newspapers carried the story that the police headquarters would be moved to a better location, but it never seemed to happen.

The fluorescent lighting flickered above, the floor was of old green tile, broken in places, and the walls were grimy, cheaply paneled. Mismatched file cabinets lined one side of the hall, inexplicably, and Mary passed a crummy bathroom on the right, its door propped open by a full trash can. She kept going ahead toward a secured door with a buzzer next to another sign, **HOMICIDE**.

She buzzed and waited to be admitted, mentally preparing herself. After a few calls, she'd been able to reach Detective Randolph, who had called her back because he was "out on a job," which she knew was police-speak for a dead body. He had agreed to meet her at the Roundhouse and was on his way, so she had shown ID and used his name to get in downstairs, and he had called a Detective Hilliard to admit her to the squad room.

In the next moment, an African-American detective in a shirt and

tie came to the door, checked her out, and opened it with a professional smile. "You must be Mary DiNunzio. I'm Detective Hilliard."

"Yes, thank you." Mary smiled back, stepping inside the waiting
area, which had only gotten dirtier since the last time she was here.
It was no wider than a hallway, with black rubbery seats and an
ancient gumball machine. Both walls were lined with the scariest
photo array ever, of fifty or so Wanted posters, men and women of
all races and ethnicities wanted for murder.

"Detective Randolf should be here any minute. Follow me, I'll
set you up in an interview room."

"Thank you." Mary fell into step beside him through the squad
room, which was empty, probably because most of the detectives
were out on jobs. The squad room was so cramped that there wasn't
enough space to pass in places, and they had to make their way
between gray desks, outdated computers, and mismatched file
cabinets.

"So I've heard your name before."

"You have?" Mary brightened. Maybe her name was finally getting around town.

"Yes, you work with Bennie Rosato."

"Right."

"We don't mind the defense bar, contrary to popular opinion."
Detective Hilliard smiled, and Mary smiled back.

"And we value the police department, contrary to popular opinion," she said, meaning it. "Detective, I've been a resident of this
city all my life and I appreciate everything you do to keep me and
my family safe."

"Thank you." Detective Hilliard grinned, more broadly, and they
stopped at the first interview room. He opened it to reveal a grimy
white box that contained a few gray folding chairs, a rickety old
table with some forms scattered on top of it, and most remarkably,
a metal chair that was bolted to the floor.

"I'll take a seat, but not that one," Mary joked, then realized it
wasn't funny.

"Ha! I can get you some coffee, but it's my duty to warn you that
it's from a vending machine."

"I'll pass, thank you." Mary entered the interview room and set her purse on the table because the floor was filthy.

"Let me know if you need anything. He'll be here pretty soon."

"Thanks."

"Take care." Detective Hilliard closed the interview room door, leaving Mary alone. She sank into one of the folding chairs and noticed above the door that there was a discreet black camera lens, probably for a video recording of interviews with suspects. On the wall to her left was a small mirror, which was undoubtedly a two-way for observing statements, and she glanced at the forms on the table, picking one up.

The form was a waiver of Miranda rights, with a list of questions with blanks for the answers: **1. Do you understand that you have a right to keep quiet, and do not have to say anything at all? 2. Do you understand that anything you say can and will be used against you? 3. Do you want to remain silent? 4. Do you understand you have a right to talk with a lawyer before we ask you any questions?**

Mary set the form aside, beginning to worry. The waiver form, the camera lens, the two-way mirror, and the chair bolted to the floor were physical reminders that her interview with Detective Randolph could have legal consequences for her. She wondered briefly if she should call John, Judy, or even Bennie, who was one of the top criminal defense lawyers in the country. Mary didn't have to be here unrepresented, after all. She could've come with legal guns blazing.

But she told herself to calm down. She was allegedly a competent lawyer and she knew enough to represent herself. If things went south, she could just terminate the interview. She knew from Bennie that there were plenty of investigations, ones that the public never heard about, which didn't turn into charges because they were handled unofficially between lawyers and police. She was hoping that Patrick's case would be one of them. She had truth and justice on her side, which should count for something.

Suddenly there was a knock on the door, and in the next moment it was opened by Detective Randolph. He met her eye with a tired smile, wearing the same dark suit he had on in court today, slightly more wrinkly. "Hi, Mary, if I can call you Mary?" he asked, extending his hand in a friendly way.

"Yes, of course." Mary stood up and shook his hand. "Thanks for coming in."

"Not at all. Call me Joe." Detective Randolph came into the room, stepping aside for a shorter, slimmer man who looked in his thirties. He was handsome, with dark almond-shaped eyes set far apart, and a great smile. His dark hair was cut in a brush cut, gelled in a hip way, and he had on a dark suit tailored close to his trim, muscular body.

Detective Randolph gestured to him. "Meet my partner, Ted Jimenez. You can call him anything you like, but don't be too nice to him. It goes right to his head. I call him *Defective* Jimenez, but he doesn't think that's funny."

Detective Jimenez smiled at Mary, extending a hand. "Hi, Mary. Nice to meet you. As far as what you should call me, don't call me Defective Jimenez. It's not that funny. Call me Joe, too. That will confuse my partner all to hell. Or we should piss him off. I'll be Young Joe and he can be Old Joe. "

Detective Randolph rolled his eyes, for Mary's benefit. "Why don't we just call him The Hot One? That's how he imagines himself. We gave him a T-shirt last year that said The Hot One. You think he didn't wear it? He never takes it off."

Mary laughed, and so did Detectives Randolph and Jimenez, but she wondered if they were being genuine or trying a comedy routine to relax her, so she would lower her guard. It was a Machiavellian trick and she remembered that Machiavelli had even tried to use it against her, but she put him out of her mind for now.

"Sit down, please." Detective Randolph gestured at her chair and sat down across from her, and Detective Jimenez took the other chair, but not before he slid a skinny reporter's notebook from his sport jacket, with the pen attached, and set it on his lap as he sat down, flipping open the front cover.

"Mary, I'm going to take notes," Detective Jimenez said, flashing her his killer smile. "I'm sure that's okay with you."

"It's fine," Mary answered, straightening in her chair. "I assume from the camera that the session is videotaped."

"Don't give us that much credit." Detective Jimenez chuckled. "The camera is broken and hasn't worked in ages. The audiotape never worked in the first place, and we don't have the budget to repair it."

"That's criminal," Mary said, and they both laughed again.

Detective Randolph crossed his legs. "Mary, I think the easiest way is for you to tell us what you know about Edward O'Brien's death. I appreciate your volunteering to come in here. I regret that you got blindsided at the shelter care hearing today. If it hadn't been scheduled, I wouldn't have testified and given my theories or the results of my investigation. It really is too soon."

"I understand that and thank you for saying it." Mary believed him, and his tone sounded genuine. "I do think you're off on the wrong track and that's why I came in today. You testified that you thought Patrick injected his grandfather intentionally and you couldn't be more wrong about that. You also testified, or at least you suggested in your testimony, that somehow I knew that and destroyed evidence of a crime. You couldn't be more wrong about that either."

"So let's talk." Detective Randolph met her eye directly.

"Exactly. That's why I came in. I could've lawyered up, but I didn't. I want to fill in the blanks about Patrick's relationship to his grandfather, about Patrick himself, and about the timeline of events leading up to Edward's death."

"I appreciate your cooperation." Detective Randolph blinked, his interest plain. "Before we begin, I have to advise you of your Miranda rights. I know you know them but I have to recite them."

"Let me ask you first, do you really suspect a ten-year-old boy of injecting his beloved grandfather with insulin, intentionally trying to kill him?"

"Yes, tentatively," Detective Randolph answered, his expression frank.

"He's *ten*."

"Mary, that doesn't negate the possibility. We've had ten-year-olds who kill in this city. According to the facts I have, including the Complaint filed in Common Pleas Court, Patrick O'Brien is a deeply disturbed ten-year-old."

Mary felt pained to hear it. It was the direct opposite of the sweet little boy she knew, but she let it go for now, changing tacks. "And you really suspect me of covering up a murder? A lawyer, a partner at my own law firm? A lifelong resident?"

"Yes. Again, tentatively."

"Why?" Mary asked, trying to understand, because the notion was so absurd.

"To protect a child you obviously care about. For all we know, *you* could have been the one who injected Edward with the fatal dose."

"That's ridiculous!" Mary blurted out, shocked. "What are you talking about?"

"Okay, I'll lay some cards on the table. In addition to Patrick's fingerprints on the syringe, we found adult fingerprints, too. We don't know whose they are."

Mary kicked herself. The prints had to be hers, since she'd picked up the syringe to throw it away. "But why would I kill Edward?"

"To get custody of Patrick," Detective Randolph answered, his tone reasonable. "I saw you in court. You want Patrick."

"But I would never kill anybody to get him!" Mary said, though she couldn't deny it was a theory, even if it was a bad one.

"Maybe so, but there are too many questions I don't know the answer to. As I testified today, the only facts I have are that Edward died of an insulin overdose early Friday morning. I don't know what happened between Thursday night and the time of your phone call to 911 on Friday night, reporting the death. By the way, I heard the audiotape of your 911 call. It's too brief to answer any questions. You only said that you were 'reporting the death of Edward O'Brien, a seventy-two-year-old and he died in his sleep.' You also asked the dispatcher to tell the patrol officers, when they came for his body, not to run their sirens because it might upset his grandson."

Mary remembered the call, and it made her nervous that Detective Randolph and Jimenez had already listened to the audiotape.

They were seriously investigating her complicity in Edward's death, and it was becoming clearer that even though she knew the idea was ridiculous, they didn't have the facts to see it her way, at least not yet.

"Mary, I'll lay all my cards on the table. I followed up with the patrol officers who came to the house after you called 911. I spoke with Officer Agabe-Diaz. He said that you had pulled some strings with Officer Diamond of the Twenty-fifth Precinct."

Mary shuddered. She remembered that she had asked for the favor, and now it was coming back to haunt her.

"I followed up with Officer Diamond. Evidently you know his mother from some case you handled for her. You called in a favor and asked him to wait to call DHS to pick up Patrick. You said you wanted Patrick to spend a night alone in the house with you, after Edward died. Why, so you could coach him on his story? You're a lawyer. You knew what he should say."

Mary could see how every single good thing she did was getting turned against her and Patrick. She had to nip it in the bud before Detective Randolph dug in his heels.

"So you're clearly very involved with Patrick after the murder. It's reasonable to assume that you were involved before, since you were the one who made the phone call. I have to suspect you, if only because there's so much information that only you have. For example, I don't know why you told the 911 dispatcher that Edward died in his sleep." Detective Randolph started to count off on his fingers. "I don't know what time you arrived at the house or why you were there. I don't know if you discovered Edward's body or Patrick did. I don't know if anyone else was present. I don't know your whereabouts at the time of Edward's death."

Mary felt her heart sink as he continued. It was even making sense to her that the police suspected her.

Detective Randolph was still talking. "I don't know what you did to clean up the scene. I don't know why you cleaned up the scene. I don't know why you threw away the insulin cartridge." Detective Randolph kept counting on his fingers. "We noticed the dust was unsettled on Edward's night table and dresser. It looked as if some items had been taken. I don't know who took them. If it was you, I don't know what you took or why. I don't know why you would wash sheets from a bed that no one was ever going to sleep in again, if you weren't trying to destroy evidence."

Mary sensed that Detective Randolph had stopped talking only because he was running out of fingers. She took a deep breath, because she knew she had a chance to clear this up. "So bottom line, there's a lot you don't know, but I can assure you, there's a perfectly reasonable explanation for everything. I didn't cover up any crime because there was no crime to cover up. If Patrick injected Edward that night, he did so at Edward's request, because that was what they did when Edward's hand got too shaky to inject himself. Patrick is a wonderful ten-year-old boy and he's innocent of any murder, *completely* innocent."

"Now it's time for you to put your cards on the table." Detective Randolph leaned forward. "Still want to talk?"

"Yes," Mary answered, without hesitation.

"First I'll Mirandize you, and then we'll get started." Detective Randolph recited her Miranda rights, then turned to the form on the table, presented it to Mary, and took her through each of the questions that she had just read to herself, asking her to answer each one in writing, then sign the bottom of the form, so the waiver of rights was knowing and valid. Mary signed her name, knowing she was doing the right thing for Patrick.

So she began a detailed account of everything that had happened, starting from the morning that Edward had hired her and stopping at the day that the police had taken Patrick into DHS custody. Detective Randolph interrupted only to ask questions and he listened without apparent judgment, while Detective Jimenez took notes nonstop. When Mary was finished, she took a stab at getting them to close their investigation, though she knew it was a longshot.

"Detective Randolph, I hope that makes it clear to you that there was simply no crime in this case. If Patrick injected Edward, it was at his request, and Patrick wasn't abused by Edward, so he had no motive to kill him. Now that you know the facts, I would expect you to shut the investigation down."

"Well." Detective Randolph's expression remained impassive. "Mary, thank you so much. That was very complete. You answered many of the questions I had."

"So I take it that's a yes?"

"No." Detective Randolph pursed his lips. "My partner and I will have to talk it over and get back to you. But you know that one critical piece is missing. I have to be able to talk to Patrick and ask him if he injected Edward that night."

Mary hadn't wanted to tell them about her visit with Patrick tonight, but she came clean. "I just visited him at his foster family's home and asked him that question. Unfortunately, he's been put on anti-anxiety medication, and there's something wrong with the dosages. He was so lethargic that I couldn't be sure he was understanding my questions. But if he injected Edward that night, it was clearly with Edward's permission."

"You may be correct, but we can't take your word for it. We can't close this investigation unless and until we talk to Patrick."

"I have to think about whether I would allow that. Let me get back to you." Mary had anticipated the request, but when it came to Patrick, her lawyerly instincts were taking over. Or maybe it was her maternal instincts. She picked up her purse and rose.

"One last question." Detective Randolph stood up, hitching up his pants. "Don't take this the wrong way, but how are you still Patrick's lawyer? I understood that you weren't declared his legal guardian today."

Mary had anticipated that question, too. "I'll get back to you about that, as well," she said, opening the door.

Luckily, she knew the best criminal defense lawyer in the city.

CHAPTER FORTY-NINE

Mary closed the door to the conference room for her emergency meeting with Bennie and John. She had called them both as soon as she left the Roundhouse, asking Bennie to represent Patrick and John to represent her. John had immediately agreed, but Bennie had agreed only to the meeting. Mary crossed to her chair but remained standing, to plead her case. Both of them were still dressed from work, though they were in completely opposite moods. John was supportive, but Bennie was cranky. Mary had her work cut out for her, to persuade Bennie to represent Patrick. Mountains had been moved more easily.

Mary cleared her throat. "Thanks for coming. Let me just explain why I called you here and why I need you both."

"No." Bennie crossed her arms, sitting in her typical seat at the head of the table. "DiNunzio, I don't want to represent your ten-year-old. You have to find him somebody else."

"Please hear me out, partner." Mary had never called Bennie that before, but she was pulling out all the stops. "You agreed to meet with me, so at least give me a chance. Fair enough?"

"Fine." Bennie sighed theatrically, then sipped coffee from her favorite mug, which read I CAN SMELL FEAR.

Mary began again. "I lost the shelter care hearing, and that means I'm not Patrick's guardian. Now, Patrick is suspected of murdering his grandfather, but I can't act as his criminal defense lawyer because

I have a conflict of interest with him, in theory. For all the police know, I could've injected Edward with a fatal dose of insulin and I'm presently under some ridiculous suspicion of covering up evidence. I asked John to be my criminal defense lawyer and he agreed."

John nodded. "I've done some criminal work, and I'm happy to represent you, if they don't close the investigation."

"God bless you," Mary said, grateful. "So that means Patrick needs a criminal defense lawyer. He can't be represented in a criminal case by Abby Ortega, his Child Advocate, because representation by a Child Advocate is confined to proceedings in Family Court. The same is true of Michael Harris, Patrick's *guardian ad litem*, who should burn in hell anyway."

John chuckled, but Bennie checked her watch, already impatient.

Mary faced Bennie, directly. "So this is where you come in. Patrick needs a criminal lawyer and I'm begging you to do it. You're the best—"

Bennie frowned. "Hold the flattery. Rewind a minute. Why would the police close the investigation, like John said?"

"I went to the Roundhouse tonight and spoke to the detectives. I told them what I knew." Mary hadn't mentioned that in her phone call because she didn't know how her former boss would react. Or rather she did know how her former boss would react, which was why she kept it from her.

"You did *what?*" Bennie asked, aghast.

"Let me tell you why, briefly." Mary put up a hand, cutting off a tirade. "The police have major proof problems with Patrick's case and they know it. I mean, consider how high the standard is in a criminal case, reasonable doubt—"

"I know the standard. Why would you ever walk into the Roundhouse and start talking? Have I taught you *nothing?*"

"How can they prove that Patrick injected Edward with the intent to kill him? They can't. Even if they could suggest that Patrick's motive was that Edward was abusing him, which he wasn't, they can't prove motive beyond reasonable doubt. I met with Cassandra Porter at the Philadelphia Children's Alliance and I know that she believed that Robertson was the abuser, so she will be vulnerable to cross-examination."

Bennie rolled her eyes. "I don't know who any of these people are—Cassandra, Robertson, whoever. I'd have to get completely up to speed on the case, yet another reason I don't want to take it, and still, none of it explains why you went to the police—"

"Let me just finish," Mary interrupted Bennie, probably for the first time ever. "I knew the police would have major proof problems and I also knew that a lot of their theories about me were based on a lack of information. I went to them to fill in the information, which rang true because it was. And I hope that given what they know about their proof problems, they'll close the investigation, but not until after they talk to Patrick."

Bennie thought a minute. "Okay, DiNunzio. I see why you went to the police and amazingly, I don't think it's legal malpractice."

"Thank you," Mary said, uncertainly.

"I agree." John sipped his coffee. "I know that our go-to is not to cooperate with the police, but this is one case where it makes sense."

"Thank you, John." Mary smiled. "You're the best."

"What's going on with you two, by the way?" Bennie frowned in confusion, looking from John to Mary and back again. "When did you get to be such good friends? The last time we were in this conference room together, you were at each other's throats."

"We made up," John answered with a smile.

"I apologized," Mary added. "I was completely wrong about him. John did an amazing job representing me in the shelter care hearing."

"Yet you lost," Bennie said flatly, eyeing them both.

"We got surprised by the murder allegations," Mary said, for them both. "So now the only problem is that they want to talk to Patrick, and he needs a great criminal lawyer. That's you."

"Sucking up to me won't work."

"I'm trying everything." Mary didn't say, *But it has before.*

"I'm too busy to take the case."

"It won't take long."

"I don't like kids. I have a dog."

"So get your dog a kid," Mary said, even though she was pretty sure it was the other way around.

"Still, I don't want it. Count me out. I want to go home."

"Bennie, if you met this little boy, you would be totally on board. He's the sweetest kid and he's had the hardest time in life. He's been physically and sexually abused, then his grandfather died, and now he's in a foster home. You wouldn't believe how much he's been through, and he's got nobody in the world to look out for him but us."

"Sympathy doesn't work for me." Bennie sipped her coffee.

"What *does* work for you? What do I have to do to get you to take his case?"

"There's nothing you can do. I don't want to take it, and I won't. I hate stepping into a case that was somebody else's. I like to control things from the beginning."

"It is the beginning of the criminal case," Mary told her, urgently. "The investigation started only yesterday. Even the detective admitted that it's preliminary, they said it in open court."

"DiNunzio, who you kidding? I saw an article about the kid online. Somebody's already trying to taint the jury pool on you."

"That was leaked by opposing counsel, Nick Machiavelli."

"Machiavelli!" Bennie's eyes flashed with recognition. "Machiavelli, that bogus pretender to some nonexistent throne?"

"Yes," Mary answered, surprised. "How do you know him?"

"First, it's not a name you forget, and secondly, I had a case against him once and he annoyed the crap out of me. Is he really your opposing counsel?"

"Yes." Mary saw an opening, knowing that Bennie was insanely competitive. "He's representing the teacher's aide who abused Patrick and he's been pulling the strings against us. He's the one who got the *guardian ad litem* hired in the shelter care hearing, and the *guardian ad litem* testified against our Child Advocate, which was one of the reasons we lost." Mary watched Bennie begin to simmer, then realized she had a trump card left to play. "And I never intended to tell anybody this, but he attacked me in his office today."

"*Attacked you?*" Bennie's mouth dropped open in outrage.

"Mary, are you serious?" John asked, appalled. "When?"

"After the shelter care hearing." Mary felt shaky, talking about it now. "I don't want to go into details because it's creepy, but he has this thing against me and he's vowing to take it out on Patrick. He tried to kiss me, but I hit him and got away but—"

"Say no more!" Bennie smacked the table, incensed. "Why didn't you tell me that? That should've been the first thing you said! You're my partner, and I'll be *damned* if I'll let anybody get away with that!"

"Really?" Mary said, touched.

"Of course! I *absolutely* will represent Patrick and we *absolutely* will win!"

"Thank you so much, Bennie. I really appreciate it." Mary glanced at John, who looked back at her with a concerned frown, undoubtedly about her revelation, but she waved him off.

Bennie was still jazzed, her face alive with animation. "I can't wait to take him down. It'll be my pleasure. I'll do it for *sport.*"

"Now here's the hard part, guys." Mary pulled out her chair and sat down. "Even though I've just asked Bennie to be Patrick's lawyer, I'm worried that I don't really have the power to hire an attorney for Patrick because I'm not Patrick's guardian. He's currently in DHS custody, so DHS has legal custody and the power to hire an attorney for him. But I thought I could beat them to the punch." She turned to Bennie. "I figured if you said yes, then I could call DHS and tell them you were on board before they even thought about hiring him a criminal lawyer."

"One problem." Bennie hesitated. "DHS could decide *not* to hire me—and they will decide against me, if you're right about Machiavelli being on the other side, pulling the strings."

"Right, Machiavelli could have Harris, the *guardian ad litem,* call DHS and refer them to an attorney. They could even manipulate the result so that Patrick gets in deeper trouble, sabotaging him."

Bennie nodded, on the same page. "We're fighting a war by proxy, and he's going to keep fighting. We have to keep outmaneuvering him."

"Okay, so how about this idea? Edward had an estate—about $350,000 in real estate, life insurance, cash, and stocks—and Patrick is the sole beneficiary. The executor is a lawyer in the Northeast named James Geltz. I've already been in touch with him to get a deposit to reserve Patrick's admission to private school." Mary realized that James hadn't called her back yet. Anthony hadn't called her either, but that was another matter. "The only party with any legal authority besides DHS is the executor and he has the power of the purse. In other words, the executor has the authority to hire a lawyer and authorize an expenditure for attorneys' fees, doesn't he?"

"If the grandfather was Patrick's legal guardian. Was he?"

"No, unfortunately, but that just means I have to move fast, doesn't it? DHS isn't going to hire Patrick an attorney because they aren't going to leap to Patrick's defense that quickly and they don't have funds to pay anybody with. They don't know about the will or the executor yet. This all just happened." Mary was trying to improvise, using Bennie and John as a sounding board. "So Bennie, now that I know you're in, how about I call the executor and ask him to hire you? I'll email him a representation agreement and get his digital signature right away. Then we're in first, before DHS wises up."

Bennie frowned. "There's only one problem. Under Pennsylvania law, a person who is convicted of killing someone who left him an inheritance is not entitled to inherit. So if Patrick were convicted of killing his grandfather, he gets nothing under the will. Since this is a real possibility, the executor would be well within his discretion to refuse to pay Patrick's defense costs. The same is true of the expenditures for private schooling you mentioned."

"Oh no." Mary grimaced. "I wonder if that's why James isn't calling me back. He could be dragging his feet."

"It's possible, and here's more bad news. Life insurance is distributable in accordance with a beneficiary designation form, not a will, but if Patrick were found guilty of Edward's murder, the insurer doesn't have to pay off to him, even though he's the beneficiary on the policy. So no life insurance proceeds are coming

Patrick's way either, which is too bad, because they often pay quickly."

Mary saw an opening. "But Patrick hasn't been convicted of murder. He hasn't even been charged."

"That's right, and it's the only wiggle room you have."

"I'll take it," Mary said, heartened. "So it's up to the executor's discretion whether he authorizes or denies, and your point is, I should expect a fight."

"Yes, and if he denies it, there's still another solution." Bennie pursed her lips. "I'll represent Patrick for free. That way we don't have to go begging to the executor. He has no power over us if we don't want our fees paid by the estate."

"Would you do it on that basis?" Mary asked, surprised. "*Pro bono?*"

"Absolutely." Bennie's blue eyes glittered with excitement. "Crushing Machiavelli is definitely in the public interest. Either way, the first step is you calling the executor."

"On it." Mary reached for her telephone, but just then, John waved his hand to get her attention.

"Hold on, ladies. I just thought of something else we might have missed." John frowned in thought. "I think there's an ethical problem if I represent Mary and you, Bennie, represent Patrick. Mary and Patrick's interests are in conflict and members of the same law firm, especially one this small, aren't generally supposed to represent codefendants in criminal matters. It runs afoul of the Code of Professional Responsibility."

Mary hadn't even thought of that as an ethical problem.

Evidently, neither had Bennie, because she was frowning. "You're right. But I know how to fix that. A Chinese Wall."

"Exactly." John nodded. "It's a borderline case, but I'd go with a Chinese Wall."

Mary had no idea what they were talking about. "I feel dumb. Could you explain to me what a Chinese Wall is?"

John smiled. "There's no reason for you to know this, it's a big-firm thing. In a situation like ours, where two lawyers in the same firm are representing criminal codefendants with conflicting interests, then the ethical way to keep both representations is to put up a Chinese Wall. It's an invisible barrier to communications within the firm. As a practical matter, it means that because I'm your lawyer, Mary, I can't talk to Bennie about Edward's murder case."

"I see," Mary said, relieved. She didn't want Patrick to lose Bennie as a lawyer, nor did she want to lose John as a lawyer.

John continued, "Conversely, Bennie can't talk to me about the murder case and that includes every last detail, like meeting schedules, phone calls, or any procedural questions about the case. It has to end, here and now."

Bennie nodded, newly grave. "Right, so John, you and I have no further discussions about the murder case, starting from this moment." Bennie turned to Mary. "By the same token, no more meetings between you and Patrick."

"Wait," Mary said, dismayed. "Why is that? I was planning on visiting Patrick to stay in touch with him."

"You can't. It is not prudent. There can't be any crosstalk between you two from this point on. If I'm Patrick's lawyer, I don't want him talking with you anymore."

John interjected, "She's right, Mary. If you keep seeing Patrick, sooner or later you're going to start to get information from each other. He could easily tell you something that Bennie told him, and if he did, you would tell me. That's a violation of the Chinese Wall. If we want to keep both representations in-house, that's what we have to do. If you ask me, it's a borderline enough case in such a small firm. I know there's case law that says we're too small for a Chinese Wall."

Bennie snorted. "Oh, please. I didn't get this far by not taking risks. It's a reasonable risk, and I'm going to run it. I think this is an ethical choice and I can defend it if I have to."

Mary kept thinking about Patrick. "But I think it's best for Patrick if I see him. I have to stay in touch. What if I promise that I won't talk about the case with him? I can hush him if he starts talking about Bennie."

John shook his head. "Mary, I'm your lawyer in the criminal matter. Follow my advice. Even apart from the Chinese Wall, it wouldn't be good for you to be meeting with Patrick. Everything you say to each other is discoverable by the police. Remember, you're not his lawyer anymore, so your conversations aren't covered by attorney-client privilege."

"I'm still his lawyer in his special education case."

"Only until Machiavelli decides to challenge that. If DHS has custody of Patrick now, they can go hire a new special education lawyer. We would have no power to stop them."

Mary couldn't accept that answer, if it meant not seeing Patrick. "We could go to the executor and get him to sign a representation agreement for me, too, guaranteeing I remain Patrick's special ed lawyer."

"Good, do that. But still, you would be vulnerable in the murder case and you would be making Patrick vulnerable, as Bennie said. You two are suspected of being in cahoots, on the murder case, with you as accessory after the fact, if not a co-conspirator. You said it, they could even believe that you killed Edward."

Mary deflated, knowing they were making sense. "So I really shouldn't see him anymore."

"Not until we get this settled. It's best for Patrick."

"Oh boy." Bennie came over and placed a hand on her shoulder, an uncharacteristically tender gesture. "Tell you what, I'll visit the kid for you," she said begrudgingly.

Mary looked up at her. "When?"

"Soon."

"Tomorrow night?"

"Fine." Bennie rolled her eyes. "Am I a good partner or what?"

"Yes, and thank you." Mary smiled, rallying. "Will you be nice to him?"

"I'll be nice to him, on occasion," Bennie answered, with a wink. "Now call the executor, and I'm leaving the room. This meeting is over, and the Chinese Wall is hereby up."

CHAPTER FIFTY

"Dammit!" Mary looked at John in frustration, her cell phone in hand. She had called and texted James Geltz again, but he hadn't answered either. "I can't reach Geltz."

"He must be out."

"This is driving me crazy. It can't wait." Mary rose, anxious. "Machiavelli isn't going to sit on his hands. He probably already called Harris to get a lawyer in place and get the jump on us."

"Where's Geltz's office?"

"In the Northeast."

"So he probably lives up there, too."

"Right." Mary knew what John was thinking and started scrolling through her phone. "Let me see if I can get his home address. I'll go up there, right now. That's not crazy, is it?"

"On the contrary, it's exactly what I would do. It can't wait. Like I told you, family law is twenty-four/seven, and Patrick is screwed if Machiavelli gets his criminal lawyer in place before we get Bennie in place."

"I agree." Mary plugged in James Geltz's name, and only a few addresses popped onto the screen. Two of the addresses were in the far suburbs, but one was in Northeast Philly, near Geltz's office. "Bingo. I know where this is. It's not that far."

"So go." John stood up, walking to the door. "I'd go with you but my brother is visiting me this week. He's actually at home, waiting for me. I picked him up after the shelter care hearing."

"Oh, sorry." Mary felt a pang of guilt, crossing to meet him at the conference room door. "I didn't realize that you were busy tonight."

"It's okay, he'll be fine. The Sixers game out in LA is on, and he loves basketball." John hesitated as if to say something, but stopped himself, and Mary realized that he was about to open up to her.

"John, what were you going to say?"

"Remember I told you that it can be difficult to be a guardian?" John stopped in the threshold, turning to her, his eyes unusually pained. "This is one of those times. He's having issues at his group home, so he's going to stay with me this week."

"Oh no," Mary said, quietly. "Is there anything I can do?"

"No, but thanks."

"What's his name?"

"Tom."

"Is he older or younger?"

"Older." John's expression tightened, his handsome features forming a professional mask again, as if that was all he wanted to reveal.

"I wish you had mentioned on the phone that you were busy. Once I had your okay, I didn't need you to come in."

"I came in for a specific reason." John lowered his voice, glancing over his shoulder. "To back you up with Bennie. I thought it would help you shame her into representing Patrick. Nobody wants to look bad in front of a witness."

"That was so nice of you. Thank you."

"What the hell happened with Machiavelli? You had to *hit him*?" John's fair skin flushed with uncharacteristic anger. "That's outrageous! You want me to beat him up for you?"

"Nah." Mary waved him off. "You've done plenty for me already. Thank you, really. Now go home and take care of your brother. I'm going to track down a wayward executor."

"Good luck," John called out, as Mary headed for the hallway.

"Good night!" Mary called back, thinking randomly that if she didn't have Anthony, she might have set her sights on John. Then again, she was only assuming she had Anthony. All she had at this point was a caterer and a dress that didn't fit, but this wasn't the time to worry on her wedding drama.

Half an hour later, Mary was in her car and speeding back up I-95, in caffeine heaven after a big cup of coffee she'd bought at a Wawa convenience store. She was surprisingly energized, even jittery after what happened with Machiavelli. Telling Bennie and John the story had brought it back to her, though she hated trivializing the attack by using it for leverage with Bennie. Mary told herself that she turned it into a good thing if it helped Patrick, and the ultimate irony was that because Machiavelli was such a pig, he had Bennie on his ass, which was poetic justice.

Mary raced up I-95 and noticed that she was approaching the exit for Geltz's neighborhood. Edward's neighborhood was only twenty minutes away from Geltz's neighborhood, but Edward's was on the west side of I-95, which served as an unofficial dividing line in this part of the city. Unlike the neighborhoods on the west side of I-95, the neighborhoods on the east were more upscale, and Mary had been there many times, visiting lawyer friends. The homes were new construction or townhomes with yards, trees, and a gorgeous view of the Delaware River, which flowed between Philadelphia and New Jersey.

Mary took the exit, followed around to the right, and let the GPS direct her to Riverlook, a fancy development designated by a stone entrance landscaped with shrubs and illuminated from tiny lights in the ground. She took a right into the development and followed the GPS to Geltz's house, getting the lay of the land. Large single-family homes were interspersed with townhomes, and their façades were of gray or beige stone, illuminated from below with tiny lights. The grounds were tastefully landscaped and manicured.

Mary found Geltz's house, which was 221 Hudson Lane, and parked at the curb, getting the first impression that nobody was home. His house was three stories tall, but the windows were dark and if it had landscaping lights illuminating its façade, they had been turned off, too. There was a circular driveway in front of the house but it was empty.

Mary got out of her car and walked up the driveway, feeling a cool breeze off the water, which must've been on the other side of the development. The air smelled fishy, and the only sounds were seagulls squawking overhead or the rumble of somebody rolling a trash can to the curb. She reached the front door and she knocked using a brass knocker, then waited for someone to answer. No one did, so she knocked again, just to make sure. There was no answer the second time, but she wasn't giving up.

Mary went back to her car, got inside, picked up her phone, and called Geltz's cell phone again. He didn't answer, and the call went to voicemail, so she left a message: "James, it's Mary again. I hate to be pushy, but it's important that I talk with you tonight, so I'm actually sitting in front of your house. Can you call me at your earliest convenience? If not, I'll see you when you get home. I'm sorry about the intrusion, but it can't be helped. Thank you."

Mary hung up, then checked to see if Anthony had called, but he still hadn't. She had no idea what he was up to, but she put him out of her mind for now. She scrolled through her email and answered a few emails from her other clients, but she was too distracted to work on anything but Patrick's case. She happened to look up and noticed an attractive middle-aged woman with a blonde ponytail, coming over to her passenger-side window, holding a small liver-and-white colored spaniel under her arm.

Mary lowered the window. "Hello."

"Excuse me, can I help you?" the woman asked, though her tone was less than helpful. "I noticed you sitting in front of the house. You've been out here for a good fifteen minutes."

"Right." Mary smiled to show she came in peace. "I'm waiting for James Geltz to get home. I've been trying to reach him but I haven't been able to. I'm an associate of his, and it's about an important legal matter."

"Did you call him on his cell?" The woman's eyes narrowed, and Mary sensed that she was trying to suss out if she had Geltz's cell-phone number.

"Yes, I called him on his cell but I haven't been able to get ahold of him. Here, let me show you my card." Mary dug in her purse, found her wallet, and extracted a business card, which she handed over. The woman squinted at the card in the relative darkness, then passed it back with a smile.

"Well, hello, Mary. I'm Ellen Moravian." The dog barked, so Mary assumed she had passed a test.

"Nice to meet you."

"Nice to meet you, too. I live next door to James, and he asked me to keep an eye on the house. That's why I came out to see who you were."

"Oh, where's James?"

"He's gone."

"What do you mean, gone?"

"He left about two hours ago. We both live alone, so we keep an eye on each other's houses when we go away."

"Did he say where he was going?" Mary asked, frustrated. She had to get a lawyer for Patrick before Machiavelli did.

"No, I didn't speak to him, he left a note in my door. That's the way we do it. I assume he went away for business or to his condo in the Caymans. He goes there quite frequently. He plays golf."

"Do you have a number where I can reach him in the Caymans, if that's where he is?"

"No, sorry."

"What did his note say?"

"Just that he'd be gone for a few weeks and for me to please keep an eye on the house and make sure that everything was okay."

"A few weeks?" Mary groaned. "Did he leave a number for you to call in case something happened?"

"No, I already know who to call. Patricia."

"What's her last name?"

"Van Marl, his secretary. She runs his life." Ellen set the dog down. "Last winter we had a power outage while James was away, so I called Patricia and she handled everything. She lives at Water's Edge, the apartment complex up the road. She would know where to reach him if he doesn't call you back."

"I'm surprised that he would leave for an extended period of time. He didn't mention anything about a trip, and we're at an important juncture in a case."

Ellen shrugged. "I know he left, I saw him from my kitchen window, putting his suitcases in the car. He had to pack in the rain. I remember thinking, how's he gonna get all those suitcases in the trunk? His trunk isn't that big."

"What kind of car does he have?"

"A Subaru sedan."

Mary blinked. "What color?"

"Brown."

"Is it old or new?" Mary asked, surprised. It struck her as too coincidental that both Robertson and Geltz had brown Subaru sedans. She flashed on the brown Subaru, zipping past her on Moretone Street and parked across from the Philadelphia Children's Alliance when she, Edward, and Patrick had gone there. Something didn't make sense.

"His car's a few years old, I think. James isn't the flashy type." Ellen's arm jerked as the dog tugged her away. "Oops, sorry. Peach has to go. Good night."

"Bye," Mary said, shaken. She had been sure that Robertson had been the driver of the brown Subaru because he had showed up right after she had followed it, but maybe Robertson wasn't the driver. Maybe Geltz was the driver and it was *his* brown Subaru that was following them, not Robertson's. Maybe Robertson didn't have a brown Subaru at all. Only Geltz did.

Mary felt baffled, her thoughts racing. She remembered that she had caught a glimpse of the driver of the brown Subaru. He'd had a mustache, like Robertson. Geltz didn't have a mustache, she remembered from his picture on the website. Mary didn't know why Geltz would follow them anyway, but she still had to find him.

She raised the window and started the engine.

CHAPTER FIFTY-ONE

"Patricia?" Mary said, to the woman opening the front door. Patricia Van Marl was probably Mary's age, in her mid-thirties, but looked younger in an oversized T-shirt that read I'VE GOT ATTITUDE TO SPARE and jeans. She was cute and petite with narrow blue eyes, pin-dot freckles over a turned-up nose, and curly red hair in a bumpy ponytail, sprouting like a fountain from the top of her head.

"Yes, I'm Patricia, who are you?"

"Mary DiNunzio." Mary handed her a business card. "Sorry to bother you at home, but it's an emergency. I've been working with James Geltz because he's the executor of Edward O'Brien's estate, who passed away recently."

"Oh yes, I remember. Deepest condolences."

"Thank you. I need to talk to James about authorizing expenditures for Edward's grandson Patrick, but James didn't return my calls, and his neighbor told me that he was out of town for a few weeks."

"No he's not." Patricia shook her head, frowning slightly. "Who told you that? Ellen?"

"Yes. She saw him leave the house two hours ago. She gave me your name and said you might know where he went."

"Man oh man, if it's not one thing, it's another." Patricia opened the door wider and gestured her inside. "Come on in."

"Thank you." Mary looked around the entrance hall, which was bright and cheery, with yellow walls, a funky umbrella stand, and a multicolored pegboard stuffed with children's jackets and raincoats. The living room beyond was well-furnished, as well as cluttered with children's toys, and the townhome complex was lovely, just down the road from Riverlook.

"I'd invite you in, but I don't want you to get sick. My husband has the flu, and my six-year-old is getting it, too. Guess who's whinier? Don't even ask." Patricia slid a cell phone from her pocket. "Let me call James."

"I've been calling him all day, but he hasn't returned my call."

"Sorry, that's not like him. He'll answer this number. We call it the Batphone." Patricia pressed a button on her speed dial. "We don't give anybody this number. He gets so many client calls on his regular cell phone. Sometimes you have to be client-free, you know? You're a lawyer, so you understand."

"Yes, I do," Mary answered, relieved. She didn't want to lose any more time to Machiavelli and she was still thinking about that brown Subaru.

"Hmm, it went to voicemail," Patricia said, holding the phone to her ear, then she said into the phone, "James, can you call me as soon as possible? I'm with a lawyer named Mary DiNunzio and she's trying to reach you about Edward O'Brien's estate. She's at my house and she needs to talk to you ASAP." Patricia hung up and started texting. "Let me text him, too. You'll see, he'll text back any minute. I call him a text maniac. I swear, it makes him feel young. Some days he'll send me so many texts, I tell him, just freaking *call me.*"

"Ellen told me he left her a note asking her to watch the house and she saw him packing suitcases in his car. He has a brown Subaru, right?"

"Yeah." Patricia checked her phone screen, puckering her lips.

"I thought so. It's funny, I thought I saw him driving the other day on Edward's street, Moretone Street in Juniata, like around one o'clock. Do you know if he went to see Edward around one o'clock that day?"

"No, I don't know. He goes to meetings out of the office, so that's possible. I don't think he had anything scheduled with Edward, though. Edward only came in the one time and got his will done. I didn't remember his name until James told me to pull his file." Patricia frowned at her phone screen, newly worried. "Hmmm. He hasn't texted back yet. Usually it's instantaneous. He dictates his texts, so they're fast but incomprehensible. It's the attack of auto-correct."

"Where can he be?" Mary kept her tone light, though she wanted to get as much information as possible. "Ellen said he has a condo in the Caymans and he goes down there for golf trips. Do you think he would just take off and do that?"

"No, not without telling me, and he wouldn't take off this week. He has meetings all day tomorrow." Patricia checked to see if the phone ringer was on mute. "I admit, this is strange. We know he's not at the house, if Ellen saw him leave. I bet he's at the office."

"Should we call the landline at the office?"

"No, he never answers that. If he doesn't answer the Batphone, that worries me." Patricia met Mary's eye, her concern plain. "I hope nothing happened, health-wise. He has afib and he had an ablation procedure last year. We even got a defibrillator for the office, just in case."

"Oh no." Mary thought it didn't square with packing suitcases, but didn't say so.

"I think I should stop by the office to check on him."

"Good idea," Mary said, intrigued. "I'll come with you, if that's okay."

"Sure, it's not that far. Stay here a sec, I'll be right back. I want to tell my husband where I'm going." Patricia left the entrance hall, hurried through the living room, and disappeared around the corner. Mary heard Patricia's footfalls on a carpeted stairwell, voices upstairs, then Patricia descended the staircase and entered the entrance hall with her purse.

"Good to go?"

"Yes, but I'm going to call the Batphone one more time." Patricia pressed REDIAL on her phone, held it to her ear, then frowned slightly. "It went to voicemail again. Let me leave a message."

"Sure."

Patricia said into the phone, "James, it's me again. I'm starting to worry about you. Mary and I are coming over to the office. I'm hoping you fell asleep when you were working or something like that. Call me as soon as you get this though and save us the trip." Patricia hung up the phone. "I'm trying."

"I appreciate that."

"Let's go. You can follow me in your car." Patricia opened the door, and they both left the house and walked down the front walk to the pocket parking lot in front of the cluster of townhomes, where Mary had parked in a space marked for visitors.

"What's the address?" Mary didn't remember Geltz's office address, though it had been on Edward's will.

"It's 2701 Gower Street. It's off of Street Road. We can park in the back." Patricia chirped a red Honda Civic unlocked, climbed inside, and backed out of the space, and Mary did the same. The two women took off, left the townhome development, hit Remington Road, then headed toward I-95, crossing under the highway to reach the east side.

Mary instinctively started looking for the brown Subaru, though at this point, she had no idea who the driver was. It seemed impossible that both Robertson and Geltz had brown Subarus, so it had to be one or the other. Geltz didn't have a mustache, so Mary stuck with her original assumption that the driver was Robertson. He was the one who had a mustache and a motive, and Geltz and Robertson didn't know each other, so it couldn't be that Geltz had lent Robertson his car.

Mary followed Patricia through the warren of rowhomes, then turned onto wider streets and the area grew less residential. They reached Street Road, one of the busiest commercial stretches in the city, its four lanes lined with McDonald's, Dunkin' Donuts, Wendy's, big box stores, and long stretches of auto dealerships glutted with new cars, slick with residual rain.

They approached Gower Street and took a left turn, passing a strip mall of four businesses; a nail salon, a dry cleaner, a martial arts studio, and on the far end, a double-wide storefront that stood out because of its navy-blue awning and painted sign, discreetly lit, LAW OFFICES OF JAMES R. GELTZ, ESQ. All of the businesses were closed except for the martial arts studio, which was brightly lit and abuzz with activity. A class of about ten men and women in karate robes were finishing up, bowing to each other and the instructor, in a black belt.

Mary followed Patricia to the right behind the strip mall and pulled into a narrow parking lot, which was packed because of the karate class. The back of the strip mall was tan brick and windowless, with metal security doors for the back entrance to each business. They drove to the end of the lot, but there was only one empty space, which Patricia pulled into. Mary turned around in the lot, went back out, took a right, and found a space on the side street in front of a truck mechanic's shop, which was closed.

Mary got out hurriedly, grabbed her purse, and hustled to the parking lot. She made her way to the back entrance, becoming edgy about what she might find inside. She hoped Geltz hadn't fallen ill and she couldn't fight the feeling that something else was going on, since he had left for a long trip without telling Patricia. Mary reached the door, and Patricia was struggling with the lock.

"Sorry about that." Patricia turned her key with a tiny grunt. "I didn't realize it was the last space."

"That's okay."

"This freaking lock needs to be replaced, I keep telling him. It takes forever to open this damn door." Patricia grunted again, and finally the door opened. She reached inside and turned on a master switch, and fluorescent light spilled from the inside. "Come on in."

"Thanks." Mary stepped inside, finding herself in a hallway with tan tiles and fluorescent lighting, containing a coatrack, metal umbrella stand, and stacked cardboard boxes.

"Follow me." Patricia closed the security door behind them and led the way down the hall, which ended in a white door. "He still hasn't called on the Batphone. I really hope he's okay. He's a good boss."

"How long have you worked for him?"

"Two years. I like it. The hours aren't bad, and the pay is decent, and it's so close to home." Patricia unlocked and opened the white door. "Come in."

"Thanks." Mary followed her through the door, which led to a hallway that was painted light blue and had deep navy carpeting.

"James, are you here?" Patricia called out as she walked ahead, but there was no response.

Mary followed her out of the hallway, which opened onto a wider hallway that had a glass-walled break room on the right, and directly opposite, a large conference room with a long walnut table. Mary oriented herself, realizing that the conference room was located at the office's storefront on the strip mall.

"James?" Patricia called again, but there was still no response.

Mary walked behind her toward a waiting room with a reception desk and cushy blue chairs arranged around two walnut coffee tables, topped with magazines. An American flag stood in a stand next to a display case with fake-gold golf trophies, and laminated newspaper articles blanketed the walls. Behind the reception area, in the far left corner of the building, was a door, presumably to Geltz's office.

"James?" Patricia opened the door, and Mary came up next to her.

James's office was empty. His glistening walnut desk set on an angle, and in front of the desk were two blue leather chairs. Bookshelves containing case reporters and an array of photographs lined the room.

"So what do you think?" Mary asked Patricia.

"I feel better. He isn't here, so he didn't have a heart attack. Funny, his desktop computer is missing. I guess he took it with him." Patricia went over to the desk, stood behind it, and looked around, moving some correspondence aside.

Mary entered the office and came over, seeing what she meant. James's desk had stacks of papers and case files around its perimeter, but its center, where a desktop computer keyboard would be, was clear. The power cord was missing, and on the floor was an empty surge protector. "Is that unusual for him to take his desktop?"

"It's not *that* unusual. He did it once last winter when he went down to the Caymans for, like, two weeks. He has a laptop but he prefers the desktop. He says he can read the monitor better."

"So that's consistent with what Ellen said, that he was leaving for a few weeks. I do need to talk to him. How do we reach him in the Caymans?"

"The Batphone or the cell. I don't even know the landline."

Mary wondered if that was where he was and she wanted more information. "Ellen also said he was single. Does he date anybody? Could he be out on a date?"

"No, he was dating somebody off and on a few months ago, but she moved to Denver."

"Does he have kids he could be with?"

"No, his daughter lives in London."

"What about his friends? Does he have any good friends he might be with?"

"Hmm, maybe so." Patricia brightened. "There are three guys he plays golf with. He could be with one of them. If it hadn't rained so hard earlier, I would've bet he was playing nine holes and had dinner at the club. Maybe they got caught on the course in the rain."

"Maybe they did. Which club does he belong to?"

"Whitestone. He *lives* there in summer. Golfers are nuts." Patricia took her phone out of her back pocket, checking the screen. "Still it worries me that he didn't return my call or text. The Batphone always works. Maybe he lost the Batphone on the course."

"Could he be en route flying to the Caymans? Then he'd have no cell service."

"That's also possible. You have to take two planes. It's a hike." Patricia scrolled through her phone.

"Or could he be with clients? Taking them out, socializing?"

"Probably not. He networks with the Vietnam vets organizations. Most of them are older, like Edward. It's not like they party hearty."

"Did he serve in Vietnam?"

"No, I never asked him why. A lot of the vets have done very well, so they're good clients and they need estate planning. He goes to all of their functions." Patricia pressed a number into her phone. "Excuse me while I call his golf buddies. I bet he's with one of them."

"Thanks," Mary said, seizing the opportunity to snoop around. She skimmed the correspondence on the desk, scanned the red case accordions, then gravitated to the photographs.

Patricia spoke on the phone. "Hello, Don, this James Geltz's secretary Patricia. Is he with you? I haven't been able to find him and I need to talk to him . . ."

Mary scanned the photos on the bookshelves behind the desk, and there were a few pictures of a pretty young girl who must have been James's daughter, as well as a bunch of group photos with men in ties holding drinks or wearing golf clothes with verdant backdrops. She looked at the faces but she didn't recognize James in the photos.

". . . You haven't seen him since when? Okay, thanks. Sorry to interrupt you. Good night . . ."

Mary picked up one of the group photos and held it up for Patricia. "Is one of these men James?"

"Sure, yes." Patricia hung up the phone then pressed more numbers into the keypad. "Dan hasn't seen him, and I'm going to try Morris. He could be with Morris."

"Thanks." Mary eyed the photo again. "In the photo, which one is James?"

"He's the man in the middle, with the mustache."

CHAPTER FIFTY-TWO

"James has a mustache?" Mary masked her alarm. "I looked him up on the website and he didn't have a mustache."

"That picture is five years and fifty pounds ago. Also, he wasn't dyeing his hair then. The clients tease him about it. They call him Grecian Formula." Patricia said into the phone, "Hi, is this Morris? Morris, this is Patricia, James Geltz's secretary. I was wondering if James is with you . . ."

Mary turned away, hiding her surprise. She set the photo back down on the shelf, her thoughts on fire. So Geltz *did* have a mustache. Then it could've been him in the brown Subaru on Moretone Street and at the Philadelphia Children's Alliance. And if Geltz had gained weight, his face would've been more fleshy, too. So was it Geltz, following Edward and Patrick? Why?

". . . You haven't seen him? I called Dan but he doesn't know where he is. I think you're right, he probably went down to the Caymans. Right, his golf bag's always in the trunk. Okay, good night. Sorry to bother you."

Mary turned around. "No luck?"

"Not yet. That was two strikes, and I'm going to try the third, but they're not worried about him. Morris told me he'd been talking about the Caymans and he thinks that's where he might be." Patricia scrolled through her phone to find another number, then called. "Cal, hi, this is Patricia, James Geltz's secretary? I wonder if he's with you. Sorry to bother you, but I have a client who needs to speak with him. He's not there? Did he mention anything to you about going down to the Caymans? Oh, okay. All right, I won't worry. Thanks a lot."

Mary remembered that the two times she had seen the brown Subaru was on Thursday afternoon between three and four o'clock, when they were at the Philadelphia Children's Alliance, and on Friday, late afternoon, when she had followed it down Moretone Street then lost it on the way to Robertson's house. She went back to the desk and looked around for James's calendar, but she didn't see one. He must have it on his phone.

Patricia hung up. "I give up. He's a big boy. He's not with them, but I'm not worried about him anymore. They think he went to the Caymans. That's probably why he took the computer."

"Patricia, let me ask you, does he have a calendar or does he keep it in his phone?"

"He keeps it in his phone, but I can access it, why?"

Mary tried to act casual. "It's funny, I'm sure I saw him driving by on Thursday between three and four, and on Friday, in the late afternoon. Do you know where he was at those times?"

"Does it matter? I really should get home. I have a child to take care of. And a six-year-old." Patricia chuckled.

"Please? Can you just check his calendar? I'm curious. It's driving me crazy."

"Okay, hang on." Patricia thumbed through her phone, then stopped, reading it. "He was out at a client meeting on Thursday afternoon between three and four and on Friday afternoon, late, but he didn't say which clients. He just put in 'client meeting.'"

"Is that typical, that he does that?"

"Sometimes." Patricia put the phone back into her pocket.

"But he has to bill time. Do you do the bills?"

"Yes, and I take care of all of the expenses for the office, too. He takes care of his own money, that's it."

"How do you know who to bill his time to, if he only writes 'client meeting'?"

"I take it from his time sheets, not the calendar. Usually when he writes 'client meeting,' he doesn't assign it to any client on his time sheets. I noticed it a while ago, but I figured, so what? He can take down time. It's his business, not mine." Patricia checked her watch. "Okay, I gotta go. Let's lock it up."

"But wait, Patricia, I'm sure it was James I saw on both of those days, watching Edward's house and following him around." Mary hadn't wanted to tell Patricia, but this was her last chance.

"Why would he do that?" Patricia recoiled.

"I don't know, that's what I'm trying to find out. I mean, he told me Edward hadn't been in for four years."

"That's right."

"So they had nothing to do with each other for four years, then all of a sudden, James starts following Edward around?"

"Oh, come on," Patricia snapped, newly defensive. "He didn't *follow* anybody. Now you're being ridiculous."

"But I know he did, I saw him."

"You *saw* my boss following his client? Are you sure it was him?"

"Yes. Last Thursday and Friday."

Patricia hesitated. "Well, I remember something minor about Edward, but it probably doesn't matter."

"What?" Mary asked, intrigued.

"I think it was on Wednesday last week, Edward called the office. He called on the landline and I took the call."

"What did he want?"

"He wanted to talk to James but James wasn't in. So then I asked him what it was in reference to, and he said that he needed a referral for a lawyer. He didn't say what kind of lawyer and I didn't ask him why."

Mary put two and two together. "That must have been when he was looking to hire me. It was for a Complaint that had just been filed against him in connection with his grandson, Patrick."

"Oh, he didn't say that. Anyway, he asked me if I knew any good lawyers and I said no. I didn't think James would want me giving referrals, willy-nilly."

"Sure, right."

"So then later, I told James that Edward had called asking for a lawyer. That's all."

"What did James say?"

"He got mad at me, asking me why didn't I find out what the matter was and why Edward wanted a lawyer. He snapped."

Mary felt stumped. "Why would he snap at you for that? Why would he care if Edward needed a lawyer?"

"I have no idea."

"So then what happened?"

"I don't know." Patricia shrugged. "I assume James called Edward and referred him to a lawyer. To you, I guess."

"No, he didn't, because our receptionist said that Edward came to me because of our website. James doesn't know me and he wouldn't refer Edward to me."

"I don't know. That's his business."

"No, but it's also my business, because of Edward. I mean, let's be real, doesn't it seem strange that James would act that way? Why would he care if one of his clients needed a lawyer?"

"Maybe he thought we were going to get fired?"

"That can't be it. If you're going to let go of your lawyer, you don't ask him for a referral."

"Well, I don't know, and I don't think it matters. I really need to get home." Patricia became impatient, which Mary understood, but couldn't let it go.

"Wait, please work with me for one more minute. Given the chronology, it seems like James was worried that Edward was going to call a lawyer, and James was following Edward around to see if he did, or what he did." Mary felt like she was onto something.

"Whatever, I really have to go." Patricia headed for the door, and Mary fell into step with her.

"But I still need to talk to James."

"I don't know what to tell you. I'm really sorry." Patricia left the office and headed down the hall, but Mary took her arm.

"Patricia, please, you're a mom. There's a ten-year-old boy in foster care and I'm trying to give him his future. If I don't talk to

James, I can't get him a new lawyer, and he can end up in foster care for the rest of his life. You've been so terrific, but isn't there any other way we can find him? Could he have gone back to the house? Should we check there?"

"There's no reason to. I called everybody who he might be with."

"Isn't there anybody else who might know where he is? Somebody who he talks to?"

"I don't think so." Patricia stopped abruptly, raking her fingers through her red curls. "Oh, wait. I know somebody we could try. He doesn't golf but they talk on the phone. Dave Kather."

"The stockbroker?" Mary didn't say so, but she remembered that Dave Kather had told her that he never talked to James. "Dave Kather was Edward's stockbroker at Cornerstone Financial."

"I'm sure. James sends all of his clients to Cornerstone Financial. They all invest with Dave. I think every Vietnam vet in the tri-county area invests with Dave, thanks to James. So Dave might know where James is." Patricia reached for her phone. "I'll call him for you."

"Hold off. I have his number." Mary was thinking steps ahead. "Do you know Kather?"

"No, never met him."

"He doesn't come by the office?"

"No."

"Have you spoken to him on the phone?"

"I don't know, once or twice maybe? I really do need to go." Patricia resumed walking to the white door that led out of the office proper.

"How do you know that James sends him clients?" Mary followed on her heels.

"I just do. James will tell me to send a client Dave's number."

"Does Dave have the Batphone number?"

"I don't know, I never gave it to him." Patricia opened the white door, and Mary went through into the tan hallway.

"When Dave called the office, does he call on the cell or the landline?"

"The cell." Patricia closed and locked the white door.

"Do you know any reason why Dave would tell me that he doesn't talk to James, when he does? I mean, Dave and James have some sort of business relationship. James refers him investment clients. Why would they want to keep that a secret?"

"They don't, they just didn't tell you about it, and I don't think it means anything. I'm sure there's email about it. I know they email each other."

"How do you know that?"

"Because I've seen emails from Dave on James's computer."

"On the desktop that's missing?"

"Not *missing*, he took it with him." Patricia led the way down the corridor, and Mary couldn't help but feel that she was onto something, but it was just out of her grasp.

"Do you have access to James's email?"

"I have access to his main email but he has a private email that I don't have access to. Not that this is any of your business."

Mary let it go. "Do you know if James communicates with Dave on the main email or the private email?"

"No, I don't. I only noticed it on the computer once or twice. I don't spy on my boss, there's no reason to." Patricia reached the security door, twisted the deadbolt, and opened it. "James is a nice old man and he does a good job for his clients. And it's not suspicious or anything that he didn't tell you the details of his personal business."

"If he calls, will you let me know?"

"Totally." Patricia closed and locked the security door, handing Mary her phone. "Here, put your number in my contacts. He'll call me when he lands. This will sort itself out."

"Thank you." Mary took the phone, scrolled to CONTACTS, plugged in her information, then handed it back. She glanced around the parking lot and noticed that it was practically empty, with only three cars left. The martial arts class must've let out, and two men stood talking between their cars, parked behind the studio.

"You're welcome."

"Thanks again for the help. I hope your husband feels better."

"That makes two of us." Patricia hurried to her car, chirping it unlocked. "Good night."

"Good night." Mary watched Patricia drive out of the lot. Her head was swimming. She felt so frustrated that she hadn't been able to persuade her that something was amiss, but she wasn't stopping there. She went in her purse, rummaged for her wallet, and pulled out a business card.

Detective Randolph's.

CHAPTER FIFTY-THREE

"Hi, this is Mary, Detective Randolph." Mary walked through the parking lot, and the men from the martial arts class got inside their cars, started the engines, and left.

"I'm busy at the moment. Can I call you back?"

"But this is important. I think there is something you need to investigate in conection with Edward's death. There's been some very fishy things going on—"

"Mary, it's late, and I'm busy."

"But just hear me out." Mary collected her thoughts. "I needed to see Edward's executor to get a disbursement from the estate, but he took off for the Caymans for no apparent reason and without telling his secretary or his friends."

"What does that have to do with anything?"

"That's strange enough behavior, and before that, he was following Edward around in his car. Edward called his office and told him that he needed a referral for a lawyer, and as soon as that happened, the executor started following Edward." Mary reached the sidewalk and walked down the street. The asphalt shone in the ambient light. "I thought it was Robertson who was following him, but now I think it was the executor."

"Mary, I'm out on a job. I don't have time—"

"But I think this is related to Edward's death. Patrick didn't do it, I swear to you." Mary walked down the street toward her car. "I found out tonight that the executor has a mustache and he drives a brown Subaru. That means it was him, not Robertson."

"Hold on. What did you say?"

"He has a mustache."

"No. What kind of car?"

"A brown Subaru. A sedan. A neighbor saw him packing his trunk and—"

"This executor, what's his name?"

"James Geltz. He's an estates attorney in the Northeast. I'm at his office now, I'm just leaving."

"You're at Geltz's office? What are you doing?"

"I'm trying to find Geltz. I was just talking to his secretary, and he left town, taking his desktop. I'm thinking he was trying to hide whatever was inside it—"

"Mary, Geltz is the job I'm on."

"*What?*" Mary gasped.

"Yes, James Geltz was found dead in a brown Subaru, parked in an industrial stretch off I-95. He died of a gunshot wound to the head, an apparent suicide."

CHAPTER FIFTY-FOUR

"Geltz killed himself?" Mary asked, stunned. "Oh no! My God!"

"Now tell me again how you—"

Mary heard nothing else. Suddenly she was shoved from behind with brute force. She flew off her feet, staggering forward. She had no idea what was happening. It came out of the darkness.

She landed facedown on the sidewalk. She broke her fall instinctively, scraping her palms. The wind got knocked out of her. Her chin hit the concrete. Her jaw reverberated with shock.

She gasped for breath. Her purse was jarred off her shoulder. Her phone went skidding under her car. She could hear Detective Randolph saying, "Mary? Mary?"

A man was upon her, his dark figure silhouetted in the faraway lights of Gower Street. She realized she was being mugged. She torqued her body around, groped for her purse, and flung it at the man. "Take it, I don't care!" she shouted, cowering.

She looked up, but the man had gone after her phone, diving under the car. She realized it was a chance to get away. She left her purse, scrambled to her feet, and bolted back toward the martial arts studio.

"Help!" Mary shouted at the top of her lungs. She ran as fast as she could. She knew the mugger wouldn't follow her. He wanted her phone and purse. Still she had to get away.

"Help!" Mary yelled. The martial arts studio was still open. Its back door stood ajar. Fluorescent lights were on inside. A man appeared in its doorway, still in his karate robes. He must have heard her cries. He ran toward her, his robes bright in the darkness. It was the martial arts instructor, with a black belt.

"Help, I'm being mugged!" Mary screamed to him, and the martial artist raced toward her. She heard footsteps behind, running hard after her. The mugger wasn't giving up. She couldn't imagine why. He had her purse and her phone. He must not have seen the martial artist. The mugger was in for a rude awakening.

The martial artist reached Mary at the back of the parking lot, taking her firmly by the arms and keeping her moving toward the martial arts studio. "I got this," he said. "Get in the studio. Close the door behind you. Call 911."

"I can't call, he's got my phone!" Mary yelled as she hurried to the open door.

"Use the phone on the desk. Go."

Mary ran to the martial arts studio. She tried to close the door behind her. It wouldn't budge, held open with a wooden wedge. She didn't have time to fuss with it. She didn't want to lock out the martial artist anyway.

She looked at the parking lot to see what happened. Light spilled from the open door, illuminating the scene. The mugger raced forward to confront the martial artist. She got a good look at the mugger's face. She recognized him from the website.

It wasn't a mugger at all.

It was Dave Kather.

CHAPTER FIFTY-FIVE

Mary gasped, terrified. She couldn't process what she was seeing fast enough. Kather was coming after her. But she had an expert protecting her. Kather would be stopped right now.

The martial artist raised his arms, lowering his center of gravity. "Stop what you're doing or I'll stop you!"

All of a sudden Kather swung his arm up. He held something in his hand. Its metallic glint caught the light. It was a weapon. He aimed it at the martial artist. Mary didn't know if it was a gun. Her heart leapt to her throat. She realized what it was a split second later. A Taser.

Kather fired the Taser. Two purplish lights flared like pinpoint explosions. Two electrified pins on wires leapt from the Taser. The pins made a hideous buzzing sound as they connected with the martial artist. He spasmed hideously, his neck wobbling and his arms flailing. He crumpled to the parking lot, still in paroxysm.

Mary screamed in horror. Kather dropped the Taser, then looked up at her. He ran toward her.

Frantically Mary tried to kick the wooden wedge from under the door. She couldn't do it. She whirled around and ran into the martial arts studio.

She saw the main entrance on the other side of the room. She sprinted across the room for it, almost tripping on the thick blue mats. She reached the door, practically threw herself against it, and tried to yank it open. It didn't move. It had been locked. The keys were nowhere in sight.

Mary looked around wildly, trying to find another exit. There wasn't one, only a front door and a back door. She was trapped. The studio was a single empty room. A wooden rail ran the length of the room, separating the mats from the spectator and office area. She was completely exposed. The only furniture in the room was the desk. Kather would find her.

Equipment and weaponry ringed the room. A rack of long wooden sticks was affixed to the wall. A life-size model of a human torso stood on a stand. Nunchucks filled an oversized bin. A ceremonial samurai sword was mounted on the wall. She had no idea how to use any of it. She would have to try. It was her only chance.

Suddenly she was plunged into darkness. Kather must've turned off the lights. She didn't know where he was. She couldn't see the weapons anymore. She couldn't hear Kather over her own ragged breath. Darkness was her enemy, light was her friend. There had to be a light switch near her. She was next to the door. With the lights on, she could see and be seen through the storefront. Somebody would drive by and discover them. She groped on the wall for a light switch. She found it and flicked it on.

"No!" Mary screamed when she saw what was happening.

Kather was midway toward her, raising a gleaming samurai sword.

Mary ran to the other corner, pushing the hanging punching bag at him. It barreled fast at Kather, but he ducked it. He kept coming, swinging the gleaming sword back and forth. Suddenly police sirens blared nearby. All she had to do was stay alive until they got here.

Mary was too terrified to even scream. She felt like she was out of breath. He kept coming toward her and she kept backing away. She started grabbing anything she could and throwing it at him, desperate. She pushed the torso stand in his path. He went around it. She grabbed a long stick and whipped it through the air. He jumped aside. She threw black pads at him. He almost tripped but kept coming, scything the razor-sharp sword through the air.

346 'I Lisa Scottoline

Mary had only one weapon she knew how to use. Her brain. If she got him talking, she could back toward the door and run away. "Kather, don't be stupid. Just run. The police are on their way. You heard me talking on the phone."

"You know too much," Kather said, advancing, but Mary kept edging away, back toward the door. He was getting closer and closer. So were the sirens. Mary prayed they got here in time.

"No, I don't know anything. What were you and Geltz up to? Stealing his clients' money? Embezzlement? Stock fraud? Here's some free legal advice. Whatever it was, you'll do less time for a financial crime than for murder. Don't be stupid. Don't kill me."

"I killed Geltz and O'Brien. One more body won't matter." Kather lunged at her with the point of the sword, and Mary side-stepped him, then turned away and ran for the door in sheer terror.

Kather caught her by the neck from behind, yanking her backwards. She couldn't breathe. Her Adam's apple compressed her windpipe. She heard herself gagging. The police sirens were only blocks away.

Kather dragged her backwards off her feet. She realized what he was doing. He was going to drag her behind the counter. He would stab her to death there, where they couldn't be seen from the window. He had killed Geltz. He had killed poor Edward. And now he would kill her.

Mary heard a primal guttural sound. She realized it was her. She could barely breathe. She spotted a stick leaning against the mirror. She saw herself in the mirror. Her eyes bulged. Her face was a mask of horror, her skin a grotesque red. She was going to die if she didn't save herself.

She made a swipe for the stick, grabbed it, and whipped it low and backwards. It connected with Kather's lower leg.

He stumbled, the stick caught between his calves. He fell to the mat, cursing.

Mary raced for the door. She gasped for breath, her chest heaving. Her throat hurt too much to scream. She made it to the door but Kather caught her from behind by her hair, yanking her down to the mat on her back.

Suddenly the sirens blared upon them. The martial arts studio lit up with red, white, and blue flashing lights. The police cruisers were here. Mary had stayed alive long enough.

Kather started to run past her for the door.

Mary thought fast and stuck out her leg, right in his path.

Kather tripped, flew forward from momentum, and banged his forehead on the wooden rail. He hit the mat facedown, knocked unconscious.

Mary got to her feet and staggered over to him. The red, white, and blue lights flashed everywhere around her. She could hear cruiser doors slamming outside, police shouting, and footsteps running her way.

She had one thing to do before they got here. She spit on Kather.

For Edward.

CHAPTER FIFTY-SIX

"Don't shoot!" Mary shouted, as loud as she could. She put up her hands as a group of uniformed police ran into the martial arts studio, their guns drawn.

"Miss, are you okay?" one of the uniformed cops said, rushing to her side and taking her arm while other uniformed officers swarmed Kather, pulled his hands behind his back, and handcuffed him just as he was regaining consciousness.

"I'm Mary DiNunzio, I didn't do anything. He tried to kill me." Mary's throat felt raw and achy.

"We saw what happened." The cop took her arm. "Come outside with me."

"He killed two people. He told me. I have to find Detective Randolph, I want to make a statement." Mary couldn't begin to process what she had just been through. She was happy to be alive, but heartbroken that Kather had murdered Edward, and Geltz.

"Come with me, hurry." The cop hustled Mary outside, where police cruisers jammed the parking lot entrance, their light bars flashing. Their sirens were off, but their high beams lit up the night and illuminated the martial artist, who was being helped to his feet by another uniformed officer.

Mary felt a wave of relief at the sight. "Officer, I want to see him," she said to the cop.

"Ms. DiNunzio, first, do you need to go to the hospital?" The cop looked her up and down with concern.

"No, I'm fine, but he may need a doctor. He was Tased." Mary walked toward the martial artist with the cop, her gait unsteady. Her knees were weak and she was shaking as adrenaline left her system. She reached the martial artist, who turned to see her.

"You made it!" The martial artist grinned with relief. "I'm sorry I wasn't able to help you."

"I'm sorry I got you Tased. I didn't realize he had a weapon. I would've warned you."

"Forget about it. All's well that ends well."

"Mary!" someone shouted, and Mary looked past the cruisers to see Detective Randolph and Detective Jimenez jogging toward her, their ties flying. The uniformed cop who had been with her waved good-bye, and Mary opened her arms reflexively when Detective Randolph reached her.

"Detective," Mary said, her chest tight with emotion, and Detective Randolph squeezed her back, then released her, beaming down at her.

"Thank God you're okay. You had me worried there."

"I'll say," Detective Jimenez added. "Mary, you almost gave Old Joe a heart attack. I think you're the first lawyer he ever liked."

"Thanks." Mary managed to smile back. "But listen, Kather told me he killed Edward, Patrick's grandfather."

"He told you that?" Detective Randolph asked, his expression going so professional that Mary worried he thought she was making it up.

"He admitted it, I swear it. I'll take a lie detector. He said it to me. He was about to kill me, so I guess he wasn't worried about me telling anyone, and he said—"

"Wait, let's not talk here." Detective Randolph raised a palm. "We'll take your statement down at the Roundhouse, if you don't need to go to the hospital."

"No, I'm fine, and I want to make a statement. I want Kather prosecuted for Edward's murder, and it's proof that Patrick didn't do it. You see, like I told you, Patrick is innocent. I can *prove* it now." Mary felt a surge of new purpose. "Detective Randolph, Kather also told me that he killed James Geltz, too. Kather killed them both, but he didn't say why. But James Geltz wasn't a suicide, no matter what it looked like."

"Really." Detective Randolph's gaze shifted to Detective Jimenez. "Defective, you owe me a cheesesteak. I want Geno's."

"Oh man." Detective Jimenez shook his head. "You lucked out."

Mary got the gist. "Detective Randolph, you didn't believe Geltz committed suicide?"

Detective Randolph pursed his lips, his demeanor back in professional mode. "I can't answer that question, it's confidential police business. Suffice it to say that my partner is handsome, but he has a lot to learn until he becomes me—"

"—and I lose a prostate?" Detective Jimenez wisecracked.

Mary couldn't joke around anymore. "So how does this work? Would you guys be the detectives on Kather's case now?"

Detective Randolph nodded. "Yes, we caught Geltz. We'll take your statement and use it for leverage to get a confession out of Kather."

Detective Jimenez nodded in agreement, eyeing Mary. "If this works the way we want it to, Kather is facing an attempted murder charge against you, for sure, and two other murder charges, potentially. In those circumstances, the D.A. may charge him with capital murder, so Kather is looking at the death penalty if he doesn't make a deal. We have all the cards. We're gonna squeeze him."

Mary knew what he meant, having been on the other side. "So you'll try to get Kather to confess by offering him a deal, no death penalty? Life without possibility of parole?"

"That's the plan. LWOP, life without parole." Detective Randolph nodded. "But you're up first. It's all on your statement."

"No pressure," Detective Jimenez added.

Suddenly the crowd of policemen around them parted, and several uniformed officers escorted a handcuffed Kather to the closest cruiser and loaded him in the backseat, slamming the door behind him. Mary felt a bitter satisfaction to see Kather slumped in the backseat, his head bent. Even if he was punished, it wouldn't bring Edward or Geltz back.

Mary, Detective Randolph, and Detective Jimenez watched in silence as the cruiser with Kather pulled away, and Mary wondered why Kather had killed them. Maybe it was human nature to try to make sense of something that senseless, or explain something that was simply inexplicable, namely that one human being would intentionally kill another, extinguishing a human life. No reason could ever be good enough for murder.

Mary felt tears come to her eyes. Usually *why* a murder was committed was what got her, almost secondary to *how* it was committed, but in this case, she wanted to know both. She wanted to know *everything* about Edward's murder, because she knew how much it cost Patrick to lose him.

"Mary, let's go," Detective Randolph said quietly, taking her arm.

CHAPTER FIFTY-SEVEN

Mary sat in the interview room alone, having given her statement. She had told every detail to Detective Randolph, while Detective Jimenez took notes, just like before. The process had taken almost two hours, and Mary knew it mattered more than ever. Her throat hurt from being choked, but she ignored the ache and kept her emotions at bay by focusing on her goal, which was giving the detectives the leverage they needed to squeeze a confession out of Kather, or failing that, to convict him at trial.

She sipped cold vending-machine coffee and waited for Detectives Randolph and Jimenez to come back. They had wanted her to go home and wait, but she didn't budge. She didn't want to call Bennie or anyone at her office, or even Anthony or her parents. It was the middle of the night and they would all be asleep, oblivious of everything that had happened to her. She didn't want to worry them, and more than that, she wanted to go it on her own. The only way to step out from Bennie's shadow was to stop relying on her.

Mary checked the clock on the wall, but it was only three minutes later than the last time she'd checked it. She looked around the interview room, but there was nothing to see and it was the exact same interview room in which she'd been interviewed earlier, when Detectives Randolph and Jimenez had suspected Patrick of killing Edward and her of covering up the crime. She paused to congratulate herself on proving Patrick innocent the very same night, without getting herself chopped into pieces by a samurai sword. Maybe someday, she'd be not only as good as Bennie Rosato, she'd be better.

She listened to the hustle and bustle going on outside the interview room, the commotion caused by Kather's arrest. He was being interviewed in the very next room, and she was dying to know what was going on, but she had to wait. The detectives had ordered her to stay inside the room and not go poking around, on penalty of being sent home. She obeyed only because she didn't want to do a single thing to jeopardize the case against Kather.

Mary was beginning to wonder if they had completely forgotten about her when suddenly there was a knock on the door and it opened. Detective Randolph entered the room with Detective Jimenez behind him, and Mary found herself rising to her feet, without really knowing why.

"Shhh." Detective Randolph quickly put an index finger to his lips, and Mary got the message. He motioned her back into the chair and sat down across from her, as did Detective Jimenez.

"What happened?" Mary asked, keeping her voice low. It wasn't difficult because her throat hurt. Her heart began to pound in her chest.

"This is completely confidential, but we obtained a complete confession." Detective Randolph's eyes flared slightly, though they looked bloodshot and weary.

"Really?" Mary wanted to cheer, but she didn't.

"We're drawing up the papers. He's in there with his lawyer and the A.D.A. It's going to take a while, but it happened. Kather confessed to your attempted murder, as well as the murders of Edward O'Brien and James Geltz."

"What did he say? Why did he do it? How did he do it? Tell me everything."

"I'll tell you as much as I can, only because you're a victim. You have to agree to keep the details confidential."

"I will, I swear it."

"Good." Detective Randolph inhaled. "I'll start backwards, chronologically. Kather lured Geltz to a meeting at the river and shot him in the head, at close range, to make it look like a suicide. He took Geltz's keys, went to his office, and took his desktop because it contained incriminating email on a private email account."

Mary had guessed as much, but didn't interrupt him to say so.

"Then he went to Geltz's house to get his laptop, for the same reason. It was raining and Kather put on Geltz's golf windbreaker and pulled the hood over his head to trick the neighbor into thinking it was Geltz. Kather took some suitcases to make it look like Geltz was going away. Kather forged a note for the neighbor to watch the house. He knew Geltz's habits and handwriting."

"So *Kather* was the one Ellen saw. Not Geltz." Mary wished she'd realized that. She thought of Abby at the Stackpoles', wearing her rain slicker with the hood.

"Kather ditched both computers in the river. We're dredging for them. I don't know if we'll find them or what we can recover from the hard drives. The truth is, we don't need them with a full confession."

"Right," Mary said, trying to take it all in. "But what about Edward?"

"Kather knew that Edward kept a house key under a stone. He knew about Edward's diabetes. He'd had lunch with him and he'd seen Edward check his blood sugar and inject himself."

"And that night?"

"Kather let himself in. Patrick was asleep when he went into the house and Kather injected Edward in his arm."

"Why didn't Edward wake up?"

"Ambien. Kather said Edward was out like a light. Kather knew about that too. He slipped out of the house before Patrick was awake."

"So Patrick found him dead that morning. That's so awful." Mary's heart broke for Patrick all over again. "But why did Kather kill Edward? And Geltz?"

"Kather had a Ponzi scheme going, and Geltz was in on it with him. You know what a Ponzi scheme is?"

"Like Madoff?" Mary asked, shocked.

"Yes, but smaller scale. People sent money to Kather to invest, but he didn't. He collected their money and sent them fraudulent statements to make them believe he's investing it, so they didn't cash out. Geltz sent clients to Kather knowing it was a Ponzi scheme, and they shared the proceeds. They were bilking money from the Vietnam vets who were Geltz's clients, like Edward. Kather and Geltz played it smart and kept it low-key. They didn't live large. They put the money in offshore bank accounts and spent the money out of sight, in foreign property. They both have big places in the Caymans and apartments in Europe too."

"That's so evil!" Mary blurted out in disgust, then she realized the dire implications. "Edward had $225,000 at Cornerstone Financial, the bulk of Patrick's inheritance. Only some of his savings were in the bank. So it's all gone?"

"Unsure, as yet." Detective Randolph frowned in sympathy. "The Feds will seize the assets, sell them, and create a fund, so maybe there'll be restitution."

"But any restitution will only be for pennies on the dollar, because the fund will have to be divided among all the Cornerstone investors. Do you know how many there were?"

"Kather's saying about six hundred, and the Ponzi scheme wasn't confined only to Geltz's clients. Kather had investors all over the mid-Atlantic area, so they crossed state lines. The returns were decent enough that nobody asked for their money and got out of the fund, but not so good that they aroused suspicion. Kather kept recruiting new investors to the fund, keeping it replenished." Detective Randolph gestured toward the door. "The Feds are here, DOJ, FBI, and the SEC. They're starting investigations for securities fraud, mail fraud, false SEC filings, even international money laundering. They have to notify investors and sort out the financials. There are going to be a lot of people like you, who find out that their life savings were stolen. But our jurisdiction is primary, due to the attempt on your life and the two murders."

Mary set the money worries aside, since Edward mattered more. "So why did Kather kill Edward?"

"Edward invested with Cornerstone about two years ago, and in time, he began seeing tiny red flags. He must have been a pretty good accountant. He started emailing and calling Kather, asking questions."

Mary remembered Kather telling her on the phone, how much he liked having an educated client. She had even agreed with him, but he had been lying the whole time.

Detective Randolph continued, "Kather tried to make friends with Edward to deflect suspicion, but Edward didn't fall for it. Kather and Geltz started to worry he'd find them out. When Edward called Geltz and asked if he knew a lawyer, they panicked."

"Why would Edward call Geltz for a lawyer, if he suspected him of wrongdoing?" Mary realized the answer as soon as she'd asked. "Oh, Edward didn't realize that Geltz was in on it, too. He suspected Kather of wrongdoing, not Geltz."

"Correct. Geltz and Kather thought Edward wanted a lawyer to go to the feds about Cornerstone. They didn't know anything about the Complaint in Common Pleas Court. Geltz got more and more panicky, so Kather killed him to silence him. Kather was going to kill you because you were getting too close to the truth. He was going to Tase you and strangle you, making it look like a botched car-jacking."

Mary shuddered. "But how did he even know where I was? He came out of nowhere. Nobody knew I was at Geltz's office."

"Kather took Geltz's second phone, a private one."

"The Batphone." Mary realized what must have happened. "Geltz's secretary Patricia was calling him to try to find him."

"Yes, and she kept saying where you were going. She told him that you were at her home, then you were going to the office."

"You would think the phone would be password-protected."

"It was, but Kather knew about the phone and forced Geltz to give him the password at gunpoint before he killed him. Kather used to call him on that phone and Kather wanted to dispose of it. He threw it in the river too."

"Oh man, what an evil guy." Mary felt suddenly so sad, at so much loss.

"I'm going to ask you not to talk to the media or leak any of this information. They're beginning to gather outside, so steer clear on your way out. The Police Commissioner and the Feds are going to hold a big press conference at midmorning, when the plea deal is signed, sealed, and delivered."

"Of course, I won't talk to the press."

"So now, it's over. Kather's going to jail for the rest of his life, without parole. The D.A. is fine with that, and so are we. The Feds will hopefully come up with some restitution for Patrick and the other investors."

Mary thought it would feel like a victory, but it didn't. It was tragic, all this needless death and destruction, over money. And Patrick had lost his beloved grandfather, derailing his entire life.

"So it's over." Detective Randolph half-smiled, in a final way.

"Not for Patrick." Mary had been working on her next step for the last two hours. She'd emailed everyone she needed, so they'd read her email as soon as they woke up. "The fact that Patrick was suspected of murdering Edward was dispositive at the shelter care hearing. We were in deep trouble as soon as you testified."

"I'm sorry." Detective Randolph looked genuinely regretful, his lower lip puckering.

"I know, and it's not your fault, but I can't let it stand. I wanted justice for Edward, and I want it for Patrick, too." Mary met his eye, unblinking. "Detective Randolph, will you help me?"

CHAPTER FIFTY-EIGHT

By eleven o'clock the next day, Mary had gone home, napped, showered, and changed, and was back in Family Court, riding up the escalator with John. She had told him, Bennie, Judy, and Anne the whole story at the office this morning, while she cut-and-pasted new papers to file with the court and called Judge Green's chambers to get back before him on an emergency basis.

"Mary, you're something else." John chuckled as they ascended to the courtroom floor.

"Never a dull moment." Mary smiled. Bright sun filled the airy space, and she couldn't help but feel that it was a new day and a second chance.

"I never filed an emergency motion in Family Court two days in a row, much less one based on after-discovered evidence."

"There's a first time for everything." Mary grinned. "Besides, there's legal precedent for the rationale. 'After-discovered evidence' will get you a new trial in criminal law, so I don't know why you can't try it in family law."

"Nor do I. That's why I'm in."

"Think of it like a legal *Groundhog Day*. We're going to keep going back to court until we win."

"I'm just glad Judge Green agreed to hear us."

"I knew he would. He's a good judge. He has to be favorably disposed toward us, if not just plain curious. The headlines this morning were too good." Mary had been all over the local news as a lawyer-heroine who almost got killed fighting for her client, a little boy wrongly suspected of his grandfather's murder.

"True, it never hurts to have momentum in the media."

"And I didn't even have to leak it. Now, let's do this." Mary stepped off the escalator as it reached the top, and John followed her.

The courtroom floor was busy, with mothers, fathers, and kids sitting in the black chairs, milling around, or looking at smartphones. Well-dressed lawyers consulted with their clients, courthouse employees in polo shirts carried documents this way and that, and large-screen TVs above the courtroom doors played on mute, with closed captioning.

Mary glanced reflexively at the TV, then did a delighted doubletake. The screen showed the Police Commissioner standing in front of a podium bearing the official symbol of the City of Philadelphia, and behind him was an array of men in ties, an American flag, and the cobalt-blue flag of the Commonwealth of Pennsylvania. The closed captioning read, NOW I'LL TURN THE PROGRAM OVER TO REPRESENTATIVES OF THE FEDERAL BUREAU OF INVESTIGATION AND THE SECURITIES EXCHANGE COMMISSION TO DISCUSS THE FINANCIAL IMPROPRIETIES AT CORNERSTONE . . ."

Mary walked up the center aisle, with a grin. "Let's hope Judge Green has a TV in chambers."

John laughed. "The way your luck is going, I think he just might."

Mary felt a surge of goodwill when she spotted their witnesses, waiting for them in front of the courtroom doors. Abby Ortega grinned at her, flagging her down, and Dr. Susan Bernardi smiled, too, since she had decided to testify for Patrick given the latest news. But best of all, with them stood Mary's star witness, Detective Joseph Randolph.

With a team like that, she knew they would win.

And in the end, they did.

For Patrick.

CHAPTER FIFTY-NINE

Everybody piled into Mary's kitchen and she and her mother got dinner ready, reheating the gravy, boiling the water for the gnocchi, and washing romaine for the salad. Her father and The Tonys sat around the kitchen island with bottles of Rolling Rock, watching the Sixers game on TV, which was your basic old-school division of labor.

Mary let it go, too happy to make a stink. Her parents had been horrified by what had happened with Kather, but that bad news had been outweighed by the good, which was that they were getting a foster grandson. Mary had insisted they have Patrick's first dinner at her house, rather than her parents', which represented a maternal changing of the guard.

Mary kept glancing at her watch, her anticipation growing, and at about ten minutes of seven, she lowered the TV and stepped in front of the screen to get their attention. "Pop and The Tonys, excuse me but I want to speak to you before Patrick gets here."

"IT'S OKAY, MARE. THEY WERE LOSIN' ANYWAY."

Feet nodded, his Mr. Potatohead glasses slightly askew. "Every season we say it's going to be different, but it never is."

Tony-From-Down-The-Block wrapped his gnarled hand around his beer bottle. "Still, you gotta believe."

"*Che, Maria?*" Her mother turned from the stove, where a pot of bubbling gravy scented the air with tomato, basil, and garlic.

"Listen everybody, I know you're all excited, but we have to remember that Patrick doesn't know you. He's meeting a lot of new people tonight, in a totally new house, and we have to be careful not to overwhelm him. Do you understand?" Mary didn't want to hurt their feelings, squelch their enthusiasm, or destroy their cultural heritage.

Feet nodded. "You want us to shut up."

Her father shrugged. "I CAN SHUT UP, MARE. I'LL ACT LIKE I'M IN CHURCH."

Tony-From-Down-The-Block looked over slyly. "Matty, you don't shut up in church. You don't shut up nowhere."

Her mother smiled, nodding, and Mary knew she understood, so she returned her attention to her father and The Tonys. "It's not that you have to shut up, but just don't go crazy when he comes in. Don't rush and hug him. Hang back. Let him come to you. He's a shy kid." Mary felt a twinge. "And you have to remember, his grandfather just died. You guys might remind him of his grandfather, so be prepared for that."

"THAT'S A CRYIN' SHAME." Her father's eyes glistened.

"The poor kid." Feet hung his head.

"Is it okay we're drinkin'?" Tony-From-Down-The-Block asked, newly worried. "We're just havin' the one, on account of our medication. The kid's Irish anyway, right?"

Mary cringed. "Don't say that, Tony. Don't say anything about his being Irish."

Tony-From-Down-The-Block frowned. "I didn't mean nothin' by it, Mare. My first wife was Irish, remember?"

"I know, I know." Mary checked the clock. It was almost seven. Suddenly the doorbell rang, and she faced her father and The Tonys one last time. "Okay, everybody stay here. I'm going to answer the door and then I'm going to bring him in here, okay?"

"GOTCHA, MARE!" Her father answered for everybody, smoothing down his T-shirt.

Mary hurried from the kitchen, rushed to the entrance hall, and opened the door to find Olivia Solo on the front step, holding his packed suitcase, and Patrick beside her. His typical alertness had returned to his eyes, so Mary assumed his medication had been adjusted, and he looked completely adorable in fresh clothes, a red Phillies T-shirt and gray sweat shorts, with his regular Converse sneakers. He held Edward's wallet and watch in his hand.

"Patrick!" Mary cried out, happy to see him.

"Mary!" Patrick smiled at her, raising his arms.

"Aw, welcome home, honey." Mary picked him up and gave him a big hug, feeling him cling to her like a little monkey.

Olivia remained stony-faced as she handed over the suitcase. "Mary, here we go. Call me if you have questions. DHS will be in touch about the training seminars. Don't forget you have to take them."

"I remember." Mary set Patrick down, took the suitcase, and stowed it inside the entrance hall. "Olivia, thank you for your help. I do appreciate—"

"You're welcome." Olivia stepped down the front step and waved good-bye. "Bye, Patrick."

Patrick didn't respond.

Mary hugged him to her side. "Patrick, say good-bye and thank you to Olivia."

"Good-bye and thank you," Patrick said obediently, and Mary felt as if she had committed her first act of motherhood, prompting a child to say thank you when he didn't really mean it.

"Patrick, *che carina*, how cute!" her mother cooed, rushing up from behind, despite Mary's lectures.

"HIYA PATRICK, I'M MARY'S FATHER, WELCOME TO THE FAMILY!" her father shouted, then Feet, Tony-From-Down-The-Block, and Pigeon Tony joined in with Italian chatter, happy noises, and hurried introductions. Patrick didn't seem to mind, dazed at the crazy people.

Mary closed the door, and Patrick was swept into the kitchen on a wave of senior citizens, and only a moment later, he was being hoisted up by Mary's father to look into the pot of gravy, a DiNunzio tradition. Her father carted Patrick around as if the boy couldn't walk, letting him watch her mother slide the gnocchi, hissing, into the pot of water. The TV stayed on in the background, and Feet pointed out certain players in the Sixers game to Patrick, then Tony-From-Down-The-Block asked him if he liked "those Irish potato candies with the cinnamon on the outside," eliciting an excited yes.

When the gnocchi were *al dente*, Mary's mother showed Patrick how she ladled hot gravy on the bottom of the serving bowl, which was one of her trade secrets, and in time Patrick placed his wallet and watch beside his plate, dinner was served, and everybody ate hungrily and happily, her family talking with their mouths full despite Mary's disapproving glances, since she was trying to raise the child with some manners.

Patrick was remarkably at ease with her family, answering questions when they were asked of him or chewing away quietly. Mary realized that he was comfortable with older adults because he was used to being around Edward, and the only word to describe the evening was happy—until she heard the front door open, and she realized that Anthony was home.

Mary rose quickly. Since they hadn't spoken, Anthony would be shocked to find Patrick here, and for her part, she had no idea what had happened at his UCLA interview or how he even felt about her or their upcoming wedding.

"Excuse me, everyone." Mary rushed out to meet him, holding her breath.

CHAPTER SIXTY

"Hey honey." Mary met him in the dining room, and Anthony looked travel-weary in a rumpled oxford shirt, sports jacket, and jeans. He peered confused at the noise coming from the kitchen, and the waning light from the kitchen windows fell on his face, bringing out the brown warmth of his eyes.

"Hey, hi." Anthony stopped in the dining room, but he didn't hug her. "Your family's here?"

"Yes. I went to court today and won. Patrick is in there, with my family." Mary hated to talk to him with everyone in earshot, then remembered that they were all hard of hearing except for Patrick.

"Wow, okay." Anthony blinked.

"I had to, honey, and I hope you understand. We can talk about it later."

"Sure, right." Anthony looked down at her, meeting her eye for the first time. "Listen, more importantly, I read that you were attacked, almost *murdered*? Is that true?"

"Kind of, but I'm fine."

"*Kind of?*" Anthony asked, in disbelief. "I didn't see it online until I landed. I called and texted but you didn't answer."

"Oh, sorry, I've been crazy busy and I didn't have my phone for a while." Mary had asked Marshall to get her a new phone while she was at court.

"What happened? Are you okay?" Anthony frowned at her with concern, so Mary assumed he still wanted to marry her, but this wasn't the time or the place to have that discussion.

"I'm fine, really. I can fill you in later."

"MARE, HOW DO YOU WORK THIS COFFEEMAKER? YOUR MOTHER WANTS TO KNOW!"

Mary looked in the kitchen to see her parents clustered around the Keurig coffeemaker, which stumped them because they still perked coffee on the stove the old-fashioned way. "Pop, I'll be right in!"

"Let's go meet Patrick." Anthony straightened up, facing the kitchen.

"Wait, what happened in California?"

"MARE, WHAT ARE THESE PLASTIC THINGS?" her father hollered from the kitchen.

"We'll talk about it later." Anthony averted his gaze. "Take me in and introduce me."

Mary started to reach for Anthony's hand, but stopped herself, not wanting to force the issue as they entered the kitchen to find Patrick pulling a chair out from under the table, dragging it over to the Keurig coffeemaker on the counter, and climbing up on top of the chair. He picked up one of the K-cups, examining it under the admiring gaze of Mary's mother, her father, and The Tonys.

"PATRICK, HOW DOES IT WORK?"

Mary didn't think he had a Keurig coffeemaker at home, and in fact, she thought she remembered seeing an old Mr. Coffee coffeemaker there.

"The coffee must be inside this, Mr. DiNunzio," Patrick answered, shaking the cup, then he found the lever on the coffeemaker and pressed it down, so that the top popped open.

"WOW! YOU'RE A GENIUS, KIDDO!"

The Tonys *ooh*ed and *ahh*ed as if Patrick had performed magic, and Pigeon Tony clapped.

Patrick grinned, placing the K-cup inside the coffeemaker. "See? It goes in here, you can tell it fits right in."

Mary whispered to Anthony, "He figured that out all by himself."

Anthony whispered back, "Children with dyslexia can have superior logical reasoning. I read a book about it on the plane."

"MARE, LOOK AT THIS KID GO!" Her father turned to her, grinning, and Mary realized that Patrick wouldn't be able to read the word BREW on the coffeemaker. Her father must've understood the problem because he pointed to the BREW button. "PATRICK, THIS IS THE BUTTON TO START IT. IT'S THE ONE IN THE MIDDLE."

"I see it!" Patrick pushed the button, then turned, his gaze shifting to Anthony.

"Patrick, great job!" Mary gestured to Anthony. "Meet Anthony, my fiancé. He lives here."

"Hi, Patrick." Anthony stepped over to Patrick, with a smile. "Welcome. We're very happy to have you."

"Thank you," Patrick said, still standing on the chair. "I'm making coffee."

"Good idea, I like coffee." Anthony slipped a hand into the pocket of his sports jacket, retrieved a gift-wrapped package, and handed it to Patrick. "I got this little present for you. I thought you might like it."

"Thank you," Patrick said, accepting the gift.

Mary caught her mother's eye, which looked suspiciously moist behind her thick glasses, and the adults fell uncharacteristically silent, mindful of the emotional subtext. Patrick tore off the gift wrap to reveal the gift, a travel chess set that Anthony must've gotten at the airport, which surprised Mary. She didn't know Anthony liked chess, he'd never mentioned it before.

"What is it?" Patrick frowned at the package, which he couldn't read.

"It's a great game called chess. It's fun and it's been around for centuries. Kings and queens used to play it."

"How do you play?"

"I'll teach it to you. It's easy. It has two sides that go to battle. One side wins."

Patrick's blue eyes lit up. "You mean, like armies?"

"Yes, exactly. Good for you."

"Cool! Can we play it now?"

"Sure," Anthony answered, pleased.

"Help me get down?" Patrick raised his arms, to Anthony.

"I gotcha, pal." Anthony reached back, without hesitation.

And watching them both, Mary was never more in love with Anthony than at this very moment. She had put him in a terrible position, but he had stepped up for Patrick. She prayed they were still getting married, but now that they were foster parents, they would have to wait until after Patrick went to bed to talk.

Mary hoped her luck would hold.

CHAPTER SIXTY-ONE

Mary held Patrick's hand as she walked him down the hall to his bedroom, their spare guest room, never used. It was ready because she'd run upstairs and put everything in place while Patrick played chess with Anthony, which had been a sweet success. After that, her parents and The Tonys had gone home amid a flurry of good-bye hugs and kisses, and it was already nine o'clock. She had no idea if that was a reasonable bedtime for a ten-year-old, but Patrick seemed exhausted and she couldn't wait to talk to Anthony, who was in their room down the hall, unpacking.

"Did you have fun tonight?" Mary squeezed Patrick's hand. In his other hand was the wallet and watch, which never left his possession the entire evening.

"Yes. I'm so full."

"I hear that." Mary smiled, knowing that Patrick would probably gain ten pounds in DiNunzio custody. "Did you like my family?"

"Yes, they're silly. It was *a lot* of people. You have a *big* family."

"They seem bigger because they're so noisy." Mary worried if he had felt overwhelmed. "By the way, I have a surprise for you when we get to your room."

"More presents?" Patrick looked up with a grin.

"Not exactly. Here we go." Mary smiled as they reached the bedroom and she flipped the light switch, revealing that she had laid out on Patrick's new bed his artwork, pens, and pencils, as well as the photographs of Edward and Patrick's mother, and Edward's rosary.

"My comics!" Patrick ran to the bed, set down the wallet and watch, and started looking through his artwork.

"All your clothes are put away in the dresser drawers." Mary gestured to the three-drawer pine dresser with a mirror on top, across the room next to a spare desk that Anthony had brought from home. "I set them up the same way you had them at home, to make it easy for you. Your other clothes and shoes are in the closet. I think I got everything you might want for now, and we'll get the rest later."

"It's all here!" Patrick busied himself with the artwork. His bedroom was situated in the north corner of the house, so it had two large windows in the front and one on the side with blue paisley curtains. The walls were soft blue, and the floors were hardwood, with a bluish-gray rug under the double bed.

"I think we should get you to bed, Patrick. Why don't you take your artwork and put it on the desk?"

"Okay." Patrick obediently picked up the artwork and took it over to the desk, then came back for the pens and pencils. "It's a big desk but I like it. I don't need a little one anymore."

"I agree."

"Do you think we can get a ruler?"

"Yes, tomorrow we'll go shopping and get you whatever you need." Mary gestured at the bathroom. "Do you need to use the bathroom?"

"I have a bathroom in my room?" Patrick's eyes widened, and Mary turned on the light in the bathroom, which she had stocked with clean towels, a fresh bar of soap, a new toothbrush, and a tube of toothpaste.

"Yes, it's all yours. Look."

"Wow!" Patrick scampered over and looked inside, his mouth dropping open at the simple white tiled bathroom. "This is for *me*? Where's yours?"

"Anthony and I have our own, in our bedroom."

"Everybody has their *own* bathroom?" Patrick turned around, his eyes even wider.

"Yes, that's how we roll." Mary smiled, remembering that her family had shared one bathroom when she was growing up. Since then, she'd gotten used to having her own bathroom, but Patrick's delight reminded her of how happy and lucky she was, all over again.

"Do you want to go to the bathroom and then go to bed?"

"I don't have to go to the bathroom."

"But you have to wash your face and brush your teeth."

"I don't do that at night. I only do it in the morning."

"I think you're supposed to do it at night, too." Mary didn't know whether to push it. She didn't have her motherhood mojo in gear, and Patrick had already gone back to the bed and was picking up the wallet, watch, and picture of Edward. He set them on the night table beside his bed, then retrieved the photo of his mother, which he put next to the picture of Edward, and finally the rosary, which he draped carefully around the frame of Edward's picture, sucking his lower lip for the first time that night.

Mary wondered if he would cry, but he didn't, and her heart went out to him. "You okay, honey?" she asked softly, going over and sitting on the edge of the bed.

"I have to say my prayers."

"Okay." Mary stood up. "Do you want me to stay or go?"

"Stay. I say them in my bed." Patrick turned back the blue coverlet and jumped inside the bed fully clothed.

"Don't you want to get undressed or put on pajamas? I can go out of the room." Mary realized that she had no idea what she was doing. Maybe this motherhood gig was harder than it looked.

"Nope, it's cold." Patrick pulled the cover up to his chin, and Mary sat back down on the bed.

"Do you want me to lower the air-conditioning?"

"No, I like it. Where is the air conditioner? I don't see one." Patrick looked over at the windows, his head swiveling on the pillow.

"It's central air-conditioning, that means it's not in the window. It comes from the vents."

"Am I going to my new school tomorrow?" Patrick sucked his lower lip.

"No, you're not starting tomorrow, but I think we can go see what it's like. How does that sound?" Mary hadn't had a chance to get the deposit, but if Kate read the newspapers, she'd forgive her.

"You said the kids at the new school don't know how to read."

"Right, they're just like you, and they're learning to read because the teachers there know how to teach them differently." Mary thought a moment. "You met my mother, you heard her speaking a different language, didn't you?"

"Yes."

"It was Italian, and she speaks Italian because she was never very good at learning English. She's very smart, but she doesn't speak the same language we do. She was never taught it, so she never learned it." Mary went with the flow, seeing an analogy and hoping Patrick did, too. "See, you can be very smart but still not speak the same language as the people around you. That's because everybody's different. And it certainly doesn't mean you're dumb, because my mother's very, very smart."

Patrick seemed to be listening, so she continued.

"You're going to like your new school and I think you'll feel happier there. The kids there don't make fun of other kids and they'll be nicer to you. And the teachers will know how to teach you in a way that you'll understand. Okay?"

"Yes."

Mary knew it was time to let him go. "Do you want to say your prayers now?"

"You have to turn off the light first. My Pops always turns out the light."

"Okay." Mary reached over and turned out the lamp, which darkened the bedroom.

Patrick closed his eyes, made praying hands, and brought them up to his chin, whispering hoarsely. "Amen," he said aloud, lowering his hands. He looked over at her, his expression solemn. "I'm done."

"Good job." Mary touched his face.

"You have a big family."

Mary remembered that he had said that before. "I guess I do. I have a sister who wasn't here tonight and I have my parents."

"And all The Tonys."

"Right, they're my family, too."

"I like them. It's funny they have the same name. *Three* people with the *same* name!"

"Pretty crazy, huh?" Mary didn't know whether to ask him how he was feeling because she didn't want to make him upset, but she wanted him to know that he could express himself. She was quickly realizing that motherhood might actually be impossible. "How you feeling, honey? Are you sad or are you happy?"

"I don't know," Patrick answered, but his voice sounded suddenly shaky in the stillness. "I miss my Pops."

"I know you do, honey. I'm so sorry about that."

"He's in heaven. My family is in heaven now."

"Yes, they are, and they're looking at you right now and making sure you're okay. That's what I believe." Mary felt tears come to her eyes, but held them back.

"I figured out how it works. I *do* have a family. Just some people have their families with them and some people have their families in heaven."

"I think you're right, honey." Mary thought of her first husband, Mike, who had passed. She realized that he would always be a part of her family, in heaven. It was a comforting insight, out of the mouth of babes.

"I wish my family wasn't in heaven. I wish they were right *here*." Patrick patted the bed next to him.

"I get that, honey, too," Mary said, heartbroken for him. "I wish that were true, too."

"I better go to sleep now."

"Okay. Good night." Mary leaned over and impulsively kissed him on the forehead, and suddenly he reached up, wrapped his arms around her, and gave her a big hug. She hugged him back, trying not to cry, and she sensed he was trying not to cry too, so she gave him another kiss on the top of the head. "I'm really happy you're here."

"Me too," Patrick said, as she released him back onto his pillow and he wiped his eyes.

"You want Anthony to come in and say good night?"

"No, he said it downstairs."

"Okay, good. Now if you want anything, I'll be down the hall." Mary rose, realizing she had reached another awkward moment. She and Anthony slept with the door open, and if Patrick slept with the door open, that meant they would have to wait until he fell asleep until they could talk.

"I'm okay."

"You want the door open or closed?"

"Open."

"Okay, good night, honey."

"My Pops always says 'nighty-night.' "

"Nighty-night, honey," Mary said softly, leaving the bedroom before her eyes welled up again.

CHAPTER SIXTY-TWO

Mary walked into the bedroom, but it was empty, which surprised her. She had left Anthony in here getting changed, because it was usually the first thing he did when he hit the house, slipping into a faded T-shirt and gym shorts. She checked the bathroom just to make sure, but he wasn't there. She got a bad feeling in the pit of her stomach. This is what it would feel like if he were gone.

She went downstairs and by the time she hit the first floor, she knew that he was in the kitchen because she could smell espresso. He made it from a silvery Bialetti espresso maker, a seven-dollar pot that brewed on the stovetop, and the first time she saw him making espresso, she realized he'd fit in perfectly with her family. But in the time they'd lived together, he'd only brewed espresso when he had to stay up late to grade papers or finish his thesis, so this wasn't a good sign.

"Hi," Mary said, entering the kitchen, and Anthony looked up from the book he'd been reading at the kitchen island, his cup and saucer at his right hand.

"Hey." Anthony placed the book flap in the pages to mark his place, then closed the book, which read *Overcoming Dyslexia*. "Is he in bed?"

"Yes."

"That sounds weird, doesn't it? This whole thing, it's just unreal. I thought it would be better if we talked downstairs." Anthony shook his head. "But first tell me what happened with Kather. What I read online scared me. He tried to *kill* you?"

"I don't want to talk about that now. We have too much to talk about." Mary had to know where they stood as a couple. "And I have to apologize. I'm sorry, I know I put you in a tough position with Patrick. It's amazing that you got him the gift, and I really appreciate it."

Anthony sighed, leaning back. "You don't have to say that. It seemed in order."

"Well, thank you." Mary pulled out the seat across from him, even though they usually sat next to each other at the kitchen island. His demeanor, and the circumstances, told her to keep her distance. The sky was turning black outside the kitchen window, and they normally would've gone outside to their back patio, had a glass of wine, and tried to find the stars through Philadelphia's electrical haze. But this wasn't one of those nights.

"I thought about it, is what happened," Anthony began, his tone quiet. His lips formed a grim line, his chin grizzly, and he seemed even more tired than before, his dark eyes sunken as if he hadn't slept in a while.

"What did you think about? Taking Patrick? And what happened with the job, did you get it?" Mary could hear herself firing questions at him, her default when she was anxious. Anthony, on the other hand, only got quieter and more introspective.

"I thought about everything. I think more clearly on planes. I don't know why, but I swear, I have real clarity in the air."

"So what happened?"

"I flew back to California and I thought about it the whole way there. What you said, what I said, what I would do in your situation, everything." Anthony nodded, as if resolving something in his own mind. "And I thought that we were both making a terrible mistake, the *same* terrible mistake."

"And? What's the terrible mistake?"

Anthony met her eye directly. "The terrible mistake is that we are not functioning as a couple. We live together and we love each other—"

"We do," Mary interrupted.

"—but we haven't come together, not really. We don't function together, at least we're not as yet. I'm as guilty of it as you are." Anthony shook his head. "The first time I went to UCLA, they started making noises about the opening in the department, and I let it be known that I wanted it. I didn't think to ask you about it, I didn't *want* to tell you about it. I knew what you were going to say. So I did it anyway. Without you."

"What did you decide?"

"Be patient, please." Anthony raised a hand, and Mary knew he wasn't trying to torture her, so she tried to shut up while he continued. "You did the same thing with Patrick. His grandfather passed away, and you decided to step up for him. On your own. You didn't talk to me about it. You could've tried to tell me, but you didn't want to."

"That's true." Mary had to admit it, now that he'd said it aloud.

"You were doing the same thing I was doing. You were functioning on your own, as if you're not part of us, and that's the thing we have to change. If we're going to get married, we have to get *married*."

"I want to get married," Mary said, a huge wave of relief washing over her.

"I know you do, and so do I." Anthony took her hand across the kitchen island, and Mary felt her eyes well up all over again.

"I love you."

"I love you too." Anthony smiled, a little sadly. "But we have to change this. What I realized, somewhere over the Grand Canyon, is that we don't have to wait to be in a church to get married. Our wedding *isn't* when we get married. We marry each other when we decide to do things together—and only together. *Now* is when we get married. Right *here*."

Mary listened quietly, not only because her heart was eased, but because Anthony was making so much sense and his emotional intelligence was one of the things she loved most about him.

"By the way, I think we make this mistake because we met each other when we were older. We're too accustomed to operating on our own. But it can't stay that way. You can't go around becoming guardians for children and installing them in our house." Anthony gestured upstairs. "As cute as Patrick is, and as deserving, there's a child I don't even know sleeping under my roof. I can't have that. That's not how married people act."

"That's not how it works," Mary said, borrowing Patrick's phrase.

"Right." Anthony smiled, less sadly. "And I can't go to UCLA and decide to interview for a job there and then come home and tell you that you have to move to California. I don't know what I was thinking. Because you can't get Mary DiNunzio out of Philadelphia."

"Aw." Mary smiled. "So what did you do about the job?"

"I interviewed, they offered it to me, and I turned it down."

"You did?" Mary felt delighted and dismayed, both at once. "Oh, Anthony, I'm so sorry. I can't believe you made that sacrifice."

"I did it, because somebody had to go first." Anthony's expression darkened. "But I'm going to ask you to make a sacrifice, in return. Patrick is here for the time being, and I'm going to welcome him. He deserves that, and I'm totally on board. But you have to give him up when the time comes. We're fostering him, not adopting him." Anthony squeezed her hand. "I don't want to start my life and my marriage with a ten-year-old child. I don't *want* a teenager in three years. When I thought about it on the flight to LA, I realized that *that* was what scared me. That you wouldn't let him go. We talked about traveling, we made plans. And when the time comes to have a baby, I want a baby of our own."

Mary felt the words resonate in her chest. "I want the same thing, I do."

"So that's the deal, then. I know it won't be easy for him, you, or me either. And you know who else it won't be easy for? Your parents, who are already in love with him."

"I told them it can't be forever."

"It can't be."

"I know. I agree."

"Good." Anthony rose with a soft smile and held Mary's hand as he walked around the island. "Here. Now. Will you marry me?"

"Aw, yes." Mary stood up and kissed him lightly, then with feeling, and she felt the love that flowed between them, binding them one to the other.

"*Now* we're married." Anthony brushed a strand of hair from her face.

"Yes, and from now on we're going to *act* married. Decisions made together. Jointly." Mary was about to kiss him again but her phone started ringing. She took it from her pocket and checked the screen to see that it was Machiavelli. She hesitated to take the call, but the Complaint in Common Pleas Court was still viable and she still wanted to back him down from deposing Patrick. "Anthony, do you mind? I should take this call."

"Go ahead. I'll meet you out back." Anthony kissed her on the cheek, picked up his cup and saucer, and went out to the patio.

Mary answered Machiavelli's call. "What do you want?"

"I read about what happened to you in the Northeast." Machiavelli sounded unusually somber. "Glad to hear you're alive, and I'm sorry about what I did in my office."

"Fine, I have to go. Never call me for a personal reason again."

"I'm not calling for a personal reason. I'm calling for a business reason."

"What is it?"

"Steven Robertson was arrested tonight for rape and sexual assault on a nine-year-old boy in his neighborhood."

"My God!" Mary said, appalled.

"I know, I'm disgusted, too."

Mary didn't know if she could trust him. "Is this true or one of your schemes?"

"Objection to form, but it's true."

"So Robertson's in jail?" Mary couldn't process it fast enough.

"Yes. He's asked me to represent him, but I declined. In addition, I'm withdrawing from representing him in the civil case against the O'Brien estate and the school district. I refuse to represent anyone who lies to me."

Mary didn't know if Machiavelli was trying to redeem himself after his conduct, or if he was trying to prove to her that he didn't know that Robertson had attacked Patrick at school. Either way, it was good news.

"You don't have to thank me, Mary."

"Don't worry, I won't." Mary realized that Robertson's arrest vindicated Patrick's side of the story, so the Complaint was less credible now, anyway.

"And don't think you won. We live to fight another day. The day I'm in court against you, you'll lose and you'll lose *big.*"

"Don't hold your breath. On second thought, do." Mary hung up, hugely relieved. Patrick wouldn't have to undergo any deposition, which was great.

Suddenly her phone started ringing again, and she looked at the screen to see that it was Lou. He was probably calling about what had happened to her, since he hadn't been in this morning when she'd filled them all in.

Mary pressed Answer. "Lou, hi. Thanks for calling, but I'm fine."

"Good, but guess who's with me at the office?"

"Who?"

"Patrick's father."

CHAPTER SIXTY-THREE

"What the *hell*?" Mary closed her office door with Lou and John inside. As soon as she'd hung up with Lou, she'd called John and asked him to come in, as her family law expert. They'd agreed to talk privately before they went into the conference room, where Patrick's alleged father was supposedly waiting.

"Mary, stay calm. We'll get this sorted." John took the seat next to Lou, crossing his leg. He still had on the clothes he'd worn to court, minus the tie and jacket, and he looked characteristically composed.

"Mare, he's right, I don't know why you're so damn upset." Lou groaned as he eased into the other chair. His polo shirt had a new mustard stain on the front, and his slacks were wrinkled. "You wanted me to find this kid's relatives, cousins, uncles, whatever. I found his *father*. I thought you'd be happy!"

"Lou, I appreciate what you did. Thank you." Mary leaned against the credenza, too antsy to sit at her desk. "But this is a huge surprise. Edward told me Patrick's father was dead. His father hasn't been in Patrick's life ever. *Patrick* thinks his father is dead. I don't know if I believe that it's really his father. That's why."

"It's him," Lou said, matter-of-factly.

"You don't know that," Mary shot back, more sharply than she intended. She couldn't begin to control her emotions. She'd rushed out of the house, grabbed a cab, and gotten to the office as quickly as she could, leaving a bewildered Anthony to babysit.

John raised a hand like a referee. "Point of law. This man's paternity is not yet established. Proceed from there."

Mary repeated, "Edward told me that Patrick's father is dead."

Lou threw up his hands. "So you said, but I looked into it. That's what you wanted me to do. Remember, you asked me to do this?"

"How did you look into it? What did you find out? How?"

"Basic police work, like in the old days. Except it was easier because nobody's hiding." Lou slid a skinny notebook from the back pocket of his slacks, then flipped the cover open. "I went to City Hall, trying to run down anybody on Edward's side. You know how many people are named O'Brien in Philly? Don't ask."

Mary leaned against the credenza, willing herself to be patient, since this was the day when nobody wanted to tell her anything quickly enough. In contrast to her, John folded his long arms and listened quietly, since he was congenitally patient.

Lou continued, "So I thought, let me look up Patrick's birth certificate, and I did. Suzanne, his mother, musta filled it out, and where the father is supposed to be listed, it says 'unknown.' So she didn't put his name on. She didn't list the father."

John interjected, "She doesn't have to."

Lou turned, surprised. "She doesn't have to put the father's name on the birth certificate?"

"No." John shook his head. "Let me give you the fundamentals of paternity law in Pennsylvania. Everything depends on the marital status of the mother at the time of the child's birth. If she's married, her husband is presumed to be the biological father unless they both give a written acknowledgment identifying another person as the biological father. If she's not married, which presumably is our situation, she doesn't have to put anybody on the birth certificate."

Mary listened, letting John's professorial tone soothe her.

"In fact, if the mother isn't married, the father is identified on the birth certificate only if both parents also sign a voluntary acknowledgment of paternity, called an AOP, or if a court has made the determination." John paused. "In my *pro bono* work, when I represent indigent unmarried mothers, I always advise them to get an AOP and get the father's name on the birth certificate. If they don't, they can't go after him for child support and he has no rights to visitation. But a single mother who doesn't intend to seek child support and who doesn't *want* the father to have visitation or other rights, is so signifying by not putting his name on the birth certificate."

Lou shook his head, frowning. "It's like it doesn't matter if he's the father."

John shook his head again. "No, the point is that the law distinguishes between a biological father and a legal father. Every child has a biological father, but not every child has a legal father. Patrick has a biological father, which may or may not be this man. But Patrick doesn't have a legal father because there's no father's name on his birth certificate. Right now, Mary is the closest thing he has to a legal parent because she was declared his legal guardian today."

Lou looked at Mary, his regret plain. "Mare, sorry I didn't let you know. I woulda but my phone ran out of battery. I left without my charger."

Mary didn't want to give him a hard time. "So tell us what you found out."

"Well, you gave me a few facts to start with." Lou glanced at his notebook. "Edward gets married in 1983 at the age of forty. He marries Patty, who's thirty-two. They have a daughter two years later, in 1985, that's Suzanne, Patrick's mother. You told me Suzanne dropped out of Penn State when she got pregnant. I assumed she was class of 2006 and I also assumed she went to the main campus because everybody wants the main campus. My niece, she woulda killed to get on the main campus—"

"So you went up there, to State College?" Mary hadn't seen this coming. It was about a three-hour drive.

"Yes, sure."

"Really?" Mary couldn't make herself sound happy about it, but she wasn't unhappy yet, either. She still couldn't believe that the man in the conference room was really Patrick's father. She was trying to process it, after a long and difficult day.

"Mare, I drove to the boonies for you. Gimme credit, would you?" Lou opened his palms in appeal, his gray eyebrows flying upward. "I went the extra mile, I thought you *wanted* to find this kid's relatives."

"I know, thank you," Mary said, too anxious to feel truly grateful. "So then what happened?"

"I went to the registrar's office, told them the situation, and since Suzanne passed, they took pity on me and showed me her records. She was in the Schreyer Honors College, a smart cookie. She lived in Atherton Hall, and I found out who the residence advisors used to be." Lou checked his pad again. "The residence advisor for her floor was Julia Thomas, and one of the girls in the registrar's office knew her. She told me that Thomas got her graduate degree and she still works at Penn State, in the admissions department. So I went there and I asked her do you remember Suzanne O'Brien and do you remember who she was dating when she dropped out?"

"But he's supposed to be dead!"

"What can I tell you? He ain't. Julia told me that Suzanne had a steady boyfriend and his name was Norman Lavigne. He sang in a band that used to play in a restaurant. Suzanne worked as a waitress in the same restaurant. That's how they met."

"I just don't believe this."

John folded his arms again, saying nothing.

Lou checked his notebook again. "The name of the restaurant is The Vines, and it's a brewpub. So I went over to the restaurant and I started asking around about Suzanne O'Brien and Norm Lavigne, and it turns out that Lavigne's father Bill owned the restaurant. Bill would be Patrick's grandfather, but he's dead and so's his wife."

"Why didn't Norm Lavigne come forward before? Why is he coming forward now? Did he ditch her when he found out Suzanne was pregnant? Or did she ditch him? How do you know he's the real—"

"Whoa, whoa, whoa." Lou put up both hands. "Mare, don't get crazy. Norm should answer these questions. He wants to."

"I don't want him to," Mary heard herself say, then couldn't believe the words had slipped out of her mouth.

"Why not?" Lou frowned, mystified.

John looked over at Mary, pursing his lips, but behind his glasses, his eyes looked knowing.

Mary answered, "Lou, I just got Patrick, I became his guardian today. He met my parents, and Anthony's on board. We're going to orientation at his new school tomorrow. He's finally going to get help. I have it all set up."

"Mare." Lou recoiled. "It's the boy's *father.*"

John shook his head. "We don't know that. Remember, Lou. We have to proceed slowly. This man could be a fraud."

"Totally!" Mary's mind raced, her emotions tumbling over one another. "He could be a *total fraud,* coming out of the woodwork because he believes Patrick has money. Or for all we know, Machiavelli sent him. Maybe it's one of his schemes. Ask yourself, why didn't DHS find this Lavigne?"

John interjected, "DHS follows if there is a legal father named in the birth certificate. If there's no legal father, they end their inquiry. They don't have the resources to search for biological fathers, especially if he hasn't surfaced in a decade." John gestured toward the conference room. "Let me do the talking when we go in there. Even if Lavigne is the biological father, he'll have to go to court to establish paternity and become the legal father. Right now we have all the cards and that's the way I want to keep it."

Lou frowned. "I don't understand what you mean."

Mary's ears pricked up, listening as John answered:

"I represent Mary, and she has to make a decision about what's best for Patrick. Even if Lavigne is Patrick's biological father, she doesn't have to hand Patrick over to him. In fact, she *can't.* Only a court can do that. If Lavigne is the biological father, he'll have to prove it by a DNA swab and petition the court for paternity. He can do that now or anytime until Patrick turns eighteen. And if Lavigne does try to do that, Mary can decide how she wants to react. She may oppose Lavigne's petition, if she wishes."

Lou frowned more deeply. "Why would she, if Lavigne is the real father? I mean, the biological father?"

"That's Mary's decision," John answered calmly. "She may not think Lavigne is an adequate parent or she may have other reasons. Mary doesn't know anything about Lavigne, and neither do I. Our job is to preserve her options. She has a legal right to make that decision. So when we go into the conference room, I don't want any of us to say anything that would negate Mary's rights."

"Okay." Lou rose slowly, then placed a heavy hand on Mary's shoulder. "Come on, he can tell you the whole story."

"Let's go." John stood up, brushing down his pants.

Mary still couldn't wrap her mind around it. "He came all the way here from State College?"

Lou squeezed her shoulder. "No, they live closer in Reading. They followed me back in their car."

"*They?*"

"Him and his wife. She's a real sweetheart. Amanda." Lou sighed, exhaling heavily. "You been under a lot of strain lately, kiddo. I don't blame you bein' upset. Let's go hear what he has to say."

"I agree." John shot Mary a reassuring look.

Lou flashed her a final smile. "Marc, look on the bright side. If you hadn't done everything you did, we never woulda known Patrick's father was really alive."

John looked over, but said nothing.

Mary set her emotions aside and opened the door.

CHAPTER SIXTY-FOUR

Everybody shook hands, introducing themselves and forcing smiles despite the undercurrent of tension. Nobody offered anybody coffee, and the air in the conference room smelled stale. Outside the window the night sky had gone black, except for the stacked squares of windows where office lights were on. They usually reminded Mary of waffles, but that was when she was in a better mood, not now.

She felt sick to her stomach because Norm Lavigne looked a lot like Patrick, and vice versa. Lavigne had a longish face with a pointed chin but his front teeth protruded slightly, an overbite that wouldn't require correction and so never got one. He had smallish blue eyes set close together, with a long nose just like Patrick, except he didn't have any freckles. His hair was a shade darker than Patrick's, medium brown and cut in shaggy layers around his ears, which contributed to a vaguely organic vibe created by his work shirt and jeans. He had on a leather bracelet with his runner's watch.

His wife, Amanda, looked about the same age, maybe thirty-something, and she was pretty, with a sweet, if uncomfortable, smile. Her greenish-hazel eyes were set far apart with only light makeup, and she had a small nose and a mouth shaped like a Cupid's bow. Her hair was dark blonde and long enough to cover her shoulders, and she had on a blue handknit sweater with oversized loops. In other circumstances, Mary would have asked her where she bought it.

John gestured Mary into the seat catty-corner to him and waited for her to sit down until he took his seat at the head of the table. The Lavignes sat on the one side of the table, behind a manila folder that was closed, and Lou sat down next to Mary, who realized that everyone had lined up into Us and Them, which was exactly how she felt.

John cleared his throat. "So, Norm, I'm representing Mary, and the best way to proceed is for me to ask you a couple of questions. Could you explain how we got here?"

"Sure." Lavigne turned to Mary. "Mary, before I go into it, we read about how you were almost killed. We admire your heroism and your dedication to Edward and Patrick."

"Thank you," Mary said, though if Lavigne was trying to charm her, it hadn't worked.

"It's hard to know where to begin." Lavigne placed his hands on either side of the manila folder.

"Begin at the beginning," John said, with a tight smile.

"Okay." Lavigne inhaled. "I dated Suzanne when she came to Penn State, almost from the first week of her freshman year. She got a job at my father's restaurant and we liked each other, right away. I would say it was love at first sight." Lavigne glanced over at his wife, Amanda, who smiled back at him.

"Go ahead, honey. You're going to have to tell them everything."

Lavigne nodded. "I had a rock band then, we played every night at my father's restaurant. It was a bad period of time in my life. I was an addict. I was on heroin. I had been using since high school. I never enrolled in college. I don't know what I was thinking." Lavigne met Mary's gaze evenly. "Maybe I do, I was thinking what every addict is thinking, which is where I get my next fix. Every addict's story is the same. The drugs reduce you. They erase your individuality. You all do the same thing, every day, day after day, and you all become the same person."

Mary nodded, but didn't say anything.

"When I met Suzanne, she was smart and fun. She was also straight and motivated. She wanted to make something of herself. She was an *individual*." Lavigne smiled briefly at the memory. "We got to be boyfriend and girlfriend. I knew she was too good for me, but there was no way I was going to stop using. She nagged me all the time, but I was functional. I thought we were doing fine. I never had any problem with denial."

Mary listened, trying not to note the similarity in tone between his voice and Patrick's, but it was undeniable.

"So she broke up with me. One day, she said, 'I can't do this, you're an addict, and that's never going to change.' She dropped out of school, she asked me not to contact her, and I didn't. I knew why she broke up with me, the whole band knew why she broke up with me. None of us hung on to any decent women because no decent woman would've put up with who we were."

John interjected, "So she didn't tell you she was pregnant before she dropped out of school?"

Lavigne shook his head. "No she didn't tell me. She didn't tell me before she left. She never told me."

"Did she tell you why she was leaving school?"

"She said she wanted to transfer somewhere else. She wasn't that happy at Penn State, she thought it was too big for her. Here, take a look at some of these pictures." Lavigne opened the manila envelope, took out some photographs, and placed them in a line on the table, turning them around to face Mary. She looked over, recognizing Suzanne's pretty and wholesome face from the photo that had been on Edward's dresser. The other photos showed a grinning Suzanne with her arm around a younger Norm Lavigne, a sexy bad boy in a black leather jacket. Mary scanned the photos and could understand why Suzanne would be attracted to Lavigne, but also why it wouldn't work.

John asked Lavigne, "Did you try to stay in touch with her?"

"No, I was high, constantly high. I fought with my parents, I was bugging them for money all the time. I blew it all on drugs. They let me play at the restaurant, that was my job. It's a never-ending cycle, a nightmare. I lost everything, I lost Suzanne and any girl-

friends after that. But then one day, my bass player died of an overdose. He was my best friend from when we both were kids." Lavigne
paused, swallowing visibly. "And that was when I bottomed out. I
went to rehab. I relapsed but I went back again and finally I cleaned
up for good. I found my faith. I'm six years clean and sober, not
even tempted. I still go to meetings because I believe in the program and I sponsor three people right now. But I'll never go back
to using, ever again."

Amanda patted his arm. "He's an amazing man and an amazing
husband, and I know he'll make an amazing father."

Mary felt her gut twist, but said nothing.

John asked, "Norm, would you submit to drug testing?"

"Of course." Lavigne didn't hesitate. "I would even agree to testing for a period of time, say, a full year. Whatever you and Mary
need to feel comfortable."

John blinked. "Good. To clarify, it's your position that you didn't
know Patrick even existed?"

"It's not my position, it's the truth," Lavigne answered, without
rancor. "I had no idea I was a father until Lou came and knocked
on my door. It blew me away. But I believe everything happens for
a reason, and I think this was meant to be."

John's eyes narrowed. "You didn't attempt to contact Suzanne
after you got clean?"

"No, I didn't know she had passed, either. Lou told me that, too.
That's a tragedy."

"You didn't look her up on Facebook, anything like that?"

"No, why would I? I had moved on and I assumed she did too.
She was someone I dated a long time ago."

"So you had absolutely no idea she had a child?"

"I had no idea. I just didn't know." Lavigne gestured to his wife.
"Amanda and I met when she hired me to design a website for her.
She makes these really cool hand-knits with big needles, and her
business just took off. I fell in love for good. We got married, and
here we are."

Mary sensed that what he was saying rang true, but it turned
everything she had believed on its head. "Do you think that Su-

zanne told her parents that you were dead? Because I was told you were dead. Patrick believes you're dead."

Lavigne inhaled slowly, his mouth a grim line. "No, I don't think Suzanne lied to her parents about me. She was close to both of her parents, and they were a great family. I think she told them the truth, and they all lied to Patrick. They told him I was dead, to protect him. I don't even blame them. I get it."

"Why do you 'get it'?" Mary wasn't sure she believed him. She could understand why Suzanne had made the decision she did, but it had denied Lavigne the chance to know his own child.

"While we were dating, she took me home to meet her parents. They didn't like me in *the least*. They were right. I was bad news and they knew it. I remember her father took me aside in the kitchen, he knew I was on drugs. He told me if I wanted to be with his daughter, I had to quit."

Mary could imagine the scene. Edward wouldn't mince words.

"I said no way, I flipped him the bird." Lavigne's fair skin flushed a pink tinge. "I'm ashamed of myself, even now, the way I treated that man. To hear that he was murdered, that's sad. I know he rests in peace, with God. He was a good man."

Mary swallowed hard.

"Ten years ago, I wasn't fit to be Patrick's father. I wasn't fit to be anybody's father. There would have been no point in telling Patrick that I was alive, nothing but a world of hurt for that child."

Mary thought that Lavigne's assumption about what had probably happened made sense. She could easily imagine Edward and his wife taking care of Suzanne and the baby. They simply hadn't anticipated that Suzanne would die, and now Edward.

Lavigne shook his head. "I wouldn't have come forward for Patrick back then, even if Suzanne had told me we had a baby. I didn't have a penny to my name and I couldn't have supported a baby. Suzanne was the responsible one. I woulda let her take on all the responsibility she could handle, even more so. Typical addict behavior."

John interjected, "So what do you do for a living?"

"It's hard to get a job with a past like mine, but I'd always been good at art—"

Mary's ears pricked up. Maybe Lavigne was where Patrick got his talent in art.

John interrupted, "Do you have a criminal record?"

"No, nothing like that," Lavigne answered quickly. "But I don't hide my addiction and that made it hard to get hired. Art doesn't pay, and I wanted to make a living. So I went back to school for graphic design and now I own my own marketing company. We do web design, direct mail, and the like. I have for the past three years, and it's doing very well. We have over $2 million in billings this year. We project growth for the next few years, I'm already planning to hire another coder. We have about twenty active clients, most of them corporate."

Amanda interjected, "My business is really small compared to his other clients."

Lavigne smiled. "But I like her the best."

Lou laughed, but Mary didn't. She didn't know how she felt. It had been such a long day, and her thoughts were all over the lot. She believed Lavigne, but she wanted to research him and verify everything he'd told them. And she didn't know what to do about the fact that he had appeared in Patrick's life, out of the blue. She thought about what John had said. She had to make a decision.

"The name of my company is Lavigne Marketing, and I employ six people. We have an office in Wyncote, outside the city, and Amanda and I own our own home. We have four bedrooms, two baths. There's a bedroom for Patrick."

John glanced at Mary, but then returned his attention to Lavigne. "Norm, let us have your position. What is it you want, vis-à-vis Patrick?"

"I'm Patrick's father. I'll take a DNA test to prove it, but I know it by the timing. We were exclusive. At least she was." Lavigne pressed his lips together, bitterly. "We're in a position to take him and raise him. Amanda and I have discussed it and that's what we want to do."

Mary felt her chest tighten. "It's not that easy. He has special needs. He has dyslexia and anxiety."

Lavigne nodded. "Lou told me that, and I would love to know

more about the details from you. Amanda and I discussed that, too, and we would be happy to take him on, just the same. He belongs with blood."

"But you have to know what you're getting into. You can't just snap your fingers." Mary heard the resentment edging her own tone, but didn't hide it. "I've won the right to be his guardian and I'm enrolling him in a private school, Fairmount Prep near the Art Museum, because it can meet his academic and emotional needs. Your taking him would disrupt everything what's set up for him."

Lavigne shook his head. "It doesn't have to. We'll keep him in whatever school you think is necessary. If this is a school that he needs to be in, then he can stay there. We'll take our cue from you. We'll work with you in every way possible, on any timetable. You can transition him from your home into ours on whatever schedule is best for him. We can meet him and get to know him, and he can get to know us."

Amanda nodded enthusiastically, her shiny hair bouncing. "Mary, I totally get what you're saying, and I work from home. If I have to drive him to school in the morning, even into Philly, I'll do that. My sister lives in the city, and I can do my knitting there, all day. And then I would take Patrick home, when school is over."

Mary didn't believe it. "You're going to do that forever?"

"If that's what it takes," Amanda said, meeting her eye plaintively. "I used to commute in town for my old job, so I don't mind. We don't want to switch him out of a school that he needs. We're not trying to disrupt his life, we're just trying to make it better."

"We can't avoid talking about money. Even if his private school tuition is reimbursed throughout his school career, you need to know that he comes to you virtually penniless. Edward had left him a substantial estate, but if you saw the news, you know that Edward's lawyer, James Geltz, and his stockbroker, Dave Kather, were running a Ponzi scheme at Cornerstone Financial. There's no money left except in the bank account. Everything that was invested, all of Edward's savings for Patrick, are completely gone."

"We're not coming forward for Patrick because of the money, so the fact that there's no money doesn't deter us. We can support him. We will make all the sacrifices that any other parents would, for his benefit."

Mary looked from Amanda to Lavigne. "But there's so much you don't know about him, what he's been through at school, even losing Edward. His life has been so difficult, even traumatic."

"You're right, we don't know him, but we want to get to know him. You'll fill us in. We're all ears. We'll help him deal with it. I'm a big believer in therapy, it saved my life. We're big on talking about our feelings. We'll encourage him to talk about his with us and with a therapist, if you think that's a good idea."

Mary couldn't wrap her mind around it fast enough. "It's so confusing for him. He just met my parents tonight and he gets along so well with older people. He's comfortable around them because of Edward."

Lavigne smiled, in an understanding way. "If he likes your parents, we have no problem with him seeing them wherever he wants to. We feel the same way about you, too. We're inclusive folks, Amanda and I. To us, it's all about Patrick. About what he needs and what he wants."

John interjected, "So do you intend to go to court and be declared Patrick's father?"

Lavigne nodded. "Yes. We called a lawyer today and that's what we intend to do. He said that we should meet with you tonight and that things will go better if we can get on the same page."

John frowned. "Your lawyer advised you to come here without him?"

"No, he wanted to come, too, but we wanted to come alone. We don't think we're on opposite sides. We believe in peace, not war. That's what I'm saying. I think we all want the same thing, what's best for Patrick." Lavigne returned to Mary, his expression softening. "Mary, I know this comes out of left field for you."

"Yes, it does," Mary blurted out.

"It did for me, too."

"And it will for Patrick."

"I know." Lavigne nodded. "Patrick and I may be father and son, but we're also strangers. It'll take some doing for us to get to know each other. I'll do the work it takes to make that happen." Lavigne smiled, tilting his chin up confidently. "We think we can offer Patrick something and we want to. We can give him a family, forever. *His* family."

Mary knew the thing Patrick wanted most was a family, and she saw the conviction in Lavigne's eyes, but she wasn't ready to respond.

John answered for her. "How about we let Mary think it over and get back to you?"

CHAPTER SIXTY-FIVE

It was after midnight when Mary got home, shut the front door behind her, and twisted the deadbolt. Light spilling from the kitchen told her that Anthony was still downstairs, waiting up for her. She dropped her purse on the floor, kicked off her heels, and padded through the dining room to the kitchen.

An empty wineglass waited for her on the kitchen island next to a small plate that held shaved locatelli, oily green Ceregnola olives, and a bulb of fennel, her go-to late-night snack. Anthony wasn't in sight, but the French doors that led to the backyard were open and she knew he was outside reading, which meant they were back to their favorite routine.

She went to the fridge, popped the rubber stopper off the Lambrusco, poured some bubbling into her glass, then put the wine back in the fridge and went outside with her glass and small plate. She stepped onto the patio and almost immediately felt herself relax.

The sky was as dark and soft as black velvet, even starry above the city lights. There was a slight breeze, its fresh snap signaling that autumn had finally arrived to stay. Anthony was sitting in one of their wrought-iron chairs reading on his e-reader, the soft glowing square reflecting upward on the handsome contours of a face she loved so well.

"Hi, honey." Mary crossed to him, set the snack plate down on the small glass-top table between them, and leaned over to kiss him on the cheek. "That was nice of you to wait up. You must be exhausted."

"I'm okay, I'm still in my time-zone warp." Anthony set his e-reader on the table next to his wineglass, looking over at her with concern. "Well? Is it really his father?"

Mary sat down in her chair, forcing a smile. "All signs point to yes. Isn't that what the Magic Eight Ball says?"

"Oh boy." Anthony sighed, a quiet sound. "Wow."

"Exactly." Mary took a sip of her Lambrusco, which didn't cheer her up, so she set the glass down. "And bottom line, I have a decision to make. But I'm not going to make it alone this time. Not anymore. We're going to make it together."

"I'm glad. I'll help you make it, and I'll think about it objectively." Anthony smiled at her, with love. "I don't want to let him go either, not really."

"You don't?" Mary smiled.

"No." Anthony's voice softened. "He gets under your skin."

"Right?" Mary felt happy to hear it. "You didn't say so before."

"While you were gone, he called for you, so I went upstairs. We had a nice talk."

"Aw, what about?"

"Honestly, everything." Anthony shrugged, shaking his head and looking up at the stars. "He talked all about his grandfather, and his comics, and World War II. He knows a lot of historical battles. I think he just wanted company. He didn't want to be alone. I held his hand."

Mary felt tears come to her eyes that she couldn't really explain. "He's sweet, right?"

"He really is. We started talking about chess, and he told me how much he liked it. He really was good at it, I have to tell you." Anthony reached across the table for her hand, and he took hers in his, holding it gently. "He picked it up so quickly, I was surprised. Anything I told him, he remembered. He soaked up the way the pieces move. He's smart."

Mary nodded. She knew if she tried to speak, she would cry.

"What's amazing about him is that he wants to learn and he wants to be taught. He didn't get impatient or bored, and at first, I thought it was about the game, but it wasn't. It was about the connection. He likes to be talked to and listened to, and his heart is so *open*."

"I know. I love that kid." Mary felt tears brimming in her eyes.

"I know you do, babe," Anthony said quietly.

"I hate to give him up, now that I finally got him."

"I know that, too."

"It just makes me want to cry."

"You wouldn't be you if you didn't." Anthony rose, coming over to comfort her. "I'm here. So go ahead and cry."

EPILOGUE

The ceremony was about to start, and Mary, Judy, and Anne listened nervously at the thick carved door, dressed in their swishy gowns, holding their fragrant bouquets, and squeezed into a small room at the church, among stacked boxes of newsletters, a rolling rack of coats, and an American flag in a wobbly stand. Sunlight poured through a small arched window, showing the dust that got stirred up only on Sundays.

Mary could hear the quartet playing entrance music and the guests talking, laughing, and coughing. The hubbub echoed in the church, so she knew that everybody was seated. She glanced at the clock, which read 9:56. Her mouth turned to cotton. Her heart fluttered in a permanent state of fibrillation. Unfortunately, she lacked oxygen because her wedding dress was too tight. She almost hadn't been able to zip it up.

"God, I can't breathe." Mary rushed panicky to a full-length mirror leaning against the wall, dismayed to see the satiny fabric of her wedding dress pulled along the waistband.

"Don't worry about it." Judy rushed to Mary's side, looking fresh and pretty in her light blue gown, which matched her eyes perfectly. Her hair was its natural blonde again, cut feathery and feminine, and she put a comforting hand on Mary's shoulder. "Mare, nobody's looking at your waist. Just carry your bouquet in front."

Anne rushed to Mary's other side, looking like a bridesmaid

model in her blue column dress, her glistening red hair braided around her head with tendrils curling around her lovely green eyes. "She's right, Mary. You look gorgeous."

Mary shook her head, worried. "But I can't breathe. I can't sit down."

Judy said, "You don't need to sit down."

Anne said, "You don't need to breathe."

"What if the dress rips?" Mary checked the clock—9:57.

"It won't, and look at yourself." Judy gestured at the mirror. "Really, you look great."

Anne said, "Yes, look. Be in the moment."

Mary looked at her reflection, trying to come into the moment. She'd had Anne to do her makeup, so it looked natural and lovely, and she'd had her hair professionally styled into a French twist with freesia woven in. She had on her favorite pearl necklace with pearl stud earrings. The delicate beads on her dress sparkled in the sunlight, and the sweetheart neckline fit well because her boobs were back. Truly, a girl couldn't ask for more.

"Gorgeous!" Anne said, her eyes shining.

"Yay!" Judy threw up her hands happily.

"I love you guys!" Mary let herself be swept up in their enthusiasm, her heart lifting. She felt so grateful, happy, and blessed that they were here, even if her sister Angie couldn't be.

"Yay!" Judy cheered, and Anne joined in.

Suddenly there was a quick knock on the door and into the room burst Mary's father and The Tonys in their rented tuxedos, looking like a flock of beloved penguins and smelling like Aqua Velva.

"IT'S TIME!" Her father gave her a big hug. "WHOA, MARE, YOU LOOK LIKE A PRINCESS!"

"Thanks, Pop." Mary hugged him back, her throat tight.

"Mare, I'm so happy for you!" Feet gave her a kiss on the cheek.

"*Maria, che bella!*" Pigeon Tony stood on tiptoe to kiss her on the cheek.

"Mare, you look like a million bucks!" Tony-From-Down-The-Block gave her a hug. "Yo, you know who looks *really* great for her age? Anthony's mother, Elvira!"

Mary smiled. She hadn't seen El Virus yet, but anything was possible. "You know that you're the same age, right?"

Tony-From-Down-The-Block winked. "So maybe I'll give the old broad a shot, huh? Does she have a boyfriend?"

"Ask her." Mary was too preoccupied to play matchmaker but she would like nothing better than to keep El Virus busy.

As if on cue, El Virus appeared in the threshold, striking a pose by putting one hand with red talons on the doorjamb, and everyone's mouth dropped open because El Virus looked awesome, for an alternative source of energy. Sequins encrusted her silver fish-scale dress, throwing off so much light that she could've powered the Northeast corridor, and the sheath was tight enough to hug her curves, which were curvier than Mary had ever realized. Extensions filled out her darkly gleaming coif, balancing out her heavy makeup, and her false eyelashes turned her smoky eyes into a five-alarm fire.

"How do I look, Mare?" Elvira asked, wiggling her hips in a sexy way rarely seen in church.

"Wow! You look great!" Mary glanced over at Tony-From-Down-The-Block, who was going to have to hit the gym if he wanted a shot.

"You do, too!" El Virus sauntered over, air-kissed Mary, and gave her a majorly perfumed hug.

Mary's mother appeared in the open door, holding Patrick's hand, and Mary felt her heart wrench. Her mother looked happy and elegant in a pale blue chiffon grown with her hair teased the way she liked, and Patrick was impossibly cute in his rented tux, since he was their ringbearer. Last week, Norm Lavigne's DNA had proven he was Patrick's biological father, and any day now, a court would declare him Patrick's legal father. It hadn't been easy to let Patrick go, but Mary and Anthony had known it was the right thing to do. Patrick wanted a family, and now he would have one.

"*Maria, che bellissima!*" her mother said, raising her arms for a hug.

"Hey, guys!" Mary hugged her back, kissing her on the cheek. "Ma, you look so nice! You ready for the big day?"

"*Si,* yes, *andiamo!*" Her mother's eyes lit up behind her glasses, and Mary ruffled up Patrick's hair. He had just moved in with his father and Amanda, and he was already liking Fairmount Prep. The DiNunzios and the Lavignes had grown closer since Edward's funeral, and the Lavignes were honored guests at the wedding today. Everyone would be at Mary's parents' house tomorrow for Sunday dinner, bonding over homemade ravioli, and Mary knew that the families would be in one another's lives, for some time to come.

"Patrick, you got the ring?" Mary kissed the top of his head.

"Yes, see?" Patrick grinned, holding up the blue satin pillow, and her gleaming gold wedding band was fastened to the center by a white satin bow.

"And you remember what to do, right?"

"I go first down the aisle. My dad said I'm the leader!"

"You sure are." Mary gave him a hug, touched.

"Andiamo!" Patrick said, and everybody laughed.

"OKAY, EVERYBODY OUTTA THE POOL!" Her father hurried into the vestibule, where he could undoubtedly be heard by the entire congregation. "TONYS, YOU GOTTA GO SIDDOWN! HURRY UP!"

Mary waited in the doorway of the room, her heart pounding. The Tonys shuffled down the aisle in their orthopedic shoes just as the quartet played the first strains of Purcell's "Trumpet Voluntary."

"PATRICK, YOU GO FIRST! HAVE FUN, BUDDY!" Her father put a gentle hand on Patrick's shoulder, and Mary watched from the doorway as Patrick faced front, squared his skinny shoulders, and went forward bravely, holding his blue pillow like a lunch tray at school.

"NOW, ELVIRA, YOU GO!"

Elvira struck a pose like an aging Madonna, then sashayed off.

"ANNE, YOU'RE ON DECK!"

Anne waited for her musical cue, flashing Mary a dazzling smile before she took her first step down the aisle, like a model on a runway.

"NOW, JUDY! OKAY, GO!"

Judy took one last look at Mary, winked, and left, leaving Mary teary.

"VEET, COME 'ERE!" Her father took her mother's arm on his left side, because all three of them were walking down the aisle together, which was what Mary had wanted. Her father had given her away at her first wedding, but she was younger then. The truth was that she owed everything she had become to both of her parents. She silently sent up a prayer of thanks that they were alive to see this day.

"OKAY, MARE, WE'RE UP!" Her father smiled sweetly at her, and she could see his hooded eyes already glistening behind his glasses as he extended his hand, which she took, then looped her arm through his.

"I'm ready, Pop." Mary tried not to hyperventilate when the music switched to "Here Comes the Bride." She leaned on her parents, and the three DiNunzios stepped into the church, arm-in-arm.

Mary felt her breath taken away as everyone turned to look at her, a veritable sea of smiles and tears, and she realized that she was looking at everyone she loved most in the world—Bennie, Lou, The Tonys, Allegra, John, Marshall, and an array of long-time clients whom she adored and who had supported her for so many years. It was all she could do to keep walking, her knees weak, and when she got partway up the aisle, she lifted her watery gaze to Anthony, the most wonderful man she had met in her entire life.

She hung on to her parents, and they propelled her forward, but all she could see was Anthony, and all she could think was that he was in her family now. She found herself remembering what Patrick had said, and she realized that she had family in heaven too. Her first husband, Mike, was with her too, walking with her, and so was her sister, Angie, an angel on earth. And Mary felt so much love and so much happiness that she thought her heart would burst, and when her parents kissed her and let her go, she practically floated to Anthony.

And they stepped into their future, together.

ACKNOWLEDGMENTS

I am so lucky and blessed to have great friends in my life, and this book is dedicated to my best friend, Franca Palumbo, Esq., who gets the biggest thanks here. We've been besties since law school and she has become one of the top special-needs lawyers in the country, because she cares so much about her clients and their families, and she works around the clock to make sure that they get the programming and support that they deserve. Franca inspired this book and helped me so much with its research, but more important, she has been an amazing and sustaining force in my life and I want to thank her here. I love you, honey!

Yet another reason to thank Franca is that she introduced me to an array of experts in the field of special education law, and I would like to acknowledge their help as well, though any mistakes in this novel are mine. Thank you to Judy Baskin, Esq., and Janet Ellis, Esq., for their guidance and expertise, as well as for their hard work and determination to make sure that Philadelphia schools meet the needs of their students.

Special thanks to the amazing Diane Reott, founder of the Pennsylvania Dyslexia Literacy Coalition, whose advocacy for children with dyslexia culminated in the Dyslexia and Early Literacy Intervention Pilot Program, just signed into law in Pennsylvania. Diane's hard work and advocacy is proof-positive that one loving mother can change the world not only for her own child but for many others, and I am indebted to Diane for taking the time to open her life experience and expertise to me, in order to inform this novel.

Special thanks to Kathleen Tana, Esq., an expert in family law who advised me every step of the way and even read pages of the manuscript for their accuracy, in addition to being a wonderful friend and fellow dog lover. Thank you so much, Kate! Thank you to Mario D'Adamo, Esq., Deputy Court Administrator, Family Court, who took the time to meet with me and patiently answer my questions about the process in Family Court. Thanks, too, to Judge Diane Thompson of Family Court, who met with me informally and gave me an idea of what life on the bench was like from her perspective. Thank you, Judge Thompson, for your dedicated public service.

Thank you to the amazing people at the Philadelphia Children's Alliance, led by the awesome executive director Chris Kirchner and Miranda Barthmus, who took the time to meet with me and answer all my questions about the endlessly good work they do for abused children of Philadelphia. Thank you to Denise Wilson, manager of Forensic Services at PCA, too. It is heartbreaking but necessary work, and they and PCA have my highest admiration.

Thank you (again) to the hardworking and handsome Detective Thomas Gaul of the Homicide Division of the Philadelphia Police Department, and to Officer Goodfellow of the Twenty-fifth Precinct of the Philadelphia Police Department.

Thank you to the brilliant and good-hearted Lisa Goldstein, M.D., a psychiatrist who treats children and adolescents and helped me inform the novel's accuracy by answering all of my questions in the clutch.

Finally, I'm a bookaholic, so I read a lot to inform this novel, including *Overcoming Dyslexia* by Sally Shaywitz and *The Dyslexic Advantage* by Brock and Fernette Eide, as well as *Machiavelli: A Portrait* by Christopher Celenza and *The Essential Writings of Machiavelli*, edited and translated by Peter Constantine.

I'm a lawyer, but criminal law wasn't my field, so I always touch base with my dear friend, the brilliant public servant Nicholas

Casenta, Esq., chief of the Chester County District Attorney's Office.

Thank you to my genius editor, Jennifer Enderlin, who is also the Senior Vice President and Publisher of St. Martin's Press, yet she still finds the time to improve every one of my manuscripts, including this one. Thank you so much, Coach Jen! And big love and thanks to everyone at St. Martin's Press and Macmillan, starting with the terrific John Sargent and Sally Richardson, plus Jeff Dodes, Paul Hochman, Jeff Capshew, Stephanie Davis, Brian Heller, Brant Janeway, Lisa Senz, John Karle, Tracey Guest, Dori Weintraub, Anne-Marie Tallberg, Nancy Trypuc, Kerry Nordling, Elizabeth Wildman, Caitlin Dareff, Elena Yip, Talia Sherer, Kim Ludlum, and all the wonderful sales reps. Big thanks to Michael Storrings, for outstanding cover design for the series. Also hugs and kisses to Mary Beth Roche, Laura Wilson, Samantha Edelson, and the great people in audiobooks. I love and appreciate all of you!

Thanks and love to my agent, Robert Gottlieb of Trident Media Group, whose dedication guided this novel into publication, and to Nicole Robson, Emily Ross, and Trident's digital media team, who help me get the word out on social media.

Many thanks and much, much love and a big hug to the amazing and wonderful Laura Leonard. She's invaluable in every way, every day, and has been for over twenty years. Laura, I love you! Thanks, too, to my pal Nan Daley and to George Davidson, for doing everything else, so that I can be free to write!

Finally, thank you to my amazing daughter (and even coauthor) Francesca, for all the support, laughter, and love.

Reading
Group
Gold

DAMAGED
by Lisa Scottoline

Behind the Novel
- "You Inspire Me": An Original Essay by the Author

Keep on Reading
- Ideas for Book Groups
- Reading Group Questions

Special Extra!
- An Excerpt from Lisa Scottoline's Next Novel, *Exposed*

*A
Reading
Group Gold
Selection*

Also available as an audiobook
from Macmillan Audio

For more reading group suggestions
visit www.readinggroupgold.com.

ST. MARTIN'S GRIFFIN

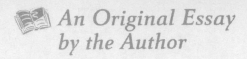

An Original Essay by the Author

"You Inspire Me"

Readers often wonder where I got the idea for a novel, and I'm always happy to explain, because there's usually a single notion that inspires me when I begin to write, and this time, my inspiration came from you.

What do I mean by that?

I mean that one day, I was talking to my friend Franca, who has been my best friend since we met in law school. We practiced law together, were pregnant together, and both quit our jobs to stay home and raise our children. I never returned to the law, because I loved being at home with my daughter, Francesca, more. After long years of struggle, I became a published author and now I get to tell stories for a living.

Thanks to you.

But Franca returned to the law, and she changed her practice entirely. She became an expert in the area of special education. She advocates tirelessly for her clients, who are children in public and private schools fighting to get the special help they need in order to acquire the basic skills that many of us take for granted, like reading.

It struck me one day that Franca changes people's lives, one child at a time. Children she represents have bright and happy futures, all because of her. And Franca works very hard, so she represents hundreds of clients.

It's the power of one woman, changing the lives of hundreds of children.

And Franca introduced me to another woman, Diane Reott, the mother of a son with dyslexia. Diane dedicated herself to her child and educated herself about all aspects of dyslexia, which at the time wasn't well known. She began to drill her son in order to improve his ability to read, and she began to notice deficiencies in the public school system, which was

falling short for dyslexic students, in addition to other students who had a wide array of learning disabilities.

Diane went on to create an organization called the Pennsylvania Dyslexia Literacy Coalition, working tirelessly to champion the needs of dyslexic children in the Pennsylvania school system. After years and years of effort, building her organization and filling the ranks with mothers and fathers just like herself, she actually got the state legislature to draft and pass House Bill 198, which was signed into law in Pennsylvania.

The new law created a pilot program to screen kindergarten students for risk factors linked to dyslexia and other reading deficiencies. The goal is to identify dyslexia and other reading issues in students as early as possible. Not only does this help these students learn to read, but just as important, as you see in my novel, since dyslexia and self-esteem are connected, the new law also builds their self-worth.

It's the power of one woman, which changed the lives of millions of children across an entire state.

The more research I did into this topic, the more I found women like Franca and Diane, and plenty of men too, all of whom were single-handedly working to better services for children with special needs and give them all of the enrichment they need and deserve to realize their fullest potential and happiness.

All of these people decided that they were going to change something for the better, for children.

In effect, they decided to change the world.

Wow.

Not many people wake up thinking that they can change the world, and there are plenty who don't even try, and I don't blame them. It's all that most of us can do to get through the day, do our job, make sure there's food in the fridge, and try to keep our hands out of the cookie jars.

I mean that literally.

I'm on a diet, as usual.

But I am so inspired by people like Franca, Diane, and many, many more of you, and you know who you are, who toil thanklessly; teach for long hours; spend your own money on things you shouldn't have to; volunteer to help at school; serve on countless committees and boards; bake cookies for after-school programs; raise money for baseball teams, band trips, and choir robes; take in foster children; or do whatever is needed, wherever it's needed.

I'm talking about every single person who decides to try to make something better and doesn't give up until they succeed.

That's you.

You may never get the credit you deserve, but I know you're there.

I see you and I celebrate you.

You inspire me.

And that's why I wrote you this book.

Ideas for Book Groups

I am a huge fan of book clubs because it means people are reading and discussing books. Mix that with wine and carbs, and you can't keep me away. I'm deeply grateful to all who read me, and especially honored when my book is chosen by a book club. I wanted an opportunity to say thank-you to those who read me, which gave me the idea for a contest. Every year I hold a book-club contest and the winning book club gets a visit from me and a night of fabulous food and good wine. To enter is easy: all you have to do is take a picture of your entire book club with each member holding a copy of my newest hardcover and send it to me by mail or e-mail. No book club is too small or too big. Don't belong to a book club? Start one. Just grab a loved one, a neighbor or friend, and send in your picture of you each holding my newest book. I look forward to coming to your town and wining and dining your group. For more details, just go to **www.scottoline.com**.

Tour time is my favorite time of year because I get to break out my fancy clothes and meet with interesting and fun readers around the country. The rest of the year I am a homebody, writing every day, but thrilled to be able to connect with readers through e-mail. I read all my e-mail, and answer as much as I can. So, drop me a line about books, families, pets, love, or whatever is on your mind at **lisa@scottoline.com**. For my latest book and tour information, special promotions, and updates, you can sign up at **www.scottoline.com** for my newsletter.

Lisa Scottoline

The Bunnies Book Club of Scottsdale, Arizona, submit their photo for Lisa's book-club contest.

Reading Group Questions

1. The title *Damaged* is appropriate for this book on many levels. In what ways do you relate the title to the different aspects of the story?

2. While *Damaged* is set within the Philadelphia School District, so many school systems across America are equally stretched and struggling. What do you think should be done to improve our nation's schools? Aside from additional funding, in what other ways can we support our teachers?

3. Mary has a strong and surprising reaction to John, the first, and only, male lawyer in the firm, when he offers to help. What do you think caused her to act so out of character? Do you think her response would have been the same if it were one of the female lawyers offering help? Why, or why not?

4. Patrick has a learning disability that has led to severe anxiety. More and more children are being diagnosed with issues such as ADHD, anxiety, and learning problems, and much has been speculated in regard to the causes. Why do you think there is such a rise in the number of children with these disorders? Do you think there is any validity to the idea that we are just doing a better job at diagnosing children, not necessarily that so many more children have problems? In what ways do you think the system is helping these children, and in what ways is it letting them down?

5. Mary (like Lisa) loves with all her heart, and attaches easily. Were you surprised by Mary's decision in regard to Patrick? How would you have reacted if you were Anthony? What did you think of Anthony's surprise for Mary? What did you think of her reaction? How do you juggle your obligations to your birth family versus your created family? Who do you think should come first, and are there any times when that priority can, or should, shift?

6. Being a working single mom, Lisa was fortunate to have her parents' help with Francesca after school, which created an incredible relationship between Francesca and her grandparents. Patrick is being raised by his grandfather. This has now become a very common situation in America. What are your thoughts about this? Do you think it is the grandparent's responsibility to step in and raise a child when the parents are unable? In what ways are grandparents better equipped to raise a child, and in what ways are they disadvantaged? How does the grandparent becoming the parent hurt or enhance the typically special grandchild/grandparent bond? What kind of relationship did you, or do you, have with your grandparents?

7. Although Mary is now partners with Bennie and bills more than she, Mary is still deferential to Bennie. Since Bennie started the firm, do you think it is appropriate that Mary concedes to her? Why, or why not? The women at Rosato & DiNunzio are very protective and supportive of one another, but that is not always the case in the corporate world. Why do you think this is? Do you think the camaraderie among the women is so strong because there were no men in the firm until recently? In what ways can women be more supportive of other women, and why is it so important?

8. Lisa always has terrific secondary characters, and Machiavelli is a true original. What did you think of him as a character? What about as a lawyer? Would you want him representing you on a tough case? Why, or why not? Do you think he crossed the line with his legal strategies, or was he just pulling out all the stops for his client?

9. Lisa has always known and promoted the importance of reading, but she learned a lot while researching the book, including how fundamental reading is to self-esteem. In what ways do you

think reading is important? Do you have creative ideas on how we can get children to read? What was your favorite book as a child? What is your child's favorite book? How have your reading habits changed over the years?

10. For fun, let's talk weddings! What kind of dress did you imagine Mary would wear on her wedding day? What about the bridesmaids' dresses? Who do you think will cry the most at Mary's wedding? Who will make the biggest scene? Who will be the craziest dancer? Who will catch the bouquet? When they eventually go on a honeymoon, where do you think Mary and Anthony will go?

*Keep on
Reading*

Turn the page for a sneak peek at
Lisa Scottoline's next novel

EXPOSED

Available August 2017

CHAPTER ONE

Mary DiNunzio stepped off the elevator, worried. Her father and his friends looked over from the reception area, their lined faces stricken. They'd called her to say they needed a lawyer, but until now, she hadn't been overly concerned. Their last lawsuit was against the Frank Sinatra Social Society of South Philly on behalf of the Dean Martin Fan Club of South Philly. Luckily Mary had been able to settle the matter without involving Tony Bennett.

"Hi, Pop." Mary crossed the lobby, which was otherwise empty. Marshall, their receptionist, wasn't at her desk, though she must've already gotten in. The aroma of fresh coffee filled the air, since Marshall knew that Mary's father and his fellow octogenarians ran on caffeine and Coumadin.

"HIYA, HONEY!" her father shouted, despite his hearing aids. Everyone was used to Mariano "Matty" DiNunzio talking loudly, which came off as enthusiastic rather than angry. On the table next to him sat a white box of pastries, as the DiNunzios didn't go anywhere empty-handed, even to a law firm. The box hadn't been opened, so whatever was bothering him was something even saturated fats couldn't cure.

"Hey, Mare!" "Hi, Mary!" "*Buongiorno, Maria!*" said his friends The Three Tonys, like a Greek—or more accurately, Roman—chorus. They got up to greet her, rising slowly on replacement knees, like hammers on a piano with sticky keys. Her father had grown up with The Tonys: Tony "From-Down-The-Block" LoMonaco, "Pigeon" Tony Lucia, and Tony "Two Feet" Pensiera, which got shortened to "Feet," so even his nickname had a nickname. It went without saying that naming traditions in South Philly were *sui generis,* which was Latin for completely insane. The Tonys went everywhere with her father and sometimes helped her on her cases, which was like having a secret weapon or a traveling nightmare.

"Good morning, Pop." Mary reached her father and gave him a big hug. He smelled the way he always did, of hard soap from a morning shave and the mothballs that clung to his clothes. He and The Tonys were dressed in basically the same outfit—a white short-sleeved shirt, baggy Bermuda shorts, and black-socks-with-sandals—like a barbershop quartet gone horribly wrong.

"THANKS FOR SEEIN' US, HONEY." Her father hugged her back, and Mary loved the solidity of his chubby belly. She would move mountains for him, but it still wouldn't be enough to thank him for being such a wonderful father. Both of her parents loved her to the marrow, though her mother could be as protective as a mother bear, if not a mother *Tyrannosaurus rex.*

"No problem." Mary released him, but he looked away, which was unlike him. "You okay, Pop?"

"SURE, SURE." Her father waved her off with an arthritic hand, but Mary was concerned. His eyes were a milky brown behind his bifocals, but troubled.

"What is it?"

"YOU'LL SEE. YOUR MOTHER SAYS HI."

Just then Feet raised his slack arms, pulled Mary close to his chest, and hugged her so hard that he jostled his Mr. Potato Head glasses. He, too, seemed agitated, if affectionate. "Mare, thank you for making the time for us."

"Of course, I'm happy to see you."

"I appreciate it. You're such a good kid." Feet righted his thick trifocals, repaired with Scotch tape at one corner. His round eyes were hooded, his nose was bulbous, and he was completely bald, with worry lines that began at his eyebrows and looked more worried than usual.

"Mary!" Tony-From-Down-The-Block reached for her with typical vigor, the youngest of the group, at eighty-three. He worked out, doing a chair-exercise class at the senior center, and was dating again, as evidenced by his hair's suspicious shade of reddish-black, like oxblood shoe polish. He gave her a hug, and Mary breathed in his Paco Rabanne and Bengay, a surprisingly fragrant combination.

"Good to see you." Mary let him go and moved on to hug Pigeon Tony, an Italian immigrant with a stringy neck, who not only raised homing pigeons but also looked like one. Pigeon Tony was barely five feet tall and bird-thin, with a smooth bald head and round brown-black eyes divided by a nose shaped like a beak. In other words, adorable.

"*Come stai, Maria?*" Pigeon Tony released her with a sad smile, and Mary tried to remember her Italian.

"*Va bene, grazie. E tu?*"

"*Cosi, cosi,*" Pigeon Tony answered, though he'd never before said anything but *bene*. You didn't have to speak Italian to know there was a problem, and Mary turned to address the foursome.

"So what's going on, guys? How can I help you?"

"IT'S NOT ABOUT US," her father answered gravely.

Feet nodded, downcast. "It's about Simon."

"Oh no, what's up?" Mary loved Feet's son Simon, who was her unofficial cousin, since The Tonys were her unofficial uncles.

"He's not so good."

"What's the matter? Is it Rachel?" Mary felt a pang of fear. Simon's wife, Ellen, died four years ago of an aneurysm, and Simon had become a single father of an infant, Rachel. When Rachel turned three, she was diagnosed with leukemia but was in remission.

"Simon will explain it. Oh, here he comes now!" Feet turned to the elevator just as the doors opened and Simon stepped out, looking around to orient himself.

"Hey, honey!" Mary called to him, hiding her dismay. He looked tired, with premature gray threaded through his dark curly hair, and though he had his father's stocky build, he'd lost weight. His navy sports jacket hung on him and his jeans were too big. She hadn't seen him in a while, since he was busy with Rachel, though they'd kept in touch by email.

"Hi, Mary!" Simon strode toward her, and Mary reached him with a hug, since she could only imagine what he'd been going through, not only with the baby, but losing Ellen. Mary herself had been widowed young, after the murder of her first husband, Mike. Even though she was happily remarried, Mike was a part of her and always would be, which suited her and her new husband, Anthony, just fine.

"It's so good to see you, honey." Mary released him, and Simon brightened.

"This office is so nice, with your name on the sign."

"Believe me, I'm as surprised as you are." Mary could see Simon was happy for her and felt a new rush of affection for him. "How's the baby?"

"I'll fill you in later." Simon's smile stiffened. "I just moved her to CHOP."

Mary wondered why Rachel had been moved, but it wasn't the time to ask. CHOP was the Children's Hospital of Philadelphia, one of the best in the country. Mary's heart went out to him. "I'm praying for her, and so is my mother. She's got the novenas on overdrive."

"I know, and she sends me mass cards, God bless her." Simon's smiled returned. "I tell our rabbi, I'll take all the help I can get."

"Exactly. She prayed for me to make partner."

"Ha! Anyway, thanks for seeing me on such short notice. Are you sure you have the time?"

"Totally. My first appointment isn't until 10:30." Mary motioned him out of the reception area. "Let's go to the conference room."

"Okay." Simon fell into step beside her, followed by her father, The Tonys, and the pastry box, which gave Mary pause. Simon was a potential client, and she wouldn't ordinarily have a client consultation with an audience, blood-related or not.

"Simon, did you want to talk alone?" she asked him, stopping in the hallway. "What we say is confidential, and it's your call whether your dad or anybody else comes in with us. They can wait in—"

Feet interrupted, "No, I wanna be there, Mare. I know what he's gonna tell you, we all do."

Tony-From-Down-The-Block snorted. "Of course we'll be there. Feet's his father, and I taught him how to ride a bike."

"I CHANGED HIS DIAPERS!"

Mary looked over, skeptically. "When, Pop?"

"THAT ONE TIME, I FORGET." Her father held up the pastry box by its cotton string. "PLUS I GOT BREAKFAST."

Pigeon Tony kept his own counsel, his dark gaze darting from Simon to Mary, and she suspected that he understood more than he let on, regardless of the language.

Simon smiled crookedly. "Mary, you didn't think we were going to shake them, did you? It's okay. They can come with."

"THIS WAY, I KNOW WHERE IT IS!" Her father lumbered off, down the hallway.

"Of course, we're all going!" Feet said, at his heels. "We're family. We're all family!"

"*Andiamo!*" said Pigeon Tony.

Mary led them down the hallway and into the conference room, where Thomas Eakins's rowing prints lined the warm white walls and fresh coffee had been set up on the credenza. The far side of the room was glass, showing an impressive view of the Philadelphia skyline thick with humidity. July was a bad-hair month in Philly, and Mary was already damp under her linen dress.

She closed the conference room door, glancing at Simon, who perched unhappily on the edge of his chair. He'd always been one of the nicest and smartest kids in the neighborhood, affable enough to make friends even though he was one of the few that didn't go to parochial school. He'd gone to Central High, and the Pensieras were Italian Jews, but the religious distinction made no difference as far as the neighborhood was concerned. The common denominator was homemade tomato sauce.

"Simon, would you like coffee?" Mary set down her purse and messenger bag while her father and The Tonys surged to the credenza.

"No, thanks. Let's get started." Simon sat down catty-corner to the head of the table.

"Agree." Mary took the seat, slid her laptop from her bag, and powered it up while her father and The Tonys yakked away, pouring coffee and digging into the pastry box.

"MARE, YOU TWO START WITHOUT US. DON'T WAIT ON US."

Mary pulled her laptop from her bag, fired it up, and opened a file, turning to Simon. "So, tell me what's going on."

"Okay." Simon paused, collecting his thoughts. "Well, you remember, I'm in sales at OpenSpace, and we make office cubicles. We have different designs and price points, though we also customize. We did $9 million in sales last fiscal year and we have forty-five employees, including manufacturing and administrative, in Horsham."

"How long have you worked for them, again?"

"Twelve years, almost since I graduated Temple, and—" Simon flushed, licking lips that had gone suddenly dry. "Well, I just got fired."

"Oh no," Mary said, surprised. Simon was smart and hardworking, a success from the get-go. "When did this happen?"

"Two days ago, Tuesday. July 11."

"Why?" Mary caught Feet's stricken expression, and her father and the others had gone quiet.

"They said it was my performance. But I don't think that's the real reason."

"What do you think?" Mary's mind was already flipping through the possible illegal reasons, which weren't many. Pennsylvania was a right-to-work state, which meant that an employee could be fired at will, for any or no reason, as long as it wasn't discriminatory.

"Honestly, my performance is great. I'm one of the top reps. I've gotten great reviews and bonuses for years. Things started to go south after Rachel was diagnosed. The final straw for them was—" Simon hesitated, and Feet came over and placed a hand on his shoulder.

"Son, the baby's going to be fine. We're all praying, and she's got good doctors. *Great* doctors."

"Thanks, Dad." Simon returned his attention to Mary, her gaze newly agonized. "I didn't let people know, but a while ago, Rachel relapsed again and she has to have a bone marrow transplant. That's why she got moved to CHOP."

"Oh, no, I'm sorry to hear that." Mary felt her chest tighten with emotion, but she didn't want to open any floodgates, especially with Feet, her father, and the others. Now she understood why they'd been so upset. Simon was in dire straits, with Rachel so ill and now him out of a job.

"Obviously, I wish the chemo had worked, but I feel great about the BMT Team at CHOP. They specialize in ALL." Simon caught himself. "Sorry about the lingo. BMT stands for Blood and Marrow Transplant Team and ALL is acute lymphoblastic leukemia, which is what she has."

"I can't imagine how hard this is to go through, for all of you."

"We're doing the best we can. My dad's there all the time, so it helps when I have to work." Simon managed a shaky smile. "It's just that as a father, you feel so helpless. I'm mean, it sounds cliché, but it's true. I know, I *live* it. You have hope, but no control. None at all. Well, you get it. You know, you see. She has to be okay."

"She will be," Feet said quietly, and Mary's father, Pigeon Tony, and Tony-From-Down-The-Block walked over, their lined faces masks of sorrow and fear. They stood motionless behind him, having forgotten about the coffee and pastries.

"SIMON, WE'LL HELP ANY WAY WE CAN. WON'T WE, MARE?"

"Yes, we will," Mary answered, meaning it. She patted Simon's hand again.

Tony-From-Down-The-Block chimed in, "We're going to get through this together." He gestured at Pigeon Tony. "He's gonna make some baked ziti for you, Simon. He's an excellent cook, like, gourmet. All you gotta do is put it in the microwave."

"Thanks, guys." Simon turned around, then faced Mary. "Anyway, I think that's the reason why they fired me."

Mary blinked. "How so?"

"Well, when Rachel was first diagnosed, my boss, Todd, was

really nice about it. I have decent benefits and they covered Rachel. I took out a second mortgage to cover what it doesn't. The meds are astronomical." Simon leaned over, urgent. "But OpenSpace is self-insured up to $250,000, which means that their insurance policy doesn't reimburse them until their employee medical expenses reach that mount. They have to pay out-of-pocket until then."

"Understood. It's like a deductible." Mary knew the basics of employment benefits.

"Exactly." Simon nodded. "But Rachel's bills alone are so high that the insurance company is going to raise the premiums."

"I see, and are the premiums going up?"

"I don't know, but I'm getting ahead of myself. After Rachel's first round of chemo, Todd kept asking me how Rachel was. I thought he was interested, like, being nice. He has a ten-year-old daughter. But then he made comments about the bills when I submitted them. And then when the first bills for chemo came in, for seven grand, he reduced my territory from three states—Jersey, Pennsylvania, and Delaware—to just Delaware."

Mary didn't understand something. "What does it matter that your territory was reduced?"

"A reduction in my territory means I can't make my sales quotas. Not only that, but the territory he gave me was more residential and had less businesses, so there was no way I could ever make quota." Simon flushed. "I tried, but no matter what I did, I was only selling a fraction of the units. For the first time in twelve years, I didn't make quota."

Mary put it together. "So your sales go down and your performance suffers."

"Right." Simon nodded. "Todd was trying to force me out, hoping that I would quit, but I didn't. I love my accounts, my reps, and my job, and I need the job."

"Of course."

"So when Rachel's pediatric oncologist told me she needed the transplant and referred me to CHOP, I told Todd and he asked how much it was going to cost. At the time, I didn't know the costs of the transplant, but the donor search alone cost like $60,000 to $100,000, and I told him that."

"To search for a match? Why does that cost so much? It didn't cost that much when we tried before, did it?" Mary was referring to a previous time, when Rachel had been considered for a bone marrow transplant and they had all registered as donors, by giving cheek swabs to collect DNA. None of them had been matches.

"It's not the costs of donating, it's the costs of finding a donor. The hospital has to contact the bone marrow donor registry to get a list of potential matches, but they have to test at least six potential donors to get one that's a perfect match. Each test costs six to nine grand. It adds up fast."

"Oh, man." Mary hadn't realized.

"Luckily, CHOP found us a match, changed Rachel's chemo protocol, and got her into remission. You have to be in remission to do the transplant."

"That's sounds like a catch-22."

"I know, but it isn't. I'll fill you in another time. Anyway, when I told Todd that Rachel needed the transplant, he fired me the next week, supposedly because I didn't make quota—for one month. The first time in twelve years."

"So it was a pretext because they didn't want to pay for Rachel's expenses? And they didn't want their premiums to go up?"

"I think so."

"That's heartless." Mary felt a surge of anger, the kind she always felt when somebody had been wronged. But here, it had happened to someone she knew and loved. Simon. And Rachel.

Feet shook his head. "They're bastards!"

"WHAT KIND A PEOPLE FIRE YOU BECAUSE YOU GOT A SICK KID? THEY SHOULD BURN IN HELL!"

"*Disgrazia!*"

Simon shook his head. "The irony is that OpenSpace wouldn't have had to pay another penny. CHOP worked with me and Aetna, and since I'm a Pennsylvania resident and the illness is life-threatening, I can use secondary insurance like the CAT Fund and

Medicaid. They cover the costs of the transplant, which is astronomical."

"How much does a bone marrow transplant cost?"

"A million bucks."

"Whoa, are you kidding?" Mary said, shocked.

"No, start to finish, it's almost a year-long process, and you can't imagine the expertise and care it takes."

"I bet." Mary got back on track. "Do you remember the comment your boss, Todd, made to you, about how much it was costing?"

"Yes, and I even have proof. I wrote down every time Todd said something to me about her bills. I didn't want to write it on my phone because it's company-issued." Simon reached into his sports jacket, pulled out a Moleskine notebook, and set it down. "I can show you right here, when and where."

"Great." Mary picked up the notebook, opened it, and glanced at Simon's characteristically neat writing, with dates and times noted. "Simon, what's your boss's full name?"

"Todd Eddington."

Mary made a note. "How long has he been your boss and what's his job title?"

"He's sales manager. I've reported to him for twelve years." Simon swallowed hard. "I thought we were friends. We used to golf together before Rachel got sick. I know his ex-wife, Cheryl. They were both good to Ellen." Simon's voice trailed off, but Mary wanted to keep him on the case.

"So does Todd make the decision or did somebody else?"

"He does. He makes a recommendation upstairs, to hire or fire, and it gets rubber-stamped by the president, Mike Bashir."

Mary made a note of the name.

"So is it legal, what they did?" Simon leaned over. "It seems so wrong to me. I understand that a transplant costs a lot, but they're going gangbusters and I worked for them for twelve years. Can they get away with this?"

"Not in my book. We can sue them for this, and we should, right away." Mary knew disability law as a result of her growing special education practice and she was already drafting a Complaint in her mind. She loved it when the law actually did justice, which happened less frequently than God intended.

"So it's illegal?" Simon leaned forward, newly urgent.

"Yes. There's a federal law, the Americans with Disabilities Act, and it prevents discrimination in employment based on disability or illness. So for example, you can't fire somebody because they have cancer—"

"But how does that apply to me? I'm not the one with cancer, Rachel is."

"I know, but the law has a special provision that applies here, though it's not well known. In fact, there's very little case law on it, but it applies to us." Mary started searching online for the statute. "It's called the 'association provision' and it forbids employment discrimination on the basis of an illness contracted by people who are *associated* with the insured employee, like their family."

"Really?" Simon's eyes widened with hope.

"Yes, under the ADA, an employer is prohibited from—" Mary found the statute and started reading aloud " '—excluding or otherwise denying equal jobs or benefits to a qualified individual because of the known disability of an individual with whom the qualified individual is known to have a relationship or association.' "

"MARE, WE DON'T GET THE LEGALESE!"

Mary explained, "It means Simon is a qualified individual under the law and he is associated with Rachel. In other words, Simon's company can't fire him because she got sick and her medical expenses are going to cost them. I have to research the cases and get more facts from you, but I think we have an excellent case here."

"That's great!" Simon threw his hands in the air.

"Thank God!" Feet cheered, and Tony-From-Down-The-Block, Pigeon Tony, and Mary's father burst into chatter, all at once. "*Bravissima, Maria!*" "Way to go, Mare! Go get 'em!"

"MARE, I KNEW YOU'D KNOW WHAT TO DO! I'M SO PROUD A YOU!" Her father shuffled over and kissed the top of

her head. "THANK GOD YOU'RE SO SMART! AND BEAU-
TIFUL!"

"Aw, Pop." Mary flushed, relieved. She couldn't have lived with
herself if she couldn't help Simon and Rachel, fighting for her life.
If there was any reason she had become a lawyer, this was it. To
help families, children, and the community as a whole. She felt as
if she had finally found her niche in special education and disability law and lately she'd come to work happier than ever before.

Simon beamed. "Mary, that's so amazing. How does that work?
Do you think I could get my job back? I really need to work."

"Okay, hold on." Mary put up her hand. "I have to study your
notebook and do my research before I can answer any of these questions for sure. And the procedure under the law is that before we
go to court, we have to file a Complaint with the EEOC, the Equal
Employment Opportunity Commission, first. Then they give us a
right-to-sue letter and we can go to court. As far as remedy, I don't
know if you can get your job back, but why would you want it? Do
you have an employment contract or a non-compete?"

"Yes, for two years, and it covers the mid-Atlantic states. So now
I can't work in sales in the area but I can't move out of the area
because of Rachel being at CHOP."

Mary saw his dilemma. "Okay, we'll see what we can do. We
might be able to get a decent settlement, then you can stay home
with Rachel during her treatment."

"But what about her medical expenses?"

"You buy COBRA with the settlement money. That covers
you both for eighteen months and you'll find another job when you
free up more."

"That would be best of all! I don't know how to thank you,
Mary." Simon broke into a huge smile.

Her father grinned. "HOW MUCH CAN YOU GET HIM,
MARE?"

Feet chimed in, "Yeah, how much?"

Mary waved them off. "Don't get ahead of yourselves. I need to
know more before we make a settlement demand and I want to see
the notebook, so I understand exactly what happened."

Simon nodded, excited. "So you'll take my case, Mary? Do you have the time?"

"Of course." Mary mentally cleared her calendar. She didn't have anything as pressing as this. This was for family.

"Thank you so much!" Simon squeezed her hand. "And I just want to say up front that I'm paying you for this. I'm not expecting you to represent me for free."

"YOUR MONEY'S NO GOOD HERE. YOU KNOW THAT."

"Simon, my father's right," Mary said, meaning it. She'd have to tell her partner, Bennie Rosato, but the days were over when she'd have to ask for permission.

"What do we do next?" Simon checked his watch. "I should get over to the hospital."

Feet nodded. "Simon sleeps there, and we trade off. We like to be there when she's up."

Tony-From-Down-The-Block added, "So she knows she's not alone."

"OF COURSE SHE'S NOT ALONE!" Mary's father's said, and she saw his eyes begin to glisten, so she rose.

"Okay, then. Let me get started so we can get a demand letter out right away. See if we can get this settled without having to file suit."

"Think we can?" Simon stood up, his entire demeanor improved. He held his head higher and squared his shoulders.

"I can't guarantee it, but I feel good." Mary gave him a reassuring hug and gathered him, Feet, her father, the remaining Tonys, and the untouched pastry while they all exchanged "good-byes, "thank-yous," and "love yous." Then she ushered them out of the conference room, down the hall, and into the elevator, giving her father one final hug.

"Mary, thanks so much!" Simon called to her.

"BYE, HONEY! LOVE YOU!"

"Love you, too!" Mary glimpsed her father's eyes mist again as the elevator doors slid closed. Something was still bothering him, but she didn't know what or why. The doors had sealed shut and the elevator rattled downward, leaving her to her own thoughts.

She felt so good that she could help Simon and Rachel, but so awful that the baby needed the transplant. Only four years old, and her young life had been a series of tests and chemo, needle pricks and IV ports. It couldn't be possible that children suffered so much, yet she knew it happened every day, in every hospital in the country.

The other elevator doors slid open, and inside was Bennie Rosato, whose appearance never failed to intimidate Mary. Maybe it was because Bennie was her former boss and a superlawyer with a national reputation, or the fact that Bennie was six feet tall and towered over Mary, or the fact that Bennie always wore a khaki power suit, or that her curly blonde hair was always in an unruly topknot, proof that she was far too sensible to care about anything as dumb as hair.

"Good morning," Mary said, as Bennie flashed a confident smile, which was the only kind she had.

"Hey, DiNunzio. I mean, Mary. What are you doing, standing here?"

"I just met with a new client," Mary answered, faking a smile.

"Tough case? You look upset." Bennie strode toward the reception desk, and Mary fell in step beside her, telling herself not to be nervous around her own partner, for no reason. Or maybe for four reasons, as above.

"Yes, tough case." Mary was thinking of Rachel.

"Tough on the law?"

"No it's just sad. On the law, it's a winner. A sales rep got fired because his daughter needs a bone marrow transplant." Mary summarized it like a legal headnote since Bennie was in a hurry.

"Ouch." Bennie grimaced as she walked. "Go get 'em, tiger."

"It's totally illegal under the association provision of the ADA. I'm hoping for a quick settlement."

"Who's the defendant?"

"Some cubicle manufacturer."

"Not OpenSpace." Bennie stopped, frowning under the gleaming Rosato & DiNunzio plaque.

"Yes, why? How did you know?"

"OpenSpace is the biggest cubicle manufacturer in the area, and you can't sue them. I represent their parent company."

"I don't understand." Mary's mouth went dry.

"You're conflicted out of the case, and I didn't hear what I just heard. Decline the representation."

> "Scottoline writes riveting thrillers that keep me up all night, with plots that twist and turn."
>
> —Harlan Coben

"Grabs her readers by the jugular and won't let go."

—*Library Journal*
(STARRED REVIEW)

"Scottoline writes terrific legal fiction with warmth, smart characters, and lots of humor and heart."

—*Booklist*

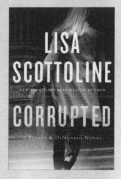

"So many plot twists, the pages seem to turn themselves."

—*People*

"One of the very best writers today."

—Michael Connelly

"Scottoline is at her best."

—*The Huffington Post*